aiseal Mór was born into a rich tradition of Irish storytelling and music. As a child he learned to play the brass-strung harp, carrying on a long family tradition. He spent several years collecting stories, songs and music of the Celtic lands during many visits to Ireland, Scotland and Brittany. He has a degree in performing arts from the University of Western Sydney and has worked as an actor, a teacher and as a musician.

Also by Caiseal Mór

THE
WELL
OF
YEARNING

BOOK ONE OF THE WELLSPRING TRIOLOGY

CAISEAL MÓR

POCKET
BOOKS

LONDON · NEW YORK · SYDNEY · TORONTO

First published in Great Britain by Pocket Books, 2004
An imprint of Simon & Schuster UK Ltd
A Viacom Company

5 7 9 10 8 6 4

Simon & Schuster UK Ltd
Africa House
64–78 Kingsway
London WC2B 6AH

www.simonsays.co.uk

Simon & Schuster Australia
Sydney

A CIP catalogue record for this book is available from the British Library

ISBN 0 7434 6856 2

Typeset by SX Composing DTP, Rayleigh, Essex
Printed and bound in Great Britain by
Cox & Wyman Ltd, Reading, Berkshire

For
my
Guardian
Angel

Acknowledgements

There's a lot of people to thank for helping me bring this novel to its conclusion. My first and foremost thanks go to my literary agent, Selwa Anthony. Her support and generous advocacy has ensured I'm still able to follow my chosen vocation.

Many thanks to Julia Stiles who has edited every one of my novels since she was Commissioning Editor at Random House Australia in 1994.

Special thanks go to Darren Nash, former commissioning editor at Earthlight Books. I first met Darren when he was a Sales Representative for Random House Australia in 1995. I have much to thank him for. He has long been an enthusiastic supporter of my work and the genres of Science Fiction and Fantasy. He's someone I'm privileged to call a friend. So it has been wonderful to also be able to call him my publisher. Thanks Darren. I'd like to take this opportunity to wish you all the best for the future.

I'd also like to thank all the folk at Simon and Schuster U.K. especially Kate Lyall Grant who took over responsibility for my novels at Pocket Books.

I'd also like to extend my gratitude to all the readers who enjoy my novels and to those who e-mail me or visit my website (www.caiseal.net). It's great to receive so much mail from so many readers. For those who haven't seen my web-page it's a great place to find out publication dates and availability of the music I've composed to accompany this trilogy. I look forward to hearing your comments on my work.

At last I'm in the midst of my favourite part of the story of Sianan, Mawn, Isleen, Lochie, Sárán and Lom. Caoimhin has been waiting patiently in the background since I wrote 'The Circle and The Cross' nine years ago. It's about time I wheeled him out.

Caiseal Mór
December 2003

If you wish to write to the author, Caiseal Mór may be contacted at the following e-mail address:
harp@caiseal.net

For information about other books and music by Caiseal Mór, please visit his website at:
www.caiseal.net

The Compact Disc of music composed and recorded by Caiseal Mór to accompany *The Wellspring Trilogy* may be ordered through amazon.co.uk or visit his website www.caiseal.net for details.

Pronunciation Guide: The Well of Yearning.

Aoife	eef-ah
Aontacht	ohn-tahkt
Áilleacht	Ah-lee-akt
Banba	bahn-va
Ban Righ	bahn-ree
Bláni	Blah-nee
Boann	boh-an
Branach	bran-akt
Brehon	breh-in
Bride	bree-dah
Caer Narffon	Car-nar-von
Caitlin	kotch-lin
Caoimhin	kay-vin
Cenn Maenach	ken mee-nahk
Cruitne	krit-nee
Cymru	kim-roo
Dearg Uila	deruk-hoola
Derbáil	der-vahl
Draoi	dree
Dulogue	doo-loge
Dun Righ	dun-ree
Dun Sidhe	dun-shee
Eagla	ah-glah
Eber Finn	ayber-finn
Eirinn	ay-rin
Eoghanacht	yo-an-akt
Eolaí	yo-lee
Éremon	ay-ra-mon
Eriu	ay-ree-oo
Fánaí	faw-nee
Feni	fee-ni

Flidais	flee-daysh
Fodhla	foh-lah
Gusán Gelt	gooh-sawn-gelit
Inisfail	inish-fahl
Inis Mór	inish-mor
Isleen	ish-leen
Leabhar Fál	lebar-fawl
Leoghaire	leeh-ree
Lochlann	lok-lan
Lom Dubh	lom-doov
Maolán	mwee-lawn
Marcán	mahk-awn
Molaise	mohl-aysh
Morcán	mork-awn
Morrigán	moh-ree-gawn
Muirdeach	mew-ah-juk
Nathair	nah-hair
Nathairaí	nah-hair-ree
Oidche	eeh-ha
Órán	ooh-rawn
Rián Ronán Og	ree-awn-roh-nawn-oge
Samhain Oidhe	sah-win-eeh-ha
Sárán	saw-rawn
Scathach	skah-hah
Sciathan Cog	skee-ah-han-koge
Sen Erainn	shen-ay-rin
Sianan	shan-nan
Síla	shee-lah
Sotar	soh-tah
Tigern Og	tee-gern-oge
Tóla	tooh-lah
Tuatha-De-Danaan	tooh-ah-hah-jay-dah-nahn

Ireland according to Binney.

The Tale-Teller's Ale

T he life of each and every mortal is filled to the very brim with unquenchable longing. Some folk long for peace from the spirits of fear that haunt the dark places of the soul. Others are consumed by the desire for material comforts to ease their passage through life. Most of us are instilled with an undeniable longing for love.

And every soul-traveller is searching. We all have our private quests. You see, before we come into this world all the Earth-born bathe in the sacred spring of the Well of Yearning.

That holy source nourishes our passions, our pain and all our pleasures. The soil of the soul must be well watered if seeds of longing are to be sown and the orchard of quests is to take root in one's heart. But not every tree that grows there bears sweet fruit.

I harvested the timber from a few of my dream-trees in that orchard. I built a quest ship. Then I set sail, seeking to satisfy the yearning in my heart. Whispering seafarers of the Otherworld crew the longship of my soul. Steady hands at the tiller, every oar pulling hard to the heave call. The singing spirit-people are masters of my soul-voyage.

I was caught up in a dream just now when you entered the house to stir me. And what a dream it was! Powerful, mystical, majestic and brief. For that's the nature of these things.

I wandered once again as a young woman, into the land of

legend, the origin of all inspiration, the birthplace of all tales. I walked in the Otherworld. I knew I was dozing but I remember thinking to myself, what is this place? Where am I?

Then I heard the music. A silver-stringed harp. Unseen fingers summoned a sweet delicate refrain. My flesh, bone and muscle rippled with breathless intensity until my giddy head was spinning in ecstatic foolishness.

The melody lifted me up. I melted into the air like the last cold winter breeze on a fresh spring morning. I ceased merely *listening* to the music. I *became* the music. My whole being was absorbed into the melody.

That honey-dipped melody the Otherworld harper called forth was stronger than life or love or any joy I've ever known.

Drowning I was, suffocating in the splendour, all goose bumps and rolling eyes. The blessed music of the Faerie folk is a cloak of skin-tingling caresses. I can still feel the wondrous enchantment of the melody. Come with me, the harp calls.

Slip away hand in hand with the One. Make ready to leave life and all its cares behind.

No more pain. No more suffering. Death is banished. Fear abated. Desires quenched. Enticements worthless.

I was just about to release my frantic grip on the pleasures and pains of the waking world. And then . . .

Then you burst in to wake me up with your heavy boots and your clumsy cloddishness.

Don't screw up your face when you look at me. It's bloody obvious I'm not what you expected to find at the end of your road.

I'm sure you've come looking for Banrigh nan h'Oidche, the Queen of the Night. But like so many others who've come before, you've wasted your journey. She's not here.

Don't fret. I may seem to be nothing more than a decrepit old woman with a cackling giggle, lapsed manners and unbridled bowel vapours, but I've a tale to tell.

2

I'll wager you a single sock you're in no hurry to be off home again with the prospect of a story left hanging in the air. And since you've come so far to interrupt my dreams of the Otherworld, I'll let you in on a secret.

There's folk hereabouts who insist I myself am one of the Faerie folk. Some attest with hand on heart that this form you see before you is merely a disguise invoked to conceal my true purpose. They say I cast enchantments on men, women, birds and other creatures. They reckon once I've sung my spell, all will do my bidding and serve me forever.

Come closer. I'll tell you something I've never told anyone else before.

That's the biggest bucket of shite that was ever shovelled off the shite hill.

And there are them that reckon my Caoimhin had a natural talent for inventing tall stories. Most people possess intolerably tiny thinking parts in their thick heads. And even those usually have to be shared with their extended family three days a week.

It's a sad fact of life that most folk let their imaginations get the better of them one way or another.

I am what I am. Nothing more. Nothing less. Though I'm probably much more than I appear to be.

Would you care to quaff a cup of storytelling from a barrel of my own home-brewed tale-teller's ale? Then rest your weary arse a while with me.

After I'm gone to dwell among the noble trees there won't be a soul living who'll know the truth of things. As it is there are few alive who could speak with experience on the subject of the Enticers and the Frighteners. But I can.

So bottle up your foolish questions. Let them ferment a while. We might have a sip from that jug at the end.

Never before have I dared speak every detail of those days. I'm nigh on my ninetieth year now so I've no fear of the Church nor of the Holy Inquisition. What I have to say about the spirits of enticement and the demons of fear you'll likely find a little hard to swallow. But in my day it was common knowledge that we mortals are nothing more than cattle to the Old Ones.

To put your mind at ease about the truth of my recollections I'll say this. When I was young I was a bookbinder, not a scribe like Caoimhin. I know what it means to keep each page in its place. I understand the importance of every tiny stitch in holding a whole manuscript together. So if my tale-telling lacks a certain skill, at least you know I've left nothing out nor embellished on the facts too freely.

This is a story rich in all the ingredients of the classic troubadour romances. There's a bitter war, a knightly quest, betrayal, intrigue, a homage to harps, a love triangle, a journey into the mystical Otherworld and a respectful appreciation for the art of making cheese.

That's not to mention a couple of pretty parables on the powerlessness we mortals imagine is our lot in life. And an illustration of the awesome life-changing potential of a blessing.

Be assured. Every word that passes by my lips is true. If you doubt me I'm willing to swear an oath of honesty on the deerskin rug where my Caoimhin so often obliged me. I never make frivolous vows on holy relics.

Folk like you with your silly mystic notions, unfounded romantic fantasies and clumsy manners rarely have any inkling about the true nature of creation. So listen well. I'm about to say something heretical.

It is through the enchantment of the Well of Yearning that the Enticers and the Frighteners first gain their hold over us. Without fear or desire there can be no longing. Mortals can do very little to avoid the feeding habits of the spirits. There are even a few immortal folk dwelling in the Otherworld who've taken a sup from the Well of Yearning. They're just as powerless for the most part. Aoife, Queen of the Night, was one of them. It was Aoife who was behind all the strife of those days, you know. Aided by an army of Ravens and the Redcaps of the North, she set out to satisfy her longing. Even one as powerful as her was driven on by the energy of the Enticers and the force of the Frighteners.

Since you likely came to my mountain hoping for a glimpse of her, take careful note of all I have to say. If you have ears to hear and a notion to listen, I'll tell you the tale of how her unbridled longing came to bring havoc to the land of Ireland.

I'll speak of her devious strategies and her shameless manipulations. You'll learn how her deepest desire was fulfilled, though not quite in the manner she had intended.

You'll find out why you're so fortunate to have found an old biddy bookbinder sitting here instead of an aspiring deity. And you'll think twice before you bow down at her shrine.

One last warning. If my ferrets leave the room it's a sign I've farted. Rest assured I won't be offended if you join them.

The Well of Forgetfulness

Outremer is the name most folk of western Christendom give to the Holy Land. In the language of the Normans it means 'the country across the sea to the east'. Not very imaginative, but that's the Normans for you.

Moses led his people there. Jesus taught his followers beneath the olive trees. And the Saracen prophet Muhammad, may Allah commend and salute him, ascended into heaven from the Rock which once supported the Temple of Jerusalem.

Clergy who preached the Crusades spoke of Outremer as a fertile land, rich and green, blessed by fountains of sweet rosewater and wine. The Lord above watched over it, they said. In that country no harm could come to any man whose faith was firm.

The truth, of course, is very different. I should know. I journeyed to Jerusalem and Egypt once on pilgrimage. I wanted to see what all the fuss was about.

In my recollection there are few green places and hardly enough rosewater to wash the dust out of a dove's eye. The wine of that country reeks of the smelly beasts that carry it to market and is thus undrinkable. The water is even worse.

Whatever inspired anyone to fight bitter wars over that barren country is one of the greatest mysteries of creation. I'll share my thoughts on that subject later. I don't mean to jump ahead.

6

Besides these obvious onerous discomforts, the whole land is plagued by hot, rolling desert sands shifted about in mighty dust storms. Fierce elemental gales swallow settlements or sweep the unwary away without trace.

One of these dry, choking tempests howls across the opening of my tale. And this storm was the kind folk from the Shali oasis would remember for generations. Its violence was remarkable. But not as remarkable as what was left behind after it blew itself out.

In the desert three days hard march south of Alexandria a wild screaming wind blasted tiny granules of sand against anyone fool enough to be abroad. One such fool was a young warrior-monk of the Order of the Poor Knights of Christ and the Temple of Jerusalem. Inexperience brought him to this place: he thought the desert would not touch him. But her sands had a song to sing for him. She lifted her voice from a gentle sigh into a scream-storm before the Templar knew what had hit him.

His cheeks burned with the stinging assault. His eyes squinted against the blast as his fingers found the protective linen band that had been snatched from his face. His world had been completely transformed into an ochre swirl of throat-burning fury. The unrelenting tempest swallowed everything in its path as the horizon melted away into a shifting, howling oblivion.

All sound was smothered in the ear-bursting rage of the onslaught.

The desert is stronger than any Saracen. She scorns the traveller who dares to cross her vastness without payment of a toll. She tortures anyone who suffers no doubt when they set off. And she destroys those arrogant few who think they have conquered her. She cooks up journeymen for her meat. She roasts them for her supper. But she leaves the feast untouched upon her table.

For the vultures.

Young Alan de Harcourt huddled beside his saddle. He wanted to weep but he was so dry with thirst he held his eyes shut tight so he wouldn't shed a single precious tear. Every drop of moisture was suddenly more dear to him than all the gold in all the venerated shrines of the Holy Land.

His nostrils were clogged with sand. His beard was heavy with dust. His surcoat of fine linen was already torn to tatters. It flapped about his body as useless as a shredded ship-sail. And worse, amidst the confusion of the sandstorm his two companions had utterly vanished. He was beginning to lose heart and his mind was filled with thoughts of death.

Alan had taken his vows as a Knight of the Temple a year earlier. He'd been told then by his Grand Master that death would likely come to him in some glorious fight against the infidel. He'd felt his heart beat faster at the thought of such an honourable passing. But now it seemed certain he would end his service to God and the Order of the Temple in an uninhabited desert far from the real conflict engulfing the Holy Land.

And what had brought him to this place? What quest had led him to a choking, solitary demise?

His life had been bartered for a book. He and his companions had come all this way to meet an Egyptian Orthodox priest. They'd been sent to purchase a manuscript wrapped in leather bindings. A deal had been quickly struck. And once the priest had received his bag full of gold, he and his camel had disappeared into the desert without so much as a backwards glance. That had been three days ago. It seemed like an eternity.

Alan tried to keep his spirits up. He told himself he and his companions might yet make it back to the fortress city of Acre if this terrible storm would only pass. But his heart told him there was no point in such wishful thinking. It was too late for hope.

Alan reached out a hand to grasp for his saddlebag. He somehow managed to open it and drag out the bundle of leather and parchment. His fingertips traced the intricate designs hammered into the leather casing of the book.

He hadn't looked upon the holy treasure he had been charged to escort. Now it was too late. His companions were gone. His horse had bolted when the saddle girths snapped. Alan was alone. More alone than he'd ever imagined possible. He could hardly believe his last moments would be so despairing.

No one would hear him cry out, even if he had the strength to do so. No one would preside over his confession. Only Heaven would hear his final fervent prayers. And once the storm had strangled him, the sands would bury his lifeless body without any rite or trace.

His life had been wasted for a collection of bound painted pages. Alan found it difficult to accept that his masters in Acre could have sent him off on such a dangerous mission without a thought for his safety.

The young knight threw off his helm so he could hug close the great book that had brought him to this place. Then he fell to his knees and prayed for salvation and forgiveness. He begged his creator not to judge him harshly for this failure.

In turn he addressed the Madonna. In Acre there was a church dedicated to Her. The chapel contained a statue of the Holy Mother bearing the infant Jesus in Her arms. Alan could picture Her face clearly. Despite the heaviness in his heart he smiled to think this statue of the Holy Mother had skin as dark as any Ethiopian's.

With the benign countenance of the Black Madonna firmly implanted in his mind, he pleaded with Her for the lives of his two companions. He asked Her to watch over them, whether in life or in death.

Then, perhaps out of sheer desperation or delirium brought on by thirst, he added one more entreaty. As he opened his mouth to speak, the wind dropped as if the desert wished to witness his parting words.

'Give me another chance,' he begged. 'Madonna rescue me from this calamity and I promise I will start my life afresh. Aid me in the completion of my task. In return I'll find a way to give my life more completely to the service of God.'

He made the sign of the cross before his breast and, before he'd finished, the storm had blown itself out. The dry hot wind of death was gone.

Alan wiped the sand from his unbelieving eyes, blinking at the scene laid out before him. He frowned deeply, wondering if he'd lost his mind.

Ten paces away was a circular stone well. Out of it bubbled the coolest clearest water sparkling like liquid diamonds. A silver cup sat on the stones, fastened to a long iron chain so it would not be stolen.

The cup beckoned to him.

Alan would have thanked the Black Madonna aloud if his tongue had not been rendered useless with astonishment. He stumbled forward, imagining the sweet cool relief that awaited him.

As he reached the well he dropped the book at his feet and scooped up the silver cup. He didn't waste a moment admiring the fine workmanship of the water vessel. He plunged it into the spring without a second thought. Then he lifted it to his lips, spilling the water carelessly down his throat, savouring every drop that fell upon his skin or washed the dust from his hands and chin.

When he could drink no more he placed the cup back on the stone, listening and laughing as the spring bubbled merrily on, spilling itself into a stone-lined ditch. He glanced up toward the green trees. And then he caught his breath with shock. If the appearance of the spring had been unexpected, the sight before him now was utterly inexplicable.

Not more than thirty paces further on lay the rim of a valley sheltered beneath the sightline of the desert floor. Green treetops peeped up from this secret oasis. The scent of date palms wafted over on the breeze.

Hugging the book to him like a long-lost friend, Alan staggered on to the edge of the oasis. There he came to an abrupt halt. The scene before him could have been plucked from the repertoire of any storyteller in Jerusalem or Alexandria. The exhausted knight could only wonder that here on the very plains of Hell lay a gateway to Heaven.

In the valley below the spring waters flowed into a deep inviting pool of sparkling coolness. All about grew lush grass and palms. Beyond the pool a great red-brown gatehouse fashioned entirely from mud rose up amongst the grasses. On the baked-earth battlements stood dark-skinned warriors in strange armour. They leaned heavily against their spears as they stared in his direction. A trumpet sounded somewhere. The massive gates of the fortification swung open.

Alan knew the oasis folk would soon be out to fetch him. As that thought struck him he felt a light hand on his shoulder. As if in a dream he slowly turned to see who was behind him. His gaze fell upon a veiled woman whose eyes shone like two enormous emeralds in her face.

She slowly reached out to him and his mouth fell open in shock. The woman touched him tenderly on the cheek with the back of her hand. Her veil fell away to reveal her clear dark skin.

Alan let the tears flow at last. Through his sobs he managed to gasp just one word.

'Madonna.'

Then the knight fell forward into the woman's arms. His vision blurred until he could no longer see anything. Perhaps he was dead or had been blinded because he was unworthy to look upon the face of the Mother of God.

He could hear her voice soft in his ear though he couldn't understand a word of what she was saying. The knight told himself his prayer had been answered. Then with a sigh he lapsed into a deep state of rest.

At that precise moment, though he couldn't possibly have known it, this Templar knight embarked upon a new stage in his great journey. His soul-voyage, his private quest, his Immrama had called to him.

All that happened afterwards became his true life. All that had been before was banished from his mind as if the cobwebs of the past had been brushed away forever.

As the saying goes, a new broom sweeps clean but an old one knows the dirty corners best.

BOUGH-SPLITTERS

Do you think you know what fear is? Do you reckon you'd recognise terror if it crept up behind you with a whacking stick? Can you be certain you wouldn't lose your stomach contents at the first taste of real fright?

I'll tell you something of what fear can do to a man. It can transform him from a strong, proud knight of renown into a useless mass of shivering goose-flesh in less time than it takes a loose-lipped gibberfish to gibber.

Redcaps inspire that sort of terror. Yes, they have an unhappy knack at frightening folk half out of their wits. And that's putting it mildly.

It came to pass three years after the events in Outremer that an old Norman knight, Hubert of Rouen, was travelling with his two retainers. They were on their way home to his humble fortification in south-eastern Ireland not far from the old Norse settlement of Wexford town.

In those days Ireland was still well forested. The Normans hadn't yet cut down most of the woodlands to build their ships and houses. They'd done some mighty damage, mind you, but not as much as they would do later. So journeying through the land inevitably involved passing through a forest now and then.

Hubert chose a place to rest for the night in a deep dark wood where the trees grew close together, ancient, gnarled and unwelcoming. Then he ordered his two servants to set up camp.

After the horses had been settled and a little blaze had been lit, the small party sat to watch the flames before they drifted into slumber.

The Normans were masters of this part of the country. No Irishman dared stand against them here. Hubert's bondsmen were drowsy; he decided to let them have their rest. No need to keep a watch this night.

The noble knight let his long grey hair fall loose around his face as he sat cross-legged by the fire. His goatee beard was plaited at the chin into a rough rope of hair. It had been a week since he'd shaved his jowls and upper lip. The untidy whiskers added to the road-weariness which could be glimpsed in his eyes. But he would have no rest this night.

After Hubert had sat motionless for a long while, he unexpectedly grasped his long hair and twisted it into a knot on top of his head. Then he tied a strip of leather round the mass of strands to hold them in place. Over this he placed his arming cap which he tied tight with two straps that met under his chin.

His two servants roused from half-slumber at his activity. They rolled their eyes at each other, wondering what the old man was up to. It was time for sleep yet he was preparing for battle. Then they noticed the concern in his eyes. There was the merest hint of fear there. Just enough to make the two men sit up straight. They'd learned to trust their master's instincts.

'Egbert,' the knight whispered in a low voice. 'There's someone nearby. It may be that brigands have been following us. Don't move suddenly, but prepare yourself for a fight.'

'Yes, my lord,' the servant replied, grasping his sword hilt tightly.

Just then Egbert coughed and a confused expression contorted his face. He leaned forward as if he were going to speak. He pointed wordlessly up into the sky. Then he fell forward

14

over the fire, an arrow in his back. Life had already fled from him as he landed among the scattering sparks.

The other servant barely had the chance to draw his blade before an arrow struck him in the chest. He was dead with four more darts in his body before he'd hit the ground.

Hubert had his shield and sword at the ready in an instant. With lightning reflexes, surprising in one so old, he parried an arrow shaft as it flew at him. Then he backed away out of the firelight into the darkness so he'd not be as easy a target. Just as his form melted in among the trees a terrifying cry warbled through the woods.

It was not a human call. To this poor Norman it sounded like a song of the satanic hordes, those evil creatures who do the Devil's bidding. And even though Hubert was a veteran of countless battles, his heart froze with fear.

'May God protect me,' he muttered as he took cover next to a venerable oak tree, twisted with age and bent under its own weight.

The knight gripped the hilt of his sword, his palms sweaty with anticipation. He wasn't frightened to be facing death. What scared him was that there might be worse things than death to be faced.

Dæmons eat souls. Every Christian knows that. And there was suddenly something decidedly dæmonic about this forest.

His breath came hard and heavy. The old knight wished he was at home. All he wanted was to sit by the hearth fire of his modest castle tower with a young serving woman to keep him company and his hunting dogs to keep him entertained.

He didn't want to die. He'd just begun to enjoy the quiet life. And perhaps because his life had been so quiet, the terror that gripped him now seemed so much more intense.

Hubert instinctively held up his shield ready to fend off a blow. His throat was dry; his eyes darted at every shadow; his ears tingled at each tiny sound.

Had it not been an unknightly thing to do he would have sobbed. Instead he leaned hard against the mighty oak, pressing his cheek to the bark. His eyes closed briefly as he offered up a prayer.

'Please God, lead me home to the bosom of my kinfolk.'

'Run!' a muffled whisper urged him.

Immediately the knight's eyes snapped open. The breathy urgency in that unearthly voice almost stopped his heart.

'Run for your life!' the invisible ally insisted.

The old man realised the voice had emanated from deep within the tree. He pushed his body away from the enchanted bough. Then he noticed a strange feature of the trunk – the great knot in its middle resembled a human face.

'Trees don't have faces,' Hubert told himself. 'I must be dreaming.'

He'd just finished speaking when a thousand little flickers of flame burst into life in front of him.

'Too late,' the tree sighed mournfully.

In the next instant a sea of torchlight floated before the old knight. Each burning lamp illumined a hideous face set framed by a mound of matted dark brown hair. And every one of these horrendous heads was surmounted by a bright red pointed hat.

But it was their eyes that set old Hubert to shivering uncontrollably.

The creatures had huge eyeballs swimming in mucus-green liquid, with dark vertical slits instead of black circles at their centre. And every foul pair flashed with immeasurable malice.

Hubert suddenly didn't care whether this was a dream or not. In a flash the Norman turned to flee as fast as his old feet could carry him.

He didn't know where he was heading and he didn't care as long as it was as far away from those terrifying creatures in the red caps. As he fled, the savage horde let up a wailing, mocking laugh that tumbled through the forest in a wave of cackling derision.

Hubert ran like he'd never run before. In no time at all he'd stumbled upon his fireplace again. His two servants were already being stripped of all their flesh by a pair of monstrous Redcaps. Both dæmons looked up from their butchery to bare rows of sharpened teeth. Then they dropped the strips of flesh they were peeling. In seconds they'd drawn enormous curved sickles from their belts. But old Hubert was already off again, dodging between the trees to escape.

Wherever he glimpsed a torch light, he made off in the opposite direction. Whenever he heard a whoop of devilish delight, he turned away from it. But he couldn't seem to outwit his pursuers.

The torch lights drew ever closer and closer with each breath. Hubert's legs were faltering. His heart beat hard in his throat fit to burst.

'Why couldn't I have stayed at home?' he reprimanded himself.

But it was already too late for regret, as I'm sure you've realised. The Redcaps had marked him for death and only a miracle could save him from that fate.

One thing I'll say for those monsters, they're cunning creatures. They weren't going to face him down while he still had some fight in him. The Redcaps enjoy nothing better than a good chase. It's a game they play. Those dæmons wear their victims down till they simply collapse in submission. The old knight was very nearly at that point when he stopped in exhaustion to lean against another oak tree.

The torches closed in around him in a circle. The Redcaps were slow about their work but soon enough he was completely surrounded by hundreds of their filthy grinning faces.

As the wild warriors encircled him, Hubert noticed another most unnerving thing about these creatures. Each one had beautiful red spirals tattooed into his face. The colour accentuated the malice in their eyes, granting them an air of brutality. The old man's stomach turned.

Hubert felt an unfamiliar warmth spread down his left leg. He touched the cloth of his britches. They were damp. Fear had emptied his bladder. In all his years as a warrior he'd never been that frightened. He was certain he was going to die a horrible, slow, agonising death.

Then an unexpected thing happened. The Redcaps stopped their advance. Inexplicably they held back a short distance to bare their pointy teeth at him and hiss.

'Come on!' Hubert bellowed. 'Get on with it! I'm not afraid to take you on.'

There must have been two hundred of them. He didn't stand a chance.

'What are you waiting for?' he screamed, frantic to get this last fight over with.

In the next breath the dæmons parted ranks from the rear. Then they all bowed low as someone passed through the crowd.

A woman emerged between the torch lights. She was elegant, dressed in a long flowing green gown which trailed behind her in the leaf fall. Her eyes sparkled with fire from beneath the folds of her cowl. Compared to the Redcaps she was no monster. Hubert felt a glimmer of hope return to his heart.

As the woman approached him the woods were illuminated with glimmering beauty. A sparkling dreamlike glamour descended upon all things. Even the nasty Redcaps transformed into gorgeous beings of light. And this Otherworldly woman was the most wondrous of them all. Her grace was unsurpassed. Her bearing unquestionably regal. The old knight realised she could be nothing less than a queen of high renown.

Hubert dropped his shield then fell to one knee. 'Who are you?' he managed to ask, his voice cracking with emotion.

'My name is Aoife,' the woman replied. 'This is my forest. All the forests are mine.'

Then she motioned for him to stand up. 'Arise brave knight,' she commanded. 'You need not kneel in my presence.'

The old knight struggled to his feet. Emboldened by her soft sweet tone he looked up into her eyes. 'Are you a woman or a dæmon-queen?'

'I was a woman once. I'm still a woman in some respects. But I must be honest with you, I'm more of a dæmon.'

She stepped forward, smiling. Then she pulled back the cowl from her head so he could see the beauteous bright red sheen of her hair and the creamy softness of her skin. The exotic silk gown was wrapped tightly about her body so the outline of her breasts was impossible to ignore.

The old knight gasped at her beauty. Desire stirred in him, reminding him of the joys of his lusty youth. In that instant his home and hearth fire were entirely forgotten. His mind strayed to another kind of fire.

'Which would you have?' Aoife asked him as though reading his mind. 'You must choose. You may go home to the warmth of your own fireside to lie with the serving girl whose duty it is to keep you fed and satisfied.' The woods-woman's eyes twinkled with mischief. 'Or you could stay here to sample the delights of my home. I offer you such pleasures as you have never known. I would grant you such sweetness as cannot be found in the realm of mortals. There is no sickness here, no death and no lingering discomfort.'

She paused to allow him to consider. But not too long.

'So what's your decision?' she demanded.

'I have travelled the wide world over, my lady,' the old knight replied. 'I have sailed the seas east of Ethiopia. I've looked on the noble women of the Tartars and ladies from the court of the Cathay kings; every one a princess to behold. But I've never met a goddess such as yourself before.'

He bowed his head. 'Do with me as you will, my lady. I am yours to command. For though you may be a dæmon from the very mouth of Hell, I cannot do less than serve you with all my heart.'

Aoife laughed in derision. And that was enough to break the enchantment she'd cast over this knight. He shook his head, suddenly remembering that the woman was a dæmon, a servant of the Devil. Better to be torn to shreds by her devilish Redcaps than spend an eternity by her side in Hell.

The old man's hands shook with fear. But his steady expression betrayed nothing of his intentions.

'You will be one of my guardians,' she told him. 'You will serve me and protect me. And I will grant you everlasting youth in return.'

The Norman's heart beat so hard in his chest he thought she must surely be able to hear its pounding. His fear was so powerful he almost felt lifted up off the ground by the force of it.

The dæmon-woman was just a dozen paces away from him now. With her every step closer his terror trebled. His thoughts scattered in every direction. He was so numb with terror he couldn't feel the hilt of his sword in his hand. His fingers barely gripped it. The weapon was slipping from his grasp. His knees felt as if they would no longer bear his weight. He let his eyes roll back as he mustered every measure of courage he had left within him.

And then he did a very Norman thing.

With a mighty war cry he thrust his blade high into the air, swung it around and ran straight at the woman. With a sweeping blow that would have been a marvel to witness in a man half his age, he brought the sword down to slash at her.

His aim was at Aoife's collarbone. But the woman had half expected this assault. She'd read her victim well. With a gentle enchanted gesture of her hand she stopped the weapon's fall in midflight. I can't tell you what spell-craft she employed but the blade glanced harmlessly aside though she hadn't so much as touched it.

The old knight's eyes widened in shock. His arm was racked with pain. The sword dropped out of his hand.

'How did you do that?' he gasped.

'I'm the Queen of the Night,' she laughed. 'I can do many things.'

She stepped forward to grasp him under the chin. Her touch was icy cold and her fingernails bit into his flesh.

'You should have chosen to join me,' Aoife told him. 'Now you will be part of my forest forever, whether you like it or not.'

Then such a strange thing happened that Hubert was too terrified to scream or make any sound at all. His entire body numbed as a prickling sensation spread across his flesh. He looked down at his feet. But he saw only the tangled roots of an ancient oak. His muscles began to twitch as bone and sinew transformed into timber.

He remembered the whispering tree he encountered earlier. He recalled the twisted face frozen in the bark.

'Do you see all these oaks?' Aoife asked him. 'Each one is a knight or traveller who refused my offer. You will have much to discuss with them during the cold winter nights that will last out your long life. For an oak may live a thousand summers.'

'A thousand years?' the Norman managed to mutter.

Then in the next instant he was a knight no more. In his stead there grew a great oak tree with one branch outstretched where a hand once held a sword. There was a wide knot in its side resembling the contorted face of a terrified man.

Aoife shrugged and turned to walk away. Her Redcap warriors fell down on their faces before her. She stood for a moment to appreciate their gesture as an intense buzzing hum filled the air. In the next breath she was bathed in a thick cloud of seething bees. She melted into the swarm entirely as she took the form of one of the countless tiny insects.

The bees soared round the newly created tree, then flew off into the depths of the forest. The loyal ranks of Redcap warriors followed. In less time than it takes to draw a dozen breaths the new oak was left alone in the darkness as if it had been there since the beginning of time.

Long after the commotion had died away, whispers of the forest folk filled the air, only interrupted by the wild fluttering of wings as a raven arrived to nestle on a low branch of the newest oak.

The carrion bird shuffled up the branch to stare at the knot in the centre of the tree trunk where Hubert's fearfully contorted face was preserved forever in bark and splinter. The raven leaned toward the knot and spoke to the oak-knight.

'You should have considered your choice more carefully,' he cawed. 'But as far as I'm concerned it's poetic justice that one of you timber-cutting, bough-splitting Norman bastards has taken the place of a fine nesting tree.'

The raven clawed the branch, tearing off a small piece of bark.

'I hope that's painful,' the bird hummed, or as near to a hum as a raven can manage. 'Every day for the rest of your life you'll have birds clawing away at you like that. It's in payment for all the trees you've caused to be killed.'

The raven spat out a lump of undigested berry pulp onto the branch.

'Now I'm off to feast on the sweet eyeballs of your two servants,' the bird declared. 'There's nothing so tasty as a newly slain Norman. Don't go running away, will you.'

The black bird spread its wings wide with a laugh that would have curdled cream. And the poor Norman knight was left imprisoned within the body of an oak to wait out the winters of the next thousand years.

The road of his Immrama had run out. The journey of his mortal flesh had ended. The ship of his soul-voyage had run aground.

Soul-Voyage

orgive me. I assumed you'd understand the meaning of the word Immrama. But I see by the dullness of your eyes and the gape of your jaw that you do not. What a bloody shame. I had held the hope of some intelligent conversation after my story's done.

I'll explain for you the Immrama as clearly as I can. This is just my understanding, mind you. You don't have to accept it if it makes no sense to you.

I've already told you that your soul and mine were born into this world, along with all the others, having bathed in the Well of Yearning. The mystical waters of that sacred spring drive us all on to seek out new experiences. In this way souls taste the wide variety of adventures open to those who walk the Earth.

At death most souls journey on to another birth to devour more experience. This is our eternal voyage. That's the Immrama. There's nothing more to it than that.

All the ancient tales suggest it's a good idea to enjoy yourself while you're sailing along on the soul-voyage. The longing we all feel from birth to death is resolved only when we draw our last breath.

So don't let it bother you too much if you don't feel entirely fulfilled or you're not completely satisfied with your lot in life. Once you're dead it won't matter any more.

You'll have rest aplenty when this life is ended. You may

even find yourself ready to return after a short sleep. But unless you're a sainted soul, it's certain you'll drink from the Well of Yearning again before you return in time.

An old Norman named William FitzWilliam taught me about these things. I'm not sure whether he truly understood them himself for there was some talk that he was mad. And it's likely my ears weren't quite ready to listen to him at that time either. But I reckon the truth passed through him to me.

Lord Will had been a knight once. He'd been a hero of the Crusades. And a lord. He'd seen many terrible battles and much hardship during his lifetime. He'd also known his fair share of joy. In his later years he became a monk and decided to live in seclusion from society. That's how he came to be with my people.

When I was a lass of twenty-one winters I'd visit him with his daily bread. I used to walk all the way out to where he had his shelter. It was a respectable distance from everyone else.

His bread was always fresh and hot, wrapped in a linen cloth. It was difficult for me to resist the urge to taste it. I never did though. The old lord needed every morsel of food for his survival. Even ascetics must eat to keep the body alive. How could I, well fed and watered, consider thieving from such as he who had devoted the remains of his life to God?

I would place the bread on the doorstep of his dwelling. Sometimes when I arrived he'd be waiting to talk to me. But most times old Will simply stayed inside. He liked his solitude. So I'd leave the bread for him, wondering how he'd fared since the last time we'd spoken.

My companions whispered that a wizard from the land of Lochlann had captured the old man's heart in a bottle. A man without a heart finds no discomfort in solitude, they said. That's why William had turned his mind to meditation and reserved his sighs for himself.

I don't know whether they were right about Will. I can only

tell you that on a cold night at the start of his third winter with us, William FitzWilliam fell into the dreaming of a powerful dream. And as the old tales tell, my dear, nothing is more powerful than a dream.

It was midday but clouds darkened the sky so much it could have been late afternoon. A young Benedictine brother stood at the window of the small monastery.

He'd pulled the leather curtain aside so he could look out to the streets of the Norse-Irish port settlement of Wexford. The rain started to fall in great sheets as he stood silently in the gloom.

His fair hair was cropped short around the crown. The style of the Benedictine tonsure left a fringe of longer hair which framed the young man's face in a halo of neat blond locks. At twenty-four he still hadn't been able to grow a full beard. Even so, every week, out of respect for the rules of his order, he shaved his face and the crown of his head. Young Harold didn't question the Benedictine rule. He simply obeyed it.

A thin stubble stood out on his chin and cheeks. He brushed his fingers over it as he tried to remember how long it had been since he'd left Glastonbury Abbey. This was his first journey outside monastic walls.

He often said afterwards that before he came to Ireland the longest walk he had ever had to undertake was to the abbot's kitchen on days when he was assigned to clean the place out. This world beyond the abbey walls was new and exciting. It beckoned to him like a birdcall at sunrise.

That's why he'd been standing at the window gazing out in awe for most of the afternoon. Harold's eyes were wide with wonder as he watched the goings-on of folk in Wexford town.

For a long while he'd managed to ignore his feelings of guilt for neglecting his teacher. But quite unexpectedly a shudder rippled through him as he glanced over his shoulder into the semi-darkness of the chamber.

From behind him, on a straw mattress set on the floor in the corner, the young monk could hear the strained breathing of the scribe Eriginas, his superior. The old man had not regained consciousness since he'd been carried off the boat from Britain. Three nights had passed since then. The scribe's fever had steadily worsened. His features had become drawn. His skin had turned grey. Even though no one had said so openly, the young monk knew Eriginas was close to death.

'Harold,' the old man whispered fitfully. 'Harold, am I going to die? What has God told you of my fate? What have you seen?'

Harold turned away from his teacher to look out at the town again. The old man was muttering in a dazed half-conscious confusion brought on by the fever. There was no reason to feel guilty for ignoring his pleas.

'It is beyond any mortal skill to save him now,' the young monk whispered to remind himself the struggle would not be a long one. 'He'll soon be gone.'

Outside, the sudden squall of rain had eased and the latest arrivals were making their way up the muddy street. A boat from Britain had unloaded its passengers and goods. The lower eastern end of the town by the wharves where vessels beached was a bustling hive of activity. With a deep sigh Harold wished he were free to walk down to the water.

He was glad to be in Ireland. All his life, for reasons which he did not quite understand, he'd longed to learn to play the harp. And this country was the land of harpers. Harold strained his ears, half expecting to hear the gentle strumming of the harp call.

27

He decided he'd seek out a teacher as soon as he was able. As this thought crossed his mind, a strange sight was revealed to him.

A veiled woman dressed in dark blue clothing stepped out from behind the blacksmith's shop. She held the reins of a black Norman warhorse and she was closely followed by two servants.

The first serving man led a lesser animal, a nevertheless well-bred beast. This fellow was clean-shaven with short cropped hair as befits the servant of a wealthy landowner. The second fellow was broad-shouldered with lanky jet-black hair and an unruly beard. He had hold of the reins of a donkey which laboured behind a fully laden cart.

Harold frowned. It was unusual for a woman to be travelling in the Norman lands with two male servants but no man of equal rank to escort her. The monk knew without question she was a woman of quality. Her rich exotic clothing marked her as such. The fine blue silk veil which concealed her face was a declaration of her rank. Her husband was likely a noble knight of renown.

As the three travellers passed by the window, Harold noticed an intriguing detail. The servant who led the cart had a short sword belted about his waist. He carried the weapon with confidence, as if he were ready to draw it in an instant. A familiar sensation washed over the young Benedictine. He trembled. And despite the fact he'd experienced this intuitive state many times before, a tinge of fear came upon him. A fear of those terrible sights he witnessed when the affliction took hold of his mind.

It had been some weeks since he'd fallen victim to a vision. He'd begun to hope God had answered his fervent prayers and removed the curse.

But he was already in the grip of the seeing-sickness again, in a strange town in a foreign country. The only man who knew how to help him was breathing his last on a mattress in the corner.

Harold's eyes glazed over and he gasped. His heart nearly stopped with the shock of the shiver erupting through every muscle in his body. He opened his mouth to beg for help but his tongue would not move. The young monk closed his eyes tight, though he knew this simple act wouldn't be enough to protect him.

In his mind's eye the woman before him threw off her veil and looked directly into his face. Her skin was dark like the finest brown ink. Her eyes, sparkling green jewels, were full of a joy tainted by hardship and tinged with cheek-reddening temptation. Fascinated, Harold opened his eyes as he dutifully crossed himself.

He'd encountered so very few women in his life, mostly old crones who would come to the abbey gates to beg. This lady stirred an unfamiliar fascination in him so he forced all his attention to the servant who led the donkey cart. To Harold's mystic eyes the man appeared dressed in a coat of mail stretching down to his knees. Over this he wore a white tunic emblazoned with a red cross.

The young monk recognised the style and manner of his dress. The stranger was outfitted as a Knight of the Templar Order.

The servant glanced up at Harold from under his flat-topped helm. And that's when something even more astounding happened.

Have you ever passed a stranger in the crowd and, though you've never seen him before in this life, recognised him? Have you ever caught a glimpse of such a stranger and been left with a longing to know that person better?

That was how the young Benedictine felt about this fellow, though it was but for an instant.

Harold was still frowning when the fit passed. Then the

strangers turned a corner, headed for the main gate of the town. In a few moments they had passed out of sight altogether. But the vision remained clear.

The young scribe was gripped by a powerful urge to run after the three foreigners.

Just then the old man coughed. 'Harold? My son. Please hear my confession.'

The young monk took in a sharp breath of surprise. He could sense immediately the venerable monk was fully awake this time. He was at his superior's side in a flash.

'I'm here,' Harold soothed as he lifted a cup of weakened ale to the old man's lips.

Eriginas drank a deep draught. His thin grey hair was drenched in sweat. His eyes were reddened and watering. His skin was like a dry piece of crumpled parchment.

When he'd satisfied his burning thirst he pushed the cup away to speak.

'How long have I been asleep?'

'Three days.'

The old scribe took another sip of the ale, closing his eyes as he savoured the aromatic sweetness. 'This ale reminds me of home. Where am I?'

'Indeed you are home. You have returned to the land of your birth. We have landed in Ireland.'

The old man frowned with frustration and his eyes filled with the fire of reprimand. 'I know that, you foolish boy! I may have a fever but I haven't lost my wits! I meant this ale reminds me of Glastonbury. The abbey is my true home.' The old man softened his tone. 'Forgive me, my lad. I'm short-tempered with this sickness. What I meant to ask is, whose house is this?'

'We've been granted the hospitality of the abbot of the Cistercian community of Wexford.'

The old man's eyes widened in concern. 'Cistercians?' he

muttered, grabbing at Harold's hand. He squeezed it tightly and spoke in an urgent whisper. 'Where are my books?'

'I have them in safekeeping as you instructed.'

'Don't let those white-robe bastards get hold of them. I've spent a lifetime collecting those manuscripts. They must not fall into the hands of the Templars.'

'I'll guard them with my life, brother.'

'If you do not, your life won't be worth living.'

'I promise I'll take care of your books.'

'Thank you, Harold,' the old man replied, suddenly relieved at the assurance. 'They're your books now. Use them wisely, if at all. There is much knowledge scribed on those pages and more wisdom in every pen stroke than a young man such as you could possibly need to draw on.'

Eriginas looked into Harold's eyes as if he was searching for something he'd lost long ago. 'Have you seen my fate?' he asked. Apprehension tainted the question.

His student nodded shyly.

'Will I die from this fever?'

Again the young monk nodded but with more gravity this time. Harold averted his eyes, unable to meet those of his master as he spoke. 'A glimpse came to me before we made landfall in Ireland.'

Eriginas let his head rest back against the wooden bedhead. He was silent for a long time as he contemplated his own passing. When at last the dying man opened his mouth to speak he had another question.

'Do you think you can continue our mission without me?'

Harold knew the old man would die soon but he hadn't really considered what he'd do with himself once Eriginas had passed away. After a moment of hesitation he found words to reply.

'If it is your wish, my teacher, I will complete the task allotted to us as if you were by my side,' he declared bravely, though there was more than a hint of doubt in his voice.

The old man smiled. 'It warms my heart to hear you say that. Though you have no idea what you're committing yourself to. Unless I'm very much mistaken, you're about to embark on a perilous adventure.'

Harold raised his eyebrows. He'd understood they'd been sent here by the Abbot of Glastonbury to establish a Benedictine community in the newly conquered parts of this wild land. But he could see by the expression on his teacher's face that this was only part of the story.

Eriginas patted the younger monk's hand as he motioned for the cup again. After he'd taken another mouthful of the ale he coughed a little. Then he grabbed Harold's hand once more.

'Your visions don't tell you everything.' The old scribe probably would have smiled with satisfaction but a cough prevented that.

'I haven't much time left,' Eriginas gasped. 'You must listen carefully to every word I have to say. You must promise not to divulge a breath of what I tell you to any of the Cistercians. They live sword in sheath with the Knights Templar. It'd be a grief to all Christendom if those brigands were to get wind of our real mission in this country.'

Harold's vision of the Knight Templar and the dark woman in the street filled his thoughts. He blinked to force the memory out of his mind.

'A lie was put about regarding our purpose so that suspicions would not be aroused when we travelled beyond the boundary of the Norman portion of Ireland,' Eriginas explained.

'I don't understand.'

The old man struggled to sit up. 'Go to the door. Make certain no one is listening.'

Harold opened the wooden door as silently as he could, then checked this way and that along the short corridor. When he was sure there was no one about, he closed the door behind him.

'All the Cistercians are at prayers,' the student reported to his superior. 'There are only nine of them and their abbot is very strict.'

'I'm glad to hear it,' Eriginas sighed. 'Come here. Sit down.'

The lad did as he was told, leaning in close to his master to hear everything that was to be said.

'Our abbot charged me with several errands,' Eriginas began. 'He was relying on me to succeed. The fate of all Christendom is in our hands.'

'You're a scribe,' Harold objected. 'I am merely your student. How could the destiny of the Christian world rest with us? What errand could you or I perform that any other monk at Glastonbury could not complete as readily?'

'My boy, we were sent here to seek out certain books. Once found they must either be returned to the abbey or destroyed.'

He waited a moment to observe Harold's reaction. When the younger monk shook his head to show he didn't understand, the old man went on.

'I have a reputation for my thorough understanding of the more obscure works kept in the libraries of the great monasteries. Indeed, I'm probably the only scribe who would be up to this task. Apart, perhaps, from you.'

Eriginas coughed again.

'You're the finest student I've ever tutored. And most importantly you've never been beyond the boundaries of the abbey before. The world outside Glastonbury means little to you. You're not easily tempted. We're a couple of rare fish in an ocean of greedy sea monsters, you and I.'

Eriginas strained to breathe but the younger man was uncertain whether his teacher wasn't also suppressing a laugh.

'The abbot considered us both to be trustworthy and learned,' Eriginas said.

'What books could bring us so far from home?'

'There are two. The first is a terrible work inspired by the

Devil himself. It is a manual of black magic known as the Book of Sigils. There are said to be three copies of this work in Ireland.'

'And what of the other book?'

'Some would say the other book is even more dangerous. There are those who blaspheme when they call it the Gospel of Thomas. They claim it was written down by the disciple Saint Thomas the Twin. Many heretics praise this book as presenting the truest doctrine of Our Lord. But it has long been denounced as a forgery by the Holy Fathers in Rome.'

'How did these books come to be here? I've never heard of them. I thought I knew the titles of all the discredited apocryphal works. Though I know nothing of manuscripts dealing with the black arts.'

'Eight hundred years have passed since the Mother Church outlawed these monstrosities,' the old man informed him. 'But the Irish were beyond the jurisdiction of Rome until the coming of the Normans. There are still yet many amongst their folk who venerate heretical doctrines as if they were the authentic word of God. These brazen blasphemers call themselves Culdees.'

The old man suddenly coughed violently. This time there was blood in his mouth. It stained his lips dark red.

Harold gave his teacher the ale cup as much to soothe the old man as to wash away the blood. When the fit had passed, Eriginas went on.

'Your duty is clear. You must find the three copies of the Book of Sigils then discover if there are any further facsimiles of it in existence. Keep them safe. However, the Gospel of Thomas must be destroyed wherever you encounter it.'

Harold's eyes widened.

'You will take all three copies of the Book of Sigils back to Glastonbury. They are to be placed in the hands of our abbot and no other. Mark my words. No other. The work was inspired by Satan. Do not be tempted to study it too closely. You will only be opening your heart to the Devil.'

'What would the Abbot of Glastonbury want with such a book?'

'We know the Knights of the Temple have at least one copy in their possession,' the old man replied in a weak voice. 'It's essential the theologians of our order have the opportunity to study the manuscript in detail so we can be prepared if the Templars use the spells against us.'

'I don't understand,' Harold interjected. 'Does our abbot intend to use the black arts against the Knights of the Temple?'

Eriginas smiled indulgently at his young student.

'You have much knowledge,' he told the lad. 'But you understand little of the world. That's my fault. Perhaps I should have educated you in the ways of men so you would be better prepared for the task ahead of you.'

He breathed in sharply as pain clouded his eyes.

'Alas, it is too late to begin now. You must trust your instincts. You must learn to rely on your gift.'

'The abbot has forbidden me to speak to anyone of my visions,' the young man protested.

'I know that. But he didn't forbid you to use them for the good of our Mother Church.'

'He warned me my visions were an affliction sent by the Devil to tempt me into evil.'

'God made all things,' Eriginas replied sharply. 'He gave you this gift for a purpose. If you don't listen to His voice then surely Satan will be sitting at his supper smiling when your soul is served up. Do not doubt for an instant that the ways of the Evil One are subtle. But the mind of God is unfathomable.'

He grunted in pain.

'Our dear abbot understands that as well as I do. He will not judge you ill if you use your talent in the service of the Almighty. Just as you must not judge him for wishing to use the Book of Sigils against the enemies of the Church.'

The scribe gasped. But after a moment he overcame the pain and forced himself to continue speaking. Now his voice was more breath than sound.

'If the Templars gain the upper hand in this matter it could spell the end of the Benedictines. Our lands will be forfeit to the Cistercians. The Church will become a mere agent of the Knights Templar. Heresy will rule as it does under the influence of the schismatic Cathars of the southern lands.'

'All because of a book?' Harold cut in incredulously.

'Knowledge is power,' Eriginas replied. 'Have I not taught you that well enough?'

The younger man nodded.

'These are but two books,' the old man agreed. 'Yet every relic or manuscript in the hands of the Temple Knights strengthens their cause. I was sent here because I am an acknowledged expert in the identification of heretical works. And because I am unlikely to be tempted by the Devil's wiles.'

The old man struggled to continue speaking.

'I've tutored you well enough for you to fill my shoes. But I'm dying. I won't be able to aid you in this quest.'

Harold shook his head. 'I don't know what I'm looking for,' he protested. 'I wouldn't know where to begin the search. Send to the Abbot of Glastonbury for another more experienced brother. I will serve him as I have served you.'

'There isn't time. You must write to Glastonbury but don't mention any matters other than the news of my passing. Only say in the letter that you will continue our mission and that I gave you my blessing. Beg our brother abbot for help. Ask him to send a trusted Benedictine to guide you.'

Then Eriginas sighed. 'But don't expect any reply before snowmelt. The year is old. All Hallows Eve is almost upon us.

The seas are becoming heavy. Passage from Britain will soon be impossible. You must do what you may to advance the search while you wait for help.'

'Surely the abbot would not want me to go off into the wilds alone,' Harold protested. 'I'm not up to such an important task. Our abbot would never have sent me off alone on such a journey.'

'God has laid this quest upon you, not the Abbot of Glastonbury. The Almighty has granted you the necessary skills and talents to help you on your way. Have no fear. Our dear abbot will send someone as soon as he is able. In the meantime you must begin this urgent search.'

Again the old man coughed. Then he sat back and laid his head on the pillow.

'You're not safe,' he strained to whisper. 'It's likely the Templars already know our real purpose in coming to Ireland. They've long had agents within the Benedictine order just as we have ours among the Cistercians. Yet they are so often one step ahead of us. They may not expect a young monk like you to undertake such a task alone. We must count on your youthful inexperience to provide a cover.'

'Brother,' the younger man pleaded, 'I've not been outside the monastery walls since I was a child. This is my first journey into the world.'

'If you follow my advice you may survive long enough to reach a part of the country where the Templars have no influence.'

The old man told Harold to make his way with all speed to the west, to always act with humility and to treat everyone he met with the utmost respect. For as the wise saying tells us, Christ often goes in the guise of a stranger. It is Heaven's way to test the hearts of those who serve the Almighty.

'When you have passed beyond the Norman lands Harold of Glastonbury must vanish. You must take a name that will make you acceptable to the Irish. Do you know our language well enough?'

'I have studied everything you taught me. I'm confident I can be understood by most Gaelic speakers. I can read their language without any problems at all.'

'I was born in the west of this land,' Eriginas told his young companion. 'So you may be sure I have passed the dialect of my country to you without error. You're a good student. Keep your ears open. Watch your back. Stay calm even under the most trying of circumstances. Be precise in every word and deed.'

The old scribe coughed again in agony but he was determined to finish what he had to say.

'Beware the lion who dresses in the clothing of a sheep. Most important of all, promise me you will survive long enough to complete this sacred mission.'

'I will do my best.'

'Then I can go to my eternal rest without remorse for having left you in such terrible circumstances,' the old man wheezed.

His cough was rasping now. The pain in his lungs had brought a bright red hue to his cheeks.

'If you need sanctuary or if you fear for your life, go to the Killibegs. Seek out my youngest sister Binney who dwells within that community. She is no longer a Benedictine nun but she is an honest woman who will ensure your safety. She will thank you for bearing the tidings of my death to her. Tell her you were my student. You'll be treated as family. But say nothing of your quest.'

Then Eriginas took a deep, shuddering breath. His jaw clenched and he growled lowly.

'I confess that I kept the truth from you. Mea Culpa, my boy. May the Lord in his mercy forgive me my pride and my foolish deceit. Binney will take care of you.'

'Where is Killibegs?' Harold pressed. 'What road do I take?'

The old man let out all the air from his lungs then smiled as if lost in a soothing reminiscence of his younger sister. But he didn't answer. Harold waited patiently for a few moments but the eyes of Eriginas were still. His chest did not stir again to take in breath. With sinking spirits the student gently shook his superior. But he could plainly see the old man was beyond any response.

'May God help me,' Harold whispered as he made the sign of the cross.

He pulled the old monk's cloak up to cover his face. Then he blew out the candle that had burned at the bedside. Harold knew he really should begin praying but he couldn't bring himself to perform that office just then.

He sat there for a long, long time until the shadows deepened in the room. His head reeled with all that had been revealed to him.

When his mind finally began to clear he considered carefully what needed to be done. He found the satchel of books Eriginas always kept close by his side. They were his private collection of rare manuscripts. The young monk had often longed for the opportunity to thumb through these mysterious works. Now they were in his care.

He swallowed hard, signing a cross once more over the corpse. Then Harold of Glastonbury stood up, pulled the cowl of his habit up over his head and went off to find the Cistercian Abbot of Wexford.

As he made his way down the corridor he worded a solemn announcement. The enormity of the situation was just beginning to dawn on him. For he was now utterly alone in the world.

At the door to the abbot's cell he paused. In a whisper he practised his speech one last time.

'Brother abbot,' he stated, listening carefully to his own words, ensuring there was gravity and sorrow in his tone but no hint of withheld secrets. 'Eriginas the Scribe, scholar, teacher and pious brother of the Benedictine order has gone to sup with the angels in Heaven.'

I was a Culdee, you know. So were all my kith and kin, including Caoimhin. You heard me right. Saint Caoimhin of the Killibegs was a heretic. Not when I first met him of course. But in time he saw the wisdom of our ways.

After he took to our customs he treated women, men and everything in between as his equals. He became a true Culdee of the old Church that had been in Ireland long before the Normans came with all their talk of Rome. But the Norman bishops wouldn't never swallow that. They point to Caoimhin as an example for all true Christians. They claim he was a man of faith who lived a life of chastity, renunciation and un-swerving devotion to the monastic rule.

They reckon he was a hermit with a holy gift for blessing the sick or turning evil-doers from the path of wickedness. A miracle-worker imbued with the Holy Spirit, they say.

Sometimes I have to remind myself this is the same Caoimhin who could hear a hissing ale barrel opened at four thousand paces. I have to shake my head when I remember he was a man who had a passion for fine food and a love of lying in bed until lunch was ready.

The truth is our Caoimhin was a man whose personal passions daily conflicted with his duties at mass. He was one of those men who didn't think ill of committing the sin of sloth since he reckoned it was the least deadly of the seven.

Let's not quibble about it. You can't deny that slothfulness slows down all the other sins – greed, gluttony, lust and the like. That is if it doesn't snuff them out entirely. So it doesn't hurt to indulge in it now and then.

Caoimhin wasn't lazy, mind you. No one could've accused him of that. If he was dishing out a particularly good shagging he could be at it all day long.

In fact he passed from this world with a smile on his face, if you take my meaning. Bless him but he didn't like to disappoint folk.

Even if he had other things on his mind he'd be there banging away at the bedhead till sun-up if you put the offer to him rightly. Always thinking of others he was.

You don't believe me, do you? Well I don't give a pig's pisser. When I was a girl they used to say a lie is either the truth waiting to blossom or a withered certainty that's finished fruiting.

Caoimhin himself used to say the scribe's ink outlasts the martyr's blood. That's why he copied down all the tales he heard, no matter how strange, unbelievable or heretical they might have seemed to him at first.

It's true he made many mistakes when he wrote down the mystical story of the Wanderers. He claimed Mawn was born of the tribes of the Feni when in fact he was a Fánaí, which is the old word for a Wanderer. It's the details he usually got wrong.

Caoimhin never really mastered our language till late in life. He freely interpreted what he heard of Mawn's tale. And he left out much of the story Lom Dubh told him because he simply didn't understand everything he'd heard.

Caoimhin was also influenced by the many books he'd read. From an ancient Christian text known as the Book of Enoch, he collected terms which he used in his retelling of the story of the Eolaí Nathairaí. They were never known as the Watchers until he struck upon that word for them.

These are simple mistakes yet they may distract some folk

41

from the greater truth held within his writings. That's the danger of the written word. Any book-tale may be interpreted in countless ways. If you take my advice you won't trust anything you read on a page.

Caoimhin's misguided Norman view of the Irish was reflected in his stark portrayal of the Druids as mystical masters of ancient ways. When in fact they were just as prone to mistakes as any other mortals. If you ask me he'd heard too many troubadour romances for his own good. I think he allowed those silly stories to influence him a little too much.

Despite these criticisms I must say Caoimhin's rendering of the tales wasn't as prejudiced as some of his fellow clergymen who claimed to be preserving our legends. At least he didn't leave out details simply because he thought the bishops wouldn't approve.

For all his faults Caoimhin was a humble man. He never wrote down anything about his own life. Instead he encouraged me to remember as much as I could of his story. He must have known they'd twist his tale around to suit their own purposes. If he'd put it all in writing they'd have rewritten it their own way in the end.

God love him, he was a devil that man. If you'd known him you'd have said there was no greater sinner who deserved a seat by the fire in Heaven.

Don't look at me like that! It's true.

I don't care what you think of me. It's the story that's important, not the storyteller. So to be getting on with it I'll tell you something of those three strangers Harold observed from the window in Wexford.

The Widow and the Wayfarers

A light mist tainted the late afternoon with a swirling mass of moist air. Distant sounds distorted weirdly. When fog closed in about her like this, Mirim could only think of her warm, dry homeland and pray she would return to its warm embrace one day.

Since they'd left Wexford town the heavens had pressed in tightly across the Earth, making their progress miserably cold and damp. Mirim drew in the reins of her stallion to bring him gently to a halt. Then she turned round in her saddle to look back along the muddy track. Her companions were both struggling on the boggy ground. One was encouraging a donkey that hauled a small four-wheeled cart full of their possessions. The other was leading a heavily laden warhorse.

Mirim's throat was dry. Her whole body tensed with anxious readiness as she scanned the fog-shrouded trees around about. She swung a leg over the rump of her mount and landed softly beside the horse. Used to wide clear skies, she felt vulnerable seated up high on the saddle when she couldn't see very far into the distance. The solid ground beneath her feet immediately reassured her.

The desert woman waited there, gripping the reins of her black stallion as she softly rubbed him below the eye. A few whispered words passed her lips to calm him but it was obvious

43

to her the mount was upset. Horses know when danger is stalking.

The young woman loosed the blue silk veil which concealed her face. Her exotic dark features were out of place in this green land where there was more rain than sunshine. Her striking dark eyes sparkled with intelligence and wariness. As she brushed two wayward strands of jet-black hair from her face, her horse whinnied.

Mirim patted him to soothe his nerves. She could sense the tension in the air too. She'd grown up around horses. She had a special kinship with them. She understood their moods. By the time her two servants caught up with her the stallion was stamping a hoof on the damp ground to show he was not happy at all. The taller, unkempt servant led his mount up beside his mistress. A glance and a frown told her he too felt uneasy.

Someone or something was watching them.

'Why have we stopped?' the clean-shaven man asked sharply, patting the donkey he'd been leading.

'Be quiet, Tom Curdle!' she snapped back.

'We can't stand around here all afternoon,' Curdle replied in annoyance. 'What's this all about?'

'Danger,' she hissed.

She turned to her other servant, lowering her voice. 'You go to the cart and guard it well. Tom will come up to stay by my side. He'll watch over my safety.'

Mirim quickly replaced her veil, ensuring her dark features were well covered from inquisitive eyes.

In that instant a horseman appeared on the track ahead of them. He must have been waiting in the trees just out of sight.

'There's no danger,' the hooded stranger declared.

The rider let his mount step forward so she could see his sunburned bearded face framed in a bright mail coif and crowned by a conical Norman helm of archaic design. He removed the helm and bowed his head.

In his old-fashioned knee-length coat of chain the warrior looked as though he'd stepped out of some tale of past conquests. Even his lance must have been at least fifty years old.

Mirim had never seen a Norman like him, except for those adventurers depicted in the great tapestry at the cathedral in Bayeux. His mail coat gleamed like silver. There wasn't a spot of rust on his helm. His leather straps and saddle were in perfect condition. A yellow dragon motif spread out down the huge Norman kite-shaped shield, the paintwork so fresh the dragon shimmered against the green background.

Even the most fastidious knight would have found it nigh on impossible to keep his armour in such a pristine state. Everyday wear and tear would have left marks that a hundred servants couldn't have polished away.

'There's no danger,' the rider repeated uncertainly. 'At least, I mean to say, you're in no danger from me,' he added, carefully replacing the helm on his head.

His voice wavered as if he suddenly doubted his own words. Then he quickly glanced over his shoulder, nervously checking the path beyond.

The Norman tried to look relaxed as he turned his mount toward Mirim. But his mare was skittish and her eyes rolled in fear. One touch from Mirim's gentle gloved hand and the mare settled. It was as if the woman had a magical gift. The Norman took no notice. He had other matters on his mind.

'My name is Lanfranc de Courcy. These days I find it necessary to regularly patrol the roads in this part of my lands.'

As the Norman spoke, another warrior appeared from the side of the road. He was dressed in a much more humble coat of mail and was mounted on a smaller horse, as befits a sergeant-at-arms.

Lanfranc shifted in his wooden saddle when he realised his greeting had not been answered.

'You've not told me your name, my lady,' he pointed out

hesitantly after an uncomfortable pause. 'I trust you have letters giving you leave to journey this road. The king has decreed none shall travel this country without his permission.'

'I have a letter from King John,' Mirim declared, reaching into her saddlebag to retrieve it.

'I'm sure you do,' the knight shot back, holding up a hand to stop her. Then he lowered his voice, indicating he didn't want anyone else to hear what he had to say. 'This is neither the time nor the place to present it. There are wild Irish raiders abroad. I would rather not be caught off guard in the open. Have you not heard of the Queen of the Night?'

Mirim shook her head.

'The Irish say she is one of their immortal gods woken from a great sleep to bring havoc, destruction and death to their new overlords.'

He waited a moment to see whether she had grasped his meaning. Then he pointed to his own chest. 'That means us. The Normans.'

He leaned forward in his saddle, his eyes darting to the left and right. There was a nervous boyish thrill in his voice as he continued speaking.

'She can't be killed, you see. The Queen of the Night has some enchantment about her. Any wound she suffers is healed almost immediately. She's the scourge of the Norman lands. I wouldn't want to have to stand against her on my own. Imagine an opponent who can't be finished off.'

Lanfranc leaned even further forward. 'It turns my marrow to water just to talk about her.' Then the knight coughed, making a pretence of clearing his throat. 'Not that I'd run off if I met her face to face, of course. I'd give her a fight worth a verse or two in the song of her life.'

'I know nothing of this Queen of the Night,' Mirim retorted flatly. 'I've come from the Latin kingdom of the Holy Land.'

'You've journeyed from the Outremer? From Palestine?'

'Yes.'

'Have you visited Jerusalem?' The Norman's eyes were lit now with childish excitement.

'Yes.'

'We have much to talk about,' the knight stuttered nervously. 'I've always wanted to go off on a pilgrimage to the Holy City. Come to my hearth and tell me your tale over a meal.'

Mirim swallowed hard before she replied. 'Please accept my apologies. I don't have time for the generous hospitality of your fine food and fireside. I'm travelling on urgent business. I seek the castle and lands of Lord William FitzWilliam. I carry dispatches of great importance to him and his family.'

There was a hint of untruth in her speech but Lanfranc didn't notice. His eyebrows had raised at the mention of the FitzWilliam name. The desert woman thought he might be shaking. But she couldn't tell whether it was from excitement, fright or the cold foggy air.

'You're going to visit Lord William?' he repeated.

She nodded.

'He's famous in these parts. I've always wanted to meet him. But I've never had a good enough excuse to go visiting. He went to the Holy Land once, you know.'

Behind him the other mounted warrior coughed to get his lord's attention.

'What is it, Stephen?' Lanfranc sighed, rolling his eyes in exasperation at the interruption.

'We should be making our way back. The place to have this discussion is within the safety of our fortifications.'

'Yes. Thank you, sergeant,' the knight barked.

'Have you forgotten the dangers which lurk in the shadows of night?'

'I've just been telling the lady about the Queen of the Night,' Lanfranc hissed in irritation.

'I was referring to other dangers,' Stephen retorted.

Lanfranc breathed in sharply. Then he swallowed hard. 'You're right. We'll discuss this when we're safe inside my chambers.'

'Alas I cannot accompany you,' Mirim protested. 'My business will not wait. Please point me in the direction of Lord William's estates and I will bless you for your help.'

'His lands are two days ride from here,' the knight laughed. 'You certainly won't make it there before nightfall. So I must insist you accompany me to my humble fortification. Spend the night as my guest and depart refreshed at dawn.'

'I cannot tarry. I must ride on.' Mirim's tone betrayed her intolerance at being told what to do.

'I can't allow you to continue your journey tonight,' Lanfranc replied firmly. 'I'm responsible for all travellers on this road. If you were to be attacked by raiders the king would have my body parts impaled on long splintery sticks in a place frequented by starving crows. That's not to mention the possible danger from other, more devilish quarters.' He shuddered at the thought.

He took a deep breath to calm himself. Then he smiled and his face lit up with an expressiveness that betrayed a softness in his character.

Mirim had never noticed this quality in any other Norman warrior. He was certainly a strange one, she told herself. Though probably harmless.

'You didn't tell me your name,' he said, his eyes sparkling with joyous apprehension.

'I am Mirim de Harcourt. I am the widow of Alan de Harcourt who was a cousin of Lord FitzWilliam.'

Lanfranc's smile widened. 'You're a widow?'

She nodded almost imperceptibly.

'That explains the veil,' he added half to himself. 'What's your business with his FitzWilliamness?'

'I've come to ask that he plead my case with the king to have my late husband's lands handed over to me. They were seized by a rival when news of my husband's death reached England.'

The Norman squinted in his boyish way. Then he cast his eyes this way and that for a few moments in a gesture of helplessness which stirred a mild sense of maternal protectiveness in Mirim. The thought struck her that if the situation had been different she might have reached out to pat his hair until he'd calmed down, just as she had done with his horse. Clearly he was having trouble making a decision.

'I know what we should do,' Lanfranc ventured at last, though he didn't seem entirely convinced. 'First of all it's too dangerous for us to be out after sunset.'

He stopped himself to make a telling correction. 'It's too dangerous for *you* to be out after sunset. I mean to say, that is unless you have a knight such as myself to guard you.' He coughed, betraying a little of his timidity.

'When we reach my tower I'll send a rider to Lord William. Then in the morning I'd be honoured if you would allow me to escort you onward to his castle.'

Though he could not see her expression behind the veil, Lanfranc sensed a change of heart come over the woman.

'Perhaps you're right,' Mirim conceded as she placed a foot in the stirrup and effortlessly launched into her saddle.

It was then Lanfranc noticed she was wearing men's britches under her cloak. He'd never seen such a thing in his life before. He was still staring at her when she spoke again.

'For the moment I accept your protection. But only because I haven't sat by a hearth fire for many weeks nor have I slept in a real bed since I departed from London.'

'A real bed?' Lanfranc echoed. 'I have a real bed.'

'Then I thank you for surrendering it to me tonight,' Mirim shot back. She gave her mount a little kick and the horse dutifully set off down the path.

Lanfranc struggled to bring his warhorse around. 'That's right!' he shouted after her, pointing. 'Just keep riding down this road. You'll be there in no time.'

He leaned back in the saddle to spur his own horse. The mare jolted forward and Lanfranc's helm tumbled off his head. The horse stamped skittishly and while the knight struggled to settle her Mirim's servants passed by and disappeared. At last the mare was steady enough for him to dismount to retrieve his helm. But he slipped clumsily out of the saddle, slid sideways and landed on his back. His lance snapped under his weight with a loud crack but fortunately without any damage to the luckless knight who'd been bearing it.

'Blast!' he hissed under his breath.

He was on his feet in seconds, searching for his helm in the grass at the side of the track. When he'd located it, he bent down low to pick it up. Just as his fingers grasped the war-hat Lanfranc heard a whistling rush nearby. He stood up sharply to find a quivering arrow stuck into a tree close by. In a breath he'd put the helm back on his head. Then, after a bit of an awkward struggle with the tight scabbard, he drew his sword.

It was this simple act that transformed the clumsy, timid Norman. If you'd seen him you would have been forgiven for thinking some magical enchantment had suddenly descended upon him.

The moment he held the blade in his hand an awesome change came over Lanfranc. Indeed, whenever he wielded this weapon his mood altered so much he sometimes didn't recognise himself. His voice deepened, his shoulders straightened and he seemed much taller and formidable. Most adversaries sued for peace at the mere sight of him with that blade.

'Come out, coward. Show your face,' he bellowed in a genuinely menacing tone.

It occurred to him that there could be more than one wild Irish raider waiting for him in the swirling fog of the forest. Or that another arrow was being notched to the bowstring even as he stood in the open issuing bold challenges.

Lanfranc looked around for his warhorse but she had wandered off down the track toward home.

'Here, Torrent,' he called, with his sword point flashing bravely at the invisible enemy. 'Come here, Torrent. There's a nice battle-nag. Who's a pretty girl, then?'

His mare didn't care about wild Irish raiders. She wanted to go home to her warm stable to listen to the midnight sighs of that lady's fine black stallion. So she ignored her master and set off down the path.

Of course Lanfranc was grateful Mirim hadn't been around to see him tumble from his horse, but with his sword drawn he was no longer fearful of what might befall him if he encountered the enemy. So he headed off into the forest to search for his hidden adversary.

Harold, the young monk from Glastonbury, stood before the abbot's door. He tapped loudly once more. His cold knuckles were red from knocking but there was still no answer. He realised the senior Cistercian brother must still be at chapel.

There was nothing else to do but wait. He had no wish to return to the chamber where the corpse of his teacher lay.

As the shadows outside began to lengthen, the air grew cooler, so Harold wrapped his monk's cowl about his head as he leaned against the abbot's door. The thought occurred to him that he should probably go to the chapel, say a prayer for the soul of Eriginas and see whether the abbot was still at his devotions. But he'd not rested properly in the three days since they'd arrived in Ireland. The journey from Glastonbury to the coast where they had taken ship had been arduous and dogged by steady rain. The sea crossing had been rough, sickening and perilous.

Harold was exhausted. Even as he stood at the abbot's door he could feel the strength draining out of him.

His head nodded against his chest no matter how much he struggled against collapsing into sleep. After a while he realised his feet were numb with inactivity and the bitter cold. So with a concession to comfort he squatted down on the floor. Then he pulled the wool of his monk's habit close around his legs. The hall was becoming dark so it was easy to shut his eyes to steal a little rest.

He breathed deeply, promising himself he would jump up wide awake the moment he heard the abbot approaching. But the abbot did not return that night. And Harold of Glastonbury slept as soundly as he had ever done in his own monastic cell at home.

This young scribe's life had always been ordered by the strict patterns of the Benedictine rule; each day was filled with the same routine of prayer, work, study and humble silence. The monastery was a peaceful, secure, serene community. Until the day he'd set out with Eriginas, Harold had known no other way of living.

The white-clothed Cistercians who had taken the two of them in were so different from any of the monks of Glastonbury. Black-robed Benedictines were forbidden to laugh or engage in witty, flippant conversation. This prohibition was thought to encourage a deeper sense of humility and foster the air of sanctity which enfolded the monastery. Cistercians, on the other hand, were always joking, playing word games and, worst of all, singing cheery songs as they went about their work. Not religious songs either. They sang light-hearted ditties they'd learned from the locals.

Eriginas had told him all Cistercians were in league with

Satan. They hid behind the cloak of white vestments but in fact they were evil, corrupt, fun-loving, lusty, lecherous and heretical. They played games in the cloisters. And, insensitive to scandal, they allowed women to attend their masses.

Under the leadership of their late brother Bernard of Clairvaux the Cistercians had risen to prominence in Church affairs. A century earlier the Benedictines had been the dominant holy order, now the Cistercians had usurped them almost completely. The white monks even had the gall to refer to their most famous brother as Saint Bernard even though the Pope had not yet officially assented to his sanctity.

Eriginas had warned his student many times of the dangers of these folk. Clearly, the old man had reasoned, the Devil himself had a hand in their sudden rise to power and influence.

The only Benedictine within a hundred miles, Harold was cast adrift among these wicked white-robes with no one to turn to for help or guidance. It is not surprising therefore that his dreams that night were unsettled as he slept at the doorstep of the abbot's chamber.

A Lion in Sheep's Clothing

T he moon was just emerging from its darkest phase so the stars were particularly bright that night as Mirim rode along. She couldn't help staring up at them, haunted by thoughts of her far-off desert homeland.

Behind her, seated on the other warhorse, Tom Curdle strummed upon a lute. The melody was one he'd learned in the land of Outremer. It was bittersweet, full of echoes of the sandy kingdoms of the east.

Many times as a child Mirim had sat gazing heavenward in wonder at the glorious never-ending stars. Though desert days were hot, dry and stifling, the nights were cool. In the evenings she had a special place she used to go to watch the sky, a place where she knew she'd be undisturbed. At the edge of the oasis there were some rough-cut stairs leading up the cliff face to a well.

Mirim would sit on the top step staring into the blue night imagining the world beyond the great desert. It was a time of peace, contentment and joy for her. How much her life had changed since then.

Each month at full moon the mystics of the desert would gather to play their drums and jangling stringed instruments while the desert wind howled in the distance. A fire would be built for them near the well while a feast was prepared. The young girl used to watch, even though unmarried women were not supposed to be out on such nights. But Mirim could not resist the temptation to catch a glimpse of the holiest person dwelling at the oasis.

Among her folk there was one woman who was not wed to any man. She was married to the well. She was responsible for keeping the spring clean. This woman also ensured all who drank from the waters acted with respect. An arcane enchantment ensured that any who drank of the waters without permission from the woman at the well would suffer a terrible punishment. The disrespectful ones were cursed to forget everything they had ever known.

When the desert mystics played their music in the moonlight the old woman would emerge from her house to sing. Even though she was ancient of years the old crone's voice always sounded like that of a girl of twenty summers.

Beneath the Irish sky Mirim softly hummed the old woman's prayer to the well while Curdle, listening carefully, accompanied her melody. Then, full of longing for her home, she recited the song of the woman at the well.

'While I am sleeping you carry off all my pain and suffering in your beautiful hands. While I am weeping you carry me like fragrant rosewater in your beautiful hands. While I was sleeping you brought me gifts of love in your beautiful hands.'

The well-woman had been old when Mirim was a girl. Her father had once told her he would be proud if she became the new well-woman when the crone passed over. Mirim had long expected that would be her destiny. In truth she'd been excited by the possibility of serving her people as well-keeper. That's why she'd learned the song.

But all her dreams had come to nothing. For she had been sitting on the steps one noontide as a terrible dust storm blew itself out. That day she had looked into the eyes of a stranger. And for the first time in her life Mirim had known the yearning of love.

The top step was her special place, her heart's home. It was there she'd seen the man who would be her husband, Alan de Harcourt.

Mirim was woken from her reminiscences as her horse stopped with a jolt. She squinted to see through the darkness. Before her was a hill surrounded by wooden posts surmounted with crudely sharpened points. Beyond the wall there was an unfinished stone tower. Firelight escaped from cracks in the palisade, betraying the presence of several guards.

Lanfranc's sergeant, Stephen, had gone on ahead at a gallop. It was he who brought the gate open to welcome Mirim and her small party in to the fort.

The desert woman dismounted and led her horse past the silent warrior. Her servants followed. No words passed between any of them. As soon as they were within the palisade the warrior slammed the gate shut then lifted an iron bar to secure the entrance.

When that was done Stephen turned to face the strangers. He'd just taken a breath to speak when the silence of the night was torn apart by a deep menacing growl which shook Mirim's stomach.

It was the fierce night call of a man-eating lion. Didn't I mention there was a man-eating lion in this story? I'm sure I listed it after the love triangle. Never mind. He's roared his way into the weave of my tale now so there's nothing I can do about it.

I'll be honest with you. I can tell you're not the gullible type. It's doubtful whether the lion actually ate anyone. At best I reckon the poor beast, if he existed at all, was just haunted by an unshakeable *reputation* for hunting people down.

This lion question vexed me for years. So I read some of the finest manuscripts on the subject of natural history. As far as large flesh-eating felines are concerned, I can confidently make one important observation. By their very nature predatory cats, and lions in particular, tend to hunt down the weak, the infirm and the slow. One way or another this qualifies almost everyone I've ever met.

Yet after conducting extensive interviews amongst my peers I haven't come across anyone who actually saw the creature with their own two eyes. To my thinking it's unlikely such a beast could have strolled around the countryside of Norman-occupied Ireland without sampling the generous abundance of suitable prey. And so leaving a trail of bones as proof of its existence.

So you see I've drawn my own conclusions about the beast, but for the sake of honesty I couldn't leave him out. Take my word for it, this flaw in the story is probably best ignored if you can manage it.

Don't treat the rest of the tale with contempt just because the wafting fishy stink of exaggeration hangs over one small detail. The lion may have been nothing more than a rumour but by Saint Columba's cat that roar was enough to soil a sober soldier's undergarments.

'What was that?' Mirim gasped when the last echo had died away.

'Probably just a couple of badgers mating,' Stephen answered after a short pause.

But the lie was painted clearly across the features of his paling face.

'I don't know what a badger looks like,' the woman replied with suspicion, 'so I have no idea what noises a rutting pair might make. But if I didn't know better I'd say that sounded like a lion.'

The warrior's eyes widened. 'Do you truly think it might be a lion?' he whispered with nervous excitement, as if he were hoping the beast wouldn't overhear him.

'I'm almost certain of it.'

'There was a rumour going about in Wexford town about a

lion harrying the countryside hereabouts. I never paid it much heed till our first night camped at this spot. Every evening since then we've heard that awful hungry roar. And then there are also the strange disappearances to account for.'

'What disappearances?'

Before Stephen could answer, the creature let out another impossibly deep growl which set their knees trembling.

'This is no time to be talking about such things,' the warrior whispered. 'His lordship can tell you all about it in the morning.'

'Aren't you concerned about your master?' the woman enquired with a frown. 'Shouldn't you be out looking to his safety?'

'Out there?' Stephen couldn't believe she was serious. 'I'm not going out there while there's a lion roaming about. I'm not a bloody fool.'

Mirim shook her head, wondering what kind of warriors the Normans had sent to occupy this country.

'I'm sure Lanfranc will be along later,' Stephen added dismissively. 'Don't worry about him. He's a knight. Any strife he gets into is his own affair.'

He was right. Lords love danger. Why else would they spend a lifetime learning how to attack anything they merely suspect of being hostile? In my opinion if you're going to build your home near a lion's den, you can't complain if you end up on his dinner table.

'I understand enough about those creatures to know they don't usually inhabit damp countries,' the desert woman noted. 'How could a lion have come to Ireland?'

'Ask Lanfranc in the morning,' the warrior replied.

Mirim was a little shocked. What kind of a sergeant-at-arms was this man to let his master face danger alone? Clearly these Normans were unlike any she had ever encountered.

'I'll lead you to the hall, feed you then show you where you can sleep,' Stephen told her. 'You'll be lodged on the second floor of the tower. It's the best we have. The roof leaks in parts and there's a terrible draught through the windows, but there's plenty of cowhide lying about to cover the gaps if need be.'

The warrior kicked the gate to make sure he'd secured it properly. Reassured, he headed to the door of the tower.

In the manner of many of his dreams Harold's slumbering mind relived the terrible sea voyage from Britain. However, in this state he recalled much greater detail than he could have possibly brought to his conscious mind.

He saw himself carrying his brother-in-Christ, Eriginas, along the stone wharf toward three Cistercian monks dressed in bright white. A fourth monk stood behind them. This last fellow hadn't actually been on the wharf that day.

Harold had never seen this old man before. But there was something strangely familiar about him. His short cropped beard was silver grey. His hair was long in the manner of a Norman nobleman and he wore a drooping moustache. His stature and demeanour gave him the air of a warrior rather than a monk. The garments of a cleric did not sit well on him.

In this dream Harold passed Eriginas into the care of the other three monks. Then he looked deeply into the old man's eyes as the scene transformed from the wharf at Wexford into a dusty desert battlefield.

'So you'd like to study the music of the harp?' the stranger asked.

But before Harold could reply the air was filled with shouts and the angry ringing of metal. Harold's heart thumped hard in his chest and he spun around on his heels. He had no idea where he was or how he came to be in this place.

The experience was unquestionably real to him as it always was with his visions. Often he found it difficult to discern the difference between events he witnessed through his special sight and those of his everyday life.

A firm hand clasped his shoulder and he was drawn to look again into the old man's eyes. The stranger was no longer wearing the white robes of a Cistercian. Miraculously he now appeared in the flowing white garments of a Knight of the Temple. There was a red cross at the warrior's breast and a larger one painted on his long kite-shaped shield. His conical helm gleamed silver. His rusted mail coat rustled beneath his knee-length surcoat.

He leaned on his sword, breathing deep and hard from exertion.

Harold opened his mouth to speak but before he could make a sound a large number of shadowy figures on horseback approached. Their forms were concealed by the clouds of dust kicked up by their horses but the young monk had no doubt they were deadly foes.

The mysterious old Templar lifted up his sword and stepped forward to stand protectively in front of Harold. In that instant the burden of the years dropped away from the old man. The veteran knight was suddenly young again. He laughed loudly in defiance of the enemy. He looked just like the other Templar Harold had seen in his vision at Wexford.

There was a ringing of metal as swords met. A mounted shadow passed by, then another. Harold heard the Templar swearing profusely as one more dark figure rode up to present a challenge. The young monk crouched low behind the Templar for fear of being discovered.

'They won't have you, lad,' Harold's protector declared confidently.

The scribe was terrified but curiosity had always been a strong force within him. He dared to look out from behind the Templar's surcoat to glimpse the enemy.

The adversary was a knight dressed entirely in black. His armour, surcoat, shield and helm bore neither device nor design.

'He belongs to us!' the black knight bellowed. 'Hand him over!'

'He's not yours,' the Templar answered sternly. 'He has work to do. He will stay with us.'

'You won't get your hands on the Book of Sigils!'

'I promise you I will,' the white knight replied.

'Lay down your sword and I may spare you,' the black knight laughed. 'If you withhold the lad from us I will certainly destroy you.'

'My life is almost done. I have no fear of you.'

'Give me the boy!'

'Why don't we let Harold decide which camp he will join?' the Templar suggested.

The Temple knight turned to look at the young monk cowering by his feet. 'Which of us would you follow? The black knights or the white?'

Harold looked up into the face of his protector. To his astonishment he saw a man not much older than himself. There were lines etched into his face which spoke of his many experiences in the world, but he had the eyes of a young man with little to be ashamed of.

As is the nature of dreams one small detail of the white knight's eyes struck held Harold's attention. The sparkles in them seemed to be spiralling designs such as might be found on a page of the manuscript of the Book of Kells.

Harold squinted to see them better but he needn't have bothered. One of the spirals suddenly exploded in size like a flower blooming all at once. Three paths led from the outer rim of the spiral to the centre.

The three paths crossed over and under one another, weaving together until they each ended in a swirling mass that reminded him of a gurgling fountain. The three fountains then spewed forth their turbulent waters again as light flowed out through the design to the edges once more.

Each pulse of energy through the spirals seemed to coincide with Harold's own heartbeat.

'There are two ways of looking at a spiral,' the white knight explained. 'One may follow the design from the outer edge to the inner circle, or from the inner depths to the outer extreme. Which do you see?'

'It flows from the centre outwards.'

'You'll be a fine practitioner of the Draoi-craft,' the knight told him.

Harold didn't understand what this term meant. Before he could ask, his attention was drawn back to the black knight mounted on a huge dark charger. The horse stirred up smoky dust as it pounded the ground furiously with one massive hoof.

Where there should have been a face the black-clothed warrior had nothing but an empty shadow punctuated by steamy breath. This enemy was a living, breathing dæmon of fear.

'Come with me,' the black knight demanded, his voice resonating evil. 'You belong to me. You and the Book of Sigils have always belonged to me.'

His breath was sulphur. His presence was like the terrifying crackling roar of a huge unquenchable fire. This was a devil come straight from the gates of Satan's kingdom.

Harold looked up at the Templar just as the white knight transformed again into an old man with a wry smile and tender eyes.

'You must decide for yourself, Harold,' the white knight shrugged. 'But choose carefully. I urge you to come to us. We have a treasure we wish to trust into your guardianship.'

The monk found himself struggling to breathe. What choice did he have? The black knight seemed the very embodiment of Satan.

Yet Eriginas had always warned him about the treachery of the Templars. The old scribe had said the Knights of the Temple were servants of the Devil.

The lad was confused. How could he possibly make a decision?

'Harold?' the old knight pressed gently. 'Harold.'

The Templar placed a hand on his shoulder to shake him but the young monk froze with fright, uncertain which path he should commit to.

'You're cold, my son,' the old knight soothed. 'Come with me. Warm yourself.'

In that moment Harold shuddered into a sudden state of wakefulness. There was a hand on his shoulder. An old man stood over him. But it was not the knight of his dream. It was the overweight, jolly-faced Brother Ollo, abbot of the small Cistercian community of Wexford. Behind him stood three other white-robed monks.

The abbot's half-closed eyes were carefully scrutinising Harold. For a moment the young scribe thought he might still be dreaming for he felt decidedly uneasy in this man's presence.

Harold felt a tug at the satchel by his side. Instinctively he snatched it away. It was then he realised Ollo had been trying to ease the books out of his grasp.

'Come into my chamber,' the abbot offered to cover his embarrassment. 'Sit by the fire, my son. You must be frozen to the very bone. What were you thinking to sleep at my doorstep at this time of year?'

The young scribe stretched his aching limbs. With the abbot's hand to help him, he stood up, tightly clutching the satchel of books Eriginas had left to him. Ollo offered to take them from him but Harold hugged the precious manuscripts close to his chest.

'Fetch some bread and beer,' Ollo commanded one of the junior Cistercian brothers. 'The lad has fasted since yesterday. He must eat something to regain his strength.'

He took the young Benedictine's arm and led him to the hearth. Once Harold was seated on a stool by the fire the abbot gave him a jug of watered ale. The young monk took it gratefully, quickly swallowing a deep draught.

'You came to tell me Brother Eriginas is dead?' the abbot offered.

Harold nodded.

'I've spent the night at prayer for your teacher. We knew there was little hope he would survive. It was a miracle he held on as long as he did.'

The abbot took the empty jug from the younger man. Then he crossed the room to refill it from a tapped barrel. Ollo continued speaking as he concentrated on the task.

'Brother Eriginas was a great man. He was a renowned scholar, a gifted scribe and a dedicated Benedictine. The Abbot of Glastonbury must have been very proud of him.'

The young Benedictine thought he heard a whisper. He turned his head to the left, tracing the source of the sound. He thought he glimpsed the faint misty outline of a man's shape in the corner of the room.

Then he heard the whispered words, 'Beware the lion in sheep's clothing.'

His teacher had used that very expression. Was this the ghost of Eriginas come back to warn him? Harold thought so.

The misty shape disappeared as Ollo returned with a full jug of watered ale. The young scribe watched suspiciously as the abbot crossed the room to take a seat on a stool beside him.

The abbot's nose was squat; his skin was wrinkled, weather-beaten and tough. But his soft, grey, low-lidded eyes were not those of a stern man. There was a certain joy in them. A joy that shone out even when he was expressing his grief at the passing of Eriginas.

'I'm sure you've learned a lot from your teacher,' the abbot commented.

'Indeed I have,' Harold replied as he took the jug.

'You must count your good fortune to have been his student. There are too few like him in these days.'

Ollo placed a hand on the younger man's shoulder. Harold gulped the weak ale to avoid the abbot's eyes. Suddenly he felt extremely uncomfortable. Ollo's action seemed almost threatening, and when he spoke again his words were uncharacteristically cold.

'We've arranged a mass to be said for the soul of Brother Eriginas. We will inter his body here in the crypt of our chapel until the Abbot of Glastonbury decrees where he should be laid to rest.'

The Cistercian removed the jug of ale-water from the young monk's hands. Then he laid it by the hearthstone and looked fixedly at Harold.

'Of course I think it fitting that Eriginas be entombed in his own country,' the abbot went on. 'The traveller came home to breathe the air of his homeland one last time.'

Harold nodded his head in agreement.

'What will become of you?' Ollo asked.

The question caught the young monk by surprise. He hadn't expected to be confronted so directly. 'I'm not sure what you mean.'

'You must think of what you will do. Now your master is no longer here to guide you, a decision must be made about your future.'

Harold frowned, silently berating himself for allowing Ollo to so easily intimidate him. He had made a promise to his teacher. And he was determined to keep his word, no matter what the abbot said.

'I will do as Eriginas commanded me before he breathed his last. I will stay in Ireland. I will travel west to establish a community as my teacher planned.'

'You can't be serious!' the Cistercian laughed. Then his tone hardened. 'The west is a dangerous place. There are brigands and Culdee heretics at every turn. A young fellow like yourself would be hard pressed to find his way along the unfamiliar paths. Would you suffer countless hardships only to arrive in a place where the people are undoubtedly hostile? It will soon be All Hallows Eve, which the Irish call Samhain. After that the weather will turn very nasty indeed. Where will you shelter?'

'God will provide for me.'

The abbot smiled but there was no warmth in the expression.

'I was young once. I believe I know what you mean.'

Then Ollo changed tack. 'Killibegs is many days' arduous journey from here,' he stated flatly.

Harold's eyes widened with surprise. 'How did you know. . . ?' he began, but realised he'd been tricked into revealing a precious piece of information.

'Do you mean, how did I know you would be headed for that place?' Ollo cut in. 'Eriginas has a sister. That's no secret. She turned into a blue-robed Culdee some years ago. Then she returned to dwell with the rest of her family at the Killibegs. I'm sure your teacher intended to speak with her. Perhaps he had hopes of bringing her back into the Mother Church as an adherent of the Benedictine rule.'

The fat Cistercian abbot took note as Harold shifted uncomfortably in his seat. Ollo had no doubt he'd guessed correctly. When he spoke again his tone was more confident.

'I suppose these books you carry were meant as a soothing gift to the heretics of Killibegs. If I'm not mistaken, your teacher hoped to bring that whole wayward community back into the fold of Rome. Doubtless Eriginas also intended you to carry on his work. Perhaps he thought you'd save the soul of his sister and his family in his name.'

The younger monk coughed. Now Ollo was certain he had struck at the truth.

'Who knows? If your master had lived, his tomb might one day have been venerated as the pilgrimage chapel of Saint Eriginas the Scribe, scourge of the heretics.'

Harold swallowed hard. Though Ollo seemed sincere, the young monk's instincts told him his life or his liberty would be in danger if he raised any word of objection.

When the abbot continued, his advice had an air of command about it.

'Of course you will wait here with us until instructions arrive from Glastonbury. You are welcome to share our humble house and hospitality.'

'I can't stay,' Harold blurted.

The abbot's half-closed eyes drained of all friendliness until they were frozen in a hard scowl. He looked like a great toad that had been robbed of its dinner.

Ollo spoke so sharply Harold resolved never again to contradict this man to his face. 'I've told you the risks involved are too great! God has provided you with this house for your shelter. Would you refuse His offer of help in your time of need?'

The abbot placed his hand on the satchel which lay across the young monk's lap. 'You have a bag full of irreplaceable treasures in your keeping. It would be folly to set off into the wilds, needlessly risking the loss of those treasures. Stay here. Allow my brothers to study the books while we wait for a reply from Glastonbury. By the time you're ready to leave we'll have copies of all your manuscripts and you will have survived the winter in good company.'

'Eriginas made me swear to continue our mission no matter what the hardship,' Harold replied, clutching at the satchel with whitening knuckles.

Ollo shrugged. Then the fat abbot smiled knowingly. 'And he made you swear not to allow any Cistercians to see his books, I'll wager.'

Harold blushed but before he could protest Ollo spoke again.

'Of course he did. But perhaps he'd been away from Ireland so long he'd forgotten how bad the weather turns at this time of year. Perhaps, as one who speaks the language fluently, he had less to fear from the Culdees. And possibly in the daze of his fever many things passed his lips which would never have been spoken by the wise Eriginas we all knew so well.'

The young monk caught the abbot's eye. There was no hint of trickery in his expression. His offer and concern seemed genuine enough. Harold had to ask himself whether he had been too hasty in his judgement of this Cistercian.

Then he recalled his dream. He knew well enough to listen to the advice of his visions. Though he couldn't be certain what this latest message meant, he knew there was a warning for him if only he could discern it.

Could he trust the Cistercians? Could he take Abbot Ollo at his word?

It occurred to Harold then that he should probably tell the Cistercian everything his teacher had said about the search for the Book of Sigils. He opened his mouth to speak but before he could do so Ollo cut in once more.

'There is something you're not telling me,' the abbot noted.

'Yes,' Harold nodded.

'I've been the leader of a monastic community for five years and a brother-in-Christ for twenty,' the old monk told him in a friendly tone. 'I know when a young monk is withholding information from me.'

Harold felt beads of sweat break out across his brow. Could the abbot have somehow discovered the true nature of Eriginas's quest? If it was not that, what else could he be expected to confess? Harold's heart beat faster as he considered the possibility Ollo might have an inkling about his strange dreams.

Such afflictions of the mind were treated as severe breaches of monastic discipline. In his youth Harold had been punished harshly by the senior clerics of Glastonbury for speaking about his visions. What if Ollo decided to imprison him as a heretic?

The young Benedictine decided it was essential he leave Wexford as soon as possible. He might have to live amongst the Cistercians for a little while, but he would depart at the first opportunity.

'What is it you have to say, young Harold?' Ollo pressed. 'What's on your mind? I can see you're having difficulty confessing this matter to me. But don't hold back. It will only be the worse for you if you do.'

'You're right,' the young scribe replied hastily. 'I agree with you. It would be foolish to set off at this time of year into a wild country I know nothing about.'

Ollo raised an eyebrow with interest.

'If I may beg the generous hospitality of your house, I would like to remain here until the Abbot of Glastonbury sends further instructions. It pains me to disobey the final instructions of my teacher, but I feel I have no choice but to follow your advice.'

'What else?' Ollo snapped.

'I'm frightened,' Harold replied, and there was such truth in those words that the abbot believed him without question.

The Cistercian scrutinised the Benedictine's face, searching for any hint of deception. When he discerned none he slapped the younger man on the back. Then he laughed loudly. 'There's no shame in that. Better men than you have baulked at wandering the wild Irish hills alone at this time of year.'

'Are you angry with me?' the young monk asked.

'I'm relieved. I suspected you weren't telling me of your reluctance to face danger alone. Believe me, you're making a wise decision.'

Harold breathed easier as the tension in his body melted away. He was so relieved he almost missed the next few words the abbot spoke to him.

'You're most welcome in this house. It's not often we play host to learned brethren bearing such rare books. You'll enjoy your stay in our little community once you've settled in.'

'I'm sure I will.'

'You never know,' Ollo added with a mischievous wink, 'you might end up preferring the white robes to the black.'

At that moment there was a knock at the door. A young Cistercian brother entered carrying a bowl of steaming warmed ale and a loaf of fresh dark bread.

'Eat your fill,' the abbot told Harold. 'Let the fire drive away the chill in your heart and the ache in your bones. I'll go to arrange a separate chamber for you so my lads won't disturb you at your private devotions.'

With that Ollo left the room. But as Harold chewed the brown bread he felt more out of place and uncomfortable than he had ever done in his whole life.

The Cruel Lordship of the Normans

he three strongest forces in this world are the force of water, the force of fire and the force of hatred. Yet one who wields the first two guided by the force of love may be a one to be reckoned with.

The Normans came from across the water bearing fire and the force of hate to Ireland so that our people fled before their savage onslaught. And few warriors of the Gael remained who would willingly stand against the foe.

Thirty years after the foreigners first set foot on Irish soil, John Lack-Land was crowned King of England at Westminster. By then nearly half the folk of this blessèd island were bowed down under the cruel lordship of the Normans.

With every passing season the strangers gained more ground. They pushed those who would not accept their domination into the west and north of this island. In the year of my story nothing seemed more certain but that the Normans would one day hold the entire country in their bloody grip.

The same morning young Harold sat eating his monastic breakfast wondering whether he'd made the right decision, another strand of events was weaving itself into the cloak of my tale.

Five days' weary walk west from Wexford a Norman knight and his foot soldiers were going about their business subjugating the natives of Ireland. But this fellow was no Lanfranc. He was cut from a different cloth entirely.

He knew no fear. That is to say, if he did he never let on about it to anyone. He hadn't shivered in anything but pleasure since the day he'd castrated his first peasant with a pair of pruning shears.

He never flinched at a fight. Mostly he started them. And though he held no allegiance to King John, Guy d'Alville was a Norman through and through.

He was certainly a man of many talents. I can testify that Guy was a superb tactician, a warrior of almost legendary ability, and one of the finest horsemen to bridle a warhorse. He was a student of poetry and marvellously skilled at the lute.

But he won't be remembered for any of these attributes. His fame lies in an aspect of his character that was somewhat less tasteful.

He was an utter bastard.

No one had a kind word for him. The nicest thing that could be said for d'Alville is that the eunuchs always spoke very highly of him. But then they had good cause to.

I know what I'm talking about. I was well acquainted with the fellow.

He was the kind of man who made you feel like your clothes needed scrubbing after you'd wished him good morning. There was a dark cloud across his back, a dark shadow beneath his feet and a darker spirit dwelling in his battle-scarred heart.

I heard he'd been a Grand Master of the Knights Hospitaller before he journeyed to Ireland. But he wasn't a pious or religious man. He was a womaniser, a thief and a scoundrel.

Guy mercilessly crushed anyone who dared opposed him. He hated those who capitulated to him. And he more or less entirely despised anyone who followed him.

His one redeeming feature was that each day he spent eight hours asleep. Eight hours in which he harmed no one. Though he snored with the force of a belching black dæmon who's just consumed a cabbage garden.

Whatever wind it was that brought him to this land may well have blown from Beelzebub's backside. But it wasn't the Devil nor any of his dark archangels who sent d'Alville here. It was the next best thing to Satan in those days.

It was the Pope.

I can't say whether or not it's true d'Alville had been charged with the mission of destroying heresy. That's only what he claimed. I reckon he was just another wanton warrior out to carve himself a kingdom in an unconquered land no matter the cost.

But he had a weapon few men possessed. It was a letter from the Bishop of Rome. And this elaborately decorated parchment scroll had a devastating effect on anyone who read it. I never saw the letter myself so I can't vouch for its authenticity nor for its contents. I only know this precious parchment could reduce a battle-hardened knight to a gibbering, gob-blubbering bucket of mush. Fear is a terrible thing. But spineless, saliva-slathering submission from a grown man is a sickening sight to see. And I suppose that will always be my clearest memory of Guy.

The terror he inspired.

Now I think of it I'd have to concede that Guy was an inspiration to many folk. He inspired some to submit. He inspired many more to repent or take the cloth in their waning years. He also inspired an unconfirmed number to disappear off the face of the earth without a trace. Indeed most departed without so much as a word of farewell to their loved ones, nor even a mumbled entreaty to a confessor. Nor any inkling of their own imminent demise.

Don't misunderstand me. I'm not implying the rest of the Normans were a gentle lot compared to him. They brought fire, fear, pillage and blood to this land in their longships. They forced our folk to pay impossible taxes. They compelled farmers to feed and quarter their foot soldiers whenever they passed by.

The Normans robbed or murdered anyone whose lands they coveted. They acknowledged no law but that of the sword. They tortured the innocent. They imprisoned the weak. They stole sheep, goats and cattle for their own flocks. In general the invaders earned themselves an awful reputation.

But it was fellows like Guy d'Alville who gave them a *really* bad name. As I said earlier, he was a Norman through and through.

Anyway, I'm sure you've understood I wasn't very fond of the man. He was handsome enough in a foreign, soldierly, emotionless-bastard sort of way. Some men are like that.

Every woman knows that behind a set of dark wet alluring eyes there is a bloody liar who could talk his way into Saint Bridget's own sandals if the desire came upon him. And every woman has met a man whose very speech could turn her mind to melted butter, at least for a while.

If she let him.

But where would we be if womenfolk submitted to such fellows without offering any challenge to their arrogance? What would become of the world if those sort of men were allowed to gallop roughshod over the cobblestones of the weak willed? Before long the very warp and weft of society would begin to unravel. No woman really wants that. It doesn't hurt to daydream a little as long as you know to look out for signs of impending nightmare.

Mark my words, Guy was the kind of man who kindled such silly dreams in certain women who should have known better and who sorely regretted their foolishness afterwards. You can take my word these dreams were the kind that swiftly transformed into the aforesaid nightmares.

It wasn't my fault I found such a rat-arsed, arrogant, two-faced, fungus-infested imitation of a man so attractive. It was an accident. Nothing more than pure chance. But there you go. That's how it was. I'll tell no more of this lest I speak of some things too soon and make a fool of myself.

I wasn't going to mention this whole business to you at all but since you know now I'll make no secret of it. Just as long as you understand I'd prefer you kept quiet about the details of my relationship with him if you don't mind. I'm not all that proud of his part in my life nor my part in his.

Anyway, you'll see what I'm on about as my story unfolds. So try to be patient. Bite your tongue in future when you're tempted to ask fool-headed questions. If you'd interrupted me just now you could have sent me right off the track of what I was saying.

As I was trying to tell you, the same morning Harold sat in the abbot's chamber eating bread and ale, Guy d'Alville launched his first attack on the native Gaelic-speaking Irish. He had a hundred men-at-arms under his command. These warriors were dressed in wine-red tunics to mark them in the colours of the d'Alville family. Guy loved that colour.

His own tunic was made of the toughest raw silk. His cloak was woven out of the lightest, finest fibres of wool such as the Turks wear. He certainly had an eye for fashion. Most genuine bastards do.

His mail coat was interspersed with brass rings so it sparkled even though the steel rings were weathered to a dull sheen from rust. His helm was of the latest design. It was flat across the top rather than rising to a conical peak. It was painted black. His shield, edged with polished steel, was smaller than Lanfranc's ancient heirloom. It was also painted in d'Alville's livery colour of wine red. Emblazoned across the length of it was a bright red, twisting winged serpent.

The Normans had only abandoned the gods of their Norse ancestors a mere two generations earlier. Men like d'Alville were rumoured to be clandestine heathens still.

I wouldn't be surprised if this one worshipped the dark gods of the north with blood sacrifices at full moon like the Saxon savages of England do.

Guy sat astride a beautiful, wild-eyed black stallion, fourteen hands at the shoulder. The saddle furniture was of blackened leather decorated with more monstrous flying creatures outlined in yellow.

His lance was black tipped with a bright red pennant that bore the design of a painted raven. And if you'd seen him that morning you might have thought he was a hero come to watch over the simple Irish folk through the dark night until the morning. You might have thought he was one of the ancient Danaan folk of the legends who still ride through Ireland at certain times of the year. Or you might have imagined him a mighty king come to drive out the Devil from the hearts of men and bring a reign of peace.

Well you'd be wrong.

Not long after sunrise Guy looked across the fields toward a hill on which stood a tiny settlement. The dwellings were all made of stone. A few had tall gables with steeply packed thatch. But three of the stone houses were square at the base with rounded rooftops built of stone.

Guy considered these poor buildings to be an indication of the barbarity of his foe. But then he'd not really met any Irish folk since he'd landed at Limerick. He'd butchered a few but he'd introduced himself first.

With a warrior's watchfulness d'Alville waited until a lone monk emerged from one of the simple roundhouses. He thoughtfully observed the man, head shaved from ear to ear, hair worn long at the back.

The strange thing about these folk, Guy thought to himself, was that they were so blatant in their heresy. Their long matted locks, blue robes and heathen customs marked them so obviously for death.

Except the women and children. They were marked for slavery.

Guy squinted to get a better look at the heretic; he gauged the fellow's worth in a fight and decided this would not be a long conflict. Satisfied that this settlement would be his first major conquest, he dipped his lance to the ground and raised his shield silently in the air.

The foot soldiers responded immediately. They'd been there half the shivering night waiting for this signal. They were keen to be about their work. Swords were drawn without so much as a whisper of steel. Helms were adjusted. Shields were readied. Hasty, half-hearted prayers were proffered. Then the Normans set off toward the defenceless community.

Even though the warriors were weighed down with weapons and armour, they hardly made a sound as they crossed the open space at the foot of the hill. These men were all hand-picked professionals, veterans of the Crusades.

The mercenaries had certainly studied their craft well. No one in the settlement suspected what was about to befall them. The goats didn't hear them coming. The dogs didn't stir. Even the geese ignored the advancing attackers until it was too late.

Guy looked on for a while, smiled, spurred his horse lightly then followed on behind his men at a leisurely pace. This would be over in half an hour. He signalled silently for his hawk to be brought to him, with a touch of boredom colouring the gesture.

Then he left his men to their work, sending his hunting bird out to bring back something tasty for his breakfast. By the time the hawk returned with a duck in its claws, his warriors were entering the walled enclosure of the hilltop settlement.

Guy yawned as he considered how to spend the remainder of the morning. When the peasant monks had been defeated, subjugated and perhaps humiliated if the mood took him, he intended to eat a fine morning meal. Then he'd have a few hours' well-earned sleep.

Unarmed heretics are certainly no match for Norman fighting men. And what's more, this was a monastic community. The men and women of this settlement were the most unwarlike of any folk. So, as Guy had expected, they offered no resistance whatsoever. Indeed there was some confusion amongst the mercenary foot soldiers as they marched up the hill. The sisters and brothers cheerily brought out bread and milk as an offering of hospitality.

By the time Guy rode up the steep path to the community a place had been arranged for his horse in the stable. His warriors were stuffing their faces with food. And many of them had removed their helms so they could chat to the locals without feeling too foolish.

The sergeant-at-arms approached d'Alville, touched his forehead with his right hand in a gesture of respect and spoke to his lord.

'The Gaels want to know whether or not we'll be staying the night,' the soldier reported merrily.

D'Alville did not reply. The kind hospitality of the heretics infuriated him. The whole attack had been an affront to his sensibilities. Not a drop of blood had been spilled nor a weapon raised in anger. That challenged his definition of honour. A storm began to brew in that secret part of him where raging gales of hatred had their birth.

'I've gathered all the people up outside their chapel,' the sergeant went on hesitantly. He knew to expect the worst when Guy didn't acknowledge a report. Bitter experience had taught him to be wary of d'Alville's silences.

Guy rode on past the warrior. The sergeant followed his lord dutifully, harbouring a growing sense of foreboding. As d'Alville approached the chapel all the inhabitants of the community sank to their knees in welcome.

As they bowed their heads, each man, woman and child offered their individual blessings. Guy grunted. He saw their respect as grovelling and feeble. These people turned his stomach with contempt.

'Have the warriors assemble,' the Norman commanded in a soft monotone.

The sergeant swallowed hard. In the next breath he was bellowing at his companions, demanding they act like the professional soldiers they claimed to be. For good measure he raised a sergeant's typical doubts about each man's parentage in the hope this might soothe d'Alville.

Now I think it is fair to say that any other Norman might have humbly thanked the Lord who dwells in Heaven above for such a swift, simple victory. But Guy wasn't like other men. It didn't seem right to him there'd been no defence offered.

He distrusted folk who yielded too easily. He'd learned from many raids on seemingly innocent, unarmed villagers that such people often a have a trick or two prepared. They just wait for the right moment to play out their strategy.

So he ordered his sergeant to split the people in two. The women and children were sent off to prepare his breakfast. The duck was given into their care. The men were forced to kneel down in a long line with caps off and heads bowed. Once that was done, Guy d'Alville passed his hunting bird back to his hawker and dismounted to walk along the line of prisoners.

He took his time, carefully inspecting his first living Irish captives. As he reached the end of the line he removed his helm. Then he took off the heavy padded arming cap he wore to cushion the helm on his head. His long black locks fell free. Guy thoughtfully stroked his moustache and pointed beard. As he did so he walked back down the line. He singled out five of the strangers.

'Kill them,' he ordered the sergeant-at-arms.

The warrior looked at his lord in horror. 'They're holy men!' the warrior reminded d'Alville. 'You never said anything about killing holy men when I took the farthing to fight for you.'

Something inside d'Alville must have snapped then, though he would never be one to give a hint of it in his demeanour. His breakfast was forgotten. A rage storm was about to erupt.

Now Guy wanted more than blood. He turned to face the sergeant. His harsh face took on a disarming fatherly expression. The Norman lord placed a mail-gloved hand on the warrior's shoulder and stared at the sergeant who'd served him well for so long. The indignity of the morning had erupted like a weed in a fertile garden bed. It was time to root it out before it strangled his honour completely.

'Which man among my warriors do you trust above all the others?' d'Alville asked in his most subdued and therefore most frightening voice.

'Martin,' the sergeant replied quickly.

'Is he reliable in a fight? Trustworthy? Follows orders without question?'

The sergeant nodded to each enquiry, sensing something awful was about to happen but praying silently it wasn't going to happen to him.

'Summon this Martin to me.'

A few breaths later the warrior called Martin was standing before d'Alville wondering what special errand the lord might have in mind for him. A gangly red Sotar dog no more than a year old sat at Martin's side, shivering with excitement.

'Are you Martin?' Guy enquired without taking his eyes from the sergeant.

'I am, my lord.'

'Are you loyal?'

'Yes, my lord. I am as loyal to you as my dog is to me.'

'Where did you come by that ugly creature?'

'I won him in a game of dice while we were waiting for your arrival in Limerick, my lord.'

D'Alville turned up his nose in distaste. 'Keep it away from my hounds. Do you understand?'

'Yes, my lord.'

'Are you an honest man?' Guy went on.

'When circumstance requires it, my lord.'

D'Alville smiled at this little jest, though his cold eyes were still fixed on his sergeant.

'You are blessed with some fine qualities,' the Norman stated. 'I promote you to sergeant-at-arms. Your first duty is to execute these five heretic monks and your former sergeant.'

Martin gulped audibly. Guy turned swiftly to face him.

'Do you have some objection to my order?'

The new sergeant immediately realised the deadly position he had been landed in. 'No objections, my lord. How would you like me to kill them?'

'By putting them to death,' the lord replied sarcastically. 'Must I think of everything? I'm sure you can come up with some method I haven't seen before. Make it interesting. It's been a slow morning. I'd like to watch the executions over my breakfast to cheer me up.'

'Yes, my lord.'

'And one last thing.'

'Yes, my lord.'

'Where are you from?'

'I'm from Brittany, my lord.'

'I hate Bretons,' the Norman grunted hoarsely.

Guy reached for the leather bottle which hung at his side. He removed the stopper and brought the vessel up to his mouth. But the bottle was empty. The Norman threw it at his new sergeant.

'Before you kill those men fetch me some water.'

'There is none,' a woman's voice cut in sharply.

Guy d'Alville turned on his heel to seek out the audacious soul who'd dared interrupt his command.

On the steps of the chapel stood a figure entirely draped in a long blue cloak. Her face was completely concealed by a hood and veil of the same colour. She leaned on an intricately carved staff decorated with strange swirling designs.

The woman was perfectly motionless as she surveyed the scene.

'Did you say there's no water?' d'Alville bellowed at her.

'Have you some problem with your hearing?' the woman retorted sharply. 'Or are you as stupid as you are brutal?'

Guy's patience had reached its limit.

'Who are you?' the Norman screamed, but the words were no sooner out of his mouth than he regretted this outward show of rage. He usually saved such outbursts for special occasions. And he knew it didn't do to let his temper get the better of him in front of the hired warriors. Guy preferred to retain an air of unpredictability in his dealings with underlings.

Before the woman had a chance to give her name, the lord held up his hand to stop her. When he spoke again he was shaking his head. His voice had regained some calm.

'It doesn't matter who you are. You'll die with these others. Take her away, sergeant.'

'You can't kill me. And you won't murder these other men,' the strange woman replied with a hint of mocking self-assurance.

'What?'

'If you attempt to harm me or any of my people, no one among my folk will fetch water for you.'

'My warriors will fetch it for me.'

'The nearest clean water source is half a day away on foot. That is unless you know the secret of our well.'

'Then reveal the secret so my sergeant can carry out his orders. I'm looking forward to a laugh over my breakfast.'

'I'll gladly tell you that when you promise to spare my brothers and myself.'

'What about me?' the condemned former sergeant-at-arms protested.

'Don't presume to ask for a reprieve on the life of that worthless creature,' d'Alville cut in.

The woman in blue lifted her head slightly before she spoke. 'What you do with your people is your own affair,' she shrugged.

Guy curled his top lip like a dog about to snarl. 'You will make your well available to my warriors, or you and all the heretics of this place will perish by the sword.'

'Your warriors will have thirsty work murdering innocent people. And if you send your mercenaries to the well they will have to fight the guardians of the waters. Mere Norman foot soldiers have no hope of defeating the well-keepers. Your men will have to walk half a day to fetch something to drink. If they survive.'

'Guardians? My men-at-arms can take on any guardians and win. These warriors are all veterans of the Crusade.'

'If the well-keepers were mortal your soldiers might stand a chance with them. But the guardians are Eolaí Nathairaí who have dwelled here since my ancestors came to this place. The Nathairaí are beyond your skill to challenge. Even if the two of them devoured a dozen of your men their hungry immortal bellies would still cry out for more.'

'Do you think I can be put off by such a tall story? Two imaginary legends that live only in the foolish heads of heretics? I've been a warrior all my life. It'd take a good deal more than a childish fright-fable to start me jittering.'

'The Nathairaí are creatures who hold immeasurable malice for our kind. They harbour a hatred you cannot possibly imagine.'

'I have a very active imagination when it comes to hatred,' Guy quipped dryly.

'The guardians were man and woman once. They bartered their souls in service to their lord. But he cheated them. They were enchanted to live beyond the mortal span of seasons in the form of shape-changing spirits.'

The woman paused. Guy knew sincerity when he heard it. And for the first time in years a little flicker of excitement passed across his heart.

He recognised the sensation immediately, though he hadn't experienced it for a long while. It was probably what he had once called fear, though I hesitate to put a name to anything he experienced in his heart. If indeed he ever knew any sensation in that organ.

As the strange woman went on, the Norman listened intently to every word she spoke. She told him how these two Nathairaí had stirred a great war between the Gaels, who were her ancestors, and the Fir-Bolg who had lived in Ireland for many generations. In the end the goddess Danu had put an end to their mischief-making. She of the Flowing Waters, Queen of all the Arts, changed them both into enormous slime-covered worms before She banished them to the bottom of the well.

A stone house was built around the opening with barred iron doors placed upon it to keep the Nathairaí captive from sunset to sunrise. Tradition maintained the creatures hated the sun, so they rarely emerged in daylight. It was said that if ever the well was left unblocked or the gates unbarred, the water would overflow. Then the creatures would certainly escape to bring trouble to the land again. And what is more, the fields around the well would flood to refill the ancient drained lough.

'We draw water before sunset but only enough to last us through the night. The waters are tainted by the Nathairaí and unfit to drink if kept still any longer.'

D'Alville squinted at the woman, trying to gauge whether she was telling the truth. But although he could not see her eyes behind her dark blue veil, he could not escape the instinct that every word she spoke was chillingly true.

'You've seen these creatures with your own two eyes?' he challenged.

'I have heard their underground cries.'

A disturbed though suitably muffled murmur passed around his warriors. Guy sensed their unrest and that was enough to stifle his own fear. He had to admire this woman for her audacity. Her story had achieved the effect she'd been hoping for. Guy knew that if he wasn't careful he could find himself in the middle of a full revolt.

A determination overcame him that he'd not be defeated by this woman. Compromise was not his favourite method of solving disputes. D'Alville only ever employed the tactic when he intended to break his word. So he decided to compromise.

'Are you the leader of these people?' Guy asked in his calmest tone.

'I am the abbess of the community of Lough Gur. My name is Sianan.'

'You're a wise negotiator. I will spare your folk if you'll open your well to me and allow my men to drink.'

'You're a reasonable man,' the abbess acknowledged, though not without misgivings. 'Your warriors shall have water.'

Then she turned to walk away from him down the hill toward the open fields below.

'Where are you going?' the Norman cried out.

'To the well. It lies in the centre of those fields down there. Are you coming or not?'

'Release these men, sergeant. Send a dozen down with buckets to bring the water up.'

Then he remembered another important matter.

'And see to my breakfast.'

It's time to enlighten you. Some of the events which shape my tale may seem near to inexplicable if you don't know something about what brought all these Norman folk to Ireland. Listen well so you won't wonder any more.

Caoimhin explained it all to me once to the best of his understanding. He was very knowledgeable in matters of history so I've no doubt he got his facts right. But he could never bring himself to accept the deeper currents that run through this world. So he never acknowledged the existence of spirits known as Enticers and Frighteners.

Perhaps it'd be best if I just start with the explanation Caoimhin gave me and leave off telling you about the spirits until later.

Do you know anything of the origins of the Knights of the Temple of Solomon or the Knights Hospitaller? Have you ever heard why the Crusades were so well supported by nobility and kings alike?

Since it has some bearing on my tale I'll start there.

A hundred years or more before Lanfranc and his lot landed on this island, certain Church fathers and an assortment of other deluded souls got together over a barrel of beer. They'd gathered in the papal alehouse to solve a persistent problem.

It was a conundrum that had been plaguing them all for some time. It had cost the Mother Church a holy fortune. The problem was an unusual one.

It was peace.

You see, most of the kings, nobles and princes of Christendom had come to the conclusion that war was an unbearable drain upon their purses. Why spend a fortune fitting out an army when you can have your bedchambers bedecked entirely in expensive hand-embroidered silk cushions for near the same cost?

So they privately declared peace on one another. Of course the nobility continued to hurl insults and accusations publicly. No Christian king wanted his subjects to know that generations of bloody feuding had ended so he could purchase a discreet, comfortable love nest in which to tickle his latest mistress.

Peace soon became a popular policy amongst the wealthy well-born. So popular that for the first time in generations all the battlefield looters went hungry. And the out-of-work warriors weren't dancing in the marketplace to celebrate either.

Now this may sound like a step in the right direction to you. No more battles. No more senseless waste of young innocent lives. No more drunken brawls at the old men's annual axe-grinding feast. No more unreasonable demands on the travelling brothels. But in fact peace was the worst thing that could have happened to Christendom. Worse indeed than the morning Duke William the Conqueror fancied a short sea voyage and ended up setting fire to most of England before suppertime.

You see, with no wars to attend there were suddenly wagon-loads of well-armed warriors hanging round the tavern long after they could afford it. Eventually a few of them got together over a midnight barrel to bemoan their fate and relive the good old days. That's when some disgruntled bugger thought of turning to professional pillage to pay the landlord's reckoning. The bleary eyes of all his comrades suddenly lit up. And his bright idea spread through the Christian world as fast as a bright idea spreading.

Soon enough all the warriors who'd been discharged from the service of their king or lord were once again roaming the countryside fully armed. What better way to keep their killing skills well practised, their bellies full and the tavern-keeper smiling?

Neither kings nor nobles could do anything about it. For as I told you they'd mostly disbanded their armies to help pay for the latest shades in bedchamber silk.

In the end, to keep the precious peace, the nobility paid off the brigand bands. In return the looters swore to avoid harming any royal or noble lands. Those who couldn't pay were considered fair game. Those who *wouldn't* pay were targeted mercilessly. And can you imagine who was at the top of the list of those who refused to part with his precious gold and silver?

It was the Pope.

Now I don't want you to think I've anything against the papacy. But by the blesséd bedposts of Bridget, popes have been making a bloody fine mess of things since the first Council of Nicæa in the early fourth century. In fact it's well known that whenever a king needs something *really* buggered up he just has to scrawl a quick note to the Vatican requesting advice.

Anyway, the Pope wasn't going to be bullied. Before you could whisper, 'Those curtains are a fetching shade of imperial purple,' there was a papal decree. No clergy were to pay the brigands' demands under any circumstances.

The Holy Papa was building a new bedchamber wing at the palace. He didn't want to have to borrow to cover the cost.

As you can imagine it only took a handful of brigand captains, mostly bearing unresolved childhood grudges against the clergy, to spark off a fully fledged campaign on churches everywhere. So the college of cardinals decided to do something about this menace to the authority and prosperity of the Church.

Each of them held an ambition to dwell in the papal palace himself one day. So they all considered it essential that the wealth of the Church shouldn't be pilfered by armed thugs.

Now a certain Bernard of Clairvaux was in the papal alehouse the night the cardinals gathered to discuss the terrible effects of peace. He was a Cistercian monk related to some of the most fashionable nobility in the Christian world.

He offered a brilliant answer to the problem. He promised to rid the countryside of brigands by placing them under the direct command of the Pope. The cardinals were all ears.

Bernard suggested it be put about that a great war had broken out in the Holy Land. It's true Jerusalem had been captured by the infidels. Some of the city's inhabitants had been put to the sword. And one or two holy places of Christian pilgrimage had been half-heartedly desecrated.

The truth was stretched a bit to fit the story. Facts were embellished. Foreigners were demonised. The usual array of hideous acts were paraded before the shocked inhabitants of the civilised world to stir up righteous ire and indignation.

In fact the Saracens had been in the Holy Land for centuries. And they'd protected the Church of the Holy Sepulchre all along. More than that, they welcomed travelling pilgrims because they respected Christian tradition.

Jerusalem had been taken by a Moslem army. That much was true. But the new masters of the Holy City had proved to be better rulers than anyone who had come before them. In fact they'd paid for the cleaning-up of all the holy shrines and sorted out the many municipal drainage problems.

Nevertheless, at the advice of Bernard, the Pope wrote to every king and noble explaining the allegedly grave situation. In his letters he reminded the warrior class of their obligations to God. He told them it was the duty of every Christian to take part in an attack on Jerusalem where the tomb of Christ had been foully defiled by Saracen invaders.

Bernard's plan was simple. A great gathering of warriors would assemble to march to Outremer, thus ridding Christendom of its brigands. As a result the attention of the general populace would be focused on matters other than the bedroom furnishings of the wealthy and pious.

The cardinals threw up their hands in glee. They thanked Bernard for his plan with the guarantee of an early sainthood. Then they packed him off on a tour of all the major market places, cathedral squares and taverns of western Europe to recruit idle warriors to the cause.

He was a great storyteller, young Bernard. He guaranteed incalculable pillage and remission of all sin to any man who vowed his life to the Crusade. And even though he didn't quote his authority to make such optimistic promises, vast numbers of wild-eyed adventurers curled their ears in his direction. He was such a good talker, in fact, that a goodly number of kings, princes and dukes got overenthusiastic and decided to join in too.

Soon a vast army set sail in crowded cattle boats to claim Palestine for the Pope. And after a few initial disasters they very nearly succeeded.

Of course these warriors hadn't changed their ways. When they arrived in Outremer they ravaged the land, then set fire to the inhabitants and finally began methodically murdering each other once they'd run out of anyone else to harass.

As I've just explained, this behaviour was the reason they were enticed off to the Holy Land in the first place. But as long as these heavily armed thugs were far away in Palestine they couldn't be causing mayhem in their own countries.

It was a brilliant strategy to rid the civilised world of the worst kinds of greedy, vicious brigands. And it worked. It worked so well some folk actually began to believe that liberation of the Holy Land was the legitimate and only reason for the Crusade.

Soon there was talk of defending the Christian city of Jerusalem against the very people who made up the better part of its population. That's when the trouble took a twist. That's when the whole business turned really nasty. And it's also when the Knights Templar came into being.

It was inevitable that sooner or later a few honest warriors would end up in the Holy Land. And when they got there they were appalled at the terrible slaughter of pilgrims taking place before their eyes. It wasn't the Saracens or the Jews who were murdering pious travellers to rob them of their purses. It was all those out-of-work warriors who'd caused the trouble in the first place.

So these few honest knights formed themselves into a company of holy soldiers who vowed to protect the pilgrim road from raiders. They granted themselves the grand title of Poor Knights of the Temple of Solomon.

The Templars were a strict bunch.

They required their warrior monks to be chaste, pure of heart, steadfast, true and brave. Upon joining the company of the Knights Templar a man gave all his worldly goods to the Grand Master of the order. Then he pledged himself to eternal poverty.

New Templars promised to not so much as look at a woman or drink wine or cut their hair or wash for ever after. Last of all they swore to always wear a shirt of goat hair against their skin and never under any circumstances to remove it.

It may not surprise you to hear that for the first nine years no more than nine warriors applied to enter the order. But then young Bernard of Clairvaux heard about them.

In no time he was off on another market-square tour of Christendom. This time he called for recruits to join the Temple Knights, an order founded, as it happened, by one of his close relatives.

And his call was heard.

From every corner of the Christian world young men, intent on escaping nagging wives or embarrassing bedchamber decorations, made their way to Jerusalem. For a long while there was a drastic shortage of white tunics, red canvas crosses and hairy goats.

All those young noblemen surrendered land and fortune to the Temple. The order suddenly became immensely wealthy. Within a year the already jittery Pope began to feel somewhat threatened by Bernard's gift of the gab.

The young Cistercian had spoken out against bedchamber

silk on more than one occasion. And now Bernard had a massive Templar army to back him up if he had a notion to refurbish the papal palace in more sedate woven cloth.

But to his credit the Pope came up with a quick solution. He called on the assistance of the black-clad Order of the Knights Hospitaller who claimed to be dedicated to providing hospitals for the sick and infirm in Outremer.

Soon enough, of course, their duties included guarding the Pope against a possible Templar takeover. Suspicions bred quickly in the lavishly curtained corridors of the papal palace. Then both orders lapsed into a century or so of clandestine warfare before they levelled charges of heresy at each other. Not many hospitals have been built or pilgrims rescued ever since.

You probably understand that heresy has always been a very serious accusation indeed. Heretics have no rights whatsoever. They forfeit their possessions to the Church. They can expect nothing less than torture and imprisonment. And on the day of their execution they count themselves lucky if there's enough timber stacked around the bonfire stake to do the job properly.

If a charge of heresy could have been proved by one order against the other the result would have been disgrace, disbandment and swift defeat. So both the Templars and Hospitallers dedicated a large proportion of their resources to gathering information about each other. Holy knights travelled to the remotest parts of the Christian world searching for evidence of misconduct. They crossed the seas to investigate incriminating tales.

Successive popes supported one camp or another according to whim and the tides of conflict. Innocent the Third, who was Bishop of Rome during the time of our tale, favoured the Templars but he was a nervy sort who never burned his bridges with the Hospital either.

To win this war of words warriors from both camps sought

out the remotest communities and followed the most unlikely roads. And when there was absolutely nowhere else left to look, they crossed the ocean to Ireland.

Monks, inquisitors, adventurers, miscreants, mercenaries and opportunists followed on. Many other foreign folk came to this island as a result. As if it wasn't crowded enough!

OLDER, WISER AND
MORE DANGEROUS

he same morning Guy was choosing victims from the innocent holy folk of Lough Gur, Mirim the desert woman awoke in Lanfranc's Norman fort. From the instant she opened her eyes she felt clear-headed and refreshed.

Even so she lay on her side in the nobleman's bed, staring at the stone walls of the chamber. She was glad of her rest. And she was in no hurry to rise up from the warmth of the bedcovers.

Directly behind her there was a large fireplace. A small blaze crackled and spat in the stone-built hearth, but it was enough to warm the entire chamber.

The smell of cooking stirred her attention. Mirim rolled over to face the fireplace. One of her servants was frying some eggs on an iron skillet. She breathed deeply, taking in the aroma as if she were already eating the meal.

'Where would I be without you?' she asked the serving man.

He looked back into her sparkling jewel-like eyes, shrugged and silently smiled. At that moment her other servant came up the stairs carrying a great bundle of firewood in both arms.

'Good morrow, my lady. I trust you slept soundly.'

'I did, Thomas.'

'We'll be ready to leave after breakfast if you wish, my lady.'

'Excellent.'

Thomas stacked the wood by the fireplace then produced a small package from the leather pouch tied at his belt. He carefully unwrapped the cloth parcel, all the while appreciatively passing the contents under his nose.

'I have a treat for you this morning, my lady,' he told her. 'It's a section of Somerset cheese. I've been saving it till it matured sufficiently.'

He placed the block reverently under his nose again, inhaling slowly. 'It's one of my best,' he sighed. 'I can still smell the fields round Cheddar Gorge and the scent of every cow that gave her milk for this. I can even bring to mind the house where I boiled it up and strained the curds.'

'If it satisfies my grumbling belly, I'll be happy,' Mirim laughed.

'Mere food fills the empty stomach. This is cheese fit for the table of King John himself.'

He took another whiff of the cheese then changed his mind. 'On reflection, this stuff is too good for that bloody tyrant. This is a cheese fit only for my lady Mirim.'

Once again she laughed. 'Tom Curdle, my belly is growling. What are you going to do about it?'

'I'll cut some cheese. If that laggard cook is finished frying the eggs I'll serve you up a feast to break your fast. I know what a noise your gut can make when it's empty. I swear I never heard such a growling come from the mouth of any beast.'

Then he leaned toward her and whispered, 'Until last night.'

As he spoke those words Lanfranc ascended the stairs to stand at the open door of the chamber. Behind him Stephen waited with his eyes cast down to the floor.

The lord had just caught the reference to growling. He was grimacing as he respectfully averted his gaze from the lady lying in bed.

Mirim had already grabbed her scarf and veil to make sure

her dark face was covered. She did not want the Norman to know too much about her just yet.

'Good morning, my lady,' Lanfranc offered graciously but the grimace had not gone.

'Good morrow, my lord. I'm glad to see the lion isn't picking you from its teeth. I was quite worried about you.'

'I've faced worse dangers,' the Norman lied. 'That lion has never dared to confront me.'

'But it has taken other folk?'

'Indeed it has, if the stories are to be believed. We often hear the Gael folk hereabouts speak of their losses of cattle and kin.'

'There are no lions in Ireland,' Mirim giggled, unable to disguise her disbelief any longer.

'They say this creature was born of a mating pair brought over from Normandy by Strongbow himself when he was regent in the time of Good King Henry,' Lanfranc informed her in an injured tone. 'It is said the beast escaped and has lived on the flesh of the Gaels ever since.'

'Were you out riding late?' Mirim asked, changing the subject so she would not offend him any further with her mirth.

'I've just now found my way home.'

'Found? Were you lost?'

Lanfranc took a sharp breath. 'I was hunting raiders half the night. I strayed into unfamiliar territory,' he hedged.

Mirim's cook offered her a bread trencher loaded with eggs and sliced cheese. She reached out to take it. As she did so the scarf slipped from her head to reveal her dark skin. Both Lanfranc and his sergeant gasped in surprise.

'Are you an infidel?' the lord hissed in horror.

The woman put the trencher of bread down on the bed beside her and slowly removed the veil. Then she turned to look Lanfranc directly in the eye. His mouth dropped open at the sight of her face. He trembled from his toes up to the crown of his head.

'You're beautiful,' he stuttered. 'Your eyes are like the dark green depths of two wells. Your skin is the colour of a fine young calf.'

Mirim laughed. 'Do you imagine all infidels to be ugly?'

'No!' Lanfranc protested.

'I am a Christian woman,' she went on. 'I was born into a Christian family. My people may have dark colouring but our hearts are much the same as yours. And though it may surprise you, the hearts of those you call the infidels are no different either.'

'Are all the women of Outremer as delightful to look upon as yourself?'

'They are, my lord,' Thomas cut in. 'But the state of the cheese-cloth covering won't tell you whether the curds are rancid.'

Mirim giggled again, hardly able to contain her amusement. But she knew a man like Lanfranc expected some decorum of her so she pulled herself together.

In the Norman world women were not supposed to ask questions or show interest in the affairs of men. A lady of nobility was rarely encouraged to offer her opinion. And women certainly did not dare laugh in the presence of a nobleman.

'May I introduce Thomas Curdle,' Mirim began politely, 'my loyal manservant, an expert in the cooking, curing and consumption of cheese. I'm willing to wager there's neither man nor woman alive who knows as much about draining curds as that fellow.'

'I meant to say, my lord,' Curdle explained, 'just because a knight wears a bright mail coat, it doesn't necessarily follow he's a fine warrior.'

Curdle realised his impudence too late. He was blushing with embarrassment before he'd finished speaking. Lanfranc's expression turned to one of deep hurt.

'Thomas isn't implying your magnificent shining armour is an indication of a lack of war skill,' Mirim declared quickly.

Her other servant stood up from the fireplace holding a bread trencher piled high with fried eggs. He walked purposefully across the chamber and bowed as he presented the meal to the Norman lord.

'Please take some breakfast,' the lady offered. 'Shali is a wonderful cook.'

The lord stared at the unkempt servant for a few moments. The man had lighter features than his lady. His eyes were blue and his hair dark brown rather than black. But he certainly had the callused hands of a man who worked hard for his daily bread.

'Where did you get these eggs?' Lanfranc demanded suspiciously. 'We haven't had eggs since we left Wexford Town. The locals refuse to barter farm goods with us, and our chickens all fell to foxes in the first week.'

Shali straightened up to stare the lord in the eye. He swallowed hard with apprehension but he did not reply. He flashed a glance at Mirim, silently entreating her intervention. But Lanfranc was not going to take such insolence from a man of low birth.

'Didn't you hear me, man? I asked you a question.'

'He will not answer you,' Mirim intervened.

'He will if I beat him for his trouble,' the Norman shot back. 'I punish disobedient servants with the back of my hand. If they become too familiar they will rob you. They will take advantage of your kind heart, my lady. You must exercise some discipline over your people.'

'He will not answer you because the enemy cut out his tongue,' she informed him solemnly. 'He was captured with my husband. Shali stayed at his master's side until my beloved died of his wounds. Then the savages returned my servant to me.'

Lanfranc lowered his gaze in remorse, unable to meet her eyes as she went on. That's how he failed to notice Shali glaring at the desert woman.

'I have never heard nor will I ever know anything of the last hours of my husband's life. Shali only opens his mouth to take food. It was a cruel joke the enemy played upon me through the terrible torture they imposed upon my loyal servant.'

The servant flashed another glance at his lady. She caught his eye then lifted her hand almost imperceptibly to reassure him.

'The Saracens are renowned for their barbarism,' Lanfranc acknowledged.

'If only it had been the Saracens who'd captured my husband,' Mirim replied. 'If it had been any other but a Christian knight fishing in the desert for ransom, perhaps my husband would now be by my side. Then I would not have been forced to travel to this cold damp country at the end of the Earth.'

Lanfranc took the trencher and moved to the windowsill to eat his meal. He stared out over the wooden palisade as he stuffed his mouth with eggs so he would not be able to speak another word of offence.

Shali went back to the fireplace to prepare a breakfast for Thomas. But as soon as he'd been given his meal Curdle carried it to the stairs and graciously offered it to Stephen.

'I have no stomach for eggs this morning,' Thomas told the Norman sergeant. 'They're bad for my digestion.' Curdle cocked a thumb in the direction of Shali the cook. 'And well he knows it! Go on. Take my share.'

The sergeant accepted the trencher with a smile. A few moments later Stephen was intently enjoying the delicious food.

'I'll be waiting in the courtyard, my lady,' Thomas told his mistress. 'If you should require anything, send the insolent mute to fetch me.'

Then Curdle disappeared down the stairs.

'Forgive him,' Mirim sighed. 'We've been journeying nearly a year from our home in Outremer. It has been a hard time. He's developed a bitter streak that occasionally finds expression. But Tom's a good man. They both are. I could never have come this far without them.'

'There is nothing to forgive,' Lanfranc replied with contrition. 'I'm humbled by your story. I'm sorry you suffered offence by my foolish tongue. I had no idea.'

'Let's forget it then,' the desert woman smiled.

The knight averted his gaze to the floor as he spoke. 'When you're ready to leave, my warriors will form an escort for you. I would be honoured if you would allow me to ride with you on the road to the FitzWilliam estates. A rider has been dispatched. Lord William will be expecting you.'

'I would gladly accept your gracious offer,' Mirim answered formally.

With a deep bow Lanfranc departed to make final preparations for the journey.

As the lord left, Mirim again caught the eye of her servant. She immediately recognised the silent disapproval in his expression.

When she was sure Lanfranc was out of earshot she spoke.

'I had no choice but to allow him to escort us,' she whispered hoarsely. 'If I'd refused he might have become suspicious. Let's just hope his messenger reaches the FitzWilliam estates and Lord William sets out to meet us immediately.'

Shali shrugged as he went about cleaning up the cooking utensils. Mirim knew he was not happy with this turn of events. But his discontent was just a reflection of his deep and genuine concern for her.

'I'm sorry I told him your tongue had been cut out.'

The servant shook his head, dismissively rolling his eyes. Then he turned his attention to dousing the cooking fire.

'Don't worry,' she reassured him. 'Lanfranc is harmless. And a Norman knight like him could be a great help to us. Our road will be easier if we don't fear attack nor need to be concerned our purpose might be discovered.'

Once again the servant shrugged but Mirim chose to ignore his apparent lack of faith in her judgement. She rose from the bed and went to his side; then, as he knelt to clean the fireplace, she touched her hand to the top of his head.

'Do not fear,' she whispered. 'I wouldn't have any harm come to you for anything in the world.'

At the same time, out on the stairs, Lanfranc put a hand on his sergeant's shoulder to indulge in some whispering of his own.

'We'll take the road to Kiltealy.'

'I've never travelled that road nor do I know any man who has,' Stephen pointed out. 'But that seems the long way round to the estates folk say the FitzWilliam rules over. Anyway, as far as I can tell, Lord FitzWilliam is merely a legend, a story told to children.'

'He may be no more than a fool's tale but this lady seems to believe he's real enough. I've agreed to escort her. But we'll take the long way round.'

'My lord, it's two days ride for a man on a fast horse to where the FitzWilliam is rumoured to dwell. If we travel at a lady's pace you can call it four. By way of Kiltealy it's five or six days at the least. Why go to so much bother?'

'I have two reasons for taking that road,' the knight explained. 'First, the lion hasn't been heard round Kiltealy so there'll be no need for me to keep watch at night. And second, that lady is the most gorgeous creature I've ever encountered. If we add a couple of days to our journey I'll have an opportunity to become familiar with her.'

'She's a lady,' the sergeant stated. 'What makes you think she'd be interested in you?'

'I'm a knight of the realm and a lord,' Lanfranc reminded him crossly. 'Providence has sent her to me. I will be her protector today, her friend tomorrow and in time I will make her my wife.'

'As you wish, my lord,' Stephen bowed.

There was resignation in his voice, possibly a touch of exasperation, but Lanfranc chose to ignore it.

'Make the preparations. You'll lead the column. Has the messenger left yet?'

'He's awaiting your word, my lord.'

'Tell him to tarry here until we've set out then to ride at his ease. If the FitzWilliam exists I don't want him fretting over the lady when we're late.'

The sergeant nodded as he continued down the stairs. It wasn't till he got outside that he allowed himself to shake his head and laugh a little at his master, Lanfranc.

Sianan waited patiently beside the stone enclosure which housed the well. Iron-barred gates blocked all access to the water. On top of the well-shaft there was a large granite slab placed squarely to seal the entrance completely. Ropes were attached to iron spikes driven deep into this slab. That's how it was winched up clear of the well-shaft when the community wished to collect their morning water.

The abbess Sianan fumbled about in the pouch she wore at her side. At last her fingers found the key to the lock which secured the iron gates. Her pride rankled at having to open this well to the Normans. But she had given her word and she didn't want to endanger the lives of any of her people. As far as she was concerned their liberty was cheaply bought whatever the price.

The lord and his men were still a long distance off, climbing down the hillside from the settlement. Their heavy war gear made the going slow.

The abbess closed her eyes to pray silently. After a few moments she heard a sound she'd rarely noticed before in this place. It was like the low hum she often listened for in her youth. Her teacher had called this mystical sound the Song of the Earth.

On this occasion there was another quality to the sound which defied any explanation. It was as if a huge creature were deep underground slowly breathing. Sianan listened closer. The hair on the back of her arms stood up in shock.

This was no song.

What she could hear was the noise created by two distinct intakes and outpourings of air. She was listening to the life signs of the great worms known to her folk as the Eolaí Nathairaí.

'Open the gates!' Guy demanded, though he was still a short way off.

Sianan felt the cold key in her pouch. Her palm sweated as she hesitated. Perhaps it was not within her authority to hand this well over to the conquerors. What if the Norman misused the privilege? What if the Nathairaí managed to escape?

She stood perfectly still as the warriors approached. She was already regretting her hasty promise to give the Normans the water they needed. She reminded herself that none of her folk had been harmed. It was her duty as abbess to offer hospitality to the strangers. It was not for her to judge their intent.

'Did you hear me? Open the well!' d'Alville bellowed.

She could not reply. The abbess was struggling to find a way out of this dilemma.

Guy walked straight up to her. 'Are you deaf?' he shouted.

'I'm not deaf. Merely careful,' she replied in a quiet, soothing tone.

D'Alville grunted before he let fly with his opinion on the legend of the well guardians.

'You surely don't expect me to believe that heathen rubbish about two worms dwelling at the bottom of the well? Every Saxon in Britain tried that one on the Norman conquerors. It was simply a story to keep us away from their water. If it didn't work for them, why should it work for you?'

'It's not just a story,' she warned.

'You're a heretic. Why should I believe anything you say?'

'I am Abbess of Lough Gur. I'm sworn to truth.'

Guy looked past her to the massive lock which held the gates shut. 'Give me the key,' he demanded coldly.

'I will give it to you gladly if you make a solemn oath first.'

'I've never heard of a conquered people extracting promises from their conquerors. I'm your overlord now. I will take possession of this well. You will swear oaths of loyalty to me. They're burning heretics in the south of France, you know. Perhaps that's what we need here. A bonfire to sort out who's an unrepentant pagan and who knows when they're beaten.'

'You must promise to return the slab then lock the gates before sunset each evening. If the Nathairaí should escape they will spread havoc. Only the rising sun will drive them back into their prison.'

'Don't lie to me,' Guy snapped. 'You'll find me a fair man as long as you treat me better than I expect you to. But I won't have a heretic trying to mislead me in front of my men. I won't have a woman making a fool of my honour. I won't tolerate a defeated enemy who refuses to submit.'

He put out his hand to receive the key.

'You have been spared the sword. Now you will relinquish the keeping of this well into my care.'

Sianan understood he had the strength to take the key from her whenever he chose to, and he would choose to eventually, no matter how much she insisted he give his word. But she could be stubborn herself, and she wasn't going to give in easily when the future well-being of her people was so much at stake.

'I will hand you the key when you have given your oath to protect my people,' she stated coldly.

D'Alville spat at her feet and grabbed at the veil concealing her face. The garment tore, immediately revealing features which had until that moment been hidden. And when he looked on Sianan's face Guy did a most un-Guy-like thing.

He took a step back and gasped in horror. And so did all his men.

The abbess was a beautiful woman. Golden strands of hair framed her face. Her skin, though unnaturally pale, was beautifully soft and youthful.

What disturbed the warriors was her eyes.

They were a startling dark blue like the little pebbles of lapis crusaders brought home for their wives from Jerusalem to prove they'd really been off crusading and not just sampling exotic bedchamber silks. The jewels that were her eyes were deep and wet like the whirlpools of the ocean.

But most disturbing of all, her eyes were as large as an otter's and the whites were hardly visible at all.

'Are you a dæmon?' d'Alville shouted as he drew his sword. 'I've never set sight on a creature such as you.'

'I am what you see,' Sianan replied with resignation. 'I am the abbess of my people.'

Guy stepped forward again to snatch at the pouch at her side. She let him have it without a struggle.

Now her secret was known she understood the trouble had only just begun. But to put up a fight would only further endanger the lives of her people.

'Seize her!' the lord commanded.

Two of his warriors strode up to her with bravado but they both hesitated just as they were about to take hold of her arms.

D'Alville covered her eyes again with the torn veil so his men would not hold back from his orders.

'See. You have nothing to fear,' he told his warriors. 'The Devil may have given her his eyes but he did not grant her all his evil enchantments.'

'You are making a terrible mistake if you think my eyes were a gift from Satan,' the woman warned.

'Silence!' the lord demanded. 'I am absolved of any promise to you. You have beguiled these simple folk into believing you are their abbess. I can forgive them. I was also taken in for a time. None of them will be punished.'

'Thank God,' Sianan whispered under her breath.

'And this well will be free of your pagan superstitions. From this day it will remain open, unlocked as proof of your heathen deceit.'

'I beg you not to let the Nathairaí escape. They are flesh-eaters. They will surely harm any they catch unawares. You don't understand what you will unleash.'

'We'll see about that,' he snarled.

Then the lord commanded the slab be winched away so water could be carried up to the settlement. When that was done he had his warriors throw Sianan into the stone enclosure but he left the slab hanging above the well.

'If these worms exist you'll be their first meal,' he informed her as he threaded the chains through the iron gates and closed the lock.

'If I hear your screams tonight I'll know your tale is true. If you've lied to me you'll face the heresy fire at dawn.'

Sianan shook the veil from her strange Otherworldly eyes. Boldly she stared at the Norman. With iron bars between them, Guy felt safe enough to ignore his discomfort.

Then his vengeful heart spoke the question he'd been asking everyone he met high and low, near and far for years. 'Do you know where I may find Robert FitzWilliam?'

'If you leave me here you will live to regret it,' the abbess stated, ignoring the question. 'You're dealing with something older, wiser and more dangerous than you can possibly imagine.'

'Your mythical worms don't frighten me.'

'I wasn't referring to the Nathairaí,' Sianan smiled. 'I was talking about me.'

Toothache

s Harold finished his monastic breakfast he felt he had no room in his belly for more. That was unusual for him. Harold loved food. He sipped at a mug of weak ale and turned his back to the fire to warm his shoulders.

The abbot's chamber was full of books. They lay scattered across the table. They were piled in the corners. A great stack of them threatened to collapse into a pile of leather and vellum. There were many more books on the shelves lining every wall.

For a moment Harold considered the wisdom of remaining in this place. Abbot Ollo's advice seemed as sound as his library was well stocked. A scribe who set to studying this collection could learn many new things. And Harold loved learning even more than having a full belly.

It was warm and comfortable here by the fire. Who could tell what lay in the lands beyond the walls of Wexford town? The only thing the young scribe knew for certain was that the nights would soon be bitterly cold.

Suddenly his rash promise to remain here seemed very sensible. He'd only pledged to stay so as to silence the abbot's insistence. Now a part of Harold, the weak part that loved warm rooms, regular meals, rules and books, breathed a sigh of relief.

How could he, an apprentice scribe, undertake the task of tracking down such artefacts as the Book of Sigils or the Gospel of Thomas? He was only twenty-four years old. He'd spent his entire life cloistered behind the grey stone battlements of Glastonbury Abbey.

It would be easier for him to sift a grain of sand from a bucketful of wheat flour than to find two manuscripts in this foreign land. He resolved to bide his time until either his dreams offered him a sign or it became obvious he'd made the wrong decision.

And as it happened, both of those things came to pass only a few breaths later. Out in the town beyond the little monastic community Harold heard a great commotion of horses and shouting.

Intrigued by the noise he went to the window to investigate. What met his eyes made his mouth fall open with surprise and a touch of the terrors.

The entire town was swarming with black-cloaked knights leading horses or bellowing orders to their squires. Each warrior wore a white cross emblazoned across his left breast to mark him as a member of the Order of the Knights Hospitaller.

The awful dream of the previous night returned vividly to Harold's mind. His heart missed a beat. He immediately knew he could not tarry in Wexford.

Instinct told him there was great peril here, though he couldn't guess exactly what form it might take. Every muscle in his body warned by its tension that he must leave without delay or face unimaginable danger.

Harold closed his eyes and took a deep breath; then, as he released the air from his lungs, he made the most difficult decision he'd ever had to make. It was one that would follow him for the rest of his days.

The dangers which lay beyond the town walls were nothing compared to the fate he might meet if he remained. He must depart immediately.

In the next instant he'd snatched up the satchel of books

Eriginas had left to him. He swallowed another mouthful of ale to steady his nerves. Then he crossed the room to lean against the door. Harold counted six breaths before silently checking the corridor.

To his relief there were no Cistercians about.

Full of hope that the white brothers were still at their breakfast, he swiftly made his way to the main doors of the monastery. All the while he looked over his shoulder, breathless with fright, expecting at any moment to be challenged or apprehended.

At last Harold found himself panting heavily against the great oak doors which shut the monks within their sanctuary. He lifted the latch and pushed, praying silently that the doors wouldn't make much sound when they swung open.

But they didn't move.

Harold leaned harder but the great oaken barriers would not budge. Sweat was beginning to break out upon his brow. His mouth was dry. His was breath was short.

From somewhere within the walls of the monastic enclosure he heard several voices raised in laughter. The Cistercians must have finished their meal. They would be upon him at any moment.

In a last desperate effort the young monk threw his entire weight behind the doors. And to his everlasting relief they swung open. He hurtled forward and landed in the mud at the bottom of three stone steps.

In a few seconds he was on his feet again, surrounded on every side by black-cloaked warriors going about their black-cloaked-warrior business.

None of them noticed him. The Hospitallers were all occupied with finding places to spend the night. So with a glance behind him to make sure his exit hadn't been noticed, Harold headed off up the main street toward the town gates.

As he passed through the Norse market gate which marked

the outer limits of the old Viking town, he realised that in his black Benedictine habit he merged into the crowd of Hospitallers. But the fact remained Harold was becoming increasingly nervous. He constantly cast glances over his shoulder, expecting Abbot Ollo to charge up and drag him back to the monastery house at any moment.

There were so many warriors making their way to their billets that everyone shuffled along, hardly moving in the press of the market stalls. Harold was sure he was going to be caught. Just as the despair became almost unbearable he noticed a strange figure standing next to a baker's stall.

The man had long brown matted hair shaved across the forehead in the style of the Culdee heretics the Benedictine had heard so much about. The stranger's beard and moustache were twisted into knotted strands. His clothes were unlike any Harold had ever seen. He wore boots of red doeskin cut to an unusual design with pointed toes and straps that held them tight to his calves. His trousers were cut from cloth of a once bright pattern. Time and weather had greyed the colour out of them and they were patched about the knees. Over these he wore a tunic of dark brown. Under the tunic was a shirt of grey linen, the sleeves of which were tied at the wrists. Over all this he wore a black cloak which shimmered with a sheen like raven feathers.

The stranger leaned on a wonderfully carved staff and stared directly at Harold. The young scribe swallowed hard. This was one of the wild Gaels from the country beyond Norman influence. Despite his apprehension, Harold was fascinated. He took note of the heretic's adornments. He had a thick band of silver around his neck and black feathers woven into his hair. And he looked as if he hadn't washed in a long while.

The stranger beckoned to Harold. The young scribe hesitated. In seconds the Gael was pushing his way through the crowd toward him. There was nowhere to run. Harold was trapped in the midst of the throng.

With seeming ease the heretic wove his way between the warriors until he was close enough to place a hand on Harold's shoulder.

'Are you planning on making a journey out beyond the walls?' the Gael asked in strained Latin.

The young scribe nodded.

'Then you'd best buy yourself some food and drink to take with you. There's nothing to be had out there in the wilds. You'll be glad of a good meal by nightfall.'

It was sound advice. Harold turned to thank the stranger but the man was already making his way off through the crowd again. In a few breaths he'd been swallowed up in the mass of warriors.

The Benedictine scribe pushed with all his might to make his way toward the baker's stall. When he got there he spent a farthing buying enough bread to fill the pouch he always wore at his side. Then he decided to risk another farthing on some more loaves which he stuffed inside his monk's robe. By moving along behind the stalls that lined the street he managed to travel faster than the rest of the crowd. At another stall he bought a water-skin filled with the local variety of watered-down ale. This cost him a third farthing. Three-quarters of a penny already spent and he hadn't even begun his journey.

Harold had hardly finished whispering thanks to the soul of Eriginas for the fifteen farthings he'd left him when the town gates loomed in front of him. They were surmounted by a platform on which stood several archers, but the gates were wide open.

The crowd thinned out here at the crossroad before Saint Dulogue's church, an old Norse chapel. None of the Hospitallers was leaving the walled town. They were heading off to find places where they could get drunk, meet the locals girls and entice them into sinful acts unbecoming of Christian women.

Those wide-open gates beckoned to Harold like a bowl of hot broth on a winter morning. Yet his heart faltered. It was not too late to turn back, he told himself. He could still weather the winter months within the walls of Wexford if he chose to do so. No disgrace in that. None of these warriors would have considered going off alone into the wilds.

He glanced back down toward the wharves where several large ships were moored and other smaller craft had been beached on the strand. The town was filling with more black shapes. Horses were being unloaded and a great siege engine rolled onto the wharf from a wide ship specially built to carry it.

Harold's mind was made up.

But when he turned to face the gate again his hopes vanished. In those precious few seconds while he'd been considering his final decision Hospitaller knights had gathered at the walls to stand guard. They were already hauling the massive timber doors shut. If he didn't make a move now, he might miss his opportunity altogether.

So with a deep, determined breath Harold suppressed all fear and marched purposefully toward the guardsmen. When no one challenged him he pushed past.

The next instant was a sweet one. He was looking out over the green fields beyond to a path that wound its way into the distance. But any joy he experienced at the sight was short-lived.

Before he knew what was happening a hand came down heavily on his shoulder, almost knocking the breath out of him.

'Where do you think you're off to?' a Hospitaller barked as he spun Harold round.

'I'm travelling on behalf of the Abbot of Glastonbury Abbey,' Harold replied nervously.

'Are you?' From under his war helm the black-robed warrior

looked the lad up and down with suspicion. The soldier's eyes were slightly crossed from years of peering out at the world from behind an iron nose-guard. 'You're a bit green to be wandering the world without someone to watch over you.'

'I was journeying in the company of Eriginas the Scribe. But he passed away last night. Now it is left to me to complete his mission.'

'And what was his mission?'

'To establish a monastic community of Benedictine brothers in the west of this country.'

The Hospitaller shook his head, trying to work out whether he'd heard right. Moments later he burst out laughing. 'Are you a madman?'

The young monk was not surprised at this reaction but he didn't have a chance to answer before the knight spoke again.

'I suppose you have a letter from your abbot giving you authorisation to pass beyond the town and letters patent from the king.'

Once again Harold swallowed hard as he fished about in his pouch. He quickly found the parchment his abbot had given Eriginas.

The knight snatched it away and began studying the document intently. But he was obviously ignorant of letters because he held it the wrong way up. Harold helpfully attempted to turn the letter the right way round but the warrior moved it quickly out of his reach.

'This all seems to be in order,' he told him briskly.

Harold frowned but didn't question the verdict. The Hospitaller was pretending he could read so he wouldn't look like an ignorant fool in front of his foot soldiers.

'Your letter seems genuine. However, I can't let you travel alone in these dangerous times.'

'Why not? Does it really matter what happens to me?'

The knight took a breath as he tried to frame an answer. The young monk had a point. The warrior leaned in close to whisper his feelings on the matter. 'It just doesn't seem right. It's dangerous out there. And you're so young and fresh-faced. I'd hate to think of what might happen to you.'

'I'm a monk,' Harold reasoned. 'I'm a simple man. What have I to fear from the people who dwell beyond this wall?'

'They're murderers and cutthroats all of them,' the Hospitaller replied. 'They'll take your life, divvy up your gold and feed what's left of you to their wolfhounds.'

'Nevertheless I am a Benedictine brother. It's my duty to go out into the world, no matter what the dangers, to spread the word of Christ before the Cistercians or the Templars beat me to it.'

The knight frowned, seeing the sense in these words but still harbouring misgivings.

'And now there are so many Hospitallers in Ireland, I surely have nothing to fear,' Harold added.

'You can be certain of that,' the knight nodded solemnly. 'Things are about to change in this country and no mistake.'

'What brought you all here at this turn of the tide?' the young scribe enquired.

'The same mission that put you on a ship and dragged you over that rough, unforgiving sea. We are here to ensure the heretics of this country bow down to Rome.'

'And if they will not?'

'I have a sword at my side that presents our argument better than pretty words may do. And there's three hundred more like it. That's not counting squires and foot soldiers we've brought along to make up the numbers and offer a fine show.'

'You've put my mind at rest,' Harold lied, casting a glance behind him to check once more that he hadn't been followed. 'But the morning is getting on. I hope to make good distance today before the sun sets. May I pass?'

The knight handed back the letter with a grudging grunt. 'Go on then. Be on your way. And God speed.'

Harold bowed, signing the cross before the warrior as he mumbled a hasty blessing. He quickly stuffed the letter into his pack, then with heart thumping in his chest he walked through the gate as if he'd done it a thousand times.

The knight watched him set off. But before the young monk had travelled fifty paces the Hospitaller felt a tap on his shoulder. It was Ollo touching him with the tip of his staff.

'Where's that boy off to?' the fat cleric asked in a low voice.

'He reckons he's going to start a monastery in the wild lands where the brigands live,' the knight laughed.

'I want him followed,' Ollo ordered. 'He has some.books in his possession which rightfully belong to me. I don't care how you retrieve the manuscripts. Set your best man to the task.'

'Is that you, Your Eminence?' the Hospitaller stuttered, recognising the face of the white-robed Cistercian. 'Bishop Ollo? When did you take to wearing cloth of that colour? I thought you were a devoted Benedictine. I must say black suits you better.'

'I am a devoted Benedictine,' Ollo replied. 'I've been here preparing the way for your invasion. My vows of service to the order occasionally require me to don the cloth of the enemy. Now do as I tell you or you'll find yourself bearing the brunt of my wrath.'

'Yes, Your Eminence,' the knight bowed.

Suddenly the warrior's expression brightened. He turned to face his foot soldiers with an uncharacteristic smile on his face. A marvellous opportunity had just presented itself. And our Hospitaller wasn't going to let it slip by.

'Toothache!' he screamed as if he'd suddenly been beset with the affliction himself.

A large man as tall as an oak and as broad as a horse stepped forward. He had a scowl permanently etched into his face. One cheek was drawn up in pain so that his right eye was buried in a deep squint. He had a tight grey cap drawn over his skull, fastened beneath his chin by two ties. On top of this he perched a green flat hat of wool rolled up in the style of the Saracens so that it clung precariously to his crown.

The man growled when he spoke. 'What do you want now?'

'Some respect for a start,' the knight suggested.

Toothache grunted. 'When does the fighting start?'

'We haven't finished unloading the ships yet,' the knight replied. 'Were you expecting to wade ashore knee-deep in blood?'

'Ankle-deep would have been fine.'

The knight rolled his eyes. 'John Toothache, I have a job for you.'

'What is it this time?'

Ollo stepped forward to interrupt. 'Hold your tongue or I'll have it torn out.'

Toothache grunted again but he was careful to avert his gaze as he did so. He recognised a genuine threat when he heard it.

'Are you sure this man is up to the task?' the cleric barked.

'He's ruthless, sly, brutal, efficient and he has a vicious streak as wide as a river,' the Hospitaller replied. 'He'll do the job.'

Ollo turned to the foot soldier to issue his instructions. 'I want you to follow that young Benedictine who just passed through the gate. Don't get too close to him. Don't let him know you're anywhere near. You will shadow him until he comes into contact with the barbarians of the west. Have you heard of Guy d'Alville?'

Toothache grunted again to indicate he had.

'He has landed at Limerick with a large force. You'll report your observations to him. Do you understand?'

Grunt.

'Those books are invaluable. But there are others held by the heretics that are much more important to me. That young fellow could very well lead us directly to a treasure-house of heretical manuscripts.'

'Can he kill him?'

Ollo had to pause to consider this strange question.

The Hospitaller knight coughed with embarrassment. He tactfully explained that John Toothache never referred to himself as 'I' or 'me'. It was always he or him. No one knew why. It was just his way.

The cleric cast a dark glance at the knight, fully expressing his lack of confidence in the choice of foot soldier. Then he turned to address Toothache again.

'If you get a chance to steal the books he carries, you are charged with dispatching him. But only after he's led you to the heretics of Killibegs.'

The bishop reached into his robe to retrieve a silver crucifix on a fine chain. His fingers held the top and bottom of the cross and the whole thing popped open. Inside there was a concealed compartment containing a small dark lump.

'There's enough poison in this pellet to kill a horse,' Ollo explained, handing the crucifix over to Toothache. 'Use it wisely.'

The foot soldier frowned. He didn't quite understand what exactly was expected of him. He wanted to be certain he knew how far he could go without raising the abbot's ire. He wasn't all that smart but John Toothache was a man who preferred to know where he stood.

'Can he hurt him?'

'Only if you get hold of the books he carries so you can return them to me. And only if he's led you to the Killibegs.'

The foot soldier nodded then added another question.

'Can he frighten him?'

'Are you an idiot?' The cleric rolled his eyes in disbelief. 'Make sure those books don't fall into the hands of the wild heretics of the west.'

'If he should come across other folk, can he kill them?'

'I don't care what you do to anyone else.'

'When do you want him to start?'

'Now!'

The big man shrugged, grabbed his pack of meagre possessions, strapped on his sword belt and, without a word of farewell or fine hunting, set off along the road after Harold.

Ollo turned to the Hospitaller. 'He'd better prove worthy of your trust or you'll be off after him.'

'Don't worry, my lord abbot. Toothache is your man. If anyone's going to bring back those books and finish the lad off, it'll be him.'

'Unless d'Alville beats him to it,' the cleric added. 'My dear friend Guy is going to sweep across this country like a plague of locusts. And he'll eat up everything in his path.'

Then Ollo whirled around and stormed off back to the monastery.

The knight wiped his brow, overjoyed the troublesome foot soldier was gone.

'That's one less madman I have to deal with. Good riddance to John Toothache. I hope the wild heretic Gaels chop him into a thousand pieces and scatter all the bits about for the ravens to feast on.'

The gates swung shut. Then the Hospitaller shrugged as he wondered once again why Bishop Ollo of the Benedictines was wearing a white Cistercian habit.

⬧⬧⬧⬧⬧⬧⬧⬧⬧⬧⬧⬧

Sianan sat in the darkest corner of the small stone well enclosure, waiting. She'd always been a patient woman. In any case, time runs differently for her than it does for you or me.

Concerned at what might happen if the Natharaí managed to break free of their prison, she twisted the torn cloth of her veil in her fingers. Her heart held no fear for her own fate nor had she any thought for her personal safety. There wasn't a doubt in her mind she would escape this situation unscathed. She'd long ago ceased to consider the possibility any harm could ever come to her.

In the enforced silence her thoughts turned to the simple Christian Culdee folk who looked to her for leadership. There were good and bad amongst them as there are with all people, but every one of them lived their life with the best of intentions. That was the only thing about them that mattered to her. That's why she had devoted her life to them. Without her hand to guide them she wondered whether any among the Culdees would allow their faith to falter.

At last she disciplined herself to stop worrying. The worms would have to be dealt with first and there was no point in planning any confrontation with them. She had no idea what they were like. She turned her mind to other matters.

In the performance of her duties it was rare for Sianan to experience such solitude. A part of her was secretly grateful for the opportunity to reflect.

She closed her eyes to rest, calming herself to drive all worry from her mind so she would be better able to find a solution to the situation. Her thoughts began to wander, bringing a thousand faces to mind. But two in particular looked out from the mist of recollection with bright eyes and unrivalled affection.

The first was her beloved teacher who had schooled her in the harp and the ways of her ancestors. He had been a Druid, a poet and an Ollamh-master of the lore. She could still recall the musty smell of the raven-feather cloak he had worn as the badge of his office.

How long ago had they parted? She tried to sum up the

seasons that had passed since his death. But it was beyond her skill or care to do so. Instead she let herself return in spirit to that terrible night when the siege of Dun Righ had separated her from him forever.

Sianan's teacher had fallen in a terrible battle. While the night sky had been lit with fiery dragon-tailed missiles launched from an enemy catapult, her teacher had journeyed on beyond the knowledge of mortal and immortal alike.

The abbess whispered an ancient prayer to herself. She had always held out hope that her teacher had gone to bide his time in the Halls of Waiting. Even after all these years tears welled in her eyes whenever she thought of him.

She'd not been there to witness her master's death. But she'd heard that her teacher's other apprentice, Mawn, had lifted up the Ollamh's harp to play a lament as the wise one drew his last breath.

Mawn. His face appeared so clearly in Sianan's mind. Mawn had been her companion since early youth. He was her soul-friend. He was her fellow Wanderer on the long road forward into the bright blue future. Together they were the Fánaí.

A smile played upon Sianan's lips as she recalled his sparkling laughter. She remembered his dark hair shaved across the forehead from ear to ear in the style of the Druids. The mere memory of those merry eyes of his was enough to still her fears and quench all concern in her heart.

She had not seen Mawn since that night either. The same siege that took her teacher away stole her best friend too. Though she was absolutely certain he had not lost his life, in all these years she'd heard only whispered word of his whereabouts.

For ten summers after they'd parted she had scoured the country hoping to hear something of his fate. But as the years rolled by she had searched less and less until eventually she had forced him from her thoughts.

Sianan's work had taken up her life since then. Time had not touched her. There were no lines etched into her face from the hardships of the years. But her heart was scarred by her loss.

The abbess reminded herself that her soul-friend must be safe. She didn't doubt that Mawn of the Dark Wet Eye was somewhere wandering in the world working some enchantment or weaving some tale. Wherever he was, the master's harp would be there also.

That harp had been a part of her teacher just as an apple is part of the tree which bore it. The fruit may fall from the keeping of the bough but it retains the flavour of the one who nurtured it.

Sianan longed to taste the apple of her teacher's music again. She yearned to breathe in the scent of his storytelling.

Just as a loving sigh was passing her lips she was stirred from her recollections by a frantic fluttering of wings beyond the bars of the well-house. Sianan sat forward with a questioning squint and listened intently.

Soon enough an answer presented itself. A huge black raven shuffled into view, dragging a small seed-sower's sack in his beak. The bird brought the bag up to the bars and let the strap fall on the grass. Then he opened and closed his beak a few times to soothe aching jaw muscles strained by the burden.

Still working his beak, the raven stepped forward to poke his head in between the bars.

'What are you staring at?' Sianan snapped.

The bird cocked his head and let out a low gurgle. With a quick glance to either side he shook out the dust from his feathers and yawned.

'You're enjoying this, aren't you?' the abbess hissed.

The raven turned, grasped the strap of the seed bag and dragged it closer. The little satchel was obviously full. When he had it close to the gap between two bars he dropped the strap again.

'Where have you been anyway? Didn't you hear what happened? Or were you off after some young chick not long out of the nest?'

The raven sighed as he cast another swift glance to left and right. He obviously wanted to make sure they were alone. The bird edged closer to the bars and stuck his head through the gap.

'I've always wondered what could possibly be alluring about a caged bird,' the raven stated in a low croaking cackle.

His voice always reminded Sianan of a fingernail scraped over a flat slate stone. He made her hair stand on end with his torturous tone.

'What are you talking about?' she shot back at the bird.

'I've never understood why mortals love to have a caged creature in their possession,' he explained. 'Even before I took on this enchantment, in the days when I walked as a man in the world, I could not fathom why folk would want to keep a fine bird behind bars.'

He coughed, cracking his beak shut several times with a loud clicking sound.

'Birds love to soar,' the raven went on, warming to his subject. 'There is no finer feeling than to fly free above the clouds, the forests or the sea. The wind takes you in her arms as she lifts you into the blue like a speck of dust. Anyone granted that experience is changed forever. Flight unchains the heart, unburdens the soul and numbs the Frightener spirits who feed on our fears.'

Once again he clicked his beak. Then he shuffled his claws in the grass before he spoke again.

'Do mortals believe they can capture the essence of feathered joy simply by placing a bird in a cage? Do they covet the power they wield over such beauty? Is caging simply a crude method to keep a rein on that which they cannot conceive of, nor truly ever control?'

He sighed again, this time much more deeply.

'When I was a boy, my mother, may she sleep untroubled, had twenty robins she kept in a large wickerwork basket. They'd been a gift from some Druid who'd voyaged over the eastern sea to fetch them for her. He must have fancied her far too much for his own good, but then Mother had that effect on men.'

'Is this going to be a long tale?' Sianan interrupted impatiently.

'Are you in a hurry to be off somewhere?' the raven asked her, looking this way and that.

'I've one or two matters I'd like to sort out before sunset,' Sianan replied with a hint of sarcasm.

'Bear with me a while. It's not often I have the opportunity to relate a story to a captive audience. You usually disappear long before I've finished talking. I understand you can't be happy cooped up in the well-house, but at least I know you're not going anywhere for a while. Indulge me this once.'

'Very well. But try not to burden your words with too much bird-wisdom. I'm really not in the mood at the present moment.'

The raven coughed to clear his throat, ignoring her disparaging tone.

'So one day I learned my mother had taken the King of the Danaans as a lover, which was her right since my father, King Brocan, was a surly old bugger with a bad temper. Mother had a basket weaver fashion a smaller cage. And when it was ready she placed one of the robins inside. It was her intention to gift the Danaan king with one of her bird brood.'

The raven peered into the enclosure. He wanted to be sure Sianan heard every word.

'I couldn't bear the thought of one feathered soul being separated from his kind, and all for a silly girlish gesture from a grown woman who should have known better. It's one thing to be a captive with kith and kin to keep you chirpy. Hardship isn't all that hard if there's someone there to share it. But it's another matter altogether to be stranded alone in a small enclosure then sent away.'

'So what did you do?' Sianan asked, rolling her eyes with growing impatience.

She recognised his storytelling style well enough. It was his intention to impart some lesson about her own predicament.

'I went to her chambers to let the bird go free,' he told her, his voice filling with a nostalgic quiver of emotion. 'It felt wonderful to grant that robin such liberty. I enjoyed it so much I let the bloody lot go. Every robin in her collection was off beyond the horizon in a flash.'

'What did your mother say when she found out?'

'Nothing,' the raven shrugged. 'She spent a hour or so beating my backside with a black-handled backside beater. Then she calmed down and didn't speak to me for a month. I got off lightly really when you consider what a bitter old biddy she was.'

He glanced swiftly to left and right. Then he added hastily, 'May her rest be calm and pleasant. May her dreams be ever peaceful and serene.'

'So what is your point?' Sianan asked.

'I've brought you a sack of sowing oats,' the raven answered cheekily, nudging the bag with his beak.

'Bird food?'

'You're a bird caught in a cage, are you not? Though I never saw a danker, wetter place to keep such a pretty one. Would you give me a song?'

'I'll sing you up a crack across your pointy forehead if you don't help me out of here!'

'Don't be threatening me with violence. You're wasting your breath. I'm not afraid of anything you can dish out to me. Not even your Draoi-craft. You may turn my bowels to brine water with your witch words but it won't bring you any closer to deliverance.'

'Are you going to free me or not?' Sianan hissed.

'How long have we known one another?' the raven countered.

'Sometimes it seems like seven hundred winters,' Sianan sighed.

'Seven hundred and fifty it must be at least,' the bird calculated. 'Maybe more. I've lost count of the true reckoning. But it's long enough for us both to recognise when a great change has come upon the land.'

'What are you cackling about now?'

'The Normans. They are like your people, the Gaels, and the Christians who came after them. They seek to subjugate this country to their customs, their laws, their tree-felling axes, their babbling speech and the senseless whining they dare to call songs.'

He clicked his beak at Sianan before he spoke again.

'Need I remind you it's your duty to ensure they do not succeed? You're one of the keepers of your people's law and lore. You have much work ahead of you if you hold any hope of helping your customs survive the tidal wave of weaponry that's about to descend upon us all.'

'The Normans have been here for a long time.'

'But twenty boatloads just tied up in Wexford. I can tell you they're unlike any that have come before them. And there's Guy with his mercenaries to consider.'

'How can I do anything while I'm trapped in the well-house waiting to be devoured by the Nathairaí?'

'True enough, I suppose,' the bird conceded. 'But you shouldn't fret too much about the Nathairaí. They're not all that dangerous, really. They're actually quite reasonable creatures compared to the Normans. Spend an evening with the Nathairaí playing Brandubh and you'll think differently about them.'

'I've heard enough tales of their ways to strike a chill in my heart. I'm fearful for what may happen to my people if they're released.'

'They may cause some harm here and there if they get out, but who can say whether they'll not do some good also? The Goddess Danu has forgotten them, as is her way. Her memory isn't what it used to be. Perhaps it's time their punishment was put behind them.'

'What punishment? Are you familiar with these creatures? I had no idea you were friendly with the Nathairaí.'

'I know them well enough. Our fates are somewhat intertwined. But I've no mind to tell that story now. I've a question for you and you must answer it truthfully.'

The raven cocked his head again, clicked his beak then fell silent for a long while until Sianan could bear the quiet no longer.

'Well what is it?' she screamed in frustration.

If a raven could have smiled the old bird was smirking gleefully now.

'Have you ever seen a caged bird?'

'Of course I have. Now let me out.'

'That's not the question,' the raven snapped. 'This is it. Did you ever grant a caged creature its liberty?'

Sianan stared down at her hands in her lap as she considered the question. She was glad the corner of the enclosure was so dark. She didn't want the bird to see her blushing.

'No,' she answered, reluctant to tell the truth but more unwilling to lie. 'I once placed two yellow singing birds together in the same cage. They sang much sweeter when they shared a home.'

'I see,' the raven sighed. 'My dilemma is this: I'm bound by the laws of my people, the Raven kind. Our queen, the Morrigán, is a strict old dear with a heart of gold. Unfortunately the gold has been hammered into the shape of a large battleaxe and frozen in a ocean of ice.'

He clicked once more. Sianan had to hold back from throwing her shoe at him for this annoying habit. But the Raven was already speaking again.

'I'll have to consult the Morrigán to ask whether I'm permitted to aid you in your time of need. I can't risk offending her. She can make a raven's life most unbearable if she suspects her edicts aren't being respected.'

'Lom Dubh,' Sianan pleaded, addressing him by his full name, 'are you trying to tell me you may not be able to help me out of this mess?'

'I'll fly off straight away to find out,' the raven promised. 'But only because I appreciate the way you say my name. It's sweet to hear it pass over soft fleshy lips instead of whistled through a long thin beak.'

He clicked.

'Say it again.'

'Don't waste a moment. My folk need me. And if I am still here after sunset the Nathairaí may find my Wanderer's heart too tempting a dish to ignore.'

'Say it.'

There was silence for a long while. At last Sianan capitulated. 'Lom Dubh,' she whispered wearily.

'You are a princess among your people, no mistake. And because you're a generous soul there's one thing I'll do for you before I depart to seek out the Morrigán.'

She didn't get a chance to ask what it was. He'd already spread his wings then lifted himself skyward to disappear from view. Sianan rushed forward to the bars of her prison to watch him soar off over the settlement.

'I'll wager you're enjoying this, you bloody-minded old bird,' she hissed under her breath.

As she spoke she heard a rumbling groan deep down within the well. The morning was not old but somewhere far below her the Nathairaí were stirring in their slumber. Sianan knew that before the sun slipped beneath the horizon they'd be awake. And she was certain the two of them would check the capstone of the well as they did every evening. This night they would find it gone.

Sianan fully expected the worst kind of trouble for her people when they did.

Harold walked about five hundred paces past the gates of Wexford town before he stopped to turn around. As he looked down the hill he noticed a big man leave. Then the gates shut.

There was a finality to that moment which chilled the young monk to the bone. And though he didn't know it just then, his fate had changed forever. Everything about him was undergoing a miraculous transformation.

Did I mention that this tale featured a miraculous transformation? Didn't I list it after the man-eating lion? I certainly meant to. Never mind. I've told you now.

Harold thought about his old life at the Abbey of Glastonbury. He wished he could be back home among the familiar sights, sounds and smells of that place. He wouldn't have minded if he'd been ordered to clean up the abbot's kitchen every day for a year instead of wandering round this strange land.

But it was too late to turn back. Harold knew he must move on to find his destiny whether it be death at the hands of some savage heretic or success at the task that had been allotted to him.

If only he could have guessed what was really in store for him he might have run screaming with fear back to Wexford town. And very likely he would have begged Abbot Ollo to let him take the white Cistercian habit. For all the good that would have done him. Our Ollo was more than just a Benedictine traitor working to destroy the Cistercian and the Templars. But you'll find out about that later.

I'm not fond of speculation. I have a story to tell. Each part in its place. Fortunately for my tale, Harold's gift of dreaming foresight hadn't revealed that much about his own future.

So he didn't have the faintest idea what lay ahead of him.

As he glanced back down at the town for the last time he noticed the large man had disappeared. Harold concluded the fellow must have been a farmer off to tend his cows in the fields.

As I'm sure I said earlier, he didn't know much about the world, bless him.

The young Benedictine took a deep breath to steady himself, then he turned sharply on his heel and strode off over the brow of the hill. He never saw Wexford town again, except of course in his dreams.

Many years later he realised just how lucky he'd been to leave at that moment. He often pondered the significance of his departure on the very day the Normans strengthened their stranglehold on the country and the Hospitallers landed their own expedition.

A hundred times he mentioned to me he'd felt a presence looking over his shoulder that morning, guiding him toward his destination, guarding him against harm. But I reckon the truth is he was a lucky bugger. The luckiest bugger I ever met.

Simple as that.

Anyway, the young scribe trudged on till noon when he rested beside a low rowan tree because it reminded him of one he used to sit under at Glastonbury. He ate some bread. He drank a deep draught of ale that made him feel a little sleepy. Then he dragged himself to his feet, yawned and stepped out again with determination. He didn't know where he was going but by Saint Fintan's feet he was making good time getting there. Such good time, in fact, that he passed Lanfranc's meagre hilltop defences a few hours later.

And he passed them quietly, not wishing to draw attention to himself.

Within another thousand paces he'd struck a crossroads in the path. That was where he discovered a man lying on his back in the grass fast asleep.

As he moved closer he recognised the stranger who'd advised him to buy food and drink back in the marketplace at Wexford. The heretic was snoring loudly with his mouth wide open. Harold thought this gave the fellow an air of savagery despite the peaceful, rested expression on his face.

He'd covered himself with his long black feather cloak up to his chin.

Our lad stopped to consider his predicament. At last he decided it was best to introduce himself. After all, if he was going to achieve his goal he was going to have to communicate with the heretics sooner or later.

There was another reason why he had to attempt to speak with this stranger. The road ahead forked in three different directions. Harold had no idea which branch of the path might lead him west.

The young scribe tried to make as much noise as he could as he stood at the crossroads. He didn't want to startle the sleeping man but he didn't want to creep up on him either in case his presence was mistaken for an ambush.

But the heretic didn't stir except to expel air from his lungs and draw it loudly back in again. Even as Harold stood worrying about which road to take the stranger slept on, oblivious.

Our young scribe coughed loudly. Then he said a prayer for travellers in his best cathedral voice.

When that failed he squatted at the side of the road to whistle, even though it was unseemly for a Benedictine brother to do so. But the stranger did not so much as show a sign of waking from his slumber.

Harold tried addressing the heretic openly with a request for help. But still the fellow paid him no heed.

At last, after more than half an hour had passed in this manner, the young traveller suppressed the concerns of his timid heart. He knelt down to stroke the feathers of the stranger's cloak. They were certainly raven feathers, he concluded. The multicoloured sheen was unmistakeable.

Then Harold picked up the staff which lay at the man's side. It was beautifully carved, with countless intertwining knots and spirals all along its length. Our scribe had never seen anything like it in his life. With apprehension he gently touched the tip of his walking staff to the man's foot.

There was no response. Harold tapped again. Suddenly the Gael opened his eyes and blinked at the sunlight.

'Am I awake?'

'Well I am, as far I can tell,' replied the smiling young Benedictine, trying to put on as friendly a face as possible. 'So I suppose you are too. But you'd know better than me. I'm sorry to disturb your rest. I'm in need of guidance.'

'Guidance, is it? Well I'm a guide and no mistake.'

'My name is Harold of Glastonbury.'

'What kind of a name is that?'

The young man recalled his teacher's suggestion that he take a Gaelic name so as to be more readily accepted by the native inhabitants. But it was too late for that now.

'It's a Saxon name. But my people were Irish. My father was a merchant who traded goods from Ireland to Britain. He was lost at sea when I was a baby. My mother died of grief shortly after. Then I was sent to Glastonbury Abbey to be cared for by the monks. The abbot of our monastery renamed me after the last Saxon king.'

Harold paused for a moment, realising he was babbling. He

hadn't given the stranger a chance to introduce himself. But the Gael didn't volunteer any information. When an uncomfortable space of time had passed, the young scribe reluctantly broke the silence.

'To whom am I speaking?'

'Didn't your folk teach you it's rude to ask questions?'

'I was raised by monks. I'm a scholar. I'm accustomed to asking questions.'

'Well don't ask any more. I don't like inquisitive folk. They set my teeth on edge.'

The stranger closed his eyes again as he drew in a deep breath through his nose.

Harold frowned with frustration. He couldn't see how he could avoid asking questions if he was to discover the right path. He stood looking hopelessly at each of the three roads ahead. Then he turned to stare back toward Wexford, and as he did so, a chill came over him. He didn't know why but he sensed return was not a possibility for him.

'How long have you been aware of your gift for the Faidh?' the stranger asked without opening his eyes.

'I thought you told me it was impolite to ask questions,' Harold replied sharply.

The man smiled broadly. He opened his eyes and fixed his gaze on the young Benedictine. Then he introduced himself, though he didn't make a move to rise.

'My name is Gobann.'

'You're a heretic.'

'I don't know about that. I'm a poet. I'm a master of the harp. And I'm considered one of the Eolaí or the knowledgeable ones.'

Gobann was looking directly at the young man now with a piercing gaze. His expression was not threatening but it was certainly unsettling. Harold decided to ask a question despite the previous reprimand.

'What's the Faidh?'

'It's an ability to hear, see or sense events that are yet to be. Some folk consider it a gift; others curse it as an affliction. The Faidh comes to us all in a different manner. Yours is still presenting itself in the form of dreams. But you may one day learn to control it if you have a little tutoring.'

'How did you know I have visions?'

'I can read these things in the face of man, woman or child. As you will be able to do one day if you put your mind to it. There are obvious clues.'

'I've always had the visions,' Harold admitted, feeling as if he were confessing a great sin. 'My abbot told me they come from the Devil. But my teacher, Eriginas, told me everything in creation is a gift from God.'

'Your teacher was right. In a manner of speaking.'

Gobann abruptly threw off his raven cloak, sat up then got to his feet. As he rose he shook the grass from his clothes. Then he arranged the cloak round his shoulders, securing it at the front with a silver clasp.

'Just over that rise there's an abandoned rath. You'll shelter there for the night amongst the fallen stones where no one can see your cooking fire. Do you have some food?'

'I have bread and ale. What's a rath?'

'In the old days folk used to build a circular wall of stone to keep the cattle in and the cattle raiders out. Within the wall they constructed their houses. But many wars, plagues and sorrows came to this island before the Normans. Now and then you may see an ancient rath where the only inhabitants are ghosts.'

'Ghosts?'

'Don't tell me you're frightened of ghosts.'

'Ghosts are the wandering spirits of sinners who have been refused entry to either Heaven or Hell.'

'Rubbish. You have much to learn, my lad. You're very lucky

134

you bumped into me. I'll put you straight on these matters, don't you worry.'

The poet stretched his neck as he rolled his head on his shoulders. The bones cracked loudly.

'I feel like I've been asleep for a thousand years,' he stated with a little laugh. 'But it can't be quite that long. Come on. We'd best be off. The one who's following you is not far behind. I want to lose him before he gets too close.'

'Who's following me?'

'How do you manage to get by in the world? Don't you know to listen to your instincts? What do you have them if it's not to pay them heed?'

'I'm a monk. My heart listens to the words of scripture, the laws of my order and the will of God.'

'You bloody Christians. You're all the same. Put your fate into the hands of some all-powerful King of Heaven and you don't have to take responsibility for your actions or your mistakes. Well you can believe what you will but don't blame me if you end up in a shallow unmarked grave unmourned and unmissed.'

'Aren't you a Christian?'

Gobann the Poet looked at the young man with growing disbelief. 'Do I look like a bloody Christian to you?'

With that the stranger snatched his walking staff from the monk. In the next breath he'd turned to walk off in the direction of the ruined rath. It was clear he'd been sorely insulted.

'Come on. The hound is hot on your scent. We don't have much time.'

Harold hurried to follow as he called out to the Gael, 'If you're not a follower of Christ, then what kind of man are you?'

'I told you, I'm a poet. Don't you have anything else to eat but bread and ale?'

'Nothing else.'

'How do you expect to survive in the wilds on just bread and ale?'

'I have faith. God is watching over me,' the young monk answered, full of conviction.

'Well somebody certainly is,' Gobann laughed. 'But I have a feeling his intentions aren't all that friendly.'

The Words' Turn

Mirim and her escort travelled far from Lanfranc's walled encampment that day. The desert woman did her best to avoid conversation with the knight. It was obvious he was trying very hard to get her attention.

Whenever he tried to make small talk she told him, very politely, that her thoughts were still with her husband. He would bow his head to apologise but it didn't stop him approaching her again a little while later.

By midday the Norman had eventually got the message that she wanted to be left to her mourning. From then on there wasn't much in the way of communication. Normans have never been very good at it anyway.

I reckon it must be something to do with their language. It's full of words that fill in space but don't really add any depth to the meaning. It's a custom among our people to listen to every syllable, out of politeness to the speaker and because it's a necessity. Miss a single word in the Gaelic language and you'll be lost entirely. We consider it respectful to be attentive to the very moment a word passes the lips. Not thinking on ahead to come up with some alternate opinion or to show how clever you are by hastily agreeing.

Among our folk a man may change his opinion on a subject when he hears how foolish his own words sound. That's quite acceptable. We believe everyone should be given the

137

opportunity to recognise their own mistakes or shortcomings. Normans, on the other hand, hold to an unsettling notion. Once they've said something it has to be upheld as truth no matter how ridiculous the assertion. They cling to their words. And they'll die defending an idea they know is worth no more than a ditch full of deer droppings. They're a proud people and that's part of the problem.

But they spend so much precious energy clinging to their silly notions with clever arguments. So much so that they sacrifice hearing most of what other folk have to say.

Watch them. They're fascinating to observe. They can drift off while you're talking to them and enter a little world of their mind's own making. Then, just when you think they're fast asleep with their eyes wide open, they pick up the conversation as if they'd never lost the thread. Of course they've missed the details which have to be repeated until the message sinks in.

Bloody frustrating it is. Perhaps that's why they spend so much time talking about the weather. It gives their poor distracted thoughts a rest from the constant threat to pride and position.

To be honest with you, I reckon this may explain why the Normans set out to invade most of Europe, conquer Sicily and pillage what little was left of the world after that. While they're lords over everyone they're not obliged to listen to anything the rest of us have to say.

A great relief it must be to their taxed little skulls to be able to completely disregard eight out of ten of the inhabitants of their lands.

But as I was saying, Mirim and her escort journeyed on until just before sunset. The air was beginning to chill when the distant thudding of a galloping horse was heard by one of the warriors in the lead.

Lanfranc quickly formed his men into a defensive arc in front of the lady and her servants. Then he prepared to meet this rider, to challenge him and, if necessary, to engage him in a fight to defend his guest.

Even when it was obvious by his white tunic that the rider was a Templar messenger, Lanfranc stood his ground. We Irish were thought by the Normans to be great tricksters in those days. He wasn't taking any chances.

'I bear word from the former estates of Lord FitzWilliam,' the rider announced. 'I must go on to the abode of Lanfranc de Courcy with all speed.'

'I am Lanfranc. What's your message?'

The rider eyed the knight with seeming suspicion. But he appeared relieved that his duty would be fulfilled without further hardship to his horse or himself.

'You're seeking the former Lord William FitzWilliam?'

'Yes,' Lanfranc confirmed.

'Why do you call him the former lord?' Mirim interrupted.

'He renounced title and lands when he took the robes of a Cistercian monk,' the messenger explained. 'His lands are now administered by the Order of the Temple.'

'I must speak with Lord FitzWilliam,' the desert woman protested. 'I have urgent papers for him to read and a favour to ask. Where may I find him?'

'He took to the life of a hermit, my lady. No one knows for certain where he dwells now. But when he departed he told the abbot of his monastery he was heading first to the Killibegs. That was three years ago in the spring.'

'Where may we find this Killibegs?'

'I know not. But ride over the mountains three days or four to the west. You may hear word of the place along the way. I've heard the folk there are Culdee heretics. And FitzWilliam was cast out of the Cistercian brotherhood for deciding to go to them.'

'I don't fear heretics,' Mirim declared. 'I've faced worse dangers on my journey to this land.'

'But the Culdees are brigands and pagans,' Lanfranc reasoned. 'It's not safe to be amongst their kind. If FitzWilliam was misguided enough to go to them, he is certainly lost to us.'

'I'd rather deal with a misguided soul than a malicious one,' the lady retorted. 'You are under no obligation to escort me any further. I thank you for your help. You've been very kind.'

Lanfranc blushed. His honour was at stake here. On the one hand it now seemed that Lord FitzWilliam was more than a mere legend and that this expedition had taken a course over the mountains into the wild lands when it should have been a comfortable jaunt to the north. He considered withdrawing his offer of safe passage.

But then it struck him that he couldn't let a noble widow-woman go off into the wild lands beyond the civilised laws of the Norman world without anyone to guard her. The word would soon pass round that he was a coward.

Which in some respects he was. But he didn't want people actually saying that sort of thing about him openly. And the fact was he wanted to impress Lady Mirim. It wouldn't have impressed her much if he set off home now with his tail between his legs.

The messenger saluted them both as he turned his mount around and rode off without waiting for any reply. Lanfranc frowned at the man's haste. Nothing annoyed him as much as a servant who didn't wait to be dismissed. But he had other matters to deal with so he didn't shout a reprimand after the fellow.

'I will ride on with you and so will my warriors,' the knight declared. 'I am a man of my word. I couldn't consider allowing you to journey onward without appropriate protection.'

'I have my two servants,' Mirim protested. 'They've taken care of me since we left Outremer. They will be sufficient to my needs.'

Lanfranc shook his head. 'I am a knight appointed by the

king to defend all who travel in his realm. Duty demands I protect your dignity with all the strength I have to call upon.'

With that he dismissed the messenger and ordered his warriors to make camp for the night.

As the cooks began to prepare a supper from the rations they'd brought with them, Mirim quietly fumed that she was stuck with this fool's presence for at least another four days. But she didn't want to raise his suspicions. So she acquiesced to his offer.

While her two servants were busy preparing her a place to sleep, she told Lanfranc it was her intention to set out again before dawn and ride until dusk each day.

'This is the last time we'll make camp while the sun still shines. I must not waste any time reaching FitzWilliam. If you or your men can't keep up, I'll ride ahead of you. Do you understand?'

'Yes,' Lanfranc stammered.

His heart fluttered with admiration for this brave, determined woman who had so recently been deprived of her husband. And, being a Norman, he wondered how much she stood to inherit.

Sianan dozed in the corner of the well-house all day. No one had brought her food since the doors had been locked but she'd let down the well-bucket when she'd been thirsty.

Close to sunset she heard a commotion outside. So she went up to the bars to see what was happening. To her surprise Sianan saw the new sergeant whose name she recalled was Martin. He was being dragged across the fields by three burly warriors.

141

The party eventually brought their prisoner to the well-house, unlocked the gates then threw him in. Two of the warriors posted themselves as guards while the third took the keys back to Guy.

The new prisoner pleaded with his comrades to let him out but they did their best to ignore him. At last when his cries became unbearable they moved to a distance where they couldn't hear him any more but could still keep an eye on the well.

'What did you do to upset your lord?' Sianan asked.

'I hesitated.'

'And for that he would feed you to the Nathairaí?'

Martin's face grew pale. He nodded.

'Seems harsh,' Sianan sighed.

The warrior shrugged then whispered, 'Are there really two serpents down that well who eat folk?'

The abbess looked away, avoiding his eyes. 'I'm afraid so.'

'How long have we got before they emerge to feast on us?'

'Plenty of time. Don't worry yourself.'

'How long?' the warrior pressed.

'Perhaps half an hour,' Sianan admitted. 'Then they'll rise up and do what giant worms love to do when they find a feast laid on for them.'

'Isn't there anything to be done? Is there no escape for us?'

'Why don't you get some rest? Calm yourself. In my experience, if you're going to have to face your worst fears you should try to get some sleep first so you can be in the right frame of mind.'

'I'm about to be chewed into tiny pieces by a couple of monstrous serpents and all you can do is advise me to have a lie-down?'

'You needn't fear the Nathairaí,' Sianan assured him. 'They won't chew you up. Worms don't have teeth. If anything they'll swallow us whole and spit out the bones once our flesh is digested.'

The sergeant gulped. Then he sat back to contemplate the horrific image forming in his mind.

'Aren't you frightened?' Martin asked her in shock.

'Not really. I intend to escape.'

'How?'

'I haven't quite worked that part out,' she admitted. 'But I can't afford to waste energy worrying about what will happen if I fail. Now do be quiet. I really must concentrate.'

Martin sat with his back against the wall, staring at her in disbelief. After a long while he spoke again. 'Are you a heretic?'

'I suppose you could call me that.'

'Are you a witch?'

'No. Not in the Norman sense of the word.'

'What are you then?'

'I am one of the Fánaí folk. We're also known as the Wanderers.'

The familiar flutter of wings distracted her at that moment as the raven, Lom Dubh, appeared at the gates. The sergeant reeled back from the huge bird in fear.

'Is this whole country populated with monsters?' he gasped.

Lom Dubh clicked his beak in annoyance. 'I hope you're not referring to me, young man,' the bird hissed menacingly. 'All your kind end up as food for my people. Warriors fall in battle. We clean up the mess. Don't forget that. If you want to stay on my good side you'll exercise some politeness.'

'Have you spoken with the Morrigán?' Sianan cut in, already impatient with the lesson in raven manners.

'I haven't been able to find her. Did you like the gift I sent you? I'm sorry he's not much company. But at least you won't be alone in your prison. And it's the best I can do until the Morrigán turns up.'

'Where is she?'

'Off in Alba somewhere taking a short rest from her duties. I wouldn't want to disturb her. She needs to build up her strength for the celebrations of Samhain Oidche. I've heard there's been a particularly nasty battle in Alba. Something to do with the Redcaps again. The field was littered with fodder, they say. The Morrigán is still sleeping off the feast.'

'What are you going to do?'

'Me?' Lom Dubh cackled. 'There's nothing I can do. Not without the approval of my queen. I'm very sorry, Sianan, but you and your friend will just have to face your fate with brave hearts. The Morrigán is not known for her tolerance of birds who act above their authority.'

'If you free us I will answer to the Morrigán on your behalf,' Sianan offered. 'I'll take full responsibility for the consequences.'

The raven clicked his beak. 'That's an interesting suggestion,' he replied. 'I'll think about it.' Then without another word he took to the wing and was gone.

Martin sat forward to watch the bird fly off. His face was deathly pale and his mouth was wide open.

'That raven was talking.'

'Yes,' Sianan told him. 'He's under an enchantment put upon him by the Goddess Danu. He killed a raven when he was a youth so he's doomed to serve out eternity as one of their kind. The Queen of the Ravens, the Morrigán, isn't the easiest soul to get along with. He's probably well justified in his caution.'

But the sergeant didn't hear the explanation. He swooned, eyes rolling as he fell forward and hit his head hard on the bars. When he'd slumped to the floor there was no further movement from him.

Sianan sighed.

'That's right. You get yourself some rest. I've a feeling you're going to need it.'

Gobann led young Harold off the road, through a wood, down an embankment then up a steep sloping hill toward the ancient rath.

'Have you no idea of the true nature of your visions?' the poet asked as they started their climb to the top of the abandoned hill-fort.

The student monk shrugged his shoulders. 'They are often prophetic, sometimes frightening and rarely insignificant. That's all I can tell you.'

Gobann stopped to draw a circle in the muddy ground with his walking staff. Then he laid the staff down across the circle, splitting the drawing into two halves.

'This is how foreigners view the passage of time and hence the whole world we live in,' the poet explained. 'The left half represents the past; the right, the future. And the stick is a symbol of this moment we're living right now. Do you understand?'

Harold nodded.

'Now I'll show you the Druid understanding of these matters.'

He picked up his staff to draw another circle. But this time he left a gap in the circumference. At that place where the join should have been he drove the stick into the ground.

'There is no past or future. There is only the circle of time wheeling its way through every waking hour and each slumbering minute. You and I who seem to exist in the present are as much a part of everything that ever was and ever will be as my walking stick is a part of the circle.'

He lifted his stick up again to follow the outline of the circle with the muddy tip.

'If one but knows the skill, one may travel around or across that circle to those parts you know only as the past and future. And that is how the visions may be explained.'

Harold considered the words for a moment but he couldn't quite understand what the stranger meant.

'I've read that Druids are pagans who sacrifice their brethren to the foul gods of their savagery,' he told Gobann.

'What?'

'I read about them once in a manuscript at the monastery. Julius Caesar wrote about the Druids in his book on the wars in ancient Gaul.'

'He was a bloody liar.'

'He was Emperor of the Romans.'

'What did I tell you? How do you think he rose to the highest office in the empire? He was a bloody liar.' Gobann laughed. 'At least you'd better hope he was. Or you may find yourself locked in a wicker basket, to be set alight as a sacrifice to an evil heathen god.'

Harold swallowed hard. The poet laughed again before he offered a piece of advice.

'If you want to know how the steeplechase was won, you'd be best to hear the tale straight from the horse's mouth.'

Gobann wrapped his cloak tighter. He looked to the sky as he sniffed at the wind. 'There are two Saxon-smelling rogues wandering about this evening,' he informed his companion. 'As well as the Norman foot soldier who was sent out to kill you.'

'To kill me?'

'What other purpose could he be pursuing but cold-blooded murder for profit? If the garrison commander had merely wanted you followed he would not have spared one of his trained warriors to the task. He would've sent a lowly squire or serving man.'

'Why would anyone want to kill me?' Harold stuttered nervously, looking over his shoulder.

Gobann shrugged and went on climbing the hill.

'I can bring to mind many plausible reasons,' the Druid called back. 'Treachery and robbery are what they all boil down to, of course. Someone, it seems, has got his eye on your satchel of books.'

'How did you know about the books?' Harold hissed, placing a protective arm around the leather case.

'Well what else would you carry in a bloody big book satchel? Badger bait? Or a block of last year's butter?'

The poet had a point, Harold conceded as he scurried along to catch up.

'We really should have waited till dark to climb this hill,' Gobann said. 'We're sure to be spotted now we're out in the open. It's too late to think about that, though. At least we don't have to worry about having a healthy sized cooking fire. Since every bandit in the district will know where you're camped, you might as well have a cheery blaze ready when they arrive.'

'I would never have suspected I was being followed,' Harold gasped. 'But you knew full well about the warrior and the two Saxons. Why didn't you say something sooner?'

'This experience will teach you to listen to your intuition,' Gobann scolded, waving a finger in the air.

Then he abruptly changed the conversation.

'What do you want from your life?'

'I don't understand,' the scribe replied.

'What ambitions have you? What dreams? What private wishes dwell within your heart?'

'I am a monk. I'm a scribe. I serve God and the Holy Mother Church. That is my only aim in this life. I can think of no better purpose. I have renounced ambition, dreams and wishes. I have no need of them.'

'Are those your words or was that the speech of another?'

'I first heard those words from my teacher, Eriginas. I recite them every day along with my prayers before sleep and upon waking.'

'You're a very fortunate man. And a rare one too,' the poet told him. 'However, since you are no longer cloistered in a monastery, you must learn about some things. Man and woman, daughter and son, friend and foe; all who breathe breath in the wide world surrender themselves to ambition, dreams, desires, fears and wishes each and every day of their lives.'

He stopped walking for a moment and looked directly into Harold's eyes. 'Those things are not evil in themselves. Yet they may twist a heart into compassionless acts of betrayal. Then one's soul is laid open to an infection of greed. Few men who are wounded on that war-field ever walk away.'

Harold was listening intently. He'd never encountered such unusual ideas.

'But one who keeps his aim upon the target and is not distracted will be plucking arrows out of fat stags all season long. Be compassionate. Don't take any action to your profit until you're certain no harm will come to others as a result. Don't claim more than your fair share. Balance out your selfish acts with gestures of generosity.'

'I'm led along my path by God,' the young scribe protested. 'As I wander the Almighty presents possibilities for me. Though I admit I often convince myself I choose the road, I don't set out to achieve anything unless it bears the seal of Our Lord.'

Gobann scoffed a little under his breath. 'You are indeed a rare one. You'll be a Druid whose name will resound down the ages.'

'I've no desire to be a Druid.'

'Who ever does? Nevertheless you're an aspiring Druid. And you'll be a champion among them.'

'I'm not a Druid!'

'Not yet. Not by any measure!' the poet affirmed. 'And it's a fine thing you know that without having to be told. Humility is a wonderful attribute. I hold high hopes for you, my boy.'

Gobann took off up the hill again. 'Have you ever thought about what you might have done if you hadn't been entered into the monastery so young?' he asked.

'How do you know I was young when I joined the order?' Harold demanded.

'You told me earlier you were left with the monks when a child. Besides, those hands of yours have never known blister or bruise. You must have been a very young boy when you went into the scriptorium.'

'I was.'

'And if you hadn't become a monk? What would you have done with your life?'

Harold frowned. He'd never considered the question. Only one life had ever been offered to him.

'I'd like to see a battle. Not to fight in it, mind you. I'd just like to watch.'

'Few folk who witness war are untouched by it,' Gobann sighed. 'And many who would rather watch often find themselves caught up in the slaughter.'

'I'd like to see the king, John of England, I mean. And the King of France. Or at least some great noble of renown. But even if I were not a Benedictine brother I would dearly love to do my teacher's bidding. I would still wish to complete the task he allotted me.'

'Let me see if I understand you. First of all you'd like to observe the senseless slaughter of young able-bodied warriors,' the poet summarised. 'Then to meet the misguided men who sent the fighters to their deaths in the first place. And afterwards you'd establish a monastic community based on rigid discipline and blind obedience to a man who lives in palatial opulence in a far-off city called Rome.'

The Druid shrugged. 'You may live to see all these things. But not if I have anything to do with it.'

Gobann climbed across the deep earth ditch which enclosed the rath. Then he turned to look the young man in the eye again.

'Now tell me why you would want to do these things.'

'To serve my sense of duty and to quench my curiosity,'

Harold told him. 'I'm a scribe. I'd like to write down what I've seen as a chronicle for others to read in the future. It's my obligation to record momentous events.'

The Gael was now standing on top of the defensive ditch. He put his hands on his hips and looked down as Harold clambered up after him.

'Battles are not my idea of momentous events,' Gobann frowned.

Just then the young scribe slipped his footing on the muddy embankment and slid face down all the way to the bottom of the ditch.

'That's what I call a momentous event,' the poet guffawed when the young man came to a stop.

Gobann's face turned serious. 'What about the harp?'

Harold frowned.

'Haven't you always had a secret, inexplicable and insatiable desire to play the harp?'

The young man's jaw dropped in astonishment. He'd never mentioned this deep desire to anyone. Ever since he'd first heard a harper play for the Abbot of Glastonbury he'd been enchanted by the instrument. But music was an unseemly pursuit for a Benedictine brother.

'How did you know that?'

'This is merely one of many things I know about you, Harold of Glastonbury.'

Then Gobann disappeared from view as he jumped down the ditch into the rath.

***

Martin, the former sergeant-at-arms, revived not long after he'd hit his head and fainted. When he came to his senses he could feel the floor of the well-house shaking violently. Dust filtered down from the roof of the little building as tiny pieces of mortar scattered everywhere.

He must have been lost in a deep dream while he'd been out to it because he sat for a long while staring up at the ceiling with a broad wondering smile on his face. Sianan was beginning to think he might have lost his mind. But then he spoke up at last.

To her relief his voice trembled with concern and his face paled. At least he didn't seem too mad, she thought to herself.

'What's going on?' the Breton warrior gasped.

'It's nothing,' Sianan assured him, but as she spoke the building shook again.

Then a deep rumbling growl rolled through the floor, rattling the iron bars on the doors and bringing down more dust.

'What do mean? This is nothing?' Martin shrieked.

'I can tell you're no fool,' she conceded. 'The truth is the Nathairaí are about to emerge from their prison deep within the well.'

'What are we going to do?'

'I haven't thought of anything yet,' Sianan admitted. 'All this noise has been so distracting. But don't panic. In my experience an answer always presents itself at the right moment. At least it always has in the past.'

'You're not convincing me,' Martin frowned.

'I've thought of one thing which could improve our chances.'

'What's that?'

'You could start praying,' she suggested. 'This is just the sort of situation that would warrant Our Heavenly Father's intervention.'

The building shook once more but this time when the dust settled there was absolute silence.

'Perhaps the Nathairaí have decided not to come up out of the well tonight,' the warrior ventured hopefully.

'Perhaps. But I reckon they're even now slithering up the long passage toward the top. They're both quite large creatures. I'm sure it's a tight fit. And worms aren't known for their nimble, quick movements.'

Martin sank to his knees without another word, clasped his hands tightly in front of him and offered up the first prayer that came to his mind. He had only been muttering for a moment when the raven reappeared at the iron gate.

'Have you come to watch?' Sianan enquired with deliberate bitterness in her voice.

'It'll be a good show,' the bird enthused. 'I saw them devour a herd of cows once. You probably wouldn't have considered it a pretty sight but my kind have an appreciation for such things. I thought the two of them were magnificent.'

'Isn't there anything you can do to help us?'

'There is something I might be able to do,' Lom Dubh conceded. 'But I need your word you'll take full responsibility if the Morrigán decides I acted without her authority.'

'I give you my word.'

'Very well then. I'll be off. I promise I won't be long.'

Then he disappeared into the sky again.

'You'd better not be!' Sianan screamed after him. 'We don't have very long.'

It was then she noticed Guy's two guards had deserted their posts, leaving their swords and shields lying in the field. At least she and Martin wouldn't have to contend with Norman warriors if they managed to escape.

At that moment the rumbling began again. Stones lining the top of the well started to fall away. In seconds the entire circle surrounding the mouth of the opening had collapsed. A strange silence followed hard on the heels of the destruction.

Martin raised his head to see what was happening. To his horror a huge black slimy bulb emerged from what was now nothing more than an ugly hole in the ground. The massive lump moved around until a shiny dark object appeared.

It was a little while before the Breton warrior realised this black blob was an enormous eye. And it was regarding him with obvious delight. Sianan sat perfectly still, unwilling for the moment to attract the attention of the monster. Martin sat still frozen by fear and the feeling he might soil his britches if he so much as twitched.

While the eye stayed focused on the Breton the rest of the awful head emerged. A great gaping mouth hove into view with lips of grey rolling fat and a dark red lolling tongue.

'What have we here?' the creature hissed. 'The well is open and we have a meal waiting for us. Has the Goddess Danu forgiven us at last?'

'She has forgotten you,' Sianan replied sharply.

The beast turned his attention to her. 'We've got one each!' he declared joyously. 'My companion will be pleased. Even a Nathair like myself can't live forever on the tiny creatures one finds crawling about deep within the earth. We like a bit of variety at our feasting table.'

'Do you truly intend to eat us both?' she asked.

The worm frowned as best he could considering he had no eyebrows.

'What else would I be doing with you? You're food. And my goodness, you smell quite delicious.'

The creature sucked in a huge noisy draught of air through what must have been his nostrils. Sianan stood up to face the monster. She had something to say before she was turned into dinner.

'I have a few questions,' she declared boldly.

'I'm sure you're consumed with curiosity. Or, to be certain, you soon will be,' the worm quipped. 'You'd like to know what manner of beast I am, wouldn't you?'

Sianan nodded.

'I don't mind telling you. It's a fair question considering you'll be my first decent meal in two hundred summers.'

The worm turned his great body round and settled his head on the shattered remains of the well.

'My companion and I were once like you. We were mortals. We were tribespeople of the Fir-Bolg whom your folk only remember in stories. Along with seven other companions we entered the service of a terrible and powerful druid-king. But we chose our master poorly.'

'Balor of the Evil Eye,' Sianan cut in.

'Have you heard the tale? If so, I won't bother repeating it.'

'But you tell it much better than any storyteller I've ever heard,' she added hastily.

'I'm glad you think so. It's the last story you'll ever hear.'

Then the creature paused to recall where he was up to in the tale.

'We were Druids once, you know. She and I.'

'She?'

'My companion's name is Isleen. I am called Lochie. I do beg your pardon. I should have introduced myself. Just because I'm an ugly great serpent who goes on a feeding rampage whenever he gets the chance doesn't mean I'm incapable of politeness. I'm just forgetful. If you spent night after night cooped up in a tiny place far beneath the Earth with only a giant she-worm for company, you'd probably suffer lapses in manners every now and then.'

'My name is Sianan. I'm abbess of the community of Dun Gur. I was a Druid once, in the days before I took to living with the Culdees of the Christian faith.'

'Once a Druid, always a Druid, I say,' the worm sighed. 'Do you limit your diet?'

'I eat no meat nor the flesh of any fish or bird,' she told him.

'I don't mind telling you what a sweet tasty treat you'll be. What about him? Is he a Druid too?'

'His name is Martin. He's a warrior from the Breton lands.'

'Isleen can have him,' Lochie decided with obvious distaste.

'To cut a very long story short,' he went on.

'I wish you wouldn't,' Sianan interjected.

'Of course you do, my dear, but I'm afraid I must. She down below is an impatient old so-and-so. I don't want her swallowing my tail in her rush for dinner.'

He paused again.

'I've lost the thread of my story. You must excuse me, I haven't engaged in such a conversation in more than nine hundred winters. It's most stimulating but a trifle challenging. All she wants to do is play Brandubh. And that's not an easy thing with only slobbering lips to pick up the playing pieces.'

'I used to be a great player of the Brandubh myself,' the abbess told him.

'Really!' the worm cried in rapturous delight. 'How wonderful it would be to have someone new to play against!'

'You could tell me the whole story in more detail over a few games,' Sianan suggested.

'That would be magnificent,' the Nathair agreed, and the abbess could see he was excited by the offer. 'Most enjoyable.'

Lochie was clearly temped to accept the invitation. Indeed it was considered mighty impolite to refuse a challenge in the ancient days when the Nathairaí were young. The Brandubh was a game enjoyed by all classes of people in the old days.

It was played on a board seven squares by seven which represented the four measures of the country with a fifth in the centre for the high-kingship. After I've told you this part of the tale I'll teach you how to play if you like. I haven't had a game for years myself.

As I was saying, Lochie was tempted to accept the challenge but common sense, a rumbling appetite and a long experience of his companion, the she-worm down below, made up his mind for him.

'Alas my hunger for flesh outweighs my desire to embarrass you at a dozen rounds of Brandubh. I hope you don't think it impolite of me but it is the nature of the Nathairaí to put their stomachs before anything else.'

He stopped again, grunting under his breath as he tried to pick up his story where he'd left off.

'You were telling me about Balor of the Evil Eye,' the abbess reminded him.

'So I was,' Lochie nodded as best he could considering he had no neck to speak of. 'Balor of the Evil Eye tricked us into becoming his servants by promising us eternal life. What he didn't tell us was that we would eventually be condemned to an eternity walking the Earth as disembodied spirits with a grudge against everyone and everything.'

He sighed deeply as though an old wound had opened in his heart.

'Most unpleasant! Then Danu passed a judgement on us for the harmless mischief we'd been indulging in to pass the time. She put us into this form to teach us both a lesson. I'm sure it wasn't meant to be forever. But she promptly forgot all about us.'

'I've been told she can be quite dithery,' Sianan nodded sympathetically.

'Then you've been told the truth and I don't mind who hears me say so. Just as long as the Lady Danu herself isn't amongst them. May her rest be ever tranquil and sublime. She has a mighty temper.'

'Did you learn a lesson from your enchantment?' the abbess enquired.

'Well I did. I learned never to trust anyone ever again. I learned that forgiveness is hard won and sometimes not worth the effort. And I learned never to underestimate the forgetfulness of a goddess.' He paused. 'Now it's time for dinner. You don't have the key to that lock, do you? It wouldn't be quite so cramped in here if I could move my tail outside.'

'I have the key,' a raven voice announced.

'What kept you?' Sianan cried out in frustration. 'I thought we were in real trouble.'

'I'm sorry. It wasn't an easy item to pickpocket,' the bird said, dropping a bunch of keys to the ground in front of the bars.

The raven bowed his head to the monster. 'Greetings, Lochie,' he offered. 'You're looking well.'

'As well as can be expected considering the circumstances. Is that you, young Lom? I see you're still wandering about in the form of a filthy black sky-scavenger. Hasn't the Morrigán released you yet?'

'Unlike Mother Danu, most ravens have long memories,' the bird shrugged. 'The Morrigán hasn't forgotten my misdemeanours against her kind. And even if she had, there's no word for forgiveness in the raven language.'

'How's that brother of yours, young Sárán?'

'He calls himself Sciathan Cog these days,' the bird snapped. 'I don't have much to do with him. He's raised the ravens of the north in rebellion against their queen time and time again. He faked his own death once to escape her wrath. Last I heard he was following some Norman around pretending to be a powerful portent of victory.'

'That's just like Sárán,' Lochie reminisced fondly. 'He always was a hothead who loved to stir up trouble. I'm looking forward to seeing him again.'

Sianan had already picked up the keys and begun fumbling with the lock. In moments she'd flung open the gates, dragging Martin behind her as she made off across the fields toward the woods.

Lochie sighed deeply as he watched them run away.

'She's a nice girl,' he commented. 'I'll bet she knows a story or two.'

'I thought she'd never leave,' the raven noted dryly. 'Aren't you going to go on after them to give them a scare?'

'There's plenty more where they came from. And anyway I'm enjoying speaking with you. Did I mention it's been an eternity since I had a decent chat with anyone? Most satisfying it is. Thanks for your help, Lom Dubh.'

'Are those two out of earshot?' the raven asked.

Lochie nodded, in his worm fashion. The bird scuttled closer.

'The truth is I'm not Lom Dubh at all. I'm his twin brother, Sciathan Cog, whom you once knew as Sárán.'

The Nathair gasped with delight. 'I'm so glad it's you, Sárán!' he exclaimed. 'I never liked your brother that much anyway. He was always so serious and far too much of a do-gooder for my liking.'

Then a question suddenly struck the worm. 'Why would you want to release us?'

'It's my sister, Queen Aoife of the Redcaps, Sovereign of the Night, who wished you set free.'

'Dear little Aoife! Why would she want us out of our hole in the ground? I'll wager she has a bone or two to pick with us.'

'She has a favour to ask of you. In return she will unburden you from Danu's curse.'

'Really? I'll have to discuss it with the loud fat squirming one down below, you understand.'

'You owe me this,' Cog hissed. 'If I hadn't brought the key you would never have broken the bonds of enchantment which were woven around this well-house.'

'I'm very grateful,' Lochie conceded. 'Don't worry, I'll talk Isleen into meeting with Aoife so we can discuss her offer.'

There was a great roar from far beneath the well enclosure. Lochie coughed uncomfortably.

'I'm sorry to break off our little talk. I really have enjoyed it

immensely. But Isleen is making unsubtle suggestions implying she wants me to move my slimy great arse. Perhaps when
she and I have finished ravaging the countryside roundabouts
we could all get together for a talk about old times.'

'And a game of Brandubh?'

'What a splendid idea!'

'I'll arrange it so the Normans track Sianan and the Breton.
They'll soon realise the pair of them have escaped,' Cog
promised. 'If you hide yourself in the woods the warriors will
walk straight into you.'

'We could pick them off while they're pursuing their two
runaway prisoners!' Lochie exclaimed. 'Thank you for all your
help. I really do appreciate it.'

'It is my pleasure. I've no love for the Normans. Their flesh
is tough and they know little of personal cleanliness. Worst of
all they're wanton wasters of the best nest-bearing trees. Just
don't harm the haughty one who calls himself their lord. Aoife
has plans for him too.'

'There's no bad blood between us then, Sárán?' Lochie
ventured, broaching the touchy subject of their former enmity
which Caoimhin recorded in his tale of the Watchers.

'Too many summers have passed by since we were enemies,'
Sciathan Cog replied. 'Even a raven can't bear a grudge forever.
You go about your business and I'll go about mine. Leave me a
tasty morsel here and there and I'll be much obliged. Haunt the
forests to scare away woodcutters and I'll call you raven-friend.
Help rid the land of all boat builders and carpenters and I
promise I'll speak to my sister on your behalf. Aid her in her
quest and you will certainly be free of the curse which you have
borne through all these passing centuries.'

With that Cog clicked his beak and spread his wings.

'The past is the past. Let's live for this day. And if we can be
allies, the endless treadmill of the seasons may pass by us all the
more quickly. Now farewell. I must be off. Take care of yourself.'

'Don't worry about us,' Lochie told him. 'We tend to instil terror in most creatures we encounter. There's not much out there that presents a threat to us. Thanks again for letting us out.'

'I couldn't bear the thought of you cooped up in there like caged birds,' the raven shrugged. 'But I had a murder of a job tricking those Normans into attacking this place. Glad it's all worked out for the best. Goodbye.'

And with that he was off to track down Guy d'Alville.

OYSTIC TRAVELLERS

Harold crawled back up the muddy eastern embankment of the rath. Once he'd reached the top he sat down on his knees to catch his breath. To his astonishment he noticed that Gobann had already lit a fire and was cooking a small animal over the flames.

'I hope you have a hunger for roast rabbit rashers,' the poet piped up cheerily.

The young scribe got to his feet and staggered, exhausted, to where the meal was being prepared. He squatted beside Gobann and stared at him in wonder.

'How did you prepare that rabbit so quickly?'

'It's a Druid trick,' the poet explained, touching his forefinger to his nose and winking. 'Comes in very handy now and then.'

'Is it devilry?'

'No. It's Draoi-craft. It's a way of being which allows one to act without needing to grab.'

Gobann stirred the coals with his walking stick.

'Everything you can see, and the rest you cannot, is in a state of either being, doing or possessing. Or subtle combinations of the three. Most folk spend their lives concentrating on doing the things they think are necessary to end up having the things they want from life.'

He paused, wondering how to word this as simply as possible.

'Other people are so caught up in their possessions or their companions that they don't tend to do a lot else but enjoy them. But a Druid who is focused on simply *being* can work within this state to attain whatsoever he should desire.'

'And what do you most desire?' Harold inquired as he dumped the satchel on the ground and lay down by the fire to rest.

The poet looked up sharply from the coals. There was a deep pain in his eyes. In the flickering firelight they twinkled with a single teardrop each.

'What did I tell you about the impoliteness of asking questions?'

'I'm sorry,' the young monk replied sincerely. 'I didn't mean to pry.'

Gobann grunted in annoyance and stood up. He lifted his staff to the sky and pointed with it toward a cluster of bright sparkles.

'Do you see that bluish-white star in the heavens?'

Harold nodded.

The poet touched his clenched fist to his heart. 'The Evening Star has watched over me since first I took the robes of the Druid order. She is the source of my inspiration. She grants to me the sacred Draoi-craft. She reaches into my very depths. She helps me to harvest words from the grain fields of my memory and the treasure-house of my learning.

'I will tell you what I desire. I wish to be reunited with my soul-friend. I long to sit with her in the Halls of Waiting, to laugh with her, to sing, to stare forever into the wells of her spirit. And to drink from the refreshing spring of her bright blue luminescence.'

The young Benedictine frowned, not understanding a word of what was being said to him.

'I'm looking for the woman of my dreams,' Gobann explained, seeing the confusion written on the lad's face. 'I haven't looked on her in a ferociously long while. But I'm on my way to meet her now. You'll meet her too. In fact you know her just as well as I do. Though you won't recognise her of course.'

'I don't know any women,' Harold replied, shaking his head in dismay.

'No, you don't,' Gobann agreed. 'Perhaps it's a bit early to be talking with you about this sort of thing. Maybe I should wait to see whether or not you survive the night.'

'Is the murderer nearby?' the scribe whispered.

'No. He's keeping his distance. But he could be waiting for nightfall to make his attack.'

The poet pointed his staff toward the east where the sky was darkening. There was a thin column of smoke visible there.

'That's his cooking fire.'

'And what about the Saxons?' Harold pressed. 'Where are they?'

Gobann sniffed the wind then winced as if he'd caught a foul stench on the breeze.

'They're nearby, I'm sorry to say. So I'll be leaving you presently. I have a longstanding quibble with their people. If I were you I'd offer the savages something to eat. It's a common saying among our people that a wolf rarely bites hard after its belly has been filled. Then after supper it sleeps without snoring.'

In the next breath the poet strode off toward the western side of the defensive ditch.

'Farewell. We'll meet again soon. I'm so glad I ran into you. You're going to be a fine practitioner of the Draoi-craft in time.'

'How do I deal with the two Saxons?'

'Don't worry too much. Those two won't do you any intentional harm. They're scholars like yourself. The real danger is they'll bore you to death with theology. Or lead you into a situation that might well cost you your life.'

Gobann stopped and stared at Harold, then asked a strange question.

'Where is the centre of the Earth?'

Harold frowned.

'I'm not sure. Isn't Jerusalem at the centre of the Earth?'

'You'll have to do better than that,' the poet scoffed.

Then he climbed the bank, and as he disappeared, the last rays of sunlight went with him. Harold was left alone in the blue-grey twilight. But the Druid called back with one last comment.

'By the way, don't tell anyone you've met me. I don't want to have to answer any embarrassing questions.'

The young scribe didn't rise from his place at the fire. He was simply too exhausted to follow after the strange traveller. What with three days of vigil over his teacher and then walking the whole day, his legs ached terribly.

There was still a little light so Harold reached across to the book satchel and untied the leather straps, flipping open the bag when he had done so. He grabbed the first manuscript his fingers touched. It was a small book a little larger than his hand. The binding was a dark red leather with a worn gold inlay of knot-work designs. The manuscript was quite thick.

As he opened the book he raised his eyebrows in surprise. Every page seemed to have only a few words written upon it in Gaelic. And the pages seemed to fly open of their own accord until they settled on one particular saying.

'A wise old cat recognises his own tail. So he isn't compelled to chase it,' Harold read aloud.

He shook his head, trying to work out what that could mean. Then he turned to the first page of this manuscript to read the title of the book.

'An Leabhar Fál.'

He translated this into the Norman-French dialect spoken at Glastonbury. 'The Book of Destiny.'

Wearily he placed the manuscript back in the satchel. He was too tired for this. He wanted to have a clear head and a good sleep behind him before he examined the books thoroughly.

He thought for a moment of the approaching Saxons. Perhaps he should seek out a place to hide. But he couldn't muster the strength. It was best to attend to the meal, he told himself. If Gobann had been concerned he would have said so.

And strangely enough, he trusted the Druid. He couldn't explain it but there was something very familiar about him.

Harold drooled as he turned the rabbit on the makeshift spit cut from a green branch. He hadn't eaten meat since the previous Christmas.

The monastic regulations of the Order of Saint Benedictine forbade the consumption of flesh except on special feast days. But Harold was so hungry he decided that this once it wouldn't hurt to break the rules.

He stretched out on his side by the fire to wait. And he didn't have to wait very long. But just as his meal was browning to an irresistible roasted crispness, the scribe heard voices. Two men were arguing heatedly in Latin.

'My dear deluded friend, Lewyn of the Lapsing Logic. I must once again contend that this world we witness is merely a manifestation of an implied but unsubstantiated common experience. You've offered no argument to repudiate that.'

'Are you saying we're all sharing this dream as if it were by common consent?'

'At last you've understood my point.'

'Have you considered that the simple fact I'm challenging your contention may be a clue to the possibility that perhaps each of us has a differing perspective on creation? So therefore we all retain a goodly measure of independence.'

'Apparently so. But can you prove it?'

At that moment two monks dressed in grey tattered habits

appeared at the top of the eastern ditch. Harold rose slowly to present his invitation in the friendliest voice he could manage considering how tired and apprehensive he was feeling.

'Good evening, brothers. Would you care to join me for supper?'

Two pairs of eyes lit up. Two bellies grumbled. And two travelling friars forgot their opposing philosophic conjectures for the time being at least.

'Would you truly have us sup with you, my son?' the larger of the two called out. 'That's very kind indeed. We've not had a crumb to line our stomachs since we became lost three days ago.'

'That's not strictly true,' his companion corrected. 'My friend here, Overton the Verbose, is well armed when waging word-war but he's got a tight fist when it comes to the facts. We ate wild garlic and blackberries for breakfast.'

'That didn't line my gut. Those berries barely touched the sides,' Overton complained.

As they made their way closer to the fire Overton's companion introduced himself.

'My name is Lewyn of Llancarfan,' he bowed. 'Blessed be the hand that feeds the wanderer.'

'Lewyn Drivel-Smith, they called him back at the monastery of Saint Caoimhin at Llancarfan. Have you heard of our patron, Saint Caoimhin?'

Harold recalled his teacher's advice to adopt a Gaelic name so as not to rouse suspicion. And quick as a flash inspiration hit him.

'I'm named after him,' he replied without a thought to the consequences.

'Are you?' Overton exclaimed with interest. 'Well this is an auspicious meeting. We've come from Wales to seek out relics belonging to our founding father. He may have been Irish but he was a civilised fellow and a good Christian.'

'He was a truly holy man,' Lewyn affirmed, rising to his favourite subject. 'When Saint Caoimhin passed away he had two tombs erected. In one of them he had his own bones interred. In the other were buried the remains of his closest friend.'

'The trouble is no one remembers which is which,' Overton cut in. 'So it's impossible to know whether one is paying homage to a famous holy man or a simple monk. Now that's what I call an act of humility if ever there was one. You must be proud to bear his sainted name.'

'I am.'

A mysterious and magical thing happened as those few words passed between the three men. Harold of Glastonbury drew his last breath. And the myth-tree of Saint Caoimhin the Scribe was seeded in the garden of legends. Folk often confused the two Saints Caoimhin so that the deeds of the former were attributed to the latter.

Our Benedictine brother had his mind on other matters of course, so he didn't mark the moment. Which I think is rather sad myself. But it was fairly typical of him.

'Sit yourselves down,' the young monk told his guests. 'I've met many Saxons but none from Wales.'

'We're not Saxons. We're Welshmen,' Lewyn explained as he took a seat by the fire. 'There aren't any Saxons in Wales. Our folk drove them out generations ago.' All the while he spoke, his eyes never once left the roasting rabbit.

'The truth is I'm half Saxon,' Overton admitted, taking a place by the blaze where he too could observe the meal slowly cooking on the spit. 'I speak the Welsh tongue but I wouldn't call myself a true Cymru Welshman.'

'You're no Saxon either,' his travelling companion noted. 'You're too civilised to be called that. You're a Welshman to the very bone.'

Our newly renamed scribe asked the travellers all about the

monastery of Llancarfan. Then he inquired about their travels as he passed the ale-skin to each of them in turn.

The friars told him about a Welsh monk named Gerald who was the son of a duke or a lord or some such. Gerald was a famous book-man. He'd written a history of Ireland and drawn extensive maps to illustrate the work. He'd also included a lot of information about the native inhabitants of the island. But alas, to the eternal disappointment of both Overton and Lewyn, Gerald of Wales had made some very obvious blunders in his manuscript. The truth was, none could say whether they were mistakes or deliberate misrepresentations. There was a rumour he'd made up some extravagant details in the hope he'd be rewarded handsomely by a Norman lord. Others reckoned he'd been offered an Irish bishopric and wrote all those awful lies about cannibalism and clergy killing to scare off the other contenders.

Both friars freely expressed the opinion that Giraldus Cambrensis, as he was known in Latin, had not visited Ireland at all. They both reckoned it likely he'd composed the entire book without once leaving the warmth of his own hearth in Caer Narffon.

'We've decided we're going to compile our own manuscript while we're here,' Lewyn explained enthusiastically. 'We've already filled a dozen sheets of parchment with notes.'

'I'm a scribe myself,' the young Benedictine told them. 'My teacher imparted a very comprehensive knowledge of the Irish language to me. Perhaps my skills might be of service to you in your task.'

This all sounds very polite but Roman clergy have this game they play with one another. A member of one order will happily promise the known world to a member of a rival order. But unless the archangels above intervene, nothing will ever come of it.

'We'd be honoured to accept your assistance,' Lewyn replied graciously.

'I still can't believe we were robbed,' Overton cut in, shaking his head with distraction as he gave out a bit of a whimper. 'All our money was taken. And our provisions.'

'Who robbed you?'

'Wild Irish bandits,' Lewyn explained. 'Savages they were. Matted hair, muddy faces, torn cloaks and desperate eyes. They waited for us a half-day's walk from Wexford. And when they came down on us from the trees we both nearly died of the shock. Swords drawn and tempers frayed, they forced us to go with them into the woods where they left us lost and alone.'

'And without so much as a handful of barley to stem our hunger,' his companion added as he gently indicated the rabbit roasting over the fire.

Our Harold. . . I beg your pardon, Caoimhin, took the hint. In no time three bellies were bulging with roasted meat and mouthfuls of Wexford ale.

Truth to tell they were so hungry none of them questioned how such a small animal could have satisfied three hungry men. But that was another Druid trick such as Gobann had mentioned.

'Where are you headed?' Overton enquired as he sat back to digest.

'West,' the young scribe indicated vaguely.

'Setting up a monastery, are you?' the fat friar laughed, not realising he'd struck so close to the truth.

'Yes,' Caoimhin replied.

The merry expression dropped from Overton's face. He didn't want to cause offence. 'Well we'll travel with you for a while if you don't mind. I for one would feel safer with another brother along to share the road.'

'It would be fine to walk with a fellow who could teach us something more of the Irish language. We both understand the speech but often miss hidden meanings or sly comments,' Lewyn added.

'Have you anything worth stealing?' Overton went on.

Caoimhin's heart raced. He knew he wouldn't be able to keep his books a secret for long. As soon as they saw the satchel slung over his shoulder they'd know what it contained.

'I've twelve farthings left from the fifteen my teacher gave to me,' the young scribe replied. 'And a copy of the gospels with commentaries. And a litany of the mass. One or two other small books. But nothing else of value.'

'The Irish don't care for books,' the fat half-Saxon sighed with relief. 'But those twelve farthings could present a difficulty.'

'Allow me to carry those coins,' Lewyn offered. 'If we're to travel together we should share everything. After all, we are holy brothers-in-Christ. We don't have the luxury of personal possessions. I'm the senior monk so I'll carry the pouch.'

Caoimhin hesitated, unsure whether he should trust these two. But he decided Lewyn was right to demand to take charge of the money. As the eldest of the three, he likely had the most experience of the world.

So the pouch was handed over. The Welshman quickly counted the little silver farthings. He was just replacing them in the leather pouch when a dreadful sound tore through the night. A low deep growl rolled over the top of the rampart like a great wave crashing in on the cliffs. The brothers' eyes widened in horror.

'What was that?' Caoimhin gasped.

'Haven't you heard about the lion?' Overton whispered.

The young scribe shook his head, his face pale.

'Well that is the roar of a creature out searching for its supper. I don't doubt it caught whiff of your rabbit. We'd best keep a good watch this night.'

'I won't be sleeping,' Lewyn admitted. 'If the lion doesn't get us, there's bandits to think of.'

'Well whether I'm going to die at the teeth of a wild animal or on the sword-point of a savage, I'm going to need some rest,' his companion yawned. 'I find tragedy less tragic after a good night's sleep.'

'You're a lazy fat oaf,' the Welshman huffed. 'You're slothful and you're lacking in any sense of duty to your fellow man.'

'If you don't worry about it, it probably won't happen.' Overton yawned again. 'And if it does happen, it's better to be fast asleep until it's well over.'

Then the fat half-Saxon lay down on his side. He was fast asleep dreaming fat half-Saxon dreams before another word was spoken. His friend scowled as he stirred the fire then wrapped the cowl about his head.

'It's going to be a long night,' Lewyn grumbled.

'Where are you headed?' Caoimhin asked.

'We were on our way to the fabled hermitage of the monks known as the Island of the Living,' the Welshman replied. 'Now we've found the road again, we're only four days journey from the lake where it can be found.'

'Why are you going there?'

'Because our founder, your namesake, Saint Caoimhin, lived there in his youth. And there is a holy man named Finbar who's said to dwell in that place. If the stories are to be believed this man knows the answer to any question put to him.'

'What are you going to ask him?'

Lewyn stopped to think for a moment.

'I don't know yet,' he confessed. 'But I'm sure I'll think of something when the time is right. In any case, I want to include a chapter in our book of travels all about the Island of the Living so pilgrims will be encouraged to visit the place.'

'Can anyone ask a question?'

'If they have one to ask, young Caoimhin.'

The scribe heard his new name pronounced and he liked the

sound of it. He wondered whether this holy man called Finbar would be able to answer his particular question.

He thanked the Lord for leading these two friars across his path. Perhaps the Island of the Living would be a good place to start looking for the two books Eriginas had been sent to find.

Our lad laid his head down, his thoughts entirely consumed by the possibility of discovering the reason for his visions. Or possibly learning some cure for the malady. His eyes shut, and despite the occasional roar of the alleged lion, Caoimhin didn't stir again till morning.

Sciathan Cog, raven-brother to Lom Dubh, was a bitter bleak-hearted old beak-bearer. Some birds said his blood was as black as the bottom of a broth pot.

And those were the ravens who liked him. He had few friends, though. As a matter of principle he never completely trusted any of them until they'd been dead at least a week.

He'd sat all day high in an oak tree watching Guy d'Alville's men ransack Dun Gur. As the sun set, a drop of drool dribbled down his beak onto the branch. When Sciathan Cog had his mind on something he could forget his otherwise impeccable raven manners.

This creature had once been the twin brother of Lom Dubh in the far-off days when they both walked on fleshy human feet. But an enchantment had been laid upon them in punishment for a terrible crime they'd committed together.

Our Caoimhin eventually wrote down their story in the tale of the Watchers so I won't repeat it now. If you want to find out more about them, seek out a copy of that manuscript and read it.

Just don't accept the whole tale as if it were gospel. As I mentioned to you earlier, Caoimhin made lots of mistakes.

All I need to tell you is that Sciathan Cog turned out the very opposite to his brother. He'd always been headstrong and self-centred. But countless winters covered only in a coat of feathers had left him with a scheming sort of hatred for anyone he chose to scheme against or hate. And that could be anyone with breath in their body, blood in their veins or the unhappy luckless predisposition for being in the wrong place at the wrong time.

He wasn't fussy who he hated.

He despised all creatures. Cog only suffered the company of trees, flowers and vegetables because they didn't run fast enough to keep him entertained.

Nevertheless he often spoke his mind to whichever tree he was perched on, simply because he had no one else to communicate with. Even a raven has to get things off his chest sometimes. Trees aren't renowned gossips either, so that was a point in their favour.

On occasion Sciathan came across some mortal who interested him. Now and then he spotted a mortal he thought might serve his purposes, a warrior with the potential to cause the kind of havoc that quickens the heart of any carrion bird. Once in a while, a very rare while, he discovered a man in whom he recognised a kindred blood-lusting treacherous heart. Guy d'Alville was that man.

There hadn't been anything like Guy walking round Ireland for the last nine generations at least. Sciathan's thorny claws clenched the branch tighter, squeezing the bark till it flaked away and fell to earth. Wicked daydreams blossomed in his long, elegantly ridged raven head as the Norman went about his business subjugating Dun Gur.

Cog had observed the imprisonment of Sianan. He would have hummed with delight if ravens had been capable of making such a sound. Instead he gave out a low satisfied gurgle of amusement. He'd never had much to do with the Abbess of Dun Gur, but she represented everything he loathed about the world. She was a druid of old, sworn to truth. She was a keeper of her people's tales and songs.

She was a Fánaí, a Wanderer. Sianan had sided with his enemies once in the dim dark past. This was enough reason to hold her in hatred and contempt. It was only fitting, he decided, that she should be locked in the well-house.

His spirits lifted as they did only when he added the name of a new target to the long list he kept in the vault of his memory. Another challenge. Another vengeance. Another joyous hunt ahead of him. He would have whistled if he'd had lips.

However, this fine mood abated when Sciathan Cog witnessed the arrival of his brother, the meddling Lom Dubh. Cog was briefly tempted to fly down to chase his sibling off. But he decided discretion would serve his scheme much better.

So he watched and waited until he saw the Nathair called Lochie emerge from the well. Then he flew off to fetch the key to the well-house. Everything was going according to his carefully planned strategy.

Now the Nathairaí were free and Aoife would be overjoyed.

'Lochie and Isleen,' the old bird cackled, speaking to the ancient oak tree in which he perched. 'Even an old bough like you is too young to know their story first-hand. Though you may have seen them once in a while or heard silly tales about them.'

The raven fell silent again to recall the old days. He brought to mind all his memories of the two creatures. They were mischievous, wicked, greedy, blood-hungry when roused to it, and wily when the occasion demanded.

From his perch he watched as the two worms rested a while. He gave a raven smirk as they circled the well-house three times and then set to smashing it into a hundred thousand pieces. It would be a goodly while before anyone could rebuild that prison.

Sciathan clacked his beak. For the first time in many winters he felt a warm glow kindle in his heart. His feathers shivered with excitement at the trouble the Nathairaí were going to cause.

As soon as the worms had made their way into the forest Sciathan spread his wings and dived from the tree in a graceful swoop. Levelling out, he glided effortlessly close to the ground and onwards to the summit of the hill of Dun Gur.

He remembered the time when this great mound had been an island in the centre of a wide lough. Long ago, when the Danaans had relinquished the settlement to the Gaels, the waters had receded and never returned.

Sciathan rose up on a breezy draught so that he was suddenly high above the ancient fort. With a keen raven eye he spotted Guy. Tucking his wings close to his side, he plummeted straight down at the unsuspecting Norman.

D'Alville had a warrior's sense of impending danger. The hairs on the back of his neck prickled, his nostrils flared, his ears focused on every sound and his eyes darted cautiously about him. But by the time he heard the rush of feathers, it was already too late to draw his sword. The raven landed, wings wide, only four paces from Guy.

Sciathan would have laughed for joy but he could only cackle. The sound was thin yet full of mockery.

'Where have you been?' D'Alville demanded. 'You told me you'd fly by my side into this fight.'

'You didn't need any help,' the raven grunted. 'I've been keeping my eyes open, which is more than you've been doing. Were you so busy with this little scrap you didn't notice my brother flying about? Are all your kind such fools you can't tell one bird from another?'

'You're a raven. In what manner are you different from your brother?'

'He is my twin,' Cog conceded. 'So I suppose I can forgive you.'

'And what did you see from your lofty vantage point?' Guy asked sarcastically. 'Did you glimpse Robert FitzWilliam? I'll wager you did not. Because he hasn't been in these parts for years, if indeed he was ever here at all.'

'He's here. I'll wager my wings on it,' Sciathan replied. 'The island of Eirinn is not large. Have no fear. We'll find him. In the meantime you've stirred up the hive and there'll be a swarm of bees gathering to give you a good stinging for poking about at their sweet home.'

'What are you talking about?'

'Your prisoners have escaped,' Sciathan hissed. 'And they've let loose a terrible curse that will devour all mortals in its path.'

'Are you going to tell me some idiot story about giant worms?' the Norman asked sceptically.

'Lochie and Isleen are their names, if you're interested. And now they're out they'll bring more havoc to this country than a hundred of your kind could ever do.'

'I don't believe you. It's a load of rustic rubbish. There's no such creature on this Earth as a serpent-worm that only emerges from his prison well to devour cattle.'

'First,' Sciathan began, 'let me point out that you probably wouldn't have believed in a talking raven until you encountered me. Yet I am here now before you. Second, when Lochie and Isleen do get out, which is rarely, they don't confine themselves to eating cows. Third, go down to the well-house yourself to see the damage they caused smashing it up. Fourth, I wouldn't go alone if I were you.'

'I will,' Guy told the bird defiantly.

'You'd better hurry. The waters have already begun to rise. By the morning the lough will have returned to its natural state, as it was before the coming of the Gaels to Ireland.'

'How did that happen?'

'Don't you take any notice of anything you're told? The stone covering the well was cast off and not replaced. After dark the waters rise. They will inevitably flood the fields. There's nothing can be done about it. The stone was shattered by the Nathairaí. I suggest you move your warriors from this place before they're trapped.'

'And where will I move them to?'

'Take up defensive positions in the forest,' Sciathan suggested. 'In the woods you'll hear the Nathairaí as they approach.'

'I'll follow that abbess,' Guy decided. 'I'm willing to wager she's off to warn Robert FitzWilliam I've come to seek my revenge. I'll track her down. She'll lead me right into his lair.'

'You're a madman,' the raven sighed. 'But that's why I like you. Very well, if you must persist in this childish game of cat and mouse with a man you haven't seen for years, so be it. I'll be your eyes and ears. I'll warn you of danger and guide you to your prey.'

'Why are you bothering with me?' D'Alville snapped. 'If you're the immortal you claim to be, you surely have better things to do than follow me round the countryside watching over my interests.'

'We have a bargain,' Sciathan cawed menacingly. 'Do you think I flew over to France to find you for the good of my health? You are suited to my purposes.'

'You promised me you'd lead me to Robert FitzWilliam,' Guy reminded the bird. 'You told me he dwelt in this land. That's why I followed you to Ireland. But I haven't seen hair or hide of him nor any evidence he ever walked upon the evil-infested fields of this country.'

'I'll do my best to help you find the fellow but when the time comes you must aid me in my quest. And that time is fast approaching. Did you know there's a huge army of black-robed knights assembling at Wexford? War has come again to Innisfail.'

'Innisfail?' the warrior frowned. 'What's that?'

'The ancient name for Ireland. It means the Island of Destiny.'

'How do you know about the Hospitallers?'

'I'm a raven. One way or another nothing escapes my attention. I've been expecting this influx of warriors for many winters. Now at last my hopes and dreams seem within grasp. I, too, have a vengeful heart and an old bitter quarrel to settle.'

'You're the Devil's servant,' Guy asserted. 'But I have no fear of you.'

'Nor should you have. As long as you keep your part of the bargain we'll remain friends and allies. But if you let me down, I'll bring all my kinfolk in. Then you'll have a clan war on your hands.' Sciathan clicked his beak. 'Do you imagine I'd think twice about sucking those tender sweet moist eyes of yours out of their sockets if you weren't of some use to me?'

Guy swallowed hard, knowing the bird spoke the truth.

'Fly off then,' the Norman told the creature. 'Do your work on my behalf. And when the time comes my sword will be yours.'

'I'll report to you in the depths of the forest on the eastern edge of the old lough. By midnight I should know the exact whereabouts of the woman called Sianan. And if it is still your desire to follow her, I will show you where to find her.'

With that the raven spread his wings and took off into the darkening sky. Guy watched the bird until it was nothing more than an indistinct dark speck among the silver clouds.

Then he issued orders for his warriors to march east immediately.

OAT-BEER

Sianan was quick to seek shelter in the dark forest near the edge of the ancient dry lough. Martin the Breton was close behind her all the way. He'd picked up a sword abandoned by one of the guards and he clung to it as though it were a dear old friend.

The two fugitives said not a word to one another till they were lying on their stomachs among the blackberry bushes. Even then it was a long while before either of them caught their breath.

'I'm going north and west,' Sianan told the warrior. 'Goodbye and good luck.'

'I'm coming with you.'

'I travel alone.'

'I can't go back to Limerick,' he told her. 'I can't show my face in the Norman lands again. I'm an outlaw.'

'I can't guarantee your safety in the western lands,' the abbess sighed. 'Many folk fear the Normans and their mercenaries. More of them hate your people for the warfare you've brought to this land. If I were you I'd make my way east to try to find a boat home.'

'If I'm caught I'll be hanged for desertion,' the Breton stated. 'That's if I'm lucky. If not, Guy d'Alville will catch me. I'm sure he'd be happy to arrange a lingering, painful death. I'll come with you if you don't mind.'

179

'I never travel in company. I prefer to remain invisible from my enemies.'

'I owe you my life,' Martin argued. 'I don't know what manner of woman you are, if you are a woman at all, but I know if your friend the raven had not come to my rescue I'd be a dead man. Until the debt is settled I'll stay by your side. You never know when a sword arm may serve you well.'

Sianan saw the determination in his eyes. 'Very well. But you'll follow my instructions without question,' she told him. 'Is that understood?'

'It is.'

'To start with we're going to cross this forest tonight. We'll sleep for a short while in the morning before we set out again.'

'Where are we going?'

'To a safe place. To a place where Guy and his warriors can't touch us.'

'Such a place doesn't exist on the face of the Earth.'

'You've not travelled the same roads I have,' Sianan laughed. 'At the Killibegs we may find sanctuary.'

'Where's the Killibegs?'

'It is a gathering of the community of the Culdee folk. They assemble in a different place each year.'

'It doesn't sound like a safe haven to me. Guy doesn't respect the ancient sanctuary of the altar. And he certainly won't hold back his sword hand where heretics are concerned.'

'Killibegs is no ordinary collection of stone huts. Nor is it even a mighty castle fortified against a siege. There's no moat or any clever defences. But neither Norman nor Gael would be able to find it if he didn't know exactly where to look.'

'Is Robert FitzWilliam there?'

'What business does d'Alville have with the younger FitzWilliam?' Sianan asked. 'Has he some score to settle?'

'I only know Guy is hunting the man. And he will not rest until he has served out his revenge on the poor wretch. I have no idea what passed between them to raise such hatred in the man. If FitzWilliam walks the land of Ireland his life will be in peril. And if we're anywhere near him our lives will be threatened also.'

'I'm beyond death, sickness and suffering.'

'What do you mean?' Martin shot back, confusion furrowing his brow.

Sianan avoided his question. 'Do not fear. My friend Robert, if he is in Ireland at all, will not succumb to the hatred of Guy. And neither will we.'

From the expression on his face, it was clear Martin was not at all convinced.

'Can you wait here for me just a short while?' he asked hesitantly.

'I can't.'

'I have a dog,' Martin told her sheepishly. 'I'd like to fetch him.'

'Do as you wish. I'll go on without you.'

'Please wait for me. I'll serve you true and so will Oat-Beer.'

'Oat-Beer?'

'That's my dog.'

Sianan considered the dangers of returning to Dun Gur. She thought of the pouch of rowan berries she kept hidden in the bedclothes. Truth to tell, she didn't like the idea of leaving without those precious life-givers. She was worried about them falling into the wrong hands or being cast out on the dunghill as rubbish by some well-meaning but ignorant individual.

For these rowan berries had been rescued from the great Quicken Tree that had grown at the Cashel crossroads seven hundred and fifty years before. Queen Caitlin of the Eoghanacht had found them amongst the ruins of the mighty bough in the long-ago days when Saxon raiders had mercilessly butchered the holy tree.

Sianan knew of no other source of berries with the same unusual properties as these. For if one but knew the method, a brew could be concocted of them that would end illness, cure all wounds and grant immortality.

They were a treasure bequeathed to her by Queen Caitlin. And Sianan had promised she would find a deserted place where men did not walk to plant new Quicken trees. But the abbess had never managed to find such a place. She'd treasured the berries in her keeping until she'd almost forgotten she had them at all. It occurred to Sianan now that she might stand in need of these Quicken berries in the days to come.

'Very well,' she conceded. 'I'll accompany you for I have one or two things I'd like to retrieve. But from now on you'll follow my orders and no argument.'

'Thanks to you, my lady. You'll never know a more loyal servant.'

Caoimhin woke from his sleep to a grey dawn. His two monastic companions were still wrapped in their travelling cloaks and huddled by the smouldering fire. Our young scribe yawned, stretched and sat up.

His first night in the wilds had been restless. He had a pain in his lower back and his nose was running from the chilly air and wood smoke.

Now he was awake, the first thing on his mind was to take another look at the little book called the *Leabhar Fál*. He opened the satchel and removed the manuscript.

Almost the moment it was free from the bag the book fell open. Caoimhin read the words on the page that was revealed to him.

'It takes a long while to dismount from a high horse.'

He had no idea what the little verse meant.

Just as he was turning the page to read the next saying, Caoimhin caught a movement out of the corner of his eye. He was suddenly certain someone was close by.

This was enough to distract him from the book. He rose silently, wrapping his cloak about him to stop himself shivering. Behind him he heard the unmistakeable crack of a twig breaking underfoot. The young monk spun round, his heart nearly stopping with fright.

A man was sitting on the mound of earth that formed a defensive wall. The mist shrouded him so that he was little more than a shape, but Caoimhin could see the fellow was looking down at him.

'Is that you, Gobann?' the scribe whispered.

'Of course it is,' the familiar resonant voice replied. 'Come up here. Sit with me a while before those two come to their senses.'

Caoimhin built up the fire a little. Then, still clutching the Book of Destiny, he climbed the steep wall. Under his breath he cursed the fact that Gobann had chosen the highest part of the embankment on which to sit.

At last, straining from exertion, the young man sat himself down beside the poet.

'I like your new name,' the Druid commented. 'It suits you well.'

'Did you hear that lion last night?' Caoimhin asked, not wondering how Gobann could have known about the name change.

'There are no lions in Ireland,' the Druid replied with absolute certainty.

'But I heard it growling in the night.'

'There are worse creatures abroad in this land than lions, I fear,' Gobann replied. 'What you heard is beyond your understanding at present. I wouldn't worry too much about it if I were you. You have more pressing concerns.'

'Any sign of the Norman warrior who was following me?'

'He's hiding in those bushes at the far end of the rath,' Gobann replied. 'But don't worry about him. I put a sleep on him for a while. He won't wake till the sun is high. But keep your knife close to hand just in case.'

'I don't have a knife. I'm a monk. I'm forbidden to own a blade.'

'No knife?' the Druid exclaimed. 'How do your folk eat your meat?'

'I've already told you, I don't usually eat anything but vegetables and bread.'

'You won't get far in this world if you don't build up your strength,' the poet advised. 'But I respect your vocation. It is well you do not find such restrictions a difficulty. It will not be a burden to you when you make your full commitment to the Druid path.'

'I have no desire to become a Druid,' Caoimhin protested.

'I felt the same way when I was your age. But believe me, that will pass and you will embrace your gifts as we all must.'

'Why are you so interested in me?' the scribe asked.

'What makes you think I am? I'm just filling in my days as best I can before I can go home again. I hope you don't feel I'm interfering in your life. But if I'm not mistaken you'd be a right mess if I hadn't been here to point you in the right direction. And your belly wouldn't be so content either.'

Caoimhin had to concede the point. 'I appreciate your help,' he nodded. 'Thank you.'

'What's that you're carrying?'

'It's a book.'

'I can see that. I'm a Druid, not a bloody fool. What's the book about?'

'I don't know. It's called the *Leabhar Fál*.'

184

'The Book of Destiny.' Gobann whistled through his teeth to show he was impressed. 'That'll be a great help to you.'

'How?'

'Don't you know anything? It works like this.'

The Druid took the manuscript, laid it on his lap and let it open at a page. Then he read the message written out in ornate Gaelic lettering.

'"Grass that hasn't grown yet is only fit to feed the unborn calf."'

'What does that mean?'

'That depends on what you take it to mean. It could mean something quite different to me than to fat Overton or to a farmer who's just had his cows stolen. The thing is, this book is a guide to the future. It's a little collection of wisdom. Let it open at any page and take the advice to heart.'

He looked down at the book again. 'I might have one more go at it,' he ventured. 'If you don't mind. I haven't played this game in a long while.'

The manuscript fell open. The Druid read the page.

'"A tiny bee may make a great bull scream."'

Suddenly the poet slammed the book. 'That's enough for now. Sometimes the *Leabhar Fál* can hit a bit too close to the mark.'

He handed the manuscript back to Caoimhin. 'Do your folk tell riddles?' he enquired.

'Yes.'

'Answer me this one.' In a low voice the poet began singing a song to a slow, sweet, haunting melody.

'Tend the fire of loving. Call upon the flames of joy. Sweep the hearth with songs. Stir the coals of memory. Hear the ocean's song. And the dark sea swell. Drink the cold wave spray. Taste the water in the well.'

Gobann stopped to catch his breath as if he hadn't done this in a long while. Then he went on.

'Bless the stones of waiting. Bless the stones of certainty. Bless the bread of friendship and the sands of the centuries.'

He paused to make sure the lad was listening.

'The mouth of a saint tells the world as it should be. The lonely heart of grieving will mourn eternally. An eye of compassion watches over earth and sea. The lively heart of giving will sing eternally.'

Once again Gobann ceased the song to take a breather. Then he sang the last verse.

'I tend the fire of loving. I call upon the flames of joy. I sweep the hearth with songs. I stir the coals of memory.'

Caoimhin's eyes were closed as the poet finished.

'That was beautiful.'

'But do you know what it's about?' Gobann asked.

The young scribe thought about it but had to admit he didn't.

'On the day you work out the meaning, your life will given to the Draoi. Then you may call yourself a Druid,' the poet told him.

Caoimhin shook his head but did not protest. 'You asked me a riddle last night,' he reminded his companion instead.

'Where is the centre of the Earth?' Gobann nodded. 'Have you worked it out yet?'

'The centre of the Earth is wherever I'm standing.'

'Well done!'

'I heard that one when I was a boy. I just couldn't recall the answer.'

Gobann grunted. Then he reached into his robe to retrieve a small parcel wrapped in fine white deerskin. He handed it to the young monk.

'What's this?' Caoimhin asked.

'It's a knife. You never know when you'll need one.'

'I'm not permitted to accept gifts.'

'That's inconvenient. I have another one for you.'

Gobann picked up a staff that lay at his feet. It was a short walking stick intricately carved though not as beautifully worked as his own. It was bound with fine strips of leather at the top into which small bone ornaments were woven. The top of the staff was whitened by some craft Caoimhin did not know. A single red jewel was set in this handle. And that jewel was as big as one of the scribe's knuckles. The remainder of the walking stick was dark brown, carved and smoothed by time.

'It's made of hazel wood. It will open many doors for you. To carry such a staff is an outward sign you are a postulant on the road to taking the vows of holy orders.'

'I've already taken holy orders,' Caoimhin protested.

'Now you're making a commitment to the Draoi path,' the poet explained. 'Your life will never be the same again. You've already discarded your old name for your real identity. You are to be congratulated.'

'How did you know I'd changed my name?'

'My dear Caoimhin,' the Gael laughed. 'It is within the capability of everyone to know anything they wish to.'

'I find that hard to believe,' the young scribe replied.

'It's not important *what* you believe. When you understand *how* to believe then you will be walking on the Draoi path.'

He stood up and shook out his cloak. 'That's enough for now,' he said, putting his forefinger to his lips. 'Your travelling companions are waking. I must be off. Look for my fire this evening and each night from now on. I'll wait for you.'

As Caoimhin got to his feet he remembered an important question he'd meant to ask earlier.

'Which road do we take?'

The poet laughed, pointing toward the distant mountains.

'Don't take any road. It's far too dangerous. Cut across country and make for those mountains. You should reach them by nightfall if you set out soon and keep a steady pace all day. I'll meet you this evening to give you directions over the pass.'

'What about the warrior who's following me?'

'He'll sleep. I'll see what else can be done to slow him down,' the Druid assured him. 'Now be off. No time for breakfast. Eat something on the way. You can put up with bread and ale for the day.'

With that, Gobann the Poet set off over the side of the sloping wall. Caoimhin watched him until he passed between the trees into the woods. Then the young scribe went back to the fire to wake his companions.

The morning was far advanced as Mirim's party approached the last settlement before the mountains. In the pouring rain Lanfranc rode beside the desert woman, his helm slung by its chinstrap over his shoulder.

Shali held the reins of the fully laden horse as Thomas Curdle led the wagon behind him. They liked to share all the tasks like that, all except the cooking. Far ahead rode the sergeant called Stephen with two men-at-arms on foot. At the rear of the column three more foot soldiers trudged along, bearing the weight of their cooking gear and armour.

Mirim's senses were on alert. She'd had an uncomfortable quiver in her bones ever since they'd met with the messenger from the FitzWilliam estates. Though she couldn't put her finger right on what it was that disturbed her, she was so absorbed in being on her guard that when Lanfranc spoke, she jumped, startled.

'It's a fine soft day,' he declared cheerily.

Mirim thought about this comment for a moment. Then

she looked skyward, blinking into the driving rain.

'Have you ever wondered why there are always clouds in the sky when it's raining?' she asked.

Lanfranc frowned, not sure he understood the question.

'I have a thought on that,' he coughed, hoping to use this opportunity to impress her. 'When it's foggy on certain days in this country I'll get home after chasing my horse to find my clothes soaked through.'

Mirim looked into his eyes, wondering whether he could possibly be serious. Surely he must have realised she was trying to lighten the conversation. She shrugged to indicate she didn't know what he was on about.

'Clouds are just mist that becomes weighed down with water until it can hold no more. When it's still light it's borne up on the breeze and empties out rain when it gets too close to the sun.'

'I also have an opinion,' Mirim stated without a hint of emotion in her voice. 'The clouds gather because the stars are shy.'

'What do you mean?' Lanfranc asked, genuinely concerned she could be so naïve.

'During the day the stars are still there behind the light blue curtain of silk which allows them to take their rest in private. Clouds are another kind of curtain. A curtain that preserves modesty.'

'I don't understand.'

'Rain is what happens when the stars are emptying out their pisspots all at once.'

Lanfranc heard the sincerity in her voice. He struggled to speak. Clearly women of the Orient were very bold and unabashed.

Mirim was just allowing a small smile to unfold behind her veil when the sound of hurried hoof-beats ahead caught her attention. In less time than you'd take to ask yourself what that noise could be, the answer was presented.

Stephen appeared through the mist, riding hard back toward them along the road. There were furrows of concern etched across his brow.

'My lord,' he called out. 'I must speak with you.'

'What is it?' Lanfranc asked excitedly. 'Is the road blocked? Have you encountered brigands?'

He put a hand on the hilt of his sword, ready to draw it. It was then Mirim noticed that even though the rain had not let up all morning, Lanfranc looked far neater than anyone wearing armour deserved to be under these conditions.

'My lord,' Stephen swallowed. 'I've just realised we've made a terrible mistake.'

The sergeant jumped down from his horse. With the butt of his lance he drew a large triangle in the mud.

'Our fortification is here.' He drew a circle around one point in the triangle. 'The FitzWilliam estates are here.' He did the same around the second point. 'And the mountain pass of Kiltealy is here.' He circled the final point. The lines that joined these places represented the only roads between them.

'We're here.' He pointed the lance butt close to the village of Kiltealy. 'That messenger couldn't have been sent from the FitzWilliam estates.'

'What's this all about?' Lanfranc asked, puzzled.

'The messenger we met on the road yesterday was leading us into a trap!' Mirim gasped, understanding the sergeant's point immediately.

'Indeed I fear he was, my lady,' Stephen replied with a hint of newfound respect for her. 'It must be brigands leading us into an ambush. No rider could have come that fast from the FitzWilliam estates. And I'll wager he would have come upon us from behind in any case.'

'Why do you say that?' Lanfranc enquired.

'Because a messenger would have been to our fortification first. Once there he'd have found we'd taken this road to avoid

190

the lion and keep the lady in your company as long as possible.'

Stephen immediately realised what he'd said. He rolled his eyes and thumped his forehead with the heel of his hand. Lanfranc simply turned pale.

Mirim grunted as the penny dropped. 'You told me we were taking this road because the direct route to the FitzWilliam estates had been washed away at a ford.'

'I'm sorry, my lord,' the sergeant offered sheepishly.

'We'll talk about it later, Stephen.'

Lanfranc turned to Mirim. 'My lady,' he began but those were the last words he spoke for a while.

'You've been wasting my precious time!' she screamed. 'And just to pacify your own terror of a lion you've never even glimpsed. If that wasn't bad enough, you decided to take advantage of our enforced company to try to talk me into your bed!'

The knight's cheeks burned with blushes. He drew a breath but got no opportunity to use it for speech.

'And now your scheming idiocy has led us straight into an ambush,' Mirim yelled.

Suddenly she fell silent. But there was a seething impending-doom air about her quiet. Lanfranc coughed, hoping for a chance to say a few words.

He didn't get one.

'You stupid buffoon!' she bellowed. 'You fool! If we all sat here in the rain for the rest of the day you'd still be more thoroughly wet than any of us. How did you gain your knighthood? Did you win it in a game of dice?'

She would have gone on at length berating the nouseless Norman, but just then Stephen drew his sword sharply and spun round as the blast of a hunting horn sounded from deep within the surrounding forest.

'Tell him all about it later, my lady. The brigands are upon us. We're under ambush.'

An arrow struck the mud at Stephen's feet. Then another. Mirim was down from her horse in a second. She drew a light half-length sword from a scabbard in her pack.

Her servant Shali was at her side in a flash, a war sword in one hand and a round shield in the other. Curdle seemed not as keen to fight, though he too had a blade at the ready.

'I'll take care of the beasts,' he declared as he gathered reins together in a bunch.

Stephen slapped his mount on the rump and the frightened animal galloped off out of bowshot. But Lanfranc sat firm in the saddle, his ears still tingling hot from the terrible words Mirim had spoken. All he felt was a crippling shame mingled with the sour aftertaste of embarrassment. And for the first time in as long as he could remember the trepidation in his heart receded so his honour could step forward.

In this state he easily admitted to himself he'd acted dishonourably. His reputation had been tarnished. There was obviously no alternative but to put some polish on it to match his immaculate armour.

Grimly he slipped his blade from the scabbard at his side. As the weapon woke from its sleep a familiar change took hold of him. Lanfranc was immediately swathed in a back-straightening, heart-bolstering cocoon of valour. With the air of one who is about to give his life for his friends, he raised the sword high in the air.

He swallowed hard, summoned his best knightly voice, then let fly with a most convincing war cry.

'For God and King John!'

The rain ceased as he spoke – as if the stars had been so surprised by his words they'd abruptly stopped emptying their pisspots. In the next breath a score of figures appeared on the road ahead, with a further twenty behind them.

Lanfranc spurred his mount on toward the brigands who blocked their path. The robbers charged at him on foot, screaming wild unintelligible curses as they raised axes, spears and swords of all kinds to strike him down.

But the Norman was undeterred. With a broad sweep of his blade he cut down the first man who came close to him. The blow shattered the man's collarbone. The brigand shrieked in agony. He teetered for a second, shocked he'd been wounded so badly. His comrades froze in their tracks, wide-eyed and faltering.

A few breaths passed in silence. The injured Irishman's legs buckled beneath him. Then, staring at his attacker with gaping mouth, he collapsed. All the way to the ground he clutched his wound as blood spilled from his body.

As the wounded warrior came to rest on his back, a dark-haired, bearded fighter pushed his way through the brigands to kneel by his dying comrade. The man sheathed his sword when he saw the awful gashing wound.

'Are you in great pain, Branach?' the dark-haired warrior asked his fallen friend.

He brushed the blood-soaked hair from Branach's eyes. When no answer but a gurgle came from the injured brigand he got up and marched over to Lanfranc with fury in his eyes.

'What the hell do you think you're doing?' the warrior demanded, disregarding the effects of Lanfranc's enchanted blade.

'I'm defending the honour of a lady,' the Norman boomed.

'You've just killed a friend of mine,' the Irishman countered.

'I'm not dead yet, Gusán,' his wounded comrade pointed out.

'You're as good as dead,' Gusán called back over his shoulder. Then he realised he should probably not have been quite so harsh. 'I'm sorry, Branach. I've a few matters to settle with this foreign fellow, then I'll give you all my attention. Now calm yourself,' he soothed.

The warrior turned to face Lanfranc again. 'There was no call to be killing anyone. We were just after stealing anything you might have to eat or removing a sackful of valuables. Nothing worth dying for.'

'Are you the brigands who've been shooting arrows at me in the woods whenever I go out to ride the king's roads?'

'That was us. Indeed it was,' the warrior admitted. 'Who'd you think it was? Redcaps? And we sent the messenger to make sure you were headed along this path so we could find a suitable spot to ambush you. I'll wager we put the wind up you once or twice in the woods with our arrows.'

'Your archers need practice,' Lanfranc noted with scorn.

'We weren't trying to hit you. Just to harass you. It worked too. You were so frightened the other evening you fell off your horse.'

'Do you yield?' the knight asked him quickly, hoping Lady Mirim hadn't heard.

'Of course we bloody well yield! Do you think any of us would want to risk losing his life over a few loaves of bread, a barrel of weak Norman ale and a handful of ha'pennies?'

'What's your name?' Lanfranc boomed.

'I'm called Gusán Gelt.'

'Are you the leader of these men?'

'It looks as if I am now. You've just murdered the wisest man amongst us.'

The Irish brigand turned round to check whether his wounded comrade was still conscious. He wasn't. A murmur passed around the assembled raiders.

'It's worse than I thought,' Gusán cried.

'What is?'

'That man owed me ten English marks over a wager. In that state, how's he ever going to pay me what's rightfully mine?'

The Irishman locked his gaze on Lanfranc. 'You have won yourself a deadly enemy,' he promised. 'As new leader of this fine company of warriors, I swear I'll be avenged on you.'

'Who said anything about you being our new leader?' one of the other brigands protested.

'There's been no discussion of it,' another declared. 'We mustn't rush into a decision.'

An old man stepped forward. 'We'll all go home tonight to consider carefully what's to be done. Then we'll meet tomorrow by the Dancing Tree to decide who will take the seat of our dear departed Branach.'

'He's not dead yet.'

'He will be by tomorrow.'

There was a hum of approval as each warrior shouldered his weapons then turned to walk off into the forest. Two brigands grabbed Branach's ankles and dragged the soon-to-be corpse off behind them.

The old man approached Gusán. He spoke in a low voice. Lanfranc had to lean forward to hear what was said.

'I'll tell you something, Gusán Gelt. And I want you think well on my words.'

He paused to be sure the warrior was listening.

'I wouldn't follow you if you were me and I was my own backside.'

Then he slapped the fellow on the shoulder. 'Don't take it too hard. My wife's roasting that young deer I ran down this morning. Why don't you stop by to share a cut with us? The night is sure to turn into a fine wake for Branach if he bleeds to death by sunset. A few drinks and a hearty meal wouldn't hurt you.'

Gusán nodded. 'Thank you. I'll be along later.'

'No you won't,' Lanfranc declared. 'You're my prisoner. I intend to bring you to the gallows at Wexford. And all your men as well.'

The old man shrugged, ignoring the Norman. Without wasting another breath he turned and marched off into the woods after his comrades. The old man waved a hand over his head in farewell. 'If you don't drop by I'll know what's happened to you,' he called back. 'Safe home.'

'Order those men to return,' Lanfranc commanded.

'Don't you listen? I'm not their leader. They won't take any notice of me.'

The Norman growled. 'Stephen! Lead a search. We'll capture every one of them if it takes a month.'

'No you won't!' Mirim cut in.

She strode over to Gusán, grabbed him by the tunic and threw him to the ground. She could be as strong as a horse when her temper was up.

'Was your messenger telling the truth? Did FitzWilliam leave the estates to go off to Killibegs?'

'He told the truth,' the brigand replied. 'Everyone knows the old lord went off to the Culdees.'

'I didn't know that,' Lanfranc objected. 'And I'm a lord in these parts.'

'You're a Norman. Why would anyone tell you what was going on? In any case you probably thought he was little more than a legend.'

Stephen blushed but Lanfranc bristled.

'Listen here, brigand, you're in enough trouble as it is. Don't add insolence to your list of crimes.'

Mirim lifted the poor Irishman up by the collar, dragging him closer to her face. The sudden move frightened Gusán out of his wits.

'Do you know the road to Killibegs?' she shrieked.

'I do,' he muttered in genuine fear for his life.

'Then you will remain with us. You will act as our guide to find the shortest possible route. And if you perform this task well, you'll be released.'

'You can't do that?' Lanfranc objected. 'He's to be hanged. He's broken the king's peace.'

'If you don't keep quiet I'll break your nose!' Mirim countered.

The Norman could see she was perfectly sincere in this intention. He sheathed his sword. As he did so his new-found courage wavered. Then it melted away as if it had never been.

'Very well,' he conceded with a stammer. 'But I insist on guarding the fellow myself.'

***

Just after noon Sianan stopped trudging through the woods and sat down heavily beside a young yew. She wiped her brow as she waited for Martin to catch up.

'We'll rest here,' she declared.

Before Martin could answer she lay back against the tree and shut her eyes. It had been a relatively easy matter to enter the settlement unnoticed. D'Alville had departed with all his troops to search for the two of them, leaving only a couple of dull-witted guards on sentry.

Sianan had to admit it had been a good idea to return. She had the Quicken berries. Martin had his precious dog Oat-Beer. And the Normans had lost their scent completely because the last thing Guy had expected was that they'd turn up at Dun Gur.

She'd picked up the tracks left by the Normans and to avoid them had chosen a roundabout route through the forest. It was hard going on foot, so she was certain a Norman warhorse would find the way impassable.

Sianan breathed easier, listening for any sounds in the woods that might betray her pursuers. The wind in the trees was all she heard for a long while. Then a light rain began to fall. As the splatter of droplets on autumn leaves filled her ears, the tension gradually drained from her body. But this state of rest did not last long. Above the steady rattle of the rain she perceived a thumping sound closely resembling the determined gallop of a warhorse.

She had hardly formed a question in her mind when the noise was upon her. Sianan opened her eyes, sat bolt upright then saw the blurred form of a gangly red-haired creature bound over a fallen log to land square in her lap.

In the next instant she was fending off the enthusiastic joyous licking of Martin's young hunting dog.

'That's enough, Oat-Beer!' she squealed, secretly delighted at the attention he was lavishing on her.

The dog barked. Sianan gripped his long snout and one of his wet floppy ears fell over his face. His eyes were full of sadness as if she'd broken his heart by interrupting his fun.

Oat-Beer was young yet, and like all dogs of the Sotar breed he was extremely playful. And he was blessed with keen eyes that could spot a puddle to jump in wherever he went.

'Call off your dog, Martin! And keep him quiet! Every Norman from here to Wexford will hear him.'

'Come here, Oat-Beer!' the Breton warrior called out, slapping his thigh.

The dog broke free of Sianan to run to his master, his disappointment forgotten in an instant.

'Why did you have to bring that wet, stupid creature with you?'

'You'll see why,' he told her. Then he turned to his dog. 'Sit, Oat-Beer.'

The animal whined with excitement as he placed his backside on the ground. He sat shivering with anticipation, wet floppy tail wagging wildly.

'Fetch!'

The red dog was off bounding through the woods, his long ungainly legs flying in every direction.

'You didn't throw anything,' Sianan frowned. 'What's he going to fetch?'

'Just wait and see,' Martin told her with a wink as he sat down against the tree to rest.

It had been a long hard trudge through the night. He was exhausted, hungry and footsore, but that didn't blunt the edge of his curiosity.

'You said you're a Fánaí. But you didn't explain what that means. What manner of woman are you?'

Sianan pulled back the cowl from her head to reveal her pale face. Her golden hair was shaved across the front of the head from ear to ear with long strands left to hang behind. Her dark eyes sparkled.

'I'm old. Ancient.'

Martin frowned. He reckoned she could be no more than thirty winters on the Earth. 'I'm not sure I understand you.'

Sianan sighed deeply. She was going to have to tell this fellow the story of her life. If she was to travel with him she would have to gain his trust.

So she began her tale. She told him it had been over seven hundred and fifty winters since her birth. She had been a Gael, a Druid and a young girl when her teacher chose her to become one of the Fánaí. A Wanderer through the ages. As the passing centuries had unfolded, her eyes had darkened and her skin paled so that she now looked somewhat different to mortals. That was the way with the Quicken Brew.

Along with her companion, Mawn, she had partaken of this Quicken Brew, a concoction prepared by the Druids of the mystical Danaan folk. These people had been the ancient inhabitants of Ireland long before the coming of the Gaels. The brew granted the Danaans their long lives, immaculate health and great wisdom. For once any mortal tasted of the Quicken Brew, they would not suffer death or ill health forever after. However, the Danaans were not spared the yearning of the heart which all souls experience. Some of them sought peace by withdrawing from this world into the realm of the Other. Many retreated into the hollow hills to sleep away the ceaseless cycles of the seasons in a deep state of dreaming. A few walked eternally among the mortal kind, stitching their fate to the banner of those who must die. But the desire for mortal company was a rare thing amongst the immortals.

'In our language the ever-living ones are known as the Eolaí. It means the knowers or the guides,' she told him.

Then Sianan explained how hard it is to love those you know will one day leave you and go on to the Halls of Waiting. That's why there were few immortals who still remained among the mortal kind. Their enthusiasm for those doomed to die had diminished down the years.

'What are the Fánaí?' Martin asked.

'Mawn and I were chosen to live on through the generations to preserve our people's laws and lore. When I was young the Roman Christians first arrived in this land. Their influence led to upheavals and wars such as had never been seen before.'

'So you're a heathen?'

'It's not that simple,' Sianan said hastily. 'The teachings of Christ are many. Not all the writings on his life are recognised by Rome. Much of the original doctrine does not contradict the Druid teachings at all. Unfortunately, those early teachings have been mostly lost to the followers of Rome.'

She explained how she had worked throughout her long life to incorporate the Druid ways into the new faith and that it had not been a particularly difficult task. Samhain Oidche, for example, had once been a Druid feast marking the passing of the old year into the new. It was a time for honouring the ancestors and the wisdom they had bequeathed to their children. The Christians had come to mark Samhain as All Hallows Eve. To them it was the night when all the wise saints of old were venerated. But in essence the feast remained a purely Druid celebration largely thanks to the work of the Fánaí and others who were guardians of the lore of the Gaels.

The Normans represented a new wave of Roman Christians.

This would be a time of great challenges for Sianan. You see, she had willingly taken on this task. But in the days of her youth she had not been aware of the full implications of her decision to become a Fánaí. Though she did not age, she felt the ravages of time on her soul.

There's a saying Sianan used to quote in those days when I first knew her. 'Weariness of the feet lasts but an hour or two. Weariness of the spirit lasts forever.'

When she'd finished her tale, Sianan stared off into the woods to avoid Martin's gaze. She hadn't told him everything about her condition but she'd said enough for now. She rarely spoke to anyone about her fate. It was sufficient that he knew she was vastly different to any mortal he'd ever encountered.

And believe me, her story is much more complicated than the simple version she gave Martin, though I won't tell the whole of it here. Caoimhin wrote it down in his tale of the Wanderers. I'm sure I've already mentioned that.

The Breton warrior considered her words for a moment before he replied.

'I don't believe you,' he told her flatly.

'What?' Sianan laughed.

'That's a cartload of old fishmongers.'

'It's the truth,' she declared, hurt that he might doubt her words.

'Prove it.'

'Very well,' she shrugged. 'Hand me that sword you're carrying.'

Martin carefully removed the short sword from his belt. He held it out to her by the blade so she could grasp the hilt.

'Don't cut yourself,' he cautioned her. 'These guardsmen's blades are very sharp.'

Sianan laughed with light-hearted mischief as she stood up to take the weapon. She gracefully swung it around her head a few times, getting a feel for the balance of the blade.

'Where did you learn to wield a sword?' Martin asked, surprised at her skill.

'There was a time in this country when all women learned something of the art of warfare,' she explained. 'It feels like an eternity has already passed since I last held a blade in my hands.'

Sianan took up the opening moves of the warrior's steps known as the Sword Dance. The movements were slow yet intensely powerful, expressions of an ancient formal style of warfare.

With perfect balance and a finely poised grace the abbess swept the short blade around. Then she turned it to rest the point against her robe near the soft flesh under her ribs. Sianan smiled at the Breton as she firmly grasped the hilt with her right hand.

'Do you still require some proof of my story?' she asked with a girlish grin.

'What are you going to do?' the warrior laughed uncomfortably, expecting to be the butt of some joke.

'Watch me carefully.'

Sianan pushed against the sword so it slowly bit into her flesh. Her expression remained calm but beads of sweat broke out across her brow. She stared directly into Martin's eyes all the while.

As a serene smile shaped her lips she put all her strength behind the hilt and pulled the blade forcibly into her body. Almost immediately she slumped onto her knees, only a muffled cry passing her lips.

Martin was at her side in an instant.

'What have you done?' he shrieked as he knelt by her doubled-up form.

He grabbed the sword, withdrew it from her flesh and flung it away as far as he could into the woods. He was utterly helpless and distraught at what he'd witnessed.

Sianan raised a bloodied hand to show him how badly she was wounded. Then she tore open her robe to reveal the ferocity of the wound. In a flash Martin removed his leather tunic, shirt and undershirt and ripped the undergarment in two. Before she could utter a word of protest he pressed the linen cloth down hard on the wound to stem the flow of blood.

'Don't fret,' she whispered in pain. 'All will be well in a few moments.'

'I can't let you do this to yourself,' he snapped. 'You saved my life. You're not going to die.'

Sianan let out an unusual noise that sounded like a giggle. Martin frowned with worry.

'Don't fret,' she assured him. 'You'll see. Just a little while longer. I don't fear death.'

Martin pushed heavier against the open wound, sweating now with the urgency of his task. Such a deep injury could quickly prove fatal. He'd seen enough battlefield wounds to know that.

'Why do you want to kill yourself?' he wept. 'Why?'

It would now be nearly impossible for them to escape Guy d'Alville. If Sianan lived she wouldn't be able to move very fast with such an awful stab in her body.

Tears welled up, clouding his vision. He'd just started to feel comfortable with this strange woman. Now it seemed he was going to lose her by her own hand.

Fearful he had not been able to stop the bleeding, Martin lifted the torn undershirt to look at the wound. And what he saw made him cough with shocked confusion. He wiped away the tears from his eyes so he could see better.

His mouth dropped open.

'What devilry is this?' he muttered.

'I told you all would be well,' Sianan replied serenely.

'Am I dreaming?' he stammered.

Sianan took his hand and placed it where the wound had been. I say where it had been because the injury was completely healed without so much as a scratch or a scar to mark it. The place where the sword had sliced into her flesh was smooth and untouched.

'How can this be?' the warrior whispered. 'Are you a dæmon after all? That wound would have ended the life of a man twice your strength.'

'I'm doomed to live,' Sianan told him. 'There is no death for me. I suffer no sickness nor any lasting injury. I'm an immortal. I'm a Fánaí, a Wanderer. I've seen seven hundred and fifty summers since I was brought into this world. And as many winters also.'

'Immortal?' Martin repeated, not quite comprehending.

'I will not die. This body has become a prison for my spirit. I must live out each day for the rest of eternity in the full knowledge my soul will never know the kind of rest a mortal such as yourself may enjoy.'

Martin touched the damp blood-stained robe. Then he examined his tattered undershirt. But he could find no words to express the inexplicable nature of this experience.

'I suffer pain,' Sianan went on. 'But even the fiercest agony loses its bite when you know it will only last a few moments. Fear no longer touches me unless it is fear for those I dearly love. Or fear of the heartbreak which accompanies the passing of a friend.'

'You just said pain does not last long with you,' Martin pointed out.

'Pain of the body is gone as quickly as it comes,' she confirmed. 'But my soul knows a kind of distress, a type of sadness, which could freeze the sun with its intensity at times. Or melt the cold heart of a mountain with its sting. That kind of pain lingers with me long and is not easily forgotten.'

Martin sat back against a tree, staring wide-eyed at his companion as she wrapped her robe about herself again. He slipped his shirt and tunic back over his head then asked a question.

'So you were not concerned for your own safety when the worms emerged?'

'I was worried for you. I didn't want to see your life ended by such a cruel one as Guy d'Alville and in such a terrible manner.'

'Your raven knew you were safe,' Martin concluded. 'Why did he help you escape?'

'You must forgive Lom Dubh,' Sianan smiled. 'He likes to play his little games with folk. There really wasn't much chance he'd have let you be consumed once he realised I was concerned for your safety. We immortals don't mean to seem callous. It just so happens we're fascinated by the fears the mortal kind suffer.'

Suddenly she put a hand to her mouth then held it out in front of her in a gesture for her companion to be silent.

'What was that noise?' she whispered.

Martin didn't have a chance to reply. In a flash the galloping gangly Sotar dog named Oat-Beer had bounded through the bushes to land at his feet. The dog dropped a canvas bag in his master's lap. The bag was full of flat Norman bread.

Oat-Beer yelped, seeking attention and gratitude. Sianan laughed aloud at the sight of this silly looking creature begging for a kind word from his master.

'He's a good hunter,' she giggled. 'No doubt about it.'

'I expected him to bring back a rabbit or a young fawn,' Martin admitted. 'But he must have found Guy's supply wagon.'

Sianan stopped smiling and all the mirth dropped away from her face. In the distance she heard a man's voice cursing and swearing.

'Oat-Beer has brought the whole of Guy's company down on us. They can't help but have recognised him,' Martin hissed under his breath.

'Lie low,' Sianan ordered. 'If we keep quiet and don't make a move, they'll miss us in the forest.'

Just as she spoke Oat-Beer stood up. Martin made a grab at the dog's neck to hold him down but the creature was too fast for him. With a playful bark Oat-Beer was off bounding away into the woods, daring Martin to chase after him.

'He thinks it's a game!' Sianan whispered in horror.

Oat-Beer's barking echoed through the woods as Martin and Sianan lay down flat against the moss around the roots of the trees. Before long they could both discern stern voices calling out to each other across the woods, steadily moving closer.

'You look over there,' one warrior commanded. 'I'll check over here where the trees are thickest. He can't have got far. Guy will have my balls for this. That was his dinner bread.'

Sianan shook her head in despair. No sooner had she done that than Oat-Beer returned, barking wildly to show his pursuers exactly where the abbess and his master were hiding.

Redcaps

J ohn Toothache slept well under cover of the bushes at the abandoned rath. Of course Gobann had put a Druid enchantment on him to help things along. Maybe that's why our Toothache dreamed of the first time he'd come to Ireland, three years earlier.

On his first sojourn into this wild land he'd been sent out with an expedition to reinforce the garrison around the monastic settlement high upon the Rock of Cashel. As the warriors had been resting after nightfall on the western side of the mountain a terrible thing had befallen them. A rain of arrows had fallen down from the trees around about, striking at anyone who moved.

Toothache took shelter behind the body of a fallen warhorse. That's where he stayed all night too. Next morning he discovered two things.

First of all, he had a toothache so agonising he could hardly stand up for the pain of it. He growled and groaned. He punched his own face in an attempt to dislodge the offending tooth. But he could do nothing to soothe the torture. In the end he swallowed a skin of ale. That helped him a little.

The second thing he noticed was that everyone else was dead. He was the sole survivor.

So John Toothache had earned a name, survived a slaughter and gained a violent disposition all at once. The violence of his moods was entirely inspired by the severity of his jaw pain.

Toothache woke suddenly from his memory-dream. The morning was already far advanced. This surprised him but he couldn't manage to drag himself up to check on the young monk he'd been following.

Rain spattered his face and smoke from his smouldering fire made him cough hard. After the fit had passed he sat up, broke wind at either end of his body, then reached for his ale-skin. When he'd swallowed a few mouthfuls to take the edge off his toothy agony, he yawned, scratched his head and screwed his face up into the usual painful scowl.

Toothache was struggling to recover from a deeply disorienting confusion. He asked himself how he could have overslept. When he broke cover to get a look at the spot where the three monks had been camped, he discovered they were gone. Their fire was just a blackened hole with a thin wisp of smoke curling upwards from it. Toothache grunted in frustration.

In a few moments he'd gathered his meagre possessions into his pack, arranged his ale-skin over his shoulder and set off, all the while wishing he was back in Wexford with its drinking-houses and hearth fires.

It was after midday but Toothache didn't worry about picking up the trail of his quarry. He knew the young monk would be heading west across the mountains. And the only mountain crossing that was passable in the rain was near the settlement of Kiltealy.

After a few hours walking he stopped to take a breather and have a bite to eat. A small wooded grove beckoned as shelter from the rain and there he sat down with his back to a birch tree. But he hadn't had a chance to unwrap his bread when he heard voices nearby speaking in a language he didn't understand. The Norman immediately drew his sword and moved to take cover deeper in the woods.

Toothache wasn't one to take unnecessary risks with his own life. He was tired and alone. He had no idea how many folk were nearby nor whether they were hostile or armed. So he decided to play safe.

He didn't have to wait long before a group of six short stout strangers approached. They all seemed to be talking at once, though the tallest of them was obviously in charge. The leader carried a great wide-bladed scythe across his shoulder and he spoke in a deep booming but jovial voice. The half-dozen strangers stopped to rest by the very tree where Toothache had been sitting a few moments earlier.

The Norman had the perfect opportunity to observe them without being seen. Their clothing was made of the finest brown or buff-coloured deerskins. Toothache knew this because he'd been apprenticed to a tanner in his youth. He had to admire the craft of these folk. He'd never seen such fine workmanship. The stitching, dyeing and cut of their tunics, trousers and boots were of exceptional quality. Each one of the strangers also wore a bright red hat of deerskin on his head. And their dark-brown matted locks of hair flowed out from underneath these unusual pointed caps.

They all wore red paint dotted on their hands in the most intricate designs. And each carried a hunting bow slipped into a sling, along with a quiver packed with arrows worn over the back on a shoulder strap. A sword scabbard fashioned from the same piece of leather as the quiver held each warrior's short-sword. They all carried sickles or scythes of one description or another. But these weren't harvest-gathering tools. These weapons were designed to sever necks, split limbs and spill lifeblood.

Fear is a powerful thing indeed. For under its influence the Norman forgot the pain in his tooth as he listened intently for any sign of threat. He found the crucifix Abbot Ollo had given him.

Without thinking he said a quick prayer then kissed the artefact. Suddenly he remembered it held a pellet of strong poison. He spat. Then he let the cross fall back against his chest to dangle on the silver chain around his neck.

He could hear the foreigners arguing heatedly. And though he couldn't understand a word of what they said to one another, the dangerous passion building between them was plain.

Suddenly the largest of them stood up with his scythe in both hands. Toothache reckoned this fellow must surely be the leader because all the other warriors bowed their heads and fell silent.

Except one.

In a rapid, unexpected move the large leader jerked his weapon into the air. Before John Toothache knew what was happening, the scythe came down hard. There was a sickening crunch followed by a gurgling gasp.

A head still wearing its red cap rolled out along the moss to land no more than five paces from where Toothache was concealed. The dead eyes of the foreigner stared at him lifeless, surprised and bulging.

In the next instant the strangers departed, leaving the poor shaken Toothache to ponder his good sense at hiding away from the view of these fierce warriors. It was a long time before the Norman emerged from the safety of his cover.

When he came out the first thing he did was prod the severed head with the tip of his sword. It rolled over to reveal the huge, monstrous, mucus-filled eyes of a Redcap warrior. The face was hideous. Toothache's heart stopped beating for fright. He could hardly draw breath for terror.

It's not that Toothache was squeamish. Indeed, no one loved the din and blood of battle more than this pain-racked soul. It was just that the whole incident had been so unexpected. He'd heard so many outlandish tales about the wild native Irish, but he hadn't really paid any heed to those stories. Now he was beginning to understand why grown men, veterans of bitter wars, slaughter and depravity, shook in their mail coats when they spoke of their adventures in the untamed lands of the west. These red-capped warriors were not at all like other men.

Toothache knelt down to examine the lifeless head. The awful face was painted with dozens of narrow red stripes. There were slivers of bone pierced through the fleshy ears, and scarred indentations in the flesh that picked out tiny delicate spiralling designs across the cheeks. The hair had been tied into beautiful strands of interwoven plaiting. These strands had been soaked in fat so they stuck together without unravelling. But it was the red cap which most fascinated Toothache.

Unable to bear the dead stare of those strange eyes any longer, he pushed the eyelids down with the tips of his fingers. Then he slipped the hat off the head.

For a moment he thought about trying the cap on for size but he soon noticed it was damp. As he held it up to his nose to sniff at it he caught a whiff of a familiar coppery odour. Toothache dropped the red hat in horror. Then he examined his hand. His fingers were stained with red. The hat had been dyed with fresh blood.

The warrior swallowed hard and stood up quickly to make certain the strangers hadn't returned.

It took a lot to get this fellow on edge, I can tell you. John Toothache was as brutal a bugger as they bred in Normandy. Yet he felt decidedly uneasy at what he'd seen.

He hurried over to the tree where the strangers had been arguing. There he saw the abandoned headless corpse propped up in the very position he himself had been sitting in only a short while before.

Lying on the moss beside the body was a beautifully carved walrus-tooth pendant fashioned in the shape of a seal cub.

There was a strip of leather threaded through the tail so the pendant could be worn around the neck. The piece fascinated Toothache. He decided it'd make a fine trophy.

He weighed the little ornament in his hand, hesitated for a breath or two, then slipped it around his neck. He touched it for luck where it hung just above his collarbone alongside the cross Ollo had given him. Then he headed off in the direction of the mountains again, following the trail of the strange brutish warriors. For they were headed toward the same destination.

Caoimhin, Lewyn and Overton headed west toward the mountains, keeping close within the wooded areas which lined the road in those days. That was before the Normans cut them down for firewood or shipbuilding.

It was the young scribe from Glastonbury who led the way. And he did it with such confidence that his two companions didn't question him even when it was almost dark.

'I've just had a thought,' Overton declared.

'What's that?' his companion asked.

'If the overriding impression one is left with is that all creation is little more than an imaginary, or at the very least misleading, realm where the senses delude us, then it's possible, in theory at least, to imply that one has a certain measure of influence over the course of events.'

Lewyn stopped in his tracks. 'Indeed I acknowledge your point,' he began. 'But that would negate the role or purpose of the deity in the web of the cosmos.'

'Unless of course the deity is inseparable from both the act and existence of creation.'

'That road runs over boggy ground, friend,' Lewyn objected.

Caoimhin had heard enough. 'We'll rest for the night at the top of that rise,' he declared.

They were all exhausted but Caoimhin suggested they should set about building a fire before nightfall.

'We'll make for the mountain pass in the morning,' he told them.

'So you've travelled this way before?' Overton asked.

'I've never been here in my life. I was given very good directions before I set out.'

'You spoke with a guide?' Lewyn enquired.

'Indeed. You could call him that. He's a native of these parts. It was he who advised me to keep away from the road to avoid brigands.'

'Sound advice,' Overton commented.

'You gather kindling, Lewyn,' Caoimhin told his companion. 'Overton and I will bring in the dry timber.'

The Welshman grumbled under his breath but he soon set about collecting the smallest twigs and the driest leaves to kindle a fire. Overton was already picking up armfuls of fallen branches to stack around the fireplace.

'I'll scout the road to make sure we weren't followed,' the young Benedictine told his companions. 'You never know what the brigands might be up to. I'll bring back some timber with me.' And he set off alone in search of the poet called Gobann.

The place they'd chosen to rest for the night was above the road. So he didn't have to walk far to where he could make out the path snaking through the forest. He found a spot where he could comfortably sit to observe the road and then he settled down to keep an eye out for Gobann's fire.

He sighed, relieved to be able to find some peace and quiet. All day long he'd had to listen to his two companions arguing with one another. They had obviously been engaged in their debate for a long, long while. But for the life of him Caoimhin couldn't work out what on earth they were arguing about.

As he breathed easier his head cleared. Then his thoughts strayed to Gobann, his mysterious yet intriguing guide. Caoimhin examined the walking staff the stranger had given him. It was certainly a beautiful piece of work. The wood was light, the carving intricate, and it could have been made just for him – it was the perfect height for him to lean on as he walked.

It hit him then that he hadn't noticed Gobann carrying this staff on the first occasion they'd met. This seemed rather odd. The walking stick was obviously quite old and had taken more than one night of woodcarving to complete.

Caoimhin wondered where it could have come from. Suddenly he began to feel uneasy about the stranger called Gobann. He'd heard so many tales about the wild heathen Irish and now all those stories returned to mind.

In those days it was not unusual to hear that some Irish king or another had beheaded his family and used the skulls to furnish his hall with drinking vessels. Or that the more savage of the western tribespeople collected the scalps of their enemies. Of course it was all just Norman gossip intended to scare off too many adventurers from staking a claim on the country and to imbue those who did work up the courage to stake a claim with an air of unquestionable valour.

None of those things ever really happened at all. Unless you count the scalping. Scalp bounty was actually a Norman idea. Some lord in the days of Strongbow offered a single English mark for every scalp of an Irish warrior that was brought to him. Well it turned out that after a few feud scores had been profitably settled, the Irish chieftains realised they could easily pull the wool over the Normans' eyes. Or should I say the pigskin?

For a while there arose a hitherto unknown fashion for short hair and shaved chins amongst the Gaels. All that excess hair was given to the tanners who turned fine circles of pigskin into quite convincing replicas of human scalps.

The result was devastating for the Normans for two reasons. First of all they soon ran out of gold English marks with which to pay the scalp bounty.

And secondly the lords of the Normans started to believe most of the Irish must have been wiped out. By that time there were already more scalps in their collections than there were Irish folk who could have possibly worn them. So the Normans launched an expedition into the west, with devastating results of course. There turned out to be a lot more Gaelic warriors than anyone could have predicted.

Our Caoimhin had heard this story too. He understood how tricky the Irish could be when they wanted. So he began to wonder. What if Gobann were leading himself and his two companions into a trap? What if he were a brigand? It was true that the poet had noticed the satchel of books. Perhaps he intended to steal them to sell at the market in Wexford.

'How do I know I can trust him?' the young Benedictine asked himself aloud.

'Do you trust yourself?' came the retort.

Caoimhin was so startled he spun round and stood up in one movement. He was gasping for breath as he held the staff in his hand, ready to strike at his potential attacker.

But all he saw was Gobann leaning against a tree with a broad grin on his face.

'You should be more careful,' the poet advised him. 'You shouldn't wander off alone with that warrior hot on your tail. There's no telling what could happen to you if he finds you alone. And to be honest with you, I'd rather you didn't come to any harm.'

Caoimhin let the staff drop. 'Why? Are you thinking you'll get a ransom for me? Is that it?'

The poet laughed and laughed until the tears rolled down his cheeks.

'Who'd pay *your* ransom?' he managed in between gasps of amusement.

'The Abbot of Glastonbury,' Caoimhin said defensively.

'Bollocks. Your abbot is a month's journey from here. Even if the sea passage were easy at this time of year, the ransom wouldn't arrive here for two months at least. And along the way there's brigands, Norman looters and bribes to be paid. I would hardly expect you'd be worth the bother to the abbot of a great monastery.'

'Then why would you care whether or not any harm comes to me?'

The poet touched a finger to his nose and winked. 'That's my concern. If you survive I might let you in on my little secret. But for the present it's best you don't know.'

'Why?'

'Because the rancid butter you can't smell won't do you too much harm.'

'That doesn't make any sense,' Caoimhin retorted.

'You're a smart lad and no mistake. Why do you think no traveller has ever made it further than halfway into this forest?'

Caoimhin shuddered with fright at the thought of what terrible monsters might dwell among the trees. But then the answer struck him and he relaxed.

'Because once you're past halfway into the forest you're already on your way out.'

'I admire your wits,' the poet grinned. 'I hope you manage to keep them sharpened.'

Then Gobann stepped forward with a finger to his lips. 'We must keep quiet. Tonight there are Redcaps in the woods making their way to a gathering of their people in the west. If you aren't careful you could get caught up in the impending war.'

'Who are the Redcaps?'

'That's a long tale which I don't have time to tell at the moment,' Gobann shrugged. 'Enough to say they are a tribe of folk who are among the most bloody, vicious, callous, cruel and disgusting creatures that were ever spawned from the clay of this Earth.'

'Are they really that bad?'

'Well to be honest they do have one or two redeeming qualities.'

'Such as?'

'They brew a very powerful mead which would kill a horse if it drank more than a cupful. And they are magnificent hosts. The Redcaps are renowned for their hospitality.'

Caoimhin shook his head in bemusement, then asked another question. 'What's the war about?'

'Blood lust, thievery, dishonesty, greed, cruelty, animosity, hatred and childish sentiment,' Gobann replied. 'The same as every other war there's ever been or ever will be.'

Then he added, 'Except of course this war has been started by the Queen of the Night who is planning to be acclaimed a goddess. So in that respect it is somewhat different from most other wars.'

'Who is she?'

'What did I tell you about asking too many questions? It won't do, you know. When you arrive at the Killibegs you won't be able to go round making enquiries with impunity. They won't stand for that sort of behaviour.'

Caoimhin squinted in annoyance, trying to work out how he would learn anything form this fellow if he couldn't pose simple questions. Then he struck on an idea.

The young monk lifted his staff to point it up the slope toward the place where his companions were preparing the fire.

'The mountain pass is in that direction,' he stated calmly.

Gobann looked at him as if he were mad. 'Don't be a fool,'

he snapped. 'The mountain pass of Kiltealy is in the opposite direction. To reach it you'll have to take to the road in the morning. The slopes are too steep from here on so you can't avoid the path. Once you've crossed the mountains you'll find more woodlands scattered on the other side. Take to them and keep yourselves concealed.'

Gobann smiled then, realising what the lad had done. 'Now I believe you're beginning to understand how we do things,' he congratulated the monk.

'I must not ask direct questions,' Caoimhin confirmed. 'I should make statements that so obviously need correcting that I learn the information I was after in the first place.'

'You have it! That way no one is offended that you're being too nosy. No one is upset that you've cast doubt on their personal reputation for knowledge or wisdom. And no one is embarrassed at lacking the wisdom or knowledge to answer your question.'

'You Gaels are a strange people,' the Benedictine observed.

'We are,' the poet agreed wholeheartedly. 'But don't forget that even though you were raised by Saxon monks, your parents were Irish. So there's more than a little strangeness about you too.'

Then Gobann stepped closer and spoke in a lower tone. 'You have a yearning within your heart which cannot be quenched.'

Caoimhin frowned. 'It's true,' he admitted. 'You know a great deal about me. You seem to have a gift for reading my thoughts.'

The poet smiled. 'Let's just say I have a certain sympathy for your predicament.'

NaThairaí

Whether it was due to the stupidity of the Normans or the luck Martin and Sianan were both born with, they were not discovered. The two warriors who'd been searching for Oat-Beer gave up looking as soon as the rain started to fall heavily.

After a long while the two fugitives decided it was not safe to continue on their journey until after sunset. However, the decision to tarry proved to be unwise. For just before the sun sank in the west the woods were filled with torches borne by warriors with drawn swords.

'Find them!' d'Alville's voice screamed with fury. 'Find them or I'll have every one of you flogged.'

Martin looked to his companion. The blood drained from his face. 'We're finished,' he whispered.

'Don't fret,' Sianan soothed. 'Situations like this often seem much worse than they are. Just keep quiet and muzzle that dog of yours. We'll find a way to avoid capture.'

But Martin knew what sort of a man Guy d'Alville really was. He'd witnessed the man's brutality first-hand on many occasions. And when he weighed up the odds of a hundred warriors to two runaways, he found the balance tipped in an uncomfortable direction.

The shouts and noise of the search party moved steadily closer to their hiding place. Martin wished he hadn't thrown away the sword. It seemed he'd stand in need of it soon enough. A few short moments later he wasn't just cursing himself for not keeping the blade close, he was calling himself a fool for having left it lying about in the forest.

'My lord!' a warrior called out. 'Look what I've found.'

Guy strode through the forest to where one of his mercenaries was standing. Martin could glimpse the scene through the tangle of blackberry bushes into which they'd retreated to hide from Guy's troops.

D'Alville held up the short-bladed sword high enough so that all the searchers could see it.

'They can't be far away,' he bellowed. 'I want every bush overturned until they're found.'

'What do we do now?' the Breton whispered.

'Hold your tongue,' Sianan hissed as she sniffed the air like a hound catching a whiff of the fox. 'There's something amiss in this forest. Something far more deadly than Guy d'Alville.'

'What?'

The abbess did not answer him. She grabbed the sleeve of his tunic and pulled him closer to the ground.

In that instant a shriek echoed through the woods. It was so chilling, so dripping with cold menacing horror that Martin almost screamed aloud in response. But Sianan had a hand over his mouth before he could make a sound.

Oat-Beer jumped down between the two of them and buried his head under Sianan's cloak. And he was so frightened he didn't make a sound either.

Dogs may sometimes seem quite foolish but when there's something worth being scared of, they know how to keep still. Sianan stroked the back of his neck to calm him.

Then there was another scream in the forest. This was followed by the rush of feet and the clumsy sounds of men fleeing for their lives. Panic spread through Guy's men like fire through dry brushwood.

Martin lifted his head slightly to catch a glimpse of what was happening. Torches were disappearing or dispersing in every direction. It reminded him of a flock of pigeons scattering before a hawk.

The night was drawing on so the air was already cold. But there was something else on the breeze which was much more chilling. Fear. And the Breton had sensed this fear before. In himself.

'It's the Nathairaí,' he stammered. 'They've crept up on us.'

Sianan shut her eyes as she listened for every sound in the woods. In a few moments she discerned in which part of the forest the worms had laid their trap.

'They're after the warriors,' she stated. 'We might yet slip by them if we're careful.'

Without another word she crawled out from under the blackberry bushes, dragging Martin and his dog behind her. Once clear of their cover, she stopped to listen to the noise again. The woods were filled with cries of agony, screams of terror and groans of confusion. But one voice was raised above the din. A strong noble voice unmoved by the frightening scenes being played out around him.

It was Guy.

'Stand your ground, you bloody cowards,' he demanded. 'You sons of spineless mice! Stand! If you break ranks they'll pick you off one by one. Hold your ground!'

Sianan lay down flat upon the earth again. The Breton followed her lead. Even his dog was crawling along in imitation of the abbess. In this manner they managed to make their way around to a point where they could see Guy's remaining men arrayed in a defensive battle formation. Some had spears levelled. Others had swords or shields raised ready to ward off the attacker. And in their midst stood a dishevelled but stern commander, a man not easily swayed by any foe.

Guy had lost his helm. There was a small gash above his

right eye. His mail coif had been pushed back to allow his long black hair to fall free. And he gripped a broken sword, snapped a hand's breadth from the hilt.

As the two fugitives watched in awe, d'Alville threw down the useless weapon. Then he snatched a lance from one of his underlings.

'Fall back into a tight circle!' the Norman lord commanded.

But his men were driven to a panic in their terror. Few among them held the same resolve as did their master. None of them had his mastery of fear.

One warrior broke ranks to make a run for it. Before he could even cry out a black shape moved with lightning swiftness. The warrior was snatched up high in the air and then he was gone. Boots, belt, mail coat and all slid down the eager throat of the enormous worm.

A great satisfied belch echoed through the forest. It followed by a low growling snarl.

This proved too much for even the hardest veterans among d'Alville's men. The tightly packed formation disintegrated in seconds, leaving the lord to hold his ground alone.

As Sianan watched, the two worms rose up to knock down fleeing warriors with their powerful tails. Some men were crushed, others thrown far into the forest. Puny bodies were dashed against mighty trees or stones. Screams were abruptly cut short, stifled in the throats of the beasts.

One or two warriors desperately stabbed at the worm adversaries but their lance tips could not pierce the thick slippery skin of the monsters. Their attacks amounted to little more than annoying itches which were soon scratched till the annoyance was eliminated.

A single warrior managed to mount himself behind the head of one worm. As he clung there for dear life he lifted up a sword, intending to plunge it into the monster. But the point struck flesh that was harder than any steel could cut. The other worm snatched at the doomed mercenary and swallowed him whole without any concern for the weapon he still gripped in his hands.

Another belch sounded through the woods as the few remaining foot soldiers scattered this way and that, panic-stricken.

In the midst of the confusion Guy d'Alville made his escape. Or as he would have probably preferred to describe it, he withdrew to better ground.

If it hadn't been for the abundance of warriors all around him he might not have survived this ambush. His foot soldiers had diverted the attention of the Nathairaí, enabling him to make his escape.

'D'Alville's made off out of here,' Sianan reported to Martin. 'And so should we.'

Before Martin could restrain her she stood up in full view of the Normans and the terrible Nathairaí.

'Come on!' she yelled. 'Run for your life!'

Neither Martin nor his faithful friend Oat-Beer had to be coaxed into that. In less time than it takes to draw two breaths, the three of them were off bounding through the forest retreating north to where a stream passed through the wood.

It was only a short distance, perhaps a hundred paces or so, but it seemed like a thousand to the Breton whose heart was pumping so hard he thought it would rise up into his throat to choke him.

In no time at all they crossed the narrow watercourse, climbed up the far bank then pushed on through the tangle of trees. The evening was already upon them, but the forest was not sleeping. All through the woods behind and before them birds were screeching wildly. It seemed even the trees were crying out in dismay for what had befallen the Normans in this usually undisturbed part of the woodland.

Of course it's just as likely the trees were overjoyed at the demise of Guy's band of warriors. Trees and birds have never had, nor will they ever have, any love for the Normans. Except of course those trees that once *were* Normans, if you understand me.

'It's not far to the edge of the forest,' Sianan called out, encouraging her companion to pick up his feet and make a further effort.

Martin's eyes were wild with terror and his chest heaved hard with exertion. Sianan was at least thirty paces ahead of him. She was a strong woman who could endure any hardship. And you must remember, she had no fear for her own safety. So this helped her keep a clear head and a calm demeanour in the worst of situations.

The wind in the trees picked up in a soulful song mourning the slaughter. The news of the disaster was already passing swiftly through the woods from leaf to leaf, branch to branch, tree to tree and stone to stone.

Martin stopped to catch his breath and get his bearings. He leaned heavily against a twisted oak for support. His dog was by his side. It was then he caught a glimpse of a dark shape flitting through the forest just ahead. He tried to call out to warn Sianan but his lungs simply wouldn't fill with enough breath.

The only sound he could muster was a whimpered bark that could have been mistaken for Oat-Beer's cry. Nevertheless it was enough to get Sianan's attention. She turned around to face him as the shadow passed between the trees not far from where she stood. She immediately discerned it was too small a creature to be one of the Nathairaí. But that didn't put her mind at ease. In an instant she was back at Martin's side.

The forest shook with a great rumble. The ground shivered. Branches rattled. Then an Otherworldly shriek lifted up on the air, cold, paralysing, full of the fury of monsters from the depths of the Earth.

Sianan spun around. Huge dark forms snaked about between the trees, pushing some aside, flattening others. Stones and soil were hurled up in every direction, scattering over everything.

The abbess grabbed her companion by the arm, trying to drag him away from this place. But Martin was frozen with horror. His legs wouldn't move. Sianan slapped him hard across the face, leaving a red mark where her palm had struck him.

That was enough to wake Martin from the spellbinding terror. He shook his head, muttered an apology then allowed himself to be led on.

And it was a good thing they moved just when they did. For had they tarried but a breath longer they would've been crushed by the weight of a tree flung far through the forest by the fury of the worms.

Fortune had preserved them in that second. But Fortune loves to tease her favourites. As Sianan stepped out to jump a log, the ground gave way beneath her weight. Unable to steady herself, she slid down into a deep hole in the earth. Her hand still gripped Martin's tightly. If he'd had time to realise what was happening he might have helped her out of this trap. But the Breton was tumbling after her before he could do anything to stop himself.

Oat-Beer saw his friends disappear into the ground so he loyally jumped in after them. No sooner had his red tail disappeared down the hole than another tree landed square on top of it, sealing the three of them in the hole as securely as if they'd been locked in the well-house once more.

The Tree of Life

G uy d'Alville ran as fast as his mail-covered legs would carry him. He ran like he'd never run before. He jumped logs, ducked low branches and pushed his warriors aside to get through the forest and as far away from the dreaded worms as possible. Along the way he stopped to snatch a sword from one of his men, leaving the fellow to fend for himself. Then he ran some more.

Now I don't want you to think it was fear that drove d'Alville. It wasn't. He was a warrior with many years' experience. He had seen enough hard battles to know when the odds were stacked heavily against him. And on this occasion the odds were nigh on bloody impossible. Once his men made a break for it, the Norman knew he didn't stand a chance against the two horrific beasts bearing down on him.

He'd watched with disbelief as several of his men had been swallowed whole. Then he'd noted the cold shock which had passed through his own body when a well-aimed blow to the head of one worm had resulted in not so much as a bruise to the black flesh. He'd been so surprised at that he'd hardly noticed he'd snapped his blade with that same blow. Retreat had become his only remaining option.

But his was not a panicked escape. Even in the midst of disaster Guy usually managed to keep a cool head.

As he fled, his warrior mind rattled through all the possible strategies open to him. He knew he couldn't run far in his heavy mail coat. Not without compromising his ability to defend himself. So he decided to find a good place to hide until the beasts had passed away from the immediate vicinity. He congratulated himself on deciding to hire so many mercenaries. They'd certainly keep the beasts busy for a while. If he was lucky the worms might have full bellies long before they'd caught scent of his hiding place.

Just then the perfect sanctuary revealed itself to him. At the edge of a small clearing there stood a huge, ancient oak. In the semi-darkness it seemed at first as though it was another huge monstrous creature with mighty arms outstretched to ward off attack. The trunk of this enormous bough was split close to where its roots tapped the Earth. This gave the impression that it was standing with two legs braced ready to receive a blow.

Guy realised that the shadowed area at the base of the tree was a deep cleft such as some oaks develop late in life. He quickly went to check whether he'd fit inside this natural space. The gap was just wide enough for him to crawl through with a bit of a struggle. But once he was inside the hollowed tree, there was plenty of room for him to stand up straight or sit on his knees.

The living cave was warm, dry and reassuring. Guy sat down to wait until the forest fell silent. He was prepared to stay here for the rest of the night if necessary. But he wasn't left alone for that long. Very soon a shuffling noise caught his attention. Then there was a cackling chuckle which echoed through the small tight chamber. D'Alville recognised the laugh immediately.

'Don't say I didn't warn you,' Sciathan Cog cawed as he stepped into the tree.

The raven was silhouetted against the twilight outside.

'I'll wager you've never seen anything like those two in your short, insignificant life,' the bird added gleefully. 'They're magnificent, aren't they?'

'Is this whole country inhabited by monsters?' Guy grunted. 'Those mercenaries cost me a small fortune. I'll be lucky if any of them are fit to fight after this.'

'You'll be lucky if *you* are,' Cog cackled. 'What makes you think you'll be safe inside this oak? Even a nine-hundred-year-old tree is just splinter wood to the worms of the well of Dun Gur.'

'How many of my men are left?' the Norman demanded. He was tiring of this raven's mocking attitude. If the bird had been a man he would've had him chopped into pieces long ago.

'A dozen of them made it out of the forest. But only because they were running so fast not even a giant worm with an unquenchable hunger could have caught them. The rest have gathered in two places.'

'Where?' Guy asked, hopeful that all was not lost.

'They have mustered together in the belly of Lochie and the stomach of Isleen,' the bird guffawed, or as near to a guffaw as a raven could manage.

'Only a dozen survived?'

'There's one or two like yourself who've found refuge among the trees. But that's all. And this hiding place won't serve you very long. The Nathairaí have good noses for their prey.'

Guy sat back against the inside of the oak, placing his head in his hands so he could think without distraction. He'd been in many disastrous military situations before. He'd seen defeat on more than one occasion. But he'd never found himself embroiled in a debacle such as this. The whole episode was more like something out of one of those ridiculous troubadour romances than a military campaign in a conquered land.

Outside there was a tremendous noise as the Nathairaí began smashing open trees, searching for concealed warriors. The Norman had no experience of this sort of warfare. He had to admit to himself he had no idea how to deal with this enemy.

So when he spoke again his voice held just the slightest trace of defeat. 'How do I escape them?'

The raven hummed with delight. 'Do you think I'd help you and risk their wrath?'

'You must help me escape. We have an agreement.'

'So far you've not kept your part of the agreement,' Cog pointed out. 'And I have little confidence you intend to.'

Guy looked at the bird. He understood the creature was bargaining with him. And he also understood he had no choice but to accept whatever terms were offered.

It wasn't that d'Alville was afraid of death. I can tell you for certain he wasn't. It was just that he had a burning desire to go on living so he could exact his revenge upon Robert FitzWilliam.

I've mentioned to you before that this was the entire focus of Guy's life. To find a certain Templar knight and make him suffer for the indignity that had been heaped upon him during some obscure episode during the Crusades.

Caoimhin referred to the story as *The Tale of the Tilecutter's Penny*. I know he wrote it down, though I've never seen the manuscript myself so I can't comment on the contents.

Anyway, as I was saying, it was Guy's hunger for revenge that gave him pause for thought. And in the end he conceded his position was not strong.

'What price are you asking for my freedom?'

'You Normans are a crude people,' Cog commented. 'Do you think everything in this world can be bought and sold like bread from a baker? And what makes you think I'd endanger my personal dealings with the Nathairaí in order to help you avoid becoming their dinner?'

'Because you need me?'

'I need you less than I need a new pair of britches,' the raven scoffed. 'You have a very high opinion of yourself, don't you? Do you really imagine it would be that difficult for me to find another bloodthirsty brigand suited to my purpose from among your ill-bred brethren?'

Guy d'Alville closed his eyes again before he replied. 'Did you intend to keep your part of the bargain? Or did you intend to discard me when I'd served your purpose?'

'Now there's a pair of questions more worthy of you,' Cog enthused. 'I have to admire distrust in any man. It's a rare and precious quality.'

The raven took a step closer. 'The truth is I don't care what happens to you,' the bird confessed. 'But my lady the queen has an interest in you. She's your only hope now. I sent a summons to her when the Nathairaí were released because I knew it would come to this.' He stepped closer again. 'But I can't be certain that even the Queen of the Night will be able to persuade the worms to let you be.'

'What manner of queen is she?' Guy asked with suspicion.

'She's a bitter one. Just like me. Her name is Aoife, or it was when we were children. She was my sister.'

'You sprang from an unusual brood,' d'Alville noted dryly. 'Why would your sister be interested in me?'

Cog shuffled a little closer so he could keep his voice low. 'She's on the lookout for a consort.'

'You mean she wants to make me king of her people?'

'Take my advice,' the raven suggested. 'If you want to live very long at all, don't ever use that word in front of Aoife. It doesn't agree with her.'

'What are the duties of a consort?'

'She seeks a mortal man to breed with,' Cog replied matter-of-factly. 'And an experienced war-leader with a strong arm to lead her armies in the coming conflict.'

'What armies?'

'Have you never heard of the Redcaps?'

Guy shook his head.

'I'd best leave it to her to explain herself. I've already told you too much. But I should tell you your name was mentioned to her at my recommendation. I spent a long while searching the world for a warrior as ruthless and bloody-minded as yourself. I don't mind telling you that when it comes to warfare and wickedness you are without peer in the world.'

D'Alville wasn't a man to succumb so easily to flattery.

'And if I agree to be her consort and war-leader, will I have the opportunity to seek my revenge on Robert FitzWilliam?'

'I'd imagine you'd pretty much be able to visit vengeance on anybody you chose so long as you performed your duties.'

A doubt crossed d'Alville's mind. 'This sister of yours, this Aoife. Is she a hag?'

'Only when she wants to be,' Sciathan Cog answered enigmatically. 'Only when she wants to be.'

Mirim and her company crossed the mountains late in the day and at her insistence they marched on into the night. She wanted to put as many miles behind her as possible.

Lanfranc did not protest. He focused all his energy on the prisoner, Gusán Gelt. In part this was so that he could assuage his guilt at having tried to trick Mirim. But he also had a personal score to settle with this man.

In the year since Lanfranc had been in Ireland he'd been harassed day and night by this band of brigands. They'd stolen provisions from his storehouse, pilfered building timbers from the construction of his tower, thieved anything forged in iron they could get their hands on, and generally made a nuisance of themselves at every opportunity.

Now that Lanfranc had one of them in his custody he was going to make the fellow pay for the indignity he had suffered at their hands. As I'm sure I've mentioned, the Normans are a very proud people. Proud to the point of utter foolishness at times.

So it was that Lanfranc rode along that night with a long rope attached to his wooden saddle. Gusán was bound by the hands to the other end of this rope so that he had to walk at a slightly faster pace than usual to keep up with his captor.

A few hours before dawn Mirim called the company to a halt at the advice of her loyal servant Tom Curdle. He reasoned that though she might be strong-willed enough to continue riding without rest, few in the company would be able to keep pace with her. So a hasty camp was set, a meal prepared and those who needed sleep were allowed to take a few hours. Mirim sat by her fire with Shali, though she said not a word to her mute servant. When the warriors had settled down to either eat or rest Curdle came to see that his lady had filled her belly.

Lanfranc had his men prepare a place for him away from Mirim's fire. He didn't want to offend her with his presence or any more foolish words. His prisoner was allowed to warm his hands beside him but the Norman wouldn't speak to his captive. Instead he sat poking the fire with the butt of a lance as he stared longingly across at Mirim.

'Never mind,' Gusán offered. 'Women are fickle creatures. She'll have forgotten all about it by tomorrow. You mark my words.'

'Shut up.'

'Listen to me,' the brigand went on. 'You've saved her a lot of bother. If you'd set out to the FitzWilliam estates it would have cost her another two days on the road. And not an easy road either in this weather.'

'What are you talking about?' Lanfranc barked.

'Once you'd arrived at the FitzWilliam estate you would have had to take the road over the mountains to find him. If you think about it, you saved her a disappointment and brought her closer to her goal.'

The Norman's expression brightened slightly.

'Once she realises that, I'm sure she'll forgive you.'

But Lanfranc was not convinced. He'd never seen a woman lose her temper so violently in all his life. He was sure he'd ruined his chances with her.

He stared across at the lady seated with her two servants. There was a heated debate taking place between Tom Curdle and Mirim. Though he couldn't hear what they were discussing, he was certain she was still venting her rage about the way she had been misled. But as they were talking he noticed an intriguing thing. The servant called Shali was seated very close to his mistress. Every once in a while the man would place a hand on the lady's shoulder in a most familiar way.

This wasn't the behaviour of a serving man, Lanfranc told himself.

'What do you think of that?' he asked his prisoner.

Gusán observed the gesture, raised an eyebrow then offered an opinion. 'They do things differently in the east.'

Lanfranc was not convinced.

After a long while Curdle stood up. Then, followed by Shali, he made his way over to the Norman's fire.

Before he spoke, Tom Curdle bowed low to pay respect to Lanfranc.

'My lord. I bear a message from Lady Mirim,' he began. 'She begs your forgiveness for her bout of temper prior to the ambush. She acknowledges that you have apologised for your deception and thanks you for your gallantry in confronting the brigands.'

'What did I tell you?' Gusán cut in.

'Shut up!' the Norman hissed. He looked the servant in the eye. 'Please pass on my regards to her ladyship. I thank her for her gracious forgiveness and her kind words. I have learned a valuable lesson. You can tell her that I will remain steadfast and true to her from this day forth. And I will honour my promise to watch over her until she has found William FitzWilliam.'

'I will pass on your words, my lord,' Curdle nodded.

Then the man stepped a little closer and lowered his voice. 'May I speak frankly with you, my lord?'

Lanfranc frowned. He was not accustomed to being addressed in such a familiar way by those of a lower rank to himself. But in this case he was willing to make an exception. Only because he still held hopes of winning Mirim's heart.

'You may.'

Tom Curdle leaned over toward the Norman. 'Lady Mirim is flattered that you would go to so much trouble to win her affections and make such effort to speak with her.'

'Is she?'

Curdle nodded. 'But if I may offer a small piece of advice? I only do so because I've known her for a long while now and feel I'm privy to her thoughts.'

'Go on.'

'Words cannot express the grief Lady Mirim suffered at the death of her husband,' the cheese-maker went on. 'She was so broken-hearted to have lost her true love before they had a chance to live out their lives together, that for a time I was certain she would not live long.'

'I see.'

'This journey to Ireland saved her from wallowing in a terrible state of melancholy. If we had not had to set out on this mission she would certainly not have survived the heartbreak of it all.'

'Shali and I have been at our wits' end trying to keep her spirits up all this time. You're not the first nobleman who has lavished his attentions upon her. But you have fared better than most. The thing is, she is most unwilling to accept that her husband is dead.'

'What do you mean?'

'I mean to say that once we have met with Lord William FitzWilliam she will no longer be able to avoid the terrible truth. She will no longer be able to imagine that her dear love is still alive.'

The Norman nodded to show he understood.

'A part of Lady Mirim is unwilling to let go of the hope that somehow, against the odds, her husband will be reunited with her. But she also knows the day is fast approaching when she will have to face her worst fears. Once she has confirmation of possession of her husband's lands, her life will be utterly changed forever.'

'What are you saying to me?'

'My lord, I don't want you to think I'm talking out of turn.'

'Get on with it!'

'I know you'll respect my lady's feelings. I know you're an honourable man. There is more to this story than I can tell you. Perhaps the Lady Mirim will discuss it all with you when she's ready. For now I beg you to try to understand what a good woman she is. And that she deserves to be treated well. She deserves to be happy.'

Lanfranc caught the serving man's eye. Then he looked across at Shali who immediately dropped his gaze to the ground.

'I understand you,' the Norman nodded. 'You need say no more. I will hold true to my promise to protect her until we reach Killibegs. Then we shall see what is to be done.'

'Thank you, my lord. And may God bless you for your kind heart.'

With that the two servants turned around to head back to their fire to get some rest.

'You're a good man,' Gusán commented once they were out of earshot. 'For a Norman.'

'Shut up.'

Sianan lay in the dark damp underground hole taking in the aroma of sweet mouldy soil. Martin lay on his back beside her with Oat-Beer cuddled up close.

'That was fortunate,' the abbess commented.

'It's an interesting interpretation of luck you have,' the Breton replied. 'What do we do now?'

Sianan stood up. There was plenty of room to move in this hollow. And it seemed to her there was a passage at the far end of the hole. But the light was so poor she couldn't make out whether the empty space extended very far into the Earth.

'We're trapped,' Martin sighed. 'In a dank tomb. With no hope of escape.'

'Do try to look on the bright side of things,' the abbess replied.

'What bright side is that? So far I've been imprisoned in a well-house haunted by two monstrous ravenous worms who could each wrap themselves round a castle tower and crush it. I've huddled under blackberry bushes all day long till I've more scratches on my skin than skin.'

He paused for breath. When he went on, his voice cracked with emotion. 'Then the worms return to devour a company of my comrades and chase me through the forest till I find myself landed in an underworld grave from which there's little chance I'll ever escape!'

'You're a warrior,' Sianan shot back. 'Surely you've had bad days before.'

'Not days like this one.'

'Things aren't so bad. This isn't just any hole in the ground.'

'I'm overjoyed to hear it.'

The abbess sighed with exasperation. 'This space has been excavated. It was specially dug out. We've fallen through an opening into the dwelling place of some creature.'

'Are you telling me I'm about to face a giant mole?' Martin shuddered.

Sianan laughed but then thought better of it. She realised that immortality had left her with a certain insensitivity to the irrational fears of mortal kind.

'No mole made this place,' she assured him. 'This is the work of nearly-human hands.'

She touched the walls of the little cavern. There were spiral designs picked out on every surface.

'Nearly human?' the Breton repeated.

'If our luck holds out these folk might be friendly. At the very least they won't be hostile.'

'And if our good fortune has dried up?'

'Then this is a dwelling place of the dreaded blood-letting Redcaps.'

'What were you saying about looking on the bright side? I'm beginning to think I would've stood a better chance of survival if I'd simply handed myself over to Guy d'Alville then stated a preference for my method of execution.'

'The Nathairaí won't bother searching for us underground,' the abbess pointed out. 'They've just spent an eternity locked in a tiny space deep within the Earth. They won't be in a hurry to follow us. Let's see whether this passage leads anywhere.'

'I'd rather sit still for a while. I'd like to pretend this is just a nasty dream.'

'As you wish. But the closer we are to the entrance, the more likely the Nathairaí will sniff us out. If we go deeper down they won't bother searching for us.'

'You present a compelling argument,' Martin conceded and hurriedly brushed himself off, edging his way forward in the dark with Oat-Beer. But he hadn't walked a dozen paces when he realised they couldn't possibly make much headway in the semi-darkness.

He fumbled about in the pouch that hung at his belt till he found a small brass box which held his flint and steel. He searched about on the floor of the cavern for splinters from the log that had given way above them. To his surprise his hands located a large branch. Martin worked quickly using the remnants of his linen undershirt, pieces of bark and tiny slivers of timber. Then he told Sianan to gather as many leaves as she could find.

The floor of the cavern was littered with them. Samhain Oidche, which the Normans call All Hallows Eve, was only a few days away. So there was an abundance of dry autumn leaf fall which had dropped into this hollow along with Sianan and Martin.

It wasn't long before Martin had a neat little blaze going. Before the chamber filled with smoke he lit his makeshift torch. He and the abbess looked around in wonder. Every surface of walls, floor and ceiling was covered in the most breathtaking spiral designs.

Some of these patterns were picked out into the packed soil. Others were carved into the exposed roots of the trees which grew above them.

Martin felt a chill in his blood. Though the workmanship was beautiful, there was something frighteningly barbaric about the spirals.

'Let's get a move on,' he told Sianan. 'I don't want to choke to death in the smoke of this fire.'

So, with Oat-Beer close behind him and the abbess taking up the rear, Martin the Breton edged toward the passage which led deeper into the Earth. Twenty paces on there was a large door constructed of oak.

Martin pushed against it, not expecting it to move at all. But it swung open easily to reveal a long flight of steps cut into a narrow descending passage.

'Are we to go deeper into the Earth?' he asked his companion dubiously.

'We could always go back to see whether the Nathairaí are finished devouring your Norman friends. Personally I'd rather face the Redcaps.'

'Who made these stairs? Who are the Redcaps?'

'They're an ancient people,' Sianan informed him. 'In the days of legend, long before I was born, they took the Quicken Brew. But in time many of them realised what a great gift death is. Slowly an anger arose in their folk. As the seasons passed they took to mischief. Then their mischief became evil. And now they're a formidable tribe of warring bloodthirsty monsters.'

Now, Sianan wasn't about to tell Martin the whole story of the Redcaps for it would've taken her a day and a night merely to relate their origins. And I won't either since Caoimhin has already written about them in his tales of the Watchers. But I'll tell you a little more about them.

Long ago when the Gaels first arrived in Ireland there were other tribes who called this land their home. Among them were the peoples of the Fir-Bolg. These tribes had been dwelling here so many generations that they had divided into distinct groups. One of these tribes was called the Sen Erainn and they made their home on the island of Inis Mór. After the Gaels arrived, the Sen Erainn agreed to join the hosts of Eber Finn, Gaelic King of the South, in his war against Éremon, King of the North, who was his brother. But the price for their aid was the secret of the Quicken Brew which certain Druids of the Fir-Bolg had in their possession. Two Fir-Bolg Druids named Dalan and Sorcha passed their knowledge of the brew to the Sen Erainn in the hope it would seal the alliance. Then the Sen Erainn fought alongside the Southern Gaels. Eber Finn gained the victory and granted the Sen Erainn sovereignty over their islands in perpetuity.

More than a thousand and two hundred winters had passed since that time. In the intervening period those of the Sen Erainn who had taken the Brew fell to fighting with their mortal brethren. In time they were banished from their island home to wander the countryside of Ireland searching out new dwellings. Some went deep underground beneath the hollow hills. Others disappeared into the vast forests which covered the land before the Normans cut them down to build ships. Some lived in the caverns high in the mountains or in small floating settlements built out upon the lakes.

But all of them shared a deepening distaste for mortal kind. The Redcaps were one tribe of these immortal Sen Erainn who had taken to a most unsavoury custom.

Their caps of deerskin were of the finest quality, well made and pleasing to the eye. Except for one detail. Every hat was dyed with fresh human blood.

Of course they didn't engage in this practice all the time. There wouldn't have been enough human blood in the whole of Ireland to keep their caps so bright. However, whenever their chieftains waged war, the Redcaps indulged in this practice to signify they'd gained a war trophy.

Of course there were those who killed a cow here and there so they could drain the blood to dye their caps. These fellows knew the terror their headgear inspired in their enemies. And what mortal could tell whether it was the blood of a cow or a human which gave their hats that distinctive tinge?

Naturally there were some among the Redcaps who went to extremes. You'll find their sort among any peoples. There were those Redcaps who reputedly drank the blood of their victims. These gruesome creatures were known as the Dearg Uila. In the old Gaelic this is pronounced Deruk-hoola. It means the blood-drinkers. Stories spread that they maintained their immortality by this practice. But that was just rubbish spread about to encourage a little terror in their enemies. The truth is they'd taken the Quicken Brew so they were doomed to an immortal fate in any case.

Well, you can probably understand why it was best Sianan didn't go into too much detail about the Redcaps. As it was she said enough to give Martin the jitters.

The three of them made their way down the long staircase cut into the earth. All the walls were covered with those same spiralling patterns, beautiful but terrifying to behold. As they progressed deeper into the cavern other designs began to appear. There were diamond shapes encased by long flowing lines, complimented by more lines running parallel and zigzag. Then there were circles and huge accumulations of dotted patterns too intricate to discern in detail.

Martin's fear soon subsided as he stared in wonderment at the workmanship exhibited all around him. A little voice of reason deep inside him called out in protest. It told him any folk who could create objects of such gorgeous intricacy couldn't possibly be the barbarous blood-letting bastards Sianan had described.

But we know that little voice was wrong, don't we?

FIRE OF THE HEART

aoimhin and his two travelling companions crossed the mountain pass before dawn. They set out early so they could slip by the settlement of Kiltealy without being noticed.

Only the young scribe had any idea there might be someone following them. But he didn't say anything to his friends. He didn't want to upset a couple of fellows who were obviously already quite nervous and jumpy.

You have to admire travelling monks. After all, there's no use holding them in contempt. That's far too easy to do. If it hadn't been for mendicant friars like Lewyn and Overton, Christianity might never have reached the heathen hordes of the world.

I must say, though, that some of these fellows had thick heads even if they had soft hearts. Take the monk known as Gerald of Wales. He claimed to have travelled to these shores, met with the inhabitants and learned the customs of our people. But it was obvious to everyone he'd probably never got much further than the Pale, the fence which bordered Norman Dublin. If he got that far.

He mentioned the barbaric habits of the Gaels such as blood feuds, baby eating and the collecting of the heads of enemies. All these customs were either exaggerated or invented. He stated that women held equal rank to their menfolk, which of course was true but nevertheless seemed barbarous to the Normans. And for all his fantastic descriptions of life beyond the Pale, there were some details he omitted. It's these which mark his book, *The History and Topography of Ireland*, as a work of fiction.

Anyone who spent any time at all in the areas of this island where the Gaels make their home would have made some mention of the Sidhe folk. The People of Peace are so much a part of our culture and our way of life that to leave out any mention of them is a major oversight, to say the least. So I contend that Gerald's book is largely full of gossip, lies and tall stories intended to stir up good Christians into a mighty lather.

Seen in the light of his manuscript the Normans were heroic knights who came to bring Christian ways to a heathen savages. There are some learned men who refer to Gerald's book as a load of boiled bulls' bollocks.

I'll leave you to guess my own feelings on the subject. But my language would not be quite so polite.

This may help you understand why I'm filled with admiration for Lewyn and Overton in their desire to produce a more reliable guide to this country. Of course their point of view was always going to be skewed. Neither of them knew much about our language, customs or culture. But the point is they were willing to learn. And that puts them apart from so many other adventurers before and since who've come to these shores loaded down with personal burdens built out of prejudice and preconception.

As I was saying, the three of them trudged through the woods lining the road west. As they walked the two Welshmen shared some of their early observations of this land and her people.

'Many folk in Britain assume the Irish hold the same traditions as we do,' Lewyn began. 'But this simply is not so.'

'The stories of the Irish are full of supernatural elements

which defy explanation,' Overton interrupted. 'And even though they claim to follow Christ they have a very strange doctrine regarding the journey of the soul after death.'

'Many of the Irish believe their soul will pass into another form, animal or human, when the body is dead,' his companion added. 'It is remarkable that a people who seem so civilised in many other respects would seriously consider the possibility that they could spend the afterlife in the form of a tree.'

'I don't find that so odd an idea,' Caoimhin commented. 'Of course it's blasphemous and contrary to the teachings of the Church. But it seems to me that life is terribly short and brutal for most people. Such a doctrine offers some hope to those who feel they may have suffered too much in this life.'

'Hope? How so?'

'Surely the Lord in his mercy wouldn't arrange things so that every time one is born into the world one had to live an existence marred by suffering. I'd imagine that spending a lifetime as a tree would be a fairly wonderful thing to look forward to after an existence in which hunger, war and illness were the dominant influences.'

'Be careful what you say, young scribe,' Lewyn warned. 'We've heard stories enough about civilised folk who've come to Ireland, been seduced by the heretical doctrines of the natives, then surrendered their immortal souls to the devilry of this island.'

'We must be observers of the customs,' Overton enthused. 'But we must be on our guard not to adopt the ways of these people. I shudder at the thought that you might find yourself outside the fold of the Church through lapsing into heathen ways.'

'Right now I'm more concerned about what will happen to me in this life than what will befall me in the next,' Caoimhin admitted. 'We should offer thanks to God we haven't heard any sound from that lion since we crossed the mountains.'

'There are worse beasts than lions in the west of this country,' Lewyn told him, lowering his voice as he did so. 'I've heard tell of vicious little people who wear red hats dyed with the blood of their victims.'

'And creatures that live in the lakes,' Overton cut in. 'When their prey comes close to the water's edge, they snatch them and drag them beneath the waves to drown them.'

'That's not to mention the evil race who dwell under the hills,' his comrade added. 'They're known as the Dun-Sidhe. And they've a terrible reputation for luring young folk off to their underworld kingdom to be their slaves, or worse.'

'What could be worse than being made a slave?' Caoimhin asked.

Lewyn blushed deeply. 'Never you mind, young fellow. It is above the dignity of a man of God to mention such matters. You'll just have to take our word for it that there are worse things than being enslaved.'

'Don't be such a prudish old fart,' Overton exclaimed. 'Tell the boy what you're on about.'

'I will not.'

Overton sighed, rolled his eyes then decided if his friend wouldn't explain then he'd have to. 'It is said the Dun-Sidhe take mortals for their lovers,' he whispered. 'And what is more, it's the women among them who are the most licentious in this regard.'

'But that is true of all Irish women,' Lewyn added quickly. 'They're without shame.'

'It could be said that Irish women are the worst monsters to be faced by any Christian man,' Overton agreed. 'Nuns live together with monks in their monasteries. They perform the sacraments as any priest would do. And they are permitted to marry whomsoever they will.'

Lewyn shuddered as his friend spoke, even though he'd

heard this report many times before. Even Caoimhin made a quick sign of the cross to banish temptation in all its wondrous variety.

Now I can't blame those poor clerics for thinking ill of Irish women. In the Norman world females are considered little less than property to be passed between a father and the poor girl's husband on payment of a dowry. But the customs of our people are altogether different. Irish women have always enjoyed the kind of freedom few Norman ladies ever dream of. We have rights to our own possessions when we marry and the right to divorce a husband who doesn't treat us with sufficient respect. Irish men think they have all the authority in our society but the fact is that it's women who make all the important decisions. We have a long tradition of taking the reins of a clan or kingdom.

Some queens among our folk have been great war-leaders also. Until the Church outlawed the practice in the ninth century, all women were expected to bear arms in battle. Some became quite adept at fighting. A few founded schools of the warrior art. The Sword Dance was conceived of by a woman, a goddess named Scathach.

You may think I'm simply boasting, but all this has some relevance to my tale. So be patient. A woman, married or not, was free to choose the father of her children. That's right. Whether she was married or not, it was her decision as to who would be the sire of her offspring. And her husband could not complain. But in practice few women ever let on about their adventures in the bedroom with men who were not officially their wedded husband.

And let's be honest. There's no sense in shying from the facts. Women are smarter than men in every regard. So intelligent, indeed, that they don't feel the need to go round boasting about their bedroom antics all the time.

Of course there are always a few who take themselves too

seriously. Queen Aoife of the Redcaps is one of those. That woman has always been troublesome, so the story goes. She stirred up a war all on her own when she was still a young girl. Accustomed to giving commands she carved out a kingdom for herself peopled by folk who held her in awe. For she is an awesome creature. No mistake.

But I've strayed a little from my story. Forgive me.

So as these three monks wandered on that day the two from Wales told all they knew of Irish women. Some of it was well founded, the rest was utter nonsense. Of course our Caoimhin, bless his soft leather walking shoes, believed everything they told him. He was such an innocent lad in those days.

That evening after they'd set their fire, the young scribe excused himself. 'I'm going for a short walk to be alone with my meditations,' he told them.

Then he strode off into the woods. Once more he found himself a spot to sit where he could look down on the path. It had narrowed to nothing more than a well-worn track but it held an immense fascination for the young scribe.

All he had learned about the Gaels from his travelling companions passed through his mind. In his heart Caoimhin was concerned for the future. The ways of the heathen Irish seemed uncouth and licentious to him. All he knew of women had been taught to him by the Abbot of Glastonbury, a man who'd never strayed outside the monastery in his eighty years. According to the old man, females were the root cause of all temptation. They were weak in matters of the flesh. That's why Satan found them so easy to influence.

But it seemed that *Irish* women were the most sinful in all creation. So Caoimhin sat down to pray, begging God to protect him from their wiles, seeking guidance so that he would be well prepared when he encountered any of them.

'How do I prevent them from enchanting me?' he asked aloud, his hands firmly clasped before his breast.

No sooner had the words of prayer formed upon his lips than an answer came to him. But it wasn't in a form he might have expected. Our young scribe was suddenly overcome by one of his visions.

Usually when the dreaming-sight came upon him he was conscious of a distinct change in his surroundings. However, that was not the case on this occasion. It happened that he simply became aware of a presence nearby. Of course he was expecting Gobann to show himself so he turned around eagerly toward the forest.

What he saw brought to mind all the tales he'd heard of the terrible devilish creatures that roamed the Irish countryside. And for a brief moment he thought Satan himself had come visiting.

Twenty paces away an ethereal blue fire swirled and licked at the empty air. But this was no ordinary flame. For a start, though tinged blue, it was almost completely transparent. And despite the fact that it caressed the low branches of the trees, the blaze did not spread or consume anything.

Caoimhin sat forward on his knees, his mouth wide open. He'd witnessed many inexplicable events in his visions but this was the most beautiful, the most incredible of all.

The indigo-tinted flames crept higher, growing in size and intensity of colour so that he witnessed shades of blue such as he could never have imagined. And though he knew he should have been frightened, he could do nothing but hum with delight.

There was no heat in this fire. It was not of this world, you see. And some force unknown to Caoimhin emanated from the heart of the blue flames, imbuing him with an overwhelming sense of peace, joy and contentment all at once.

The sounds of the forest ceased. The breeze dropped to stillness. All the tiny hairs across the back of the young scribe's arms stood up in a rush of tingling pleasure.

As Caoimhin drew an ecstatic breath his nostrils filled with the strong scent of roses. His lips were coated with the subtle residue which remains after sacramental wine has been imbibed.

He realised this most heavenly of visions could not possibly be the work of the Devil. Yet he couldn't deny the blue fire had a distinct feminine quality about it. Perhaps, he thought, he was in the presence of the Mother of God.

Caoimhin's heart beat like the booming drum of a war galley speeding onward into battle. Each time he exhaled, the intensity of the experience increased until he was sure his heart would burst with rapture.

Then, when he was certain he could withstand no more of this joyous convulsion, a shape formed itself within the very epicentre of the mystic fire. A figure veiled in sky-hued blues, clad in the most gorgeous indigo, emerged from the living flames.

The scribe fell down upon his face with his hands covering his head. But he couldn't keep his eyes from the woman for long. He drew three long slow breaths to still his heart then raised his face again to look upon this creature of immeasurable beauty.

'Queen of Heaven,' he whispered.

The woman smiled serenely but offered no reply. Her face was fairer than that of any living soul he'd ever known. And yet there was a quality about this woman that seemed all-too-human.

It was then Caoimhin noticed there were faint designs etched upon her gorgeous countenance. Her hands also bore these patterns. Her eyes flashed with mischief.

This wasn't exactly what he'd expected from the Holy Virgin who'd brought Our Lord into the world. He began to suspect this vision might be some hellish trickery after all.

As that doubt entered his mind the woman laughed. The

sound was like the delicate tinkling of the highest harp strings, merry, free and uplifting. And when she finished laughing she spoke.

'I've been waiting for you,' she whispered.

The words struck Caoimhin like an arrow to the chest. As he felt the wind knocked out of him the wondrous vision vanished like a candle snuffed out.

The scribe rose shakily to his knees. His gaze was drawn toward the heavens where a bright star shone out in the firmament. There was a blueness to its light which affirmed its relationship with the ethereal fire.

Caoimhin heard a footfall, looked to where he'd seen the miraculous vision and saw a familiar face.

'Gobann!' he exclaimed.

The poet smiled. 'So you've seen her?'

'Who was she?'

'You know her as well as I do, my dear friend. But it remains to be seen whether you'll recognise her the next time she crosses your path.'

'What manner of being is she?'

'All in good time, my boy,' Gobann soothed. 'All in good time.'

a Tooth for a Tooth

ohn Toothache cursed his luck. Then he cursed his toothache. He always blamed his painful affliction whenever things didn't go exactly as he wished them to.

Although he'd marched with all speed to catch up with his quarry he'd been unable to find them anywhere along the road. That was partly Gobann's doing but of course Toothache had no idea of the power of the Draoi-craft.

He crossed the mountains two hours after dawn. When he made enquiries at the settlement of Kiltealy he was disappointed to find that no one had seen hide nor hair of the three travelling friars. He also asked about the red-hatted warriors. But his question was only met with pale faces, worried glances and barred doors.

He knew the monks must have made the crossing to the west so he set out again with renewed vigour, determined to pick up the scent. He'd walked all night, so by midday he found he had to rest. As I've said before, the woods round those parts were still quite thick in those days before the trees were sacrificed to build Norman ships. So he found himself a place beside the road where he'd not be seen by any travellers.

In a hollow overshadowed by an ancient yew he lay down to ease his aching limbs. But he didn't dare shut his eyes in case he fell into a long sleep. He certainly didn't want to lose any more ground to the monks.

He fumbled about for the pendant he'd taken from the body of the strange warrior. He lifted it up over his head so he could have a closer look at the workmanship. It was certainly an unusual carving. The seal was very lifelike, its eyes almost twinkling with delight as any living seal's might do. Though he appreciated the workmanship, John was no craftsman himself. The only thought that came to his mind was gratitude that none of his teeth was as large as the average walrus's. He slipped the pendant back over his head, took a mouthful of ale then yawned.

It was halfway through this yawn that an unnerving sensation descended upon him. The sensation that he was not alone.

There was a muffled sound high in the branches above him. Toothache looked up quickly but he couldn't see anything. He shrugged, closed his eyes and breathed deeply again. In that very second there was another noise. His eyes snapped open just as a bright red hat fell from on high to land in the fallen leaves not three steps away from him.

Before Toothache could get to his feet six fierce warriors dropped down from the tree, each landing squarely on his feet with a spear at the ready. As one they gave a short sharp war cry. The surprised Norman didn't have a chance to call out in despair before four flashing spear points were pressed into his chest, forcing him hard back against the trunk of the tree. A fifth warrior picked up his red hat, tucked his tangled brown locks under it then spun round to confront his captive.

The war-captain's murderous eyes were wild, malicious and full of rage. Grey-green mucus gathered at the corners and swam across the pupils. The Redcap leaned toward Toothache, reaching out a hand covered with spiralling red tattoos. He fingered the silver cross for a moment then noticed the other adornment hanging there.

The war-leader snatched at the walrus tooth, lifting it so that the leather strap dragged his captive's head forward. Nose to nose the two adversaries faced each other. The twisted scowl fell away from the Norman's face as he forgot all his pain. This was death staring back at him. This was a hideous, shrieking, agonised death.

The Redcap said something in a language Toothache could not understand. The Norman stared back without making a sound. The war-captain repeated his question, his tone clearly indicating he was at the end of his patience.

When his prisoner still gave no reply, the Redcap screamed the same phrase again. Toothache's blood turned to ice but he couldn't have brought himself to make a sound even if he'd understood the strange words.

The war-captain tore the pendant from around Toothache's neck, easily snapping the leather strip that held it in place. In the next breath the other four warriors dived on their captive and pinned him down. Then they bound his hands tightly in front of him.

Once he was disarmed and laid face down on the mossy ground with a heavy foot at his back to keep him there, the Redcaps ripped his possessions apart, searching for anything that might be of value to them.

The war-captain tucked Toothache's meat knife into his belt then gave the Norman's sword to one of his followers. The warrior lifted it up, jubilantly crying out as he swung it round his head. His companions ducked this way and that, laughing all the while.

The rain began to fall and every drop was like a little speck of ice on Toothache's face. He screwed up his features again, submitting to this indignity but determined he would not die without taking one or two of these wild men with him.

As the strangers passed his ale-skin around, the warrior whose foot pressed down on Toothache's back released the weight of his boot a little. Without hesitation Toothache rolled over, kicking the Redcap to the ground with such force the ale-skin flew from his hands and landed in the dirt.

With a great effort the Norman dragged himself to his feet just as a spear point lunged toward him. He caught the iron tip between the ropes which bound his hands at the front. Then with all his strength he kicked the warrior who held the spear hard in the groin. The Redcap doubled up and let go of the weapon. Toothache quickly loosed the spear from his bindings. Then he spun round as another weapon flew up into the air. It was a short-handled double-edged axe.

Toothache glimpsed it just in time to avoid the blow. As the warrior who wielded it lost his balance, the Norman grabbed the handle in his restrained hands. He wrenched it from the Redcap then he swung it about him to keep the other warriors at bay.

But the strangers only laughed at him as they stepped back out of his swing. Each time he brought the weapon round they did a little mocking dance to show him his attack was entirely ineffectual. At last one of the red-hatted warriors let his guard slip, straying within the deadly arc of the terrible weapon.

The axe bit deep into his shoulder, cutting through leather jerkin, flesh and bone to lodge deep into his body. The fellow screeched in agony then fell back with the axe still embedded in his flesh.

The handle slipped from Toothache's grasp. In the next breath he was set upon and once more pushed to the ground with joyous whooping hoots from the strange warriors. His hands were bound behind him this time, and for good measure the Redcaps tied his feet together too. When that was done they lifted him up to stand with one warrior on either side of him.

Then Toothache witnessed a sight that would haunt him for the rest of his days. One of the Redcaps placed a foot upon his fallen companion and pulled the battleaxe free from his body with loud laughter. He waved the weapon round in front of the Norman then stuck the handle through his belt. When he'd done that he offered a hand to the man who had taken the blow.

Toothache shook his head. Surely the warrior he'd struck must be dead, or at least mortally wounded. But to his horror a hand jerked up from the body and the wounded man was pulled to his feet. Where the axe had hit him his leather jerkin was split and bloodstained. But there was no sign of any injury. The flesh was clean and unscathed. Toothache's eyes bulged from his head in disbelief.

He would have stood there a while longer, staring in disbelief, but there was no time for the shock to take hold of him. Before he'd had a chance to absorb what had happened, he was lifted up to shoulder height by five pairs of rough, tattooed hands.

Then the Redcaps began their run, bearing their burden as if he were no more than a sack of oats brought in at harvest time. All Toothache could do was wonder where they could be taking him.

Martin followed on after the abbess as she led the way down the dark staircase into, it seemed, the very bowels of the Earth. At length they came to a sharp twist in the staircase and then the passage widened into a chamber twenty paces across.

That was when Martin noticed a stack of new rush-lights piled by the wall. He picked up a bundle of them, handed one to Sianan then touched the end of it to his flame. The lamp sputtered into life, widening the reach of light into a broad circle. But this increased visibility made the Norman warrior baulk. All around the walls on tall stakes were impaled what looked like lumps of shadowy wax.

Some instinct told Martin not to go near. But he was overcome with curiosity. He went over and held up his own makeshift torch to one of the objects.

He immediately recoiled in disgust and horror. The lump stuck upon the pole was a matted, blood-soaked mass of rotting flesh and hair which had once been a human head. White grinning teeth mocked him from beneath the folds of what were once a young warrior's lips. The eyes were nothing but empty sockets. The ears had been torn off completely.

Sianan touched a hand to her companion's shoulder, which startled him so much that he dropped his torch. The light went out the moment it hit the damp floor of the chamber.

'Come along,' the abbess whispered, handing Martin her light then selecting another from those he was holding under his arm. 'If you don't want to end up like those poor souls, we'd best get a move on.'

He nodded, eyes still staring with shock. Then he swallowed hard and followed on behind the abbess of the Otherworldly eyes.

After that the going was much slower. They had both become extremely cautious. The corridors grew increasingly damp until, much to the delight of Oat-Beer, they encountered a few scattered stagnant puddles. The dog rolled around in every one but he must have sensed their danger for he made no sounds or squeals of delight.

The air was heavy, stifling and fetid, so Sianan guessed they were nearing a barred gate or door which stopped the flow of air. Sure enough, within a thousand paces from the bottom of the staircase, they came across a wide pool of water. At the other side stood a huge oaken door three warriors wide and as tall as a man seated on a Norman warhorse. There were no signs of any sentries but that was not surprising to Sianan. After all, who would dare to enter such a place of fear? Who would be so bold as to venture into the depths of the world? And who would have ignored the warning signs planted at the bottom of the stairs?

Only a fool with his dog and a Fánaí of the immortal kind would have acted so brazenly. But even they did not expect to escape without facing trouble.

'How deep is that pool, do you think?' Martin asked the abbess.

Sianan shrugged. 'I'm more concerned with what's behind that door. Since there's no other way for us to go, we must find out.'

It was Oat-Beer who pushed them on. His love of puddles drew him to the edge of the pool. Before Martin could restrain him, the dog was off, tail wagging, bounding through the water. Just as he was about to reach the other side, Oat-Beer tried to stop himself but instead slid through mud and crashed against the door. It slowly creaked open. And the enticing gap proved too much for the red Sotar's curiosity.

In a flash Oat-Beer was through the doorway. Martin took off after him without a thought for his own safety. The abbess cursed under her breath but she was close behind.

Sianan pushed through the door, holding her torch aloft to illuminate the scene on the other side. The view stopped her heart for a second.

This was a massive storeroom larger than any chamber she'd ever seen in all her immortal years. Along the walls were tall racks loaded with every kind of weapon. Halberds, war sickles, bearded axes, swords, shields, bows, and spears of varying lengths and styles were all stacked in groups.

While Sianan stared open-mouthed, Oat-Beer was already sniffing excitedly around the door on the far side of the chamber, about a hundred paces away. There was obviously something on the other side that interested him.

The abbess hurried over and knelt down beside the red Sotar. 'What is it? What do you smell?'

The dog whimpered with excitement as he scratched at the floor. Martin pushed hard against the door.

'There's no sense in asking him. We'd best find out for ourselves.'

'We've been very lucky so far,' Sianan pointed out. 'We haven't met any guards nor been challenged. I just hope our luck holds.'

The Norman stopped pushing. Beads of sweat stood out on his forehead. He wiped them away and took a deep breath to prepare himself for the worst.

'There's no sense in worrying,' Sianan reassured him. 'If we're going to get caught, there's not much we can do about it.'

'That's a fine attitude. Just remember, if one of us is going to die it's going to be me,' Martin retorted. 'Now give me a hand with this door.'

Together they heaved against it until it moved enough for Oat-Beer to squeeze through. It was a few more seconds before Sianan and the Breton could follow.

What they saw came as another surprise. This chamber was as large as the armoury but it was a storage place for all kinds of food. Dried meat was laid out along one wall. The dog was already taking his fill of that. Along the other were loaves of travellers' bread solid as any biscuit, and row upon row of salted fish, cheeses and barrels of honey. At the far end of the chamber were huge casks filled with mead.

Between these casks were two doors. One was ajar enough to allow light to spill into the storage room. And the sound of many voices. Redcap voices. The room beyond was a small guardroom.

Martin collected a sack of dried meat, bread and salted fish. Then he found a water-skin to fill with mead. Once he had these he joined Sianan at the door.

'What are they talking about? I can't understand a word they're saying.'

She held up her hand to urge him to keep his voice down.

'It's an ancient dialect. I can barely understand it myself,' she whispered.

She turned her attention back to the conversation between the guards. Her eyes told Martin that something she had heard disturbed her greatly.

'We must find a way out of here,' she hissed under her breath. 'We haven't much time.'

'What's happening?'

'War is brewing,' Sianan replied. 'By Samhain Oidche the whole of this country will be under the threat of bloody conflict.'

'But Guy's warriors were all scattered by the Nathairaí,' the Breton reminded her.

'It's not Guy we have to worry about. It's Aoife, the Queen of the Night and Sovereign of the Redcaps.'

A Certain Charm

The raven named Sciathan Cog left Guy d'Alville stewing inside the tree trunk for a long, long while. During his period of confinement the Norman listened to the gut-wrenching sounds of the Nathairaí tearing up the forest in their relentless search for suitable dinner morsels.

Not that Guy was moved by anything he heard. As I've said, fear wasn't an experience d'Alville ever allowed to get the better of him. He was a warrior. And successful practitioners of that craft can't afford to be subject to the skittery-jitters.

That's not to say there aren't warriors out there who do tremble from time to time. It's just that Guy had developed a thick skin where fright was concerned.

There were obvious risks involved in the pursuit of his chosen profession. The odds were always stacked against his survival into old age. However, he'd never relished the idea of growing old, so that wasn't really a consideration. In fact it was an affront to his dignity to consider passing from this world in his own bed, comforted by some coddling relative.

He desired an honourable death in battle more than anything, so he had long ago ceased to be concerned about dying. Once he'd defeated that fear he realised there wasn't really anything else to be frightened about in life.

He'd had his honour defiled and he'd survived. He'd been

disowned by the Order of the Knights Hospitaller, yet he'd managed to restore his fortunes to a certain degree. He was a self-reliant man who could look after himself. He'd never needed the company of others, nor had he much enjoyed having them about. He never felt lonely.

As for the afterlife and the possibility of eternal damnation, that didn't concern him either. He'd long since come to the conclusion that this life was a realm of pain and suffering. He couldn't imagine any punishment worse than having to be born into this world all over again. And what, you may ask, if he had nothing to look forward to but an eternity imprisoned in the hellish kingdoms of Satan's infernal dungeons? Guy had a feeling the Devil wouldn't let one such as himself languish in any place of punishment for too long. He knew he'd be a valuable asset to a fallen angel who wanted to stir up trouble in the world.

Yes, that was Guy all over. There was something not quite right about the way he saw things. If all the terrors described in scripture didn't move him to live a better life or to fear God's unfathomable wrath, what could?

I can tell you, even two rampaging serpents eager to devour every muscle, sinew and bone in his body didn't stand a chance of getting to Guy d'Alville. The only thing that worried him was that he might be killed before he had a chance to end the life of Robert FitzWilliam.

The circumstances surrounding their feud makes an interesting tale. Caoimhin told it all in *The Tilecutter's Penny* so I'll just mention a few details. It so happened that Robert FitzWilliam went off to the Holy Land and enlisted in the Knights Templar as soon as he'd saved up the gold marks to do so. While he was there he was caught up in an intrigue involving the theft of certain holy relics.

Indeed it was Robert who liberated those sacred items from the clutches of the Knights Hospitaller, thus disgracing the man who was charged with returning the objects to Rome. And if you've been listening carefully you will have guessed that the Knight Hospitaller who ended up being punished for his incompetence was none other than Guy d'Alville. Robert FitzWilliam had turned Guy's world upside down. And no man who did that ever escaped his wrath for long.

Whenever d'Alville found himself in a difficult or hopeless situation he'd focus his every thought on his hatred for Robert FitzWilliam and he'd dream of the sweet revenge that would one day be his. So it was on this occasion. Guy sat back in his living oaken gaol to await the return of Sciathan Cog. And all the while his thoughts were consumed with hatred for his enemy.

It was almost dawn by the time the Nathairaí came very close to where he was hiding. They were ripping up root and branch in their frenzy and generally making a terrible row.

Guy heard the racket and resolved it would be better to face them on open ground than to risk being crushed as they tore up his tree. At least he'd be able to look into the eyes of death at the last. And if he could do that he might see some way of avoiding its bite.

The Norman crawled out from the timber cave. He brushed off his tunic and arranged his mail coat neatly about his body. He wasn't going to face his fate looking dishevelled. Then he lifted up the sword he had taken from one of his warriors. It was a poor blade but it would have to do. He had no other. His fine sword made of beaten steel had been shattered by the monsters in his first encounter with them.

Guy wondered whether it would be better to wait beside the tree. Then he realised his legs were a little stiff from sitting in a confined space for so long. He moved out into a clearing where the grass was smooth and the ground even. With the din of wormish destruction going on not far away, he calmly began to stretch his muscles, readying himself for the impending fight.

When Guy was a young man he'd been tutored in swordsmanship by an older Hospitaller who'd been an Irishman. This fellow had instructed Guy in the Sword Dance.

Now don't get it into your head that the Sword Dance was some silly jig performed at parties. It wasn't anything of the sort. It was serious. To most warriors it was a sacred meditation practice which granted grace and focus to the fighter. And if the dance was practised diligently it ensured victory more often than not. For knights who lacked the knowledge of the dance were placed at a distinct disadvantage. Indeed Guy always attributed the early successes of his military career to this mystical series of movements. If he hadn't known about it he would most certainly have fallen in battle before he was old enough to even aspire to greatness as a warrior.

D'Alville held the weapon in his left hand. Then he settled his breathing and connected with the sensations coursing through his body. All the while the Nathairaí crashed about, coming ever closer. But Guy had practised these moves before countless battles and in the most trying of circumstances.

The Sword Dance always calmed him. It prepared him for the fight and for death if that should be the outcome. On this occasion it allowed him to limber up his sore muscles and to acquaint himself with a weapon he had not handled in battle before.

When he felt ready he took a step backwards with his left foot, stretching his right leg as he bowed low with the blade upturned behind him. This was the opening move of the dance. It was graceful, smooth and typical of the dance as a whole.

Every warrior who practised these movements interpreted them according to his nature. Not surprisingly, Guy's personal style was acutely focused, ruthless, cunning and direct. These qualities pretty much summed him up in all his other dealings with the world. So you see, for a devoted practitioner of the

Sword Dance it was an easy matter to gauge one's opponent through his movements.

A sharp-eyed master could size up an opponent before he'd finished executing the opening bow. And then he could lure the enemy into defeat by playing on his weaknesses. Guy was especially capable of reading any man who stood against him.

Gauging the war-worth of a worm was an entirely different matter of course. But the basic principle was probably much the same.

In any case, d'Alville had not managed to make it halfway through the dance before one of the monsters encountered him. However, rather than inspiring the creature to a rage of blood-lust, the sight of this Norman preparing himself for death had a captivating effect on the creature.

The worm waited at the edge of the clearing, transfixed by the exhibition of grace, single-mindedness and supple strength. Not until Guy had finished his practice did the Nathair speak.

'You're a gifted warrior,' she hummed with delight. 'I'd almost forgotten how wonderful it is to watch a fighter at his dance.'

D'Alville turned to face the worm as she sensuously slithered from the cover of the trees to coil in the clearing a short distance from where he stood.

'Don't even think of using that worthless weapon against me. You wouldn't even get a chance to raise it to strike the first blow.'

Guy stepped back awestruck at the glistening skin and deep wet eyes of the terrible creature.

'Surely you don't expect me to submit to you without a fight?' the Norman asked.

'If you insist,' she sighed. 'But it won't do you any good. You'll be lining my stomach with the rest of the warriors soon enough.'

'Those mercenaries cost me a small fortune to equip, train

and bribe,' D'Alville told her coldly. 'I'm more than a little disgruntled at the way you squandered my investment.'

'You were their lord?'

'Indeed. My name is Guy d'Alville.'

He bowed low. But don't be thinking Guy had suddenly turned polite. He was taking the opportunity to observe his adversary. And he thought he might have discovered her weakness.

'I'm known as Isleen,' the Nathair told him. 'I was a beautiful woman once, you know. I used to have every man in the land lusting after me. Of course I was very selective in my choice of male company.'

'I'm sure you were. I'm also extremely careful which worms I spend my time with,' he quipped.

'There's no need for such insolence,' Isleen reprimanded him gently. 'It ill becomes such a magnificent specimen of manhood.'

Then she sighed deeply as she raised her head up on her fat ugly worm body, desperately trying to seem as alluring as she had once been.

'If I could have but one wish it would be that I be granted the body of a young woman again,' she purred, or as near to a purr as a Nathair can manage. 'It's been an age since I dallied in a den of delight with a young fellow such as yourself.'

'I prefer my women petite, demure and compliant,' Guy shrugged. 'I don't know whether we'd hit it off.'

'You're mocking me, you bastard!' Isleen shrieked.

Then with a great sweep of her tail she swung her body round, flattening trees, sending soil flying in every direction. But Guy unflinchingly stood his ground as the worm vented her fury on the forest.

When she'd calmed a little she turned to face him again. With a mighty effort she stretched herself out to encircle the Norman completely.

'You can't escape,' Isleen informed him in a low enticing tone.

'I certainly couldn't leap over you,' Guy replied. 'Your belly's so full of my warriors it's bulging fit to burst.'

'I haven't had a decent meal in over three hundred winters,' she snapped. 'The last time I escaped the well all I had to feast on was scrawny cattle. Surely you don't begrudge me a few footmen. In any case, I was just considering whether I should spare you. So I advise you to guard your tongue.'

She softened. 'You amuse me. I haven't been amused for such a long time. It's been an eternity since I had a handsome warrior such as yourself to fritter away the days with.'

'What makes you think I'd be grateful if you spared me only to force me to fritter with you on a daily basis. You're an ugly worm. You're not an attractive young woman any more, if you ever were.'

Isleen began to pant with rage and her eyes ran with a vile black liquid that stank of rotting flesh.

'You ignorant savage!' she shrieked. 'Do you think you're the first invader I've faced? I've seen them come and go. First it was the Danaans. They were no match for me. Then I enticed the Gaels to come here. Look at what a mess they've made of things.'

She closed in on him, tightening the circle of her body.

'Now you Normans come along with your fancy ideas of chivalry, your ignorance of even the most basic bodily cleanliness, and your inane poems portraying romantic love. I may be a worm who has spent the best part of the last thousand winters underwater in a hole deep beneath the ground, but even I've had the misfortune to hear the drivel that passes for storytelling in your country.'

'I'm not an expert on the arts of music or taletelling,' Guy conceded. 'But I wouldn't take too much notice of the opinions a belching, stinking, snot-eyed beast might have on the subject.'

'I'll tear you apart, you filthy little Norman dog!' she bellowed.

Isleen swung her tail around, lashing it at the impudent nobleman. Guy was ready for the blow. He placed the sword down with the hilt stuck into the soil and the blade directed into the air. When her tail came down, the fury of her attack forced the weapon to bite deeply into her flesh. Isleen instantly let out a blood-thickening cry that shook the very ground on which she rested.

As he rolled out of the way of her rage, Guy felt his guts tremble from the intensity of her painful exclamation.

'I'll crush you like a blackberry under my boot,' she promised.

'It must be a long while since you needed a pair of boots,' d'Alville answered.

'Be silent, you insignificant creature!' she growled. 'You're not making this any easier for yourself.'

Guy laughed. 'I'm about to be digested by a filthy repulsive worm of indescribable stench. What do you suggest I do to make that experience easier?'

Isleen squealed again as she pulled her tail up close to her head so she could observe the wound. It was a deep gash but it was already healing. For Isleen was just like Sianan: no weapon could wound her. In seconds the blood had stopped flowing. She licked the wound with a great lolling grey tongue. That's when Guy saw the gash had completely disappeared.

'You can't do me any harm,' she scoffed. 'I'm no mortal creature. I'm beyond death.'

The Norman stepped back, ready to run, but the Nathair swiftly coiled herself around him again.

'I think it would be wise of you to treat me with some respect,' she cautioned him.

His eyes flashed with mischief. 'I'm beginning to see the sense in that,' he conceded, dropping the sword.

Isleen paused. In that second Guy d'Alville worked his charm on her. His eyes twinkled with just a hint of interest. The worm shuddered with delight.

'That's a good boy,' she cooed. 'Now you're beginning to understand.'

He was a bastard and no mistake. He knew how to get a woman longing after him. He knew how to turn her heart toward him.. He had a certain charm about him, that one, despite his less than attractive way of dealing with the world. Even a woman who'd been trapped under enchantment as a monstrous serpent for over a thousand years could be worked under his spell.

'I don't want to hurt you really,' Isleen told him, a touch of vulnerability in her voice.

As she spoke, Guy d'Alville knew he had a chance of survival.

'I may be ugly to look upon,' she went on. 'But beneath this slimy skin the heart of a woman still beats with passion.'

SPIRITS

t's no use putting this off any longer. I've avoided this matter as long as I could. I knew you'd likely treat the whole subject with scepticism so I've only hinted at it till now. But that just won't do.

If you want to know the fullness of this tale I'll have to explain a few things. To begin with, I don't mind admitting that although I often felt their presence I didn't hold much belief in spirits when I was young. Now I'm much wiser.

It's difficult to know where to start when introducing the Enticers and the Frighteners into a story. I'll begin with an obvious example of their influence. It will best illustrate my meaning.

Lanfranc de Courcy had always been a bit of a coward. Naturally he didn't think of himself as one. Whenever he stared into a looking glass or caught a glimpse of his reflection in the still waters of a pool, he had nothing but admiration for the face presented to him.

He'd been sired from a long line of noble warriors. His great-grandfather had landed in England with Duke William the Conqueror. His lineage had fought alongside the Norman kings in every major conflict since that time. With the exception of poor Lanfranc. Good King Henry had recognised our boy's potential and elevated him to the noble rank of knighthood. But then the king had promptly passed from this world, leaving a bitter son, Richard, to take up the crown.

The Lion-Heart had immediately cleared the court of all his father's favourites to make room for his own friends and courtiers. So Lanfranc had found himself granted lands in Ireland and ordered to leave England on the next boat.

This was not the direction he'd wished his life to take. He'd always imagined himself a brave crusader defending travellers in the Holy Land from the savage Saracens. The general opinion of his friends was that Ireland was no more than a stagnant backwater peopled by an uncouth, argumentative race. The tale doing the rounds was that the Irish insisted on washing themselves every day in the interests of cleanliness.

Lanfranc had shuddered at first to hear such tales of savagery.

So while Richard had been away fighting his crusade, Lanfranc had set off for his new homeland. Thus he'd missed out on the most glorious adventure of the age. And he was ruefully aware of the fact.

Despite this setback to his ambitions, our lad had continued to hold some hope Ireland would provide an opportunity for gallantry, advancement and adventure. But when King John ascended the throne after Richard's untimely death, his ambitions had melted away.

The new king had withdrawn his support for an expansion into the Gaelic-speaking parts of Ireland. It was simply too expensive for the English crown to maintain such a policy. The royal coffers were empty and the people had nothing to offer in taxes after the deprivations of Richard's costly wars.

So Lanfranc had begun constructing his stronghold, all the while warding off brigands, patrolling the roads and convincing himself he was of some use to his king. But his heart had been heavy and he had longed for the lively life of London.

Then Mirim had arrived. Like some lady in distress from the

troubadour tales, she seemed to offer an opportunity to test his honour, temper his courage and tempt his heart. It would be fair to say, and I'm sure Lanfranc would agree with me if you asked him, that he really didn't have his feet planted firmly on the ground in those days. He was a dreamer.

Not that there's anything wrong with that. If it weren't for dreamers this world would be a dull place indeed and the Otherworld would serve no purpose whatsoever.

However, a warrior can't afford to let himself be distracted by foolish notions based on silly stories uttered entirely for the entertainment of courtly ladies. Our Lanfranc had had an unusual upbringing for a knight and this may explain why he turned out as he did. He'd been fed fantastic, often exaggerated stories of his ancestors' exploits. He'd been nourished with notions of chivalry, gallantry and honour which really had no practical application in the world of warfare. Nor were there many remaining adherents to the tenets of these fine ideals, no matter what the troubadours might try to tell you.

All of which put Lanfranc at a disadvantage when dealing with his contemporaries. Men such as Guy d'Alville. So even if he'd not been haunted by a spirit, he'd still have found life quite challenging.

You see, my dear, Lanfranc de Courcy owned an object which had been passed down to him from generation to generation since before the time of the Conqueror. It was a powerful, mystical relic which imbued any who possessed it with an air of invincibility.

It was his great-grandfather's sword.

Now I've already mentioned that this weapon had a remarkable effect on Lanfranc whenever it was withdrawn from its scabbard. But there was more to this blade than the mighty confidence it inspired in its bearer.

You see, Lanfranc's sword was inhabited by a spirit.

Laugh if you like. I can see you know little of such matters.

So it may profit you to listen with particular attention to everything I'm about to say.

What are spirits? That's hard to say. I may never know the absolute answer to that question. But I'm certain they exist. I've sensed them since I was a girl too young to know aught but fascination and fright.

I feel their presence even more now that I'm old and my life may be coming to a close. Spirits are here in this house even as I speak. They're everywhere.

But they're not what you might expect them to be. They're not the same as ghosts. Ghosts are a different breed altogether. Ghosts are nothing compared to spirits.

This was a difficult concept for me to grasp at first. And I'm probably much brighter than you are. So I'll forgive you if you don't latch on immediately. Whisht and listen. I'll keep this as simple as I can.

Consider the cows. Imagine we're all cattle. A good farmer keeps his milkers happy. He sleeps them in a warm part of the house or in a byre of their own if he's wealthy. Each day he takes them out into the fields where the lushest grass is growing.

A good farmer keeps a watch over his cows to make sure no harm comes to them from wolves or cattle thieves. And when their udders are bulging with milk he relieves the discomfort by draining out every last drop.

In the same way the spirits keep an eye on us. Every day they lead us into the fields of desire or disquiet to feed us up with fear or infatuation. Then at night they make sure we're bedded down all snug and safe. They often bait us with dreams and nightmares while we rest, but they prefer that no real harm come to us.

And, the same as cattle, we're largely unaware our keepers have only the daily milking in mind. For that's why the spirits keep us. They milk us for the soul-light that fires up our existence. That's the purest food of all for them. It's the sweetest nectar.

There are two tribes of these beings which feed on the light of the soul. One tribe are called the Áilleacht. Then there are those known as the Eagla. The first tribe are Enticers and the second are Frighteners.

The unenlightened among the mortal kind refer to these spirits as angels and dæmons. But such simple titles deny the true nature of these feeders. They're neither good nor evil – though they employ tactics that may seem benevolent or malevolent according to their will – they simply are.

It's the nature of Enticers to draw their nourishment from the soul-light kindled by infatuation and the like. They present themselves as beautiful, compassionate, alluring beings. Folk often find them so attractive it's assumed the Enticers must be servants of God. But they're not pure angelic forms. That's just the appearance they take on to inspire awe, obsession, worship and love. Those are the emotions they feed on.

Frighteners, on the other hand, feast on fear, anger, insecurity and apprehension. They rarely present themselves as pretty creatures. They want us to tremble. So they often appear as ugly, threatening, intimidating, uncouth or ghastly. That's how they earned a reputation for being minions of Satan.

But I urge you not to think of them in such simplistic terms. The world is a far more complicated place than it may at first appear. The holiest of saints is as much a slave to these two tribes as the rest of us.

So the Church fathers can't be entirely blamed for creating a doctrine based on fear and enticement. That's how they came to believe that Hell is a place of torment and Heaven a realm of eternal pleasures. Which is only part of the story. Such men of the cloth are merely dancing to a tune played for them by the feeding spirits.

Whenever you or I react to the Enticers or the Frighteners,

whether it be with admiration or awe, deference or dread, they feast on those feelings and build up their strength. And let's make one thing perfectly clear: the Enticers are no better than their brethren the Frighteners.

The strongest and the oldest of these spirits are the most influential. They may steal the reins of the soul entirely. Then they'll set it off galloping wildly across ethereal fields of beauty or terror till you drop dead from exhaustion. Or until you meet some other murderous misadventure. Or you simply wear out.

Even a well-fed spirit is always looking to the next meal, arranging enticements or rousing fears. It's in their nature to do so. They may turn our lives to their whim if we allow it.

And there's no use denying it, most folks let them do just that. Spirits are ever leading us back and forth between the sweet grass that grows in the Fields of Enticement and the dark shadows that harbour horror in the Forests of Terror.

Now here's the interesting part. This is a great secret known to only a few. The spirits don't like this information spread about too freely. So you'll forgive me if I drop my voice to a whisper.

Each of us has our own personal Enticer and our own private Frightener. Generally they're not very forceful or greedy. They don't like to draw attention to themselves. So most folk never come to any awareness of them at all.

Many everyday objects are also inhabited by them. A spirit that takes up residence in a stone or tree has little opportunity to feed. So they tend to be more desperate and demanding than others of their kind.

Harps are most often inhabited by Enticers. I'm sure you'll agree that such instruments are the perfect abode for a being which feeds off feelings of admiration and appreciation. Harps are almost always given a name. That's done to acknowledge the spirit dwelling within.

For obvious reasons swords are more likely to be the abode

of a Frightener. Weapons, too, may attain a name in acknowledgement of the terrifying teeth-chattering trouble they cause.

But occasionally an ancient bored spirit sets itself a challenge and takes up residence in an object which at first seems contrary to its desires. A harp that holds a fear spirit can rouse folk to war with no more than a few notes from its droning bass. Such instruments attain a fame and fearsome reputation unparalleled among their kind.

And what of a sword which has an Enticer within? Such blades are revered far and near and coveted like no others.

Well it just so happened that Lanfranc possessed such a sword. Whenever he drew it from its scabbard he was overwhelmed by the immense power of the Enticer. And so were his adversaries. Those brigands were an exception but they'd been harassing Lanfranc for months. They'd likely grown accustomed to his awesome transformation. Though it's true the Gaels were generally less intimidated by such weapons than other folk because they understood the truth behind the illusion.

The spirit of Lanfranc's blade had a name. It was called Tóla the Flood. It fed on the awe it aroused in others. It imbued our boy with an heroic stature of which he was quite obviously undeserving. Thus his armour sparkled and he remained immaculately clean no matter what mishaps he'd become embroiled in.

But there was another interesting thing about Lanfranc. The moment he returned the blade to its scabbard his own personal Frightener, a minor spirit compared to that of Tóla, took to feeding once again. This would throw him into panicked states of confused fear and nervous clumsiness.

There you have it. He's a perfect example of someone who has a hungry spirit feeding off him. The tricky thing about an Enticer such as Tóla is that they move on from their host whenever there isn't enough food available to satisfy their insatiable hunger.

Swords tend to acquire new owners faster than harps because spirits of fear are much more impatient than spirits of entice- ment. And because it's easier to get yourself killed if you're wielding a weapon than if you're plucking a harp string.

But Lanfranc's sword had been in his family for generations. It was an Enticer content to bide its time waiting for the right moment to move on. And since the time of the first de Courcy that moment had not yet arrived.

All the participants in my story have, at their hearts, Enticers and Frighteners which drive them on to indulge in various follies. They may seem awesome and all-powerful, but, let me assure you, the spirits who attach themselves to us mortals are small fry indeed.

Denizens of the Otherworld have far greater, more influential spirits attached to them. Indeed, the mightiest Enticers and Frighteners are to be found latched onto the folk of the Faerie realms. Queen Aoife, like most monarchs both mortal and immortal, was dominated by a spirit of enticement. She was renowned for her beauty, her winning speeches and her feminine wiles. But she wasn't entirely ruled by her Enticer. She had come to an understanding of how to use the strengths of her feeding spirit to gain her heart's desires.

Lochie and Isleen were also inhabited by extremely powerful Enticers. Before they fell out with Danu, those two could boil up a pot full of charm that'd have you crying for more. Let's not forget they enticed the tribespeople of the Gaels to sail to Ireland. That's why Danu changed them into awful-smelling ugly great worms. It was a way of making things difficult for their Enticer spirits.

The spirits within a god or goddess such as Danu have attained a much deeper state of soul-feeding than is possible for the minor spirits in any of us. You see, the deities have almost always come to an arrangement with their feeders. It's a mutually beneficial agreement to live together in harmony.

Gods and goddesses are granted immense power by their spirits. Mortals worship deities. And worship is the purest nourishment any Enticer or Frightener can aspire to. You'll see what I'm on about as this whole story unfolds.

As I've said, we mortals are as insignificant as cattle to the Enticers and the Frighteners. They milk us of our emotions. And when our milking days are ended, they may choose to slaughter us for meat or put us out to pasture as is their whim.

All this is fine enough while the two tribes of the Enticers and the Frighteners are at peace with one another. They may even work together in alliance. Have you noticed how some folk turn to fine food for solace whenever they're frightened? Or how some stave off insecurity with fancy clothes? That proves the spirits work together. But there are times when they go to war, and then the world of mortals is shaken to the very core.

Perhaps you've guessed that the coming of the Normans, the rising of the Redcaps and the mischief of Queen Aoife coincided with a bitter rivalry which arose between the two tribes of spirits. And if you didn't guess, you certainly know now. You'll see what I'm getting to as I go on. Be patient.

Sianan and Martin stayed by the guardroom as long as they dared. They resisted trying the other door in the storage chamber until it seemed certain they'd be discovered. The door swung open noiselessly.

Before them was a staircase. A draught of fresh air hit their faces. They didn't need to discuss whether this was the direction in which they wanted to head. It wouldn't have made any difference if they had wanted to discuss it. Oat-Beer was already off up the stairs like a flash. And it was just as well.

As he disappeared there was a noise at the door to the guard-room. Sianan turned in time to catch a glimpse of a Redcap staring wide-eyed back at her. In an instant he was gone back into the chamber from whence he'd appeared.

Seconds later hunting horns were sounding throughout the underground fortress. The noise turned Martin's flesh to ice, caressing his very bones with pure terror. He shivered visibly, the blood draining from his face and his jaw hanging open. His Frightener was enjoying a tasty treat.

The abbess had gone a dozen steps when she realised he wasn't behind her. She rushed back to where the Breton was standing immobilised by fright. She grabbed his shoulder and shouted, 'Run!'

He didn't need to be told twice. The two of them were up the steep spiralling stairs and headed for another door before you could shriek, 'I may need to change my undergarments'.

This entrance, like all the others they'd encountered, was unlocked. If Martin had been able to muster enough breath and piety he probably would have thanked the Lord in Heaven for that. But his own personal Frightener was feeding, so supplication was probably the last thing on his mind just then.

The door gave way easily to a heaving push from Sianan. It swung open to reveal a dark chamber, wide at the floor and rising to a high pointed ceiling. The whole room was con-structed with layer upon layer of stone gradually tapering to the top. However, neither Martin nor the abbess noticed the fine details of its intricate architecture. They didn't get a chance. As they entered the chamber they heard shouts, cries and shrieks in the passage behind them. The Redcaps were already on their scent.

Opposite the doorway leading from the stairs there was another narrow passage. There was no other way out of the chamber. Martin edged his way into this corridor with his torch raised to light the way.

He'd only had a glimpse inside when he excitedly turned back to report what he'd seen.

'I can see daylight at the end of this passage!'

'Then what are you waiting for? Let's get ourselves out of here.'

Oat-Beer led the way of course, but being a creature of smaller build he didn't find the passage too difficult. The other two crawled along the narrow low stone-lined corridor on their hands and knees, having discarded their now useless torches.

Though they had no light to guide the way, beneath their hands they could make out beautiful spiral designs carved into the solid rock. If the circumstances had been different they might have stopped to caress the walls and ceiling of this corridor. The same designs covered these surfaces also.

Martin's dog had disappeared into the light long before the abbess and her companion emerged from that place. When they finally came out, Oat-Beer was barking enthusiastically and running round in circles for joy of being out of that confining underground world. Sianan struggled to quieten him, but it wasn't till Martin offered him a piece of dried meat that the dog stopped barking.

By then Sianan had surveyed the scene. The passage they'd just travelled along exited from the side of a small grass-covered mound. On the other side of the tiny hill there was a line of trees. There were no signs anywhere about of any destruction. She sighed with relief at the realisation that the Nathairaí were a long way off.

Even so Sianan's senses were on edge. Ears, eyes and nostrils strained for any hint of danger. There was nowhere for them to run. If they fled into the forest they'd be heading straight into the home ground of the Redcaps. If they tried to cross the pastures ahead or follow the road, they'd be outrun in no time. As I've already told you, the Redcaps can sprint like the wind when the mood takes them.

'How in the name of Lady Danu herself did you escape?' a raven voice cawed in the tree above.

'Lom Dubh? Is that you?'

'Who else would it be sitting in the branches cackling down at you?' the bird snapped.

In a flurry of feathers he leaped off his perch and landed a few feet in front of Sianan. He cocked his head this way and that as he sized the two of them up.

'You're bloody resourceful, you Fánaí,' he stated respectfully. 'That well-house was good and locked. How did you get out?'

'You brought us the key,' the abbess frowned. 'Didn't you?'

'Twasn't me,' he replied.

'Don't play games with me. Half the Redcaps of the Otherworld are on our tail. I haven't got time for your teasing.'

'I'm telling you I didn't bring the key. I couldn't find it. I thought you were well and truly done for. Especially after I saw the Nathairaí smashing up the woods and devouring those bough-splitting Norman bastards.'

'A raven saved us,' she mumbled as realisation dawned on her.

'Sciathan Cog!' they both said together.

'Now why would he want to release us?' Sianan asked herself. 'I'd have thought he'd want to see us swallowed whole. He's never had any time for me.'

'It wasn't you he was after setting free,' Lom Dubh told her. 'It was the worms. Aoife must have some use for them. And she wouldn't want folk knowing it was Cog that released you.'

'Why?'

'She's counting on the fact that you'll pass on word of the Nathairaí near and far. She's after spreading panic through the land.'

In that instant Sianan froze. Her intuition had spoken to her long before her other senses were aware of horsemen on the road.

'We can't stop here chatting all day,' she gasped. 'There are Redcaps coming. And I'm sure I smell Normans on the breeze. There are riders approaching. Have we any hope of escape?'

'How would I know? I've been off watching the destruction of the tree-cutting foreign devils. I only flew in here when I heard the blast of the Redcap war horns.'

'Didn't you think to look for us?'

'The well-house is shattered. I was sure you were gone. Forgive me but ravens are creatures who are mournful by nature. I simply assumed the worst. There are some things even an immortal can't be expected to survive and a meeting with the Nathairaí is one of them.'

The horsemen were not far off now. Sianan's first instinct was to hide. But she knew they'd be discovered easily enough, whether it be by Redcaps or Normans. There was no escaping the approaching trouble from both directions.

The hurried hoof-beats made her heart sink. But she was frozen by indecision. They were caught between the anvil and the hammer. Neither option seemed that attractive.

'Hadn't we better find some cover?' Martin urged.

'It's too late for that. The foreigners are already upon us.'

'She's right,' Lom Dubh agreed. 'I'll be up there watching if you need me. Then I'll be off to find the Morrigán. I think she'd best know what's going on.'

'Thanks for all your help!' Sianan hissed sarcastically. 'We'd be better off with your wicked brother here to stand by us.'

'Would you be able to tell us apart?'

With that the raven spread his wings and soared back up into the branches where he wouldn't be seen. Oat-Beer dropped his dried meat to bark defensively in the direction of the thudding horses.

'For the love of Blesséd Mary, be quiet!' the Breton urged.

He dragged the dog by the collar, trying to get him to come with them back to the cover of the hill. But the dog resisted him every step of the way.

Then before he knew it, two horsemen appeared. These were Norman warriors, no doubt about it. Their swords were drawn and they were on the lookout for trouble.

'They're Guy's men!' Martin cried out in despair.

He was distraught and confused, so he can be excused for not spotting that these warriors weren't dressed in burgundy tunics.

'You there!' one of the riders challenged them. 'Stand your ground in the name of King John.'

Sianan stopped in her tracks and turned round to face the foreigners.

'What business have you on the king's highway?'

The abbess cursed her indecisiveness. If they'd hidden themselves a few seconds earlier they'd not have been detected. There was no hope they'd outrun the warriors now. So she made a decision.

'Run, Martin,' she said in a low voice.

'What?'

'Run!' she repeated, this time with a hint of panic in her voice. 'Run!'

***

The Nathair named Isleen coiled into a tighter circle around Guy so that there was only an area five paces across in which he could stand. The warrior stared steadfastly into the worm's huge watery bulging eyes.

'What are you intending to do with me?' he asked forthrightly.

'I may eat you now,' she replied. 'Or I may decide to keep you for a while. I'm hoping to find someone who can break this enchantment.'

'Who could do such a thing?'

'Only the Goddess Danu who laid the spell upon me. She's forgotten me. But I intend to talk her into giving me back my more elegant shape of former times.'

As she spoke another bulbous head appeared behind her. It was her companion, Lochie.

'Who are you talking to?' he enquired.

'Just a mortal,' she snapped. 'Leave me alone. It's none of your business.'

'Are you going to eat him or not?'

She didn't answer but left him in no doubt that his presence was not welcome. 'Jigger off,' she hissed.

'If you're not going to eat him, I will,' the other worm told her flatly. 'He smells better than any of the others. Perhaps he's had a wash recently. His companions left a nasty taste in my mouth.'

'You can't have him.'

'Isleen has found a new boy to play with,' Lochie mocked.

In a flash of pent-up frustration Isleen spun round and turned on Lochie with rage.

'Do you know what it's been like trapped in that well with you for over a thousand years? It's been like no other experience I ever had in all my long seasons on this Earth. You're repulsive. You think of no one but yourself. You drone on day after day about the past as if it were all that mattered.'

Lochie rose up with an arched back to challenge her. But she wasn't in the least perturbed. This contempt had been building up in her for an age and now she was free of the well-house she wasn't going to hold back for anything.

'You cheat at Brandubh. And you thought I didn't notice! You reckon you're so bloody smart.'

'If you caught me cheating, why didn't you confront me about it?'

'Because I couldn't be bothered getting into another row with you. It was easier to let you think I hadn't noticed. You're so intolerably stupid!'

'I'm the one who convinced Sciathan Cog to help us,' he stated coldly. 'If it had been left up to you we'd still be rotting at the bottom of that hole with empty bellies and no hope of escape.'

That was enough for Isleen. She gathered up a huge gob of grey sticky phlegm and spat it at her companion. Lochie shifted out of the way of the repulsive missile just in time. It clipped a tree, taking off several branches as it scattered in a splashing explosion of mucus.

In the next breath Lochie spat his own bracken-green blob of mouth poison. But Isleen was not so fast as he was. The gob hit her in the right eye, spattering Guy with gallons of dank, stinking liquid.

The Norman shook the globs of mucus out of his hair as he tried to prevent his stomach from turning out its contents.

Isleen was shrieking in a high-pitched wail of rage. Guy had to cover his ears to prevent them bursting with the intensity of the cry.

The female Nathair swung her tail around, slamming it into a stand of trees. The boughs disintegrated into countless deadly splinters which flew in every direction. One piece as thin as a finger and as long as a man's arm slapped d'Alville across the cheek, cutting his face open in a deep slash. He made no sound to acknowledge his pain but gingerly touched the wound before he placed his palm over it to stop the bleeding.

As he was pressing on the cut he saw his chance to escape. The two worms had wrapped themselves about one another in a violent tussle. Their heads were close together as they each continued to spit.

And for the moment they'd forgotten all about him. They had centuries of accumulated disdain to unleash. Now their bellies were full there was no reason to hold back any longer.

Guy knew he might not get far but he had to make a run for it. In a desperate dash he headed for the edge of the clearing. And he would have made it into the woods if Isleen had not torn up another tree, smashing it into kindling with one sweep of her terrible tail. The debris scattered over the whole clearing, raining splinters and soil on everything.

A great slab of a tree trunk flew up into the air in an arc. When it came down it struck Guy across the shoulders, causing him to fall forward onto his face. He was lucky not be crushed, but the blow was glancing and he was knocked aside. Even so it took him a few moments to recover the breath that had been knocked out of him.

When he could manage it he lifted himself up onto his knees to stand. But his head was swimming with dizziness and the earth seemed to be rolling under him like a ship on the sea. He fell forward on his face again. He lay on the ground for a moment, then, determined to survive, forced himself to his knees.

Suddenly he saw a hand offered to him. He took it and was helped to his feet. Guy's vision was still blurred and his senses were confused, but he could just make out the shape of an old woman dressed in a short green cloak trimmed with rabbit fur. She was standing before him smiling sweetly.

'Don't worry. You're safe now,' the old woman soothed. 'I won't let anything happen to you.'

'I must sit down,' the Norman slurred. 'I've been wounded.'

The stranger led him over to a tree. She sat him down with his back to the trunk where he could witness everything taking place in the clearing. The Nathairaí were still locked together in a fighting embrace. Their ancient feud had so overtaken them, the worms hadn't noticed the old woman.

'I'll put a stop to your pain in a moment,' the crone promised.

She was completely ignoring the terrible fight. Before Guy could protest she placed a hand on his cheek. He felt a burning sensation all around the bloody gash and his head cleared a little.

'Who are you?' the Norman asked, still groggy.

'I'm the one who sent for you,' the old woman explained with a cackle.

Without any further explanation she hobbled over to the centre of the clearing. When she got close to the warring worms she raised her staff in the air then spoke in her croaking crone's voice.

'I command you to be quiet.'

The Nathairaí didn't notice her. They just kept hurling spit at each other. So she raised her staff again. When she spoke a second time her words shook the trees with a mighty boom of stern impatience.

'Will you two be silent!'

The worms shivered, uncoiled themselves and shrank away from the crone in fear. Their bulging eyes widened impossibly at the sight of this frail-looking old woman. At last Lochie lifted his head to speak.

'Danu?' he ventured tentatively. 'Lady Danu, is that you?'

Martin heard his companion cry out to him. But he was so breathless and his heart was beating so hard in his ears that he couldn't be sure if she was serious. Did she really think they could run away from danger approaching on both sides?

How could either of them hope to outrun mounted Norman warriors and countless raging Redcaps? He let go of

Oat-Beer's collar and sank to his knees in submission.

That was the very moment the underground fortress spilled out its angry hordes like a stinging swarm of bees hurrying out of the hive to vent their fury. Indeed these Redcaps were very much like bees. They were entirely devoted to their queen and each one carried a sickle for a sting.

Sianan ran to the Breton's side and tried to drag him to his feet. But she couldn't move the man.

'Get up, you fool!' she screamed. 'You must run!'

But Martin had given up all hope of escape. For a man who'd seen countless conflicts and untold dangers on the battlefield, he was, on this occasion, easily disarmed.

So it was to Sianan's everlasting relief that when the Redcaps emerged from their subterranean home the first thing they spied were two Norman warriors mounted on a pair of fine chestnut geldings.

The two warriors sized up the situation in one glance. 'Ride back. Get help!' called one to the other.

His soldier was off in a flash, leaving the first warrior to face the horde alone in a futile gesture of defiance. Futile it was perhaps, but it bought everyone a little time.

The Redcaps had the Norman surrounded in moments. They were armed with every kind of weapon, from long swords to fighting axes to vicious sickles curved like the crescent moon and mounted on short poles. The Norman warrior swallowed hard. He'd faced Saracens of the east who'd been armed with these terrifying blades. Now he wished he'd been the one to ride off for help.

The enemy raised their weapons high as the circle around him tightened. But the blows he expected to rain down on him did not come. Instead the Redcaps raised a chant calling more of their kindred from beneath the Earth. There must have been four hundred of them gathered round the Norman by the time the horde spotted Sianan and Martin.

In a second the underworld warriors had surrounded them also. Then their chant rose to a shout of hatred.

'Ro! Horo! Horo Ro!' they cried as one, spitting contempt with every syllable.

And if Martin had thought he was frightened before he was certain he knew real fear now. These folk were the wildest, most savage fighters it had ever been his misfortune to encounter. Their skin was covered in red tattoos that mimicked the designs he'd seen carved into the walls deep inside their fortress. Their hair was long, matted and unkempt. Their clothes were simple hides tanned to soft leather or of fine doeskin stained from constant wear. They wore a variety of armour thieved from many knights and warriors over a long period of time – a strange mixture of styles, sizes and materials that had been patched together more for adornment than defence.

Their faces were smeared with red mud in patterns and shapes that showed their wild Otherworld eyes to the most fearsome advantage. Most had bare feet. A few wore shoes, taken from Norman victims, no doubt. In their battle rage they each seemed tall and menacing. But none of these warriors would have stood much taller than Martin's shoulder.

As suddenly as they had appeared from underground the Redcaps ceased their chant. Absolute stillness filled the sir. Not a bird call nor a leaf fall interrupted the silence.

Countless pairs of mad staring eyes fixed on their victims as surely as an archer sets his sights upon the target. Martin felt his bowels turning to water with the tension.

As it happened he didn't have the opportunity to lose control of his bodily functions. In a breath the Redcaps fell upon the Norman warrior in a frantic orgy of flesh-hacking and bone-splitting.

The poor man had hardly a chance to scream out. His horse hit the ground before a froth of fear had formed at its mouth. Sickles raised high to swing down with sickening slashes as the warrior was torn into a thousand tiny pieces of steaming flesh.

These gruesome chunks were flung triumphantly aloft or impaled on the keen points of the Redcaps' deadly sickles. There was a joyous rush as every underworld fighter shoved forward to dip his hat in the bloody mess.

Martin fell to his knees. Sianan closed her eyes, unable to watch. The whole spectacle must have lasted less than twenty breaths but it seemed to her to go on for hours.

When at last the Redcaps finished their sport with that poor Norman the entire crowd gathered silently around Sianan and the Breton. Then they started up their deadly chant again, singing softly at first then rising steadily to an unstoppable crescendo. And long before it had reached that savage peak Martin wished they'd just get on with it and put an end to this torture. He took Sianan's hand.

'Thank you for saving me from the worms,' he shouted above the war chant. 'I'm sorry it came to this. Take care of Oat-Beer for me.'

'I'm not sure even an immortal can be ripped to shreds by those sickles and yet survive,' she admitted. 'I afraid Oat-Beer may have to fend for himself.'

The morning was far advanced as Lanfranc rode along at the head of the column with his prisoner in tow. The knight hadn't spoken a word to anyone all morning. He'd been lost in deep contemplation.

For our dear Lanfranc had realised he'd fallen in love with the Lady Mirim. She was everything he'd ever hoped for in a wife. She was tough, intelligent, determined and courageous. Her winning wit intrigued him. Her adventurous spirit had earned his respect. Her down-to-earth directness was refreshing, though perhaps a little too forceful for his liking. But that was a minor thing, he told himself. She'd soon learn to curb her ways once they were married.

Not only was she the most beautiful woman he'd ever laid eyes on, she had royal connections. Well, that's to say she had a letter signed by King John, which was a start. A wife such as Mirim could change his life. If he married her he might see himself returned to court in England or Normandy.

Best of all she was a widow with a claim to lands. Her wealth could be the very tonic for his troubles. With Mirim by his side Lanfranc imagined his life turned round for the better. For the first time in years he was touched by a very Norman twinge of ambition.

He allowed his mind to wander to a future where he had no debts to pay, a lordly land to administer and a gorgeous woman to share his bed. It was a sweet daydream which swallowed his mind completely.

He was so lost in his daydream that he didn't hear the galloping scout at first. The rider cried out his warning in a frantic voice. It was a rude awakening for our dear Lanfranc. Like it or not he was dragged out of his pleasant musings.

'There's trouble ahead!' the scout screamed.

The lord muttered an obscenity at the man's grating shriek.

'Can't I enjoy my private thoughts even for a few seconds without some bloody interruption?' he grumbled in a low voice so no one else would hear.

Then he reluctantly raised his eyes to face his scout. 'What trouble?'

'Strangers,' the scout reported. 'Strangers wearing red caps.'

Then, without pausing to halt his mount or offer a fuller

report, the scout rode on toward the rear of the column.

'Where are you off to?' Lanfranc demanded to know.

'Jerusalem,' came the reply.

The scout didn't look back and he was never seen again.

'Very well,' the Norman replied as he held up his hand to halt the column. 'I'll ride on to see what the trouble is.'

'Redcaps?' Gusán stuttered. 'Did I hear him say Redcaps?'

'Sounded like it,' Stephen shrugged.

Gusán planted his feet firmly on the ground and refused to walk another step. However, even though he dug his heels into the ground, he was still dragged along by Lanfranc's horse.

'I'm not going where there's Redcaps!' the Irishman shrieked.

'What kind of a warrior are you?' his Norman captor snapped back.

'One who wishes to live to see the dawn,' the brigand replied. 'I'll stay here with the others. Don't make me go with you.'

Stephen held up his hand and this time the column came to a stop. Mirim looked up from her own daydream as her mount shuffled to a halt.

'What's happening?' she called out. 'Why have we stopped?'

'Trouble ahead,' Lanfranc answered. 'You should stay here with your servants. It looks like brigands again. Don't worry, I'll deal with it.'

Without waiting to hear her protests he spurred his horse so that Gusán had to run to keep up whether he liked it or not. Once or twice the poor man nearly stumbled as the pace quickened.

'Have a care!' he cried out. 'Your warhorse has twice as many legs as I do. And *she* doesn't know what's in store for her.'

Lanfranc ignored the protests, inwardly pleased the brigand was in discomfort. But his satisfaction was short-lived. All of a sudden they came to a bend in the path and there, much to Lanfranc's surprise, were hundreds of warriors indeed wearing red hats as had been reported. And they were slowly closing in on two unarmed wayfarers.

Our dear chivalrous Norman didn't stop to consider what to do. With a broad sweep he unsheathed his sword, then with another he sliced through the ropes which bound Gusán to his saddle.

'Don't let that one escape,' he told his sergeant-at-arms. 'Guard him well. I'll sort this out.'

Lanfranc spurred his horse on but the Redcaps didn't seem to take any notice of him. So, raising his blade high above his head, he called out the name of his sword. He usually found that was enough to draw anyone's attention.

'Tóla!' he cried.

The entire mass of warriors froze as if touched by the fingers of an icy paralysing wind. Then one by one they turned round to face the bold challenger, the two intruders forgotten for the moment.

There was malice in each pair of Otherworldly eyes and a rasping hiss at the back of every Redcap throat. That's how Lanfranc got his first sight of these folk. And he was immediately put in mind of dæmons.

'Leave these travellers alone, you devils, or I'll unleash my blade upon your throats.'

The Redcaps stepped back, seduced by the enchantment woven by the Enticer spirit which dwelled within the Norman's sword. Only one of their number dared defy Lanfranc.

He was a little larger and fiercer-looking than the rest. He was probably a leader of some sort, or perhaps he aspired to be. He certainly carried a more ornate sickle than his brethren. The elegantly curved blade was inlaid with a gold filigree of spiral design.

The large Redcap roared in his most terrifying voice then

charged forward, sickle raised high. It was clear he intended to sweep the Norman off his horse with one heavy downward stroke.

Sianan looked away, unable to watch the devastating cut of the fearsome weapon. But she needn't have cringed. Under the protection of Tóla, our boy Lanfranc was too quick for the creature.

The knight spurred a subtle signal to his warhorse. She obediently took a step to the left. The sickle missed its mark. And before it had struck the ground Lanfranc swept his sword round in a graceful arc. The blade connected with the nape of the Redcap's neck, neatly and almost noiselessly decapitating him.

The other Redcaps hissed with horror, shrieking wildly to one another in their own spitting language. Then in less time than it takes to draw three startled breaths they began deserting the scene.

Sianan looked up, unable to believe what was happening. On the ground there was a Redcap lying in a spreading pool of his own blood. One of Aoife's hitherto invincible warriors had been put to death.

The Redcaps were of the immortal kind. Yet here before her very eyes Sianan could plainly see that one of their kindred had been killed. This was an important development which gave her another reason to make to the Killibegs with all speed.

She had no time to realise the implications for her own unnatural span of years. The flaw in her immortality would not concern her until later. But once again I'm skipping ahead of my tale. Forgive me.

Like flocks of seagulls taking to the wing the Redcaps dispersed. A wave of terror such as they'd never known overtook them. Some threw off various bits of assorted armour or their shields as they ran. Others abandoned their sickles and their swords. But not a one among them dropped his cap.

'Stop in the name of King John!' Lanfranc commanded.

But the dæmon-warriors wouldn't have stopped even if they'd understood a word of what he'd said. Nor would they have halted even if they'd had any respect for King John. In seconds they were melting into the woods to vanish completely.

'Why do so few of the folk of this country ever manage to work up the courage to face me?' the Norman whispered to himself in frustration. 'I haven't had a real fight since I landed on these shores.'

'You're a bloody hero!' Gusán whooped, tears running down his cheeks for joy and relief. 'They'll sing songs about you, Sir Lanfranc, my dear saviour. You'll be remembered forever as the man who beat off a whole army of Redcaps without so much as a flinch.'

'Be quiet!' the Norman demanded, losing his patience. 'And keep your place.'

The knight was beginning to feel a headache erupting in the centre of his forehead. All this yelling really didn't agree with him.

Gusán leaned against the rump of Lanfranc's horse to catch his breath and take in what he'd seen. Finally the brigand sank to his knees, overcome by events, and there he took the opportunity to rest.

By now Lanfranc was already in a heated discussion with the two rescued strangers. A red dog was barking defensively, frothing at the mouth with excitement.

'Call off that animal!' the Norman demanded.

Martin reached into the sack of food he'd pilfered from the Redcap stronghold. He placed another piece of dried meat under Oat-Beer's nose. The dog took the tasty morsel then sat down to chew at it enthusiastically.

'Now be quiet. There's a good lad,' the Breton admonished him.

'Who are you? And what's your business travelling this road?' Lanfranc demanded.

Sianan stepped forward, careful to keep her cloak over her head so the foreigner could not glimpse her Otherworldly features.

'I am the abbess of the community of Dun Gur,' she told him. 'We're travelling to the Killibegs. And we have no time to waste with pleasantries. I have important news for the elders there concerning the force of Redcaps you've just driven off.'

The Norman regarded her with suspicion as he sheathed his sword. Sianan immediately noticed the change which came over him. Suddenly he didn't seem quite so intimidating, and when he spoke again there was a waver in his voice that hadn't been there earlier.

'Everyone seems to be going to the Killibegs,' he mumbled. Then he turned his attention to her companion. 'What about you? Unless I'm mistaken, you're wearing the tunic of a Norman foot soldier. Are you a deserter? Who's your lord?'

The Breton stepped forward to bow. He was still formulating his lie as he straightened up.

'My name is Martin. I was travelling with the entourage of Guy d'Alville. Our company was attacked in the forest. Many warriors were slaughtered. Out of a hundred I fear I may be the sole survivor. I was lucky to escape with my life.'

'Was it that band of frightful brigands?'

'No, my lord. Something far more frightening than mere men.'

'You encountered the lion?' Lanfranc gasped, his hand reaching to the hilt of his sword again.

Martin shook his head in confusion. 'What lion?'

'Never mind. It's a long story. What was it your company ran into? What could have routed and slaughtered a hundred Norman men-at-arms?'

Sianan grabbed the Breton's arm to silence him and answered Lanfranc herself.

'An army is massing to attack the Norman and Irish settlements of this island. If we waste more precious time standing about discussing the matter, they will overrun the country. I must get to the Killibegs.'

'What's your business there?'

'There are folk in that community who may be able to help prevent this army from marching. It's the gathering place of all the warrior-chiefs of the west for the feast of Samhain Oidche. I must go on with all speed. I have no more time to waste. Please excuse my haste. I am truly grateful to you for rescuing us.'

Mirim rode up just as the abbess mentioned the Killibegs. She waited until Sianan had finished speaking then cut in before Lanfranc had a chance to ask any more questions.

'We're journeying to that community,' the desert woman announced. 'You may travel with us if you will guide us on the way. Only Gusán here has ever been to Killibegs.'

'He won't be able to help you, my lady,' Sianan bowed. 'The Killibegs is not a permanent settlement. Each year before the feast of Samhain the people of that community find a new place to sit out the winter. This year it will be at the summit of an ancient rath. They are working to make the buildings habitable even now. Samhain Oidche is nearly upon us.'

'Will you take us there? I am seeking William FitzWilliam.'

'The Orchard Keeper?' Sianan asked. 'I know him well.'

'I have urgent letters for him,' Mirim informed the woman. Sianan took a step forward and bowed again.

'I will guide you to the Killibegs in exchange for your protection. But we must go with all speed.'

Lochie laid his head on the ground, his bottom lip drooping onto the grass. Isleen stretched out down beside him, contrite and subservient to the withered crone. The bent old woman straightened up as best she could.

Then she laughed.

Lochie grumbled with indignation, though it wasn't loud enough that the ancient one might take offence. He didn't want to do anything to set the Goddess Danu off into another fury. The last time they'd upset her she'd changed them into the hideous forms they now inhabited.

'My lady,' he ventured, 'it has been so long since we were placed under your punishment. We've learned our lesson. We won't cause any more trouble in the world. I promise.'

'I promise also. I give my oath on it,' Isleen added hastily.

'I'd almost forgotten about you two,' the crone told them. 'It was all so long ago.'

'So long ago,' Lochie echoed.

'We've suffered so much in that filthy well under the ground,' Isleen told her. 'It was dark and damp. There was no decent food to be had.'

'We had to sustain ourselves on earthworms, frogs and little fishes that strayed into our subterranean spring from the loughs to the north,' her companion added.

'I heard you escaped once before,' the old woman noted.

'That was an age ago,' Lochie replied. 'Three hundred winters have passed since then. And we only got a few bony cows for our trouble that time. If we hadn't been tricked by that cursed Columcille into returning to the well we'd still be wandering about the land feeding on fresh flesh.'

'You've gone on a terrible rampage since you were let out this time, I'm told,' the crone reminded him.

'We're very sorry,' Isleen cut in contritely. 'It's just that we'd been locked up for so long we went a bit wild once we were released. We had a lot of frustration to get out of our souls.'

'We'd been locked up too long,' Lochie ventured. 'If you don't mind me saying so.'

'Hold your lolling great tongue!' Isleen hissed at him.

'What's that you say?' the old woman asked. 'Did you say you'd been imprisoned for too long? Are you questioning the wisdom of Danu?'

'No, lady!' both worms sputtered.

'He only meant that we'd long ago learned to behave ourselves,' Isleen explained. 'We'll be good from now on. We'd be willing to make oaths upon it.'

'I'm glad to hear that. But I don't have the patience to hear your pitiful pleas for clemency. I have urgent business to attend to.'

As the crone spoke, a great black raven flew down from the trees and landed at her feet.

'Sárán!' Lochie exclaimed. 'Thank you for bringing the Lady Danu to us. I am eternally in your debt. Please beg her on our behalf to consider releasing us from the terrible bonds of punishment.'

The old woman laughed. The raven cackled. Both were obviously very amused at the worm's words. Lochie didn't see the joke.

'Lady Danu, is it not enough that we have suffered our sentence for so long? Have we not paid for our misdeeds? Is it not time for you to grant us our freedom?'

'You have made a serious mistake,' the raven told him derisively.

'I thought we'd agreed to put the past behind us, Sárán? Why have you changed your mind?'

'My name is Sciathan Cog,' the bird informed him flatly. 'I do not answer to the name my mother gave me.'

'You filthy scavenger!' Isleen spat. 'You always held us in contempt. You've turned the Lady Danu against us!'

'You can't seem to help making fools of yourselves, can you?'

Cog laughed.

At that the old woman stepped forward. She threw off the cowl that covered her head, and the air exploded in bright red light which stung the worms' eyes. Both of them had to turn away. But Guy didn't flinch, although he was awestruck as the light engulfed the old crone in such intensity that every tree, leaf and bough was bathed in the furious glow. Even when the old woman's bent back straightened he made no show of his astonishment.

When her eyes brightened to a deeply sparkling green, he pretended he didn't notice. When her shoulders broadened as if a weight had been lifted from them, he forced a yawn. When her skin smoothed of all wrinkles, her lips swelled to a sensuous fullness and her green cloak transformed into a gorgeous flowing gown of the same colour, he turned away as if he hadn't noticed.

'Don't you recognise me?' the woman asked the worms as the red glow faded.

The Nathairaí both stared up at her. As the ruddy luminescence dissipated, the same tint of colour lingered as an echo in the woman's long curling hair.

'My name is Aoife,' she declared. 'I am the daughter of Brocan, the King of Sleep, who you tempted into eternal slumber. And I have returned to share this part of my Immrama with you.'

ISLANÞ OF THE SAINTS

I don't care what the travelling mystics claim. They're all disgruntled petty-minded individuals in any case. How many times have I heard some wandering monk proudly declare that he thoroughly comprehends the Immrama?

Those kind of people reason we should all endeavour to end the timeless cycle by breaking free of the ever-turning wheel of existence. They often take to the monastic life seeking solitude from the world. They imagine they will better witness the whole of creation by separating themselves from it. But doing nothing is not the way to God. Not a God who dressed us in fidgety flesh in the first place.

Those spirits of enticement and fear I mentioned earlier can't be simply starved to death by separating oneself from the source of such experiences. Solitude diminishes the hold Enticers may have over us but it can't snuff the spirits out entirely. Indeed, the yearning for enticements grows ever stronger the longer the separation, the more austere the solitude. As for Frighteners, they thrive on the soul who embarks on a secluded life.

Lochie and Isleen had become so tainted by the Frightener spirits attached to them while they'd dwelled within the well that they had transformed into the very embodiment of fear. Their isolation had accentuated that effect. All the enticements of this world had become but a bitter memory for them. All

300

their longing had boiled down to a yearning to return to the days of their youth. What folly! Yet not so different from many folk who call themselves holy.

The truly holy ones of this world are those who know of the mystical journey but don't feel the need to convince anyone else of it. Indeed, they often won't even bring the subject up in polite company. They're simply content to enjoy the voyage. Or to let the Immrama take them where it will. The voyage is the story.

That's what Caoimhin had just begun to understand about his own life. So many unexpected circumstances had arisen since he'd arrived in Ireland, he no longer questioned where the path was leading him, he simply followed it.

He and his two brother monks set out before dawn that day, hoping to cover as much ground as possible. But they were also eager to find some shelter from the driving rain that had set in during the night.

Since Caoimhin's encounter with the shining blue lady he was immune to the mindless chatter of his companions. But he'd started to cough in the night as the cold driving rain had chilled him to the bone. The damp air was settling on his lungs and he wasn't up to travelling far that day. But he wasn't one to complain. He grew silent as they trudged along, conserving his energy for a coming battle with the cough.

An hour after they set out he and two companions chanced upon a young woman bringing in her cows to the milking. Caoimhin was not surprised by her response to their questions but he was certainly relieved they might have a warm place to sleep that night.

'You'll find the island you seek in the middle of the lough down there,' the woman told them. 'I've never been there myself for women are forbidden to take the boat across. But if you follow this path it'll lead you to the waterside where the boatman awaits.'

They thanked her and hurried off with renewed enthusiasm for their adventure. And they hadn't gone much further when they glimpsed the waters of the lough dimly sparkling in the reflection of the grey dawn.

The rain hadn't ceased but a break in the clouds illuminated the land all around so that the countryside could have been mistaken for the plains of Heaven. Caoimhin took in the sight without comment. He simply followed on after the Welshmen, content to be taken wherever the road led him. He could feel a fever beginning to grow across his forehead, so he was glad a sanctuary was in sight.

They came to the edge of the lough an hour after dawn. By the time they got there a dozen hopeful pilgrims were already milling about the beached boats. Everyone had their shawls wrapped tight about their heads to keep out the cold.

The dangling corners of long green and brown cloaks dragged along the ground as each man paced about to keep warm, mumbling personal prayers as he went. There were no women to be seen anywhere.

Caoimhin coughed. His lungs were succumbing to the wet, cold, heavy air, becoming tighter by the minute. Pebbles crunched beneath his boots but he didn't notice the sound. His gaze was firmly set on the small island wrapped in a wreath of fog and grey water.

Brother Overton paddled about in the icy shallows for a while then squatted to splash water on his face as if he didn't mind the cold at all.

The Welsh monk, Lewyn, approached one of the boatmen, an old man with long flowing white hair and a belly-length beard.

'Will you take us across to the pilgrim island?'

The Gael shook his head soberly. Then he made a loud declaration in a steady gravelled voice.

'I don't take any man who hasn't got a small white pebble on his person.'

A murmur passed around the assembled Gaels and they moved in closer to listen.

The boatman stared intensely at Lewyn. Lewyn stared back, rising to the unspoken challenge. After a short while their eyes stung but each man still dared the other to blink.

At last the Welshman could take no more. He shut his eyelids with a slow squint then pushed the heel of each hand into the sockets.

'We'll find some pebbles and be back in a moment,' he said grudgingly.

The Gael laughed uproariously. Every other Irishman in earshot joined in.

'Not here you won't,' the boatman stated confidently. 'There hasn't been a white pebble found in this lough for generations.'

Lewyn shook his head. 'There must be three white pebbles somewhere hereabouts. The shore is littered with tiny stones.'

'He's telling you the truth,' Overton confirmed. 'There's a few scattered grey rocks, many darker stones and countless black pebbles. But the whitest thing in the water at the moment is my toes.'

'Where do we find white pebbles?' Lewyn sighed as he turned back to the boatman.

'I have a bag of them,' the Gael replied. 'I'll give you three so you can be taking a seat in my boat.'

Lewyn frowned in confusion at the ways of the Irish. Still, he was relieved this fellow would take them across to the holy isle so he offered a friendly smile.

'Have you any Norman farthings?' the boatman asked.

The Welshman's smile turned back into a suspicious frown. 'We've a bag of them,' he stated.

'It won't cost you that much!' the Irishman guffawed. 'One farthing for each pebble. That's a reasonable price.'

'Three farthings!'

The gathered crowd muttered as one, confirming the fairness of the bargain.

'You don't want to risk the boatman's curse, do you?' an old farmer called out.

'Of course not,' Lewyn replied quickly. 'Has he some skill at cursing?'

'He cursed the toenails off my father once,' a younger man noted.

'He cursed my uncle's manhood,' another added. 'And the old man never spent a night with another woman as long as he lived.'

'Your father was in his nineties,' a third chirped up. 'It's little wonder he'd misplaced his manhood.'

'But the curse did its work. There's no denying it.'

Lewyn held up his hand to still the argument he could see was brewing.

'I don't want the burden of a curse on my head,' he exclaimed.

Then the Welshman placed the back of his right hand against his forehead to show the palm to everyone present. This was the way Normans assured folk that they were sincere. But the gesture had an alarming effect on the assembled Gaels.

Most of the Irishmen hissed or spat. Some started making strange gestures of their own in the air before their faces. Only one man – the boatman – made any approach to the Welshman and he held his left arm up in defence as if expecting a vicious blow.

'Have you got a headache?' the Irishman shrieked with genuine fear in his voice.

'No,' Lewyn shrugged. 'I was just giving you the palm of my hand. It's to show I've nothing to hide. I don't want you to curse us. I don't want to upset you at all. A curse is a terrible thing to inspire in another human spirit.'

'No headache?' the boatman insisted.

'Not even a twinge.'

'No females and no headaches allowed on the holy island,' another Gael added.

'Three farthings it is then,' Lewyn stated as he reached into his pouch. He retrieved the coins, then with appropriate solemnity counted them out into his hand. 'Three farthings,' he declared.

'Three farthings,' he confirmed again as the coins dropped one by one into the boatman's palm.

'Three farthings,' the Gael nodded and grasped his hand tightly round them.

'Three white pebbles,' the Welshman demanded.

'Three white pebbles.'

The boatman reached into his pouch to retrieve the expensive stones.

Lewyn took the three white pebbles. He immediately handed one to Overton. The half-Saxon studied it for a moment then quickly put it away in his own pouch.

'That cost a bloody fortune,' he muttered indignantly. 'Three-quarters of a penny for three white stones. I told you to let me deal with the Gaels. But you wouldn't listen.'

Lewyn rolled his eyes skyward in a silent prayer for patience, then he gave the other pebble to Caoimhin, offering, as he did so, an opinion.

'Clearly this custom is merely just a manifestation of the implied but as yet, in my opinion, unsubstantiated phenomenon known as a religious experience.'

'Three farthings,' Caoimhin sighed with resignation.

'Three more bloody mystics,' the boatman hummed, happy now to show them to their seats.

'We only have nine coins left,' the young monk reminded his Welsh friend. 'Perhaps I'd better take care of them.'

Lewyn untied the pouch from his belt without a hint of protest and passed it to the young Benedictine.

'I willingly give them into your keeping, Master Caoimhin.'

That done, they made their way to the boat. As he was stepping into the vessel the Welshman felt a strong hand on his shoulder. It was the boatman.

'Are you certain none of you has a headache?' the Gael asked suspiciously.

'I'm sure.'

'Very well then.'

'I have a head cold,' the young scribe admitted. 'And I can feel a cough rising in my chest which may prove nasty.'

The boatman squeezed Lewyn's shoulder tighter as he squinted at the younger monk.

'But you've no headache?'

'None.'

The boatman released his grip. The Welshman shook himself of the touch.

The three travelling brothers were the last of nine to take their places in the boat. As soon as they had settled, the boatman took up a long pole from the rear of the tiny vessel. Then he gracefully pushed the boat away from the shore.

Caoimhin sat opposite a young, wild-eyed, bedraggled Gael who smirked for a long time at the Benedictine before he finally opened his mouth to speak.

'You've never been across to the holy isle, have you?'

Caoimhin shook his head in confirmation.

'I didn't think so,' the Irishman grinned, showing all his teeth and the wide rotted spaces between them. 'Are you seeking for something in particular?'

'We're searching for the famous holy man called Finbar.'

'Then your three farthings were well spent. For it's Finbar who's our boatman.'

Lewyn looked up in surprise.

'Are you Saint Finbar?' Caoimhin asked shyly.

'Three pebbles are a burden best shared,' the boatman replied enigmatically. 'I have a bag full of them. The weight of them bears down hard upon my shoulder.'

'Ask him a question,' the young Gael whispered to the Benedictine brother. 'He'll answer anything you put to him. There's nothing he doesn't think he knows.'

'The price of my wisdom is one white pebble for each question,' the boatman announced. 'One question each.'

The three monks cast their eyes at one another, silently agreeing Lewyn should speak first. Without a moment's hesitation the Welshman spoke.

'What's God like?'

'Are you trying to trick me into using a metaphor?' the boatman barked.

But before Lewyn had a chance to reply, the Gael continued. 'Metaphor is the work of Satan. No educated man indulges in it. It poisons the mind with pride in the same way a woman poisons a man's loins with her lust. And, as every Devil-fearing Christian knows, metaphor is the horrible hearth fire where Satan warms his porridge before he sets off to work each morning.'

The boatman-saint wiped a little of the froth of excitement from the corner of his mouth. Then he leaned on his pole and serenely pushed the tiny vessel onwards.

After a few moments he spoke again. This time his speech came from the heart in an unexpected confessional flood. 'I admit it. Forty years of solitude, living the life of a boating hermit, hasn't endowed me with a single ounce of holiness. I'm not any more saintly or humble for my self-imposed retreat from the world. I haven't developed a gift for miraculous healing or for visions of the future.'

No one spoke. All eyes were politely averted. No one can be comfortable when forced to hear the confession of a saint. But

Finbar paid their discomfort no heed. He launched into his story with immeasurable regret in his voice.

'When I was a young man the Dark One had an icy grip on my balls. Ravaged by guilt, shame and fear I didn't dare let the thought of a woman cross my mind lest I end up roasting my bare arse before the bottom-basting breakfast fires of Beelzebub.'

He pushed on the long bladeless oar again.

'I wandered the world not so much searching for God but rather running from the Devil.'

'And did you find God or Satan?' Caoimhin asked.

'That's two questions.' the boatman snapped. 'You're only permitted one question each.'

The young Benedictine shrugged. 'Did you find God?'

Finbar took Caoimhin's pebble before he answered.

'Yes.'

Then the boatman went back to pushing on his oar.

'Well tell us what he's like,' Lewyn pressed.

'You've already asked me that.'

'You didn't answer.'

The boatman winked. 'But I did, you see. I told you exactly what he's like.'

Lewyn frowned. 'You're a bloody liar! You never found God. What kind of a holy man charges a farthing for his wisdom and a ride in his boat?'

'A well-fed, satisfied holy man with a healthy appreciation for the manner in which God has arranged his creation. That's what kind of holy man I am. I'm never going hungry again. I'm abstaining from abstinence. That rubbish is for witless wandering mystics like yourself.'

Lewyn fumed, repeating the word 'Liar' under his breath for the rest of the journey. But Finbar simply grinned. He'd noticed Overton hadn't asked his question but he was certain these three weren't much of a challenge.

As the boat struck the pebbled beach of the island the half-Saxon leaned close to the boatman.

'Where lives the holiest man you know of?' Overton asked as he handed over his pebble.

'On the other side of this island,' the boatman replied solemnly. 'His name is Holy Michael and he's the holiest man who ever set a holy foot on the holy soil of Ireland. He lives in a holy cave and he wears nothing but the poorest and holiest of garments. Nor does he eat any more food than is absolutely necessary for his survival and the continuation of his holy reputation.'

'We'll go and visit him then,' Caoimhin stated.

'He's probably still asleep. He got himself mightily drunk last night. Made a bit of a fool of himself.'

'The holiest man you know got himself drunk last night?' Lewyn cut in incredulously.

'Mad drunk he was. By God, that Michael can murder a barrel of beer like none other. But he doesn't look after his personal appearance. That's how he came to be known as Saint Michael of the Unkempt Beard. Last night, just before he threw up his dinner and collapsed, he swallowed a bucket of the finest ale without once coming up for air.'

'We're wasting our time on this island,' Lewyn cried. 'Will you take us back to the other shore so we may continue our journey?'

'Have you three white pebbles?'

'Are you going to charge us three farthings to take us back?' the outraged monk shrieked.

'I am.'

'Why didn't you tell us that before we left?'

'You didn't ask me. And as it is I've answered a whole lot of questions without demanding payment in pebbles. So count yourselves lucky I'm in a generous mood.'

The boatman put his arm around Lewyn. 'What use are

farthings to you when you're out there amongst the western savages? They don't value them. If you had a hundred farthings you couldn't buy yourself a fartful of flour out there in the wilds. I'm just relieving you of an unnecessary burden.'

'When do you return to the far shore?' Overton asked.

'Give me time to get a few drinks into my skin,' Finbar told him. 'It's a mighty cold morning to be punting out across the water with a curragh full of tight-fisted mystics. Bring your farthings. I'll have three white pebbles set aside for you.'

'Let's visit this Holy Michael while we're waiting,' Caoimhin suggested. 'I've something on my mind I'd like to ask him.'

Lewyn grunted.

Lochie and Isleen were so stunned that this woman wasn't the Goddess Danu that they simply lay where they were in wonder for a long time. All that while neither of them made any sound at all. But their surprise soon turned to rage at the way Aoife had tricked them.

'You were nothing but a slip of a girl when I first took you under my wing,' Isleen snapped when the shock had at last subsided. 'And you're no better now.'

'But things have changed since you first went off down the well,' the red-haired woman declared. 'The Redcaps elected me to be their sovereign. They were Fir-Bolg once just like my kinfolk. My father was the king of our people. So according to the Brehon laws of succession I'm eligible to rule. I'm already known far and wide as the Queen of the Night.'

'The Redcaps were of the Sen Erainn tribes from Inis Mór,' Lochie noted. 'They might have been Fir-Bolg but there was enmity between your father's folk and their king, as I recall.'

'Time heals all wounds,' Aoife reminded him with a reprimanding wag of her finger. 'You'd do well to bear that in mind.'

She stepped toward them, utterly unconcerned by their wrath. 'You see, my dear worms,' she continued, 'I've vanquished my feeding spirits. They work for me now. And in return I see they're well looked after. My Enticer and my Frightener feast better than they ever have before. So they're content to aid me when I call on them for assistance.'

'What have you got planned?' Lochie cut in. 'I've an awful feeling you're driven by a terrible ambition.'

'I intend to make a few changes in my life,' Aoife informed him, her voice full of girlish excitement. 'My Enticer suggested it to me. The Frightener wasn't so keen on the idea to begin with. But now we all strive together toward a single aim.'

'You'll never be anything more than a foolish child with a greedy heart,' Isleen declared.

'Don't be so quick to criticise. You're the one walking about in the form of an ugly worm.' Aoife squinted, then cocked her head in mock realisation. 'You don't really walk, do you? It's more like a slither.'

'I'd be happy to teach you a thing or two about slithering,' Isleen screamed, rising up and opening her mouth wide.

But before the angry worm had a chance to strike, Aoife raised her staff high in the air. A great bolt of bright red lightning charged out from the tip. Like a whip it struck the Nathair across the face. The worm fell back shrieking with agony.

'Don't burn me!' Isleen cried out, cowering in fear.

Aoife observed the mighty creature with dispassion, a wry smile on her face. When the worm had calmed down a little and stopped her whimpering, the Queen of the Night issued a stern warning in a voice that boomed through the woods.

'You behave yourself and I won't need to punish you.'

'I'll behave. I promise!'

'What about you?' the queen asked, turning to Lochie.

'I'm as well behaved as ever,' he hastily replied. 'I wouldn't dream of challenging you, I wouldn't.'

'You can see I've spent a long time nurturing my Frightener. He's quite impressive, isn't he?'

'Very impressive,' Isleen assured her. 'Terror seeps from your very pores. I'll wager the Redcaps tremble when they worship at your feet.'

'That's right. And soon enough all the folk of this land will do the same. I've been caring for the growth of both my spirits. Though I haven't decided which I favour. What do you think? Enticer or Frightener?'

As she spoke Aoife's face transformed into the most glorious shining countenance Guy had ever laid eyes upon. Every strand of her hair was perfection. Her lips were redder than any rose, her skin as pale as fresh cream, her eyes as green as a springtime garden and twice as alluring.

'Well?' she asked the Norman. 'Do you like what you see?'

For once in his life d'Alville was speechless.

He was utterly awed by her seemingly pure beauty and the giddy joy of being in her company. He bowed deeply, and while his eyes were lowered he allowed himself to stare at the exciting shape of her legs outlined in the folds of her gown. His heart beat faster as her overwhelming presence drowned him in a wave of desire.

'I've never known a woman like you,' he told her, his voice cracking slightly.

And I can attest that he was telling the truth. He didn't care Aoife might be some beast wrapped in a snakeskin of enchantment. The scent of roses wafted round her. The promise of other pleasures beckoned with her every tiny gesture.

Guy experienced a longing to touch this woman even if it

were only with the very tip of one finger. For she was joy, ecstasy and worldly delight enfolded into one breathtaking creature.

Then just as suddenly as the glow of wonder had descended upon Queen Aoife it disappeared. She was still beautiful, make no mistake about that. Her dreamlike allure lingered on. But it wasn't as intense or all-pervading as it had been a few moments earlier.

The queen threw her head back with delight as she laughed at her stunned audience.

'I've been a busy girl,' she hummed, overjoyed at her own mastery of enchantment. 'Of course, I've still a lot of work to do before I attain my ultimate goal.'

'You wish to be the High-Queen of Ireland?' Lochie guessed.

Aoife scoffed at him. 'Don't be a fool. I've bigger fish to fry. Ireland is such a bloody backwater. Nothing ever happens here any more. Not like the old days.'

'So you have an ambition to become a goddess?' Isleen gasped. 'You'll build your strength here in this land, sure enough. But you have your sights set on the wider world.'

'Now you're thinking like the scheming female I used to know in the old days,' Aoife smiled. 'There may be some hope for you yet.'

'What do you mean?'

'Danu is asleep,' the queen explained. 'None dare wake Her. You know what Her temper's like. In the meantime you're trapped in this form until She's ready to open Her pretty peepers again. But I wouldn't count on Her remembering you two in Her dreams.'

Aoife's tone softened. It was time to win over these two as allies.

'The Lady Danu is as forgetful as She ever was. Few folk bother to worship Her these days. Even fewer ever call on Her

313

for help. Even when they do She doesn't respond. Almost none who are living have ever encountered Her. Apart from us of course. Do you know what happens to a goddess once the decline sets in?'

'She sleeps more and walks the world less,' Lochie replied. 'All the ancient ones turn to slumbering after the weight of the passing seasons has become too great to bear. And She's older than all of us or any of the other gods and goddesses. She's the Mother of the Gods.'

'Indeed,' Aoife nodded. 'But Ireland stands in desperate need of a goddess of Her stature in these trying times.'

'What of the Morrigán? What of Bride and Eriu? What of Boann and Banba?' Isleen asked. 'And where is Fodhla? Are they all asleep?'

'They are slumbering or they're gradually losing interest in the world,' Aoife confirmed. 'They're the most venerable of the immortals after Danu. But they're fading into the Otherworld and there they indulge the entreaties of mortals less and less.'

'I can't believe the Morrigán would ever fade from this world,' Lochie objected. 'She loves battle too much. And there will always be battle here.'

'It's true,' the queen agreed. 'The Morrigán will always have the battle-slain to feed on. Her position cannot be challenged. But even she sleeps more and feasts less. She cares less for the mortal kind now than she ever has. I'm sure she won't object to a new goddess who promises to stir up war and save her the bother. It'll be a small matter to bring her into alliance with me.'

'What of the others?' Isleen countered. 'They'll soon wake when they discover what you're up to. Then you'll have all the old goddesses against you.'

'Bride has been adopted by the Christians. Saint Bridget they call her, Midwife to the Mother of Christ. She seems content enough with their petty adoration. Eriu is isolated, under siege from the Normans. So she won't oppose anyone who plans to stop the advance of the foreigners. Boann is still about tending to the cows. But folk are beginning to forget her and she's become as witless as any milk-giver in her old age.'

'That lot were already on the way out when we were turned into worms,' Lochie agreed. 'The coming of the Gaels was accompanied by the strains of mourning music for them.'

'The ancient Eolaí will sleep more and more,' Aoife confirmed. 'In the future there'll be room for younger deities to take their places. Such as myself.'

It didn't take Caoimhin and his companions long to find the holy man's cave by the southern shore. Deep, dark and depressingly damp it was.

Its entrance lay where the lough waters lapped the little island. And no wonder this saint was left alone for so much of the day. The whole place reeked of stale ale and the congealed sweat of an old tankard-tosser. The three companions stood at the mouth of that cave for a long while.

They each wondered which of them should go in first and thereby risk the everlasting contempt of his own nostrils. But only Caoimhin had anything pressing to ask of the holy man. The other two had lost interest in this unfruitful journey. Perhaps if he'd not had a head full of mucus to filter out the stink, our young adventurer might not have gone in either.

But he also had a scribe's curiosity to drive him on. So he blessed his stuffy nose then got down on his hands and knees to crawl into the cave. Let us not forget everything was new to him. He was walking his first free steps in the wide world. Or in this case crawling. In any event, when you're young you'll do almost anything for a bit of entertainment.

Caoimhin struggled along the cave passage until he caught a glimpse of firelight. Then he heard a pained groan followed by a discreet yet unmistakeable belch. In front of the fire was a man lain out on his back with his hands on his chest in an attitude of prayer.

'Excuse me,' the young Benedictine ventured. 'I'm sorry to disturb you.'

'Are you really?' came the reply in a voice both sonorous and masterful.

'I am.'

'Well bugger off, then. I drank too much last night. I'm having a devil of a time keeping off this headache.'

'I was told women and headaches are banned from this island,' Caoimhin noted, hoping to lead the conversation on. 'Is that true?'

'It is. And well you know it. What kind of a fool asks a question he already knows the answer to?'

'Sorry.'

'Now bugger off.'

'But I've travelled far to hear the words of a wise and holy man such as yourself. Won't you sit with me a while and talk?'

'No. I'm tired of all you Saxon and Norman mystics coming to Ireland searching for sanctity. Don't you have stories of your own? Why do you feel the need to come here disturbing the peace of our country with your silly spiritual quests.'

'I have a great respect for your ways,' the young monk protested.

'That's shellfish shite. For the most part your folk only take in what suits you. The rest of the time you only listen to whatever your feeble minds perceive to be the truth. And then you go away with your own misguided understandings of what it all means anyway. We're not the same people. Your folk are like little children run amok in the house of a honey-gatherer.'

'I don't know what you mean.'

'Let me put it another way,' the hermit sighed. 'There is a saying among my people: "To go to Rome is little profit, endless pain. The master you seek in Rome you find at home or seek in vain."'

The lad didn't have an opportunity to comment before Michael went on.

'What's the great attraction to this country in any case?' he asked. 'It rains almost every day of the year. Every meal consists of roast pork, curly kale, cheese, milk and oatcakes. Or limited combinations of them. The women all think they've some God-given duty to make the lives of their menfolk a hell on Earth. And the forests are inhabited by the immortal spirits of a race who hold an intense hostility to all the tribes of the Gael.'

He paused for breath and rubbed his forehead.

'So most evenings after a monotonous supper and an argument with the wife, the only thing a man has to look forward to is a walk in the pouring rain through a haunted wood where he's likely to be torn limb from limb by a monstrous creature that even the Devil wouldn't accommodate in the depths of his fiery realm.'

'Your people have such wonderful stories and songs,' Caoimhin offered sheepishly.

'And what about your people? Don't you have your own stories and songs?'

'Actually my parents were Irish.'

'Then bugger off home and listen to them. Leave us poor folk in peace!'

Clearly this conversation wasn't getting him anywhere and Caoimhin still had a question to ask. The young monk recalled the boatman's fee of a farthing for each question. He wondered whether this was some tradition among the heretic Irish.

'I've got farthings in my pouch. Will three of them compensate you for your trouble?'

There was a strained silence followed by what Caoimhin thought was a noise resembling a low grunt.

'Why didn't you say so?' the old man grumbled. 'You could have saved me a lot of misery and spared yourself a cartload of unspoken curses if you'd mentioned those farthings earlier.'

The venerable Michael rolled over to face his visitor. His eyes widened as he stared into the young man's face.

'So you're troubled by visions, are you?' the saint observed.

'How did you know?'

'It's painted across your peepers as plain as the spirals on a carpet page of the sacred gospel Book of Kells.'

'Is there any way I may overcome this terrible affliction?' Caoimhin begged. 'Is there some cure for the malady? How may I find rest from the awful torment of my visions?'

The old hermit looked his visitor up and down. Then he looked him down and up and from side to side to make sure he hadn't missed anything.

Michael coughed. He scratched his head. He yawned. Finally he turned away from his visitor once again.

'I'm not going to tell you. Bugger off.'

'But you surely know the answer. Don't you?'

'Of course I do.'

'Please tell me. I beseech you.'

Michael of the Unkempt Beard rolled over again to sit up on his knees. In the flickering light Caoimhin could see how the old man had earned his strange epithet. This fellow had only to roll his eyes down toward his chin to be reminded what he'd eaten for supper the previous evening. Perhaps even the previous week.

The young Benedictine felt his stomach begin to turn in rebellion. He blessed his snotty sniffer for not detecting the full strength of the stench. Then Michael spoke, distracting Caoimhin from his queasiness.

'Look here, young self-proclaimed mystic journey-vision fellow,' the holy man began. 'I searched most of my adult life for the answer to your question. Do you think that after all the emotional bowel-looseness and spiritual dung-fights I've experienced I'm just going to roll over and tell *you* what I discovered? As simple as that?'

There was a short uncomfortable silence.

'Find out for yourself,' Michael concluded sharply.

'You don't know, do you?' Caoimhin realised aloud. 'You're still suffering yourself, aren't you? You don't know how to escape the visions.'

'Bugger off.'

'Where did you get your reputation for holiness? You're an old drunk.'

'I'm as sober as a goat!' Michael snapped, deeply offended at the accuracy of the accusation. 'And I'm as holy as a barrel wholly full to the brim with holy water.'

'You're a fraud. Holy men live lives of abstinence, devotion, meditation, contemplation and service to others. They don't go round getting drunk then throwing up their dinner in their beards.'

'Well maybe if they did every once in a while, they'd be that much the holier,' the old man ventured defensively. 'Holy men need to relax now and then too, you know.'

'Your advice isn't worth three farthings.'

The sainted Michael's face edged into a squint. Then he imagined those three precious farthings walking out the door in the young Benedictine's pouch. It wasn't a vision he relished.

'I'll give you your three farthings' worth,' the holy man conceded hastily. 'But only because I've a thirst that wouldn't be quenched by any flood the God of drowning sinners and salt pillars could send against me. And three farthings is accounted a fortune in the local alehouse.'

'How can I find peace from my affliction?' Caoimhin pressed.

'For a start, get away from this island as quick as you can. This is a place of strong drink, dancing and all those things which help a man forget the drudgery or melancholy of life. Men come here to be healed, not to find peace. Once they've been healed they go home again. Unless they've stayed too long.'

'What are they healed of?'

'Sobriety for the most part,' the old man sniggered. 'But some come to be purged, however briefly, from the company of their wives, the tyranny of their honour or the weight of their farthing pouches.'

'Is that why you came here?'

'I came here to get drunk. I just haven't managed to get away yet.'

'How long has it been since you first arrived?' Caoimhin asked, trying to sound sympathetic.

'Twenty years.'

'That's a long while to be getting drunk.'

'I've always had a terrible problem with ale. I can never get enough,' Michael admitted. 'I really should try to take a few days away from it. Perhaps next summer.'

Then the old man leaned forward and gazed intently into Caoimhin's eyes.

'You'll only find peace when you've found a purpose,' he stated confidently.

'How do you know?'

'I'm guessing,' the old boy shrugged with a giggle. 'It's the only thing I can think of that I haven't tried yet.'

'How *did* you come to be known as a holy man?'

'I can outdrink any man or beast. I can throw up all day long without flinching. I can fall over flat on my face and still have enough wits to find a soft place to do it. And above all I have visions which grant me an aura of mystical power. I can read a man's heart or foresee his imminent demise.'

Then Michael laughed wildly, revealing a touch more of the maniac than had been evident thus far.

'You'll be like me one day. Not eternally drunk and unkempt, of course. That's not what I'm referring to at all. I mean you'll have folk searching the land craving a few timely utterings from your gifted lips. And when they come crawling hands and knees into your home, do you know what I'd advise you to tell them?'

'What's that?'

'Bugger off.'

Caoimhin didn't need to be asked again. He turned around and made his way out of the cave without so much as a kind word of farewell. And that was very unlike him, I can tell you.

'Wait a moment!' the saintly old souse called out after him. 'There's one other thing you could try.'

The young Benedictine stopped still.

'Find the Brown Book of Aontacht.'

'What's that?' Caoimhin replied, a hint of hope in his voice.

Old Michael had to wait for the echoes to die away before he explained.

'Less than a day's footfall from here, north and east, there's a holy gathering of heretics. They have in their possession an ancient manuscript composed in the time of Saint Declan the Pious. Some say it was scratched into the parchment by his own hand.'

Once again the holy man waited till the sound of his voice had ceased reverberating around the walls.

'This book is reputed to hold the answer to every question that has ever been asked or could ever be conceived. I went to that gathering once but was told only a select few have the privilege of viewing the pages. Sadly I was not considered worthy. But you may be permitted to thumb the leaves. You're a scribe, after all.'

'How did you know I'm a scribe?'

'Because you ask so many bloody questions.'

'What's the name of the community where I may find this book?'

'Killibegs.'

The name echoed around the chamber as if a hundred unseen voices were passing it along mouth to ear. When the whispering echoes finally faded, Caoimhin marvelled at the coincidence then added one last thing.

'Bless you!'

He took three farthings out of his pouch then tossed them back toward Michael.

'And may God bless you also, young scribe,' the old saint replied as the coins skipped, tinkling, across the stone floor. 'Don't forget to return to tell me what you see in that book at the Killibegs. I'd dearly love to know.'

Caoimhin's mind was already racing with anticipation. His heart was overflowing with the desire to press on. Then and there he resolved that if he ever had a chance to clap eyes on the Brown Book of Aontacht, he'd visit this old man again to share what he'd discovered.

Goddess

Mirim asked Tom Curdle to relinquish their second horse so Sianan could ride beside her for the remainder of the journey. The desert woman was glad to be able to escape the company of males for a short while.

As the two women rode together the abbess related what had befallen herself and Martin. Well, that's to say she revealed as much of the story as she thought it was safe to.

Along the way Shali, the mute servant, kept a close eye on the two of them, never for a moment letting Mirim out of his sight. Sianan couldn't help but notice his attention to his lady. And she wondered at his devotion.

At Mirim's prompting, the abbess spoke of her Culdee community and the ways of her people. When Sianan had explained they were considered heretics by most Roman Christians, the desert woman raised an eyebrow.

'Are you heretics?'

The abbess laughed. 'We're simple folk. Our ways are different. This island was cut off from the rest of Christendom for many centuries. We developed our own understanding of the scriptures and we kept many books which the Roman Christians discarded. But in essence we hold the same values and beliefs as our brethren from across the waters.'

'Why do they seek to bring you to their ways? If there are so few differences between your practices and theirs, can't you all learn to respect one another?'

This wasn't an easy question for Sianan to answer. You see, the whole point of the heresy accusations levelled against us Culdees and the other nonconformists of Ireland was that we didn't recognise the Pope as the supreme Holy Father of the Church. We preferred to look to our Irish elders for guidance. And when it came to matters of personal belief, we encouraged our people to search their own hearts for the answers.

But then we had a very different view of the world from the foreigners. The ancient faith of the Druid days had not died. There were many who still held that the soul passes on at death to another form, be it human or animal. And I've already mentioned the Enticers and the Frighteners. That doctrine alone was enough to set us apart from the rest of Christendom. Heaven and Hell were real enough places in our estimation. But they were more the products of one's own imagination than of some all-powerful vengeful being who looked down from on high. God wasn't understood to be one who waited to strike down dissenters with bolts of fiery lightning. Nor to delegate that task to some cardinal in Rome or some archangel from the seventh plane of Purgatory. But I'll not press our beliefs on you.

Enough to say that our understanding of God, and everything He created, was completely at odds with the Church of Rome. And we were stubborn in clinging to our independence.

Sianan answered the question by stating that the Culdees and other so-called heretics of Ireland had long traditions of their own. And our people were not always willing to abandon the ways of our ancestors.

Then the abbess asked the desert woman a few questions of her own. And one in particular showed she had a sharp eye and a keen intuition.

'The silent one who watches over you is very handsome,' she began. 'Is he your husband?'

Mirim froze. 'What makes you say such a thing?'

'He looks at you with genuine adoration and concern,' Sianan shrugged. 'I would say he worships you.'

'We've travelled together for a long time,' the desert woman explained nervously. 'He was at my husband's side when he was killed.'

As she spoke Shali moved far enough ahead of them to be out of earshot. He turned and his eyes sparkled with admiration as he bowed his head slightly.

'That was the look of a man who has more than a passing knowledge of you,' Sianan noted.

'Are you suggesting I have been unfaithful to the memory of my husband?' Mirim snapped. 'Are you accusing me of neglecting the duty of mourning?'

'Not at all,' the abbess assured her. She lowered her voice. 'I'm suggesting he is your husband.'

Mirim closed her eyes, quickly wiping away a tear. Of course Sianan noticed this but she kept silent. It was a long while before the desert woman turned to the abbess.

'Look into my eyes,' she begged.

This placed Sianan in a difficult position. She had not revealed her Otherworldly eyes to anyone in the party. She didn't want to cause a stir.

'Lady,' she requested, 'I will keep your secret if you will promise to keep mine.'

As she spoke the abbess pulled back the cowl of her blue cloak so her face was uncovered. Then she turned to look directly into Mirim's eyes. The desert woman gasped at what she saw.

'What manner of woman are you?' Mirim whispered as Sianan pulled the cloak around her head once more.

'I'm no different from any other,' the abbess began. 'In every respect I'm the same as you. Except one.'

Sianan paused. This moment was always difficult for her.

Some folk simply did not believe her story. Mortals were less accepting than they used to be in the days when she'd taken the Quicken Brew. Most people found the idea that immortals walked the Earth incredible. Others, narrow-minded folk for the most part, attributed her gifts to the Devil. Some just considered her to be mad.

'In what respect are you different from me?' Mirim pressed.

'I will not die.'

'I don't understand.'

'I'm immortal.'

The desert woman fell silent, struggling to take in what she'd been told. But let me assure you the statement wasn't beyond her understanding. Nor did she doubt the truth of it for a moment. Her people were not strangers to those who claimed immortality.

'I had a feeling there was something very unusual about you,' Mirim admitted. 'In my country there are said to be a few folk such as yourself. Indeed, I may have met another of your kind.'

'Another?' Sianan gasped. 'Who? What was his name? Was it Mawn?' Her heart raced at the prospect that this stranger might have encountered her soul-friend. Perhaps she could tell where he was dwelling.

Mirim caught the urgency in the woman's voice and noted it. Then she asked the obvious question. 'Is he your husband? This one called Mawn whom you seek?'

'He was meant to be my companion. We were supposed to spend the seasons together keeping one another company. But we were separated during a great battle. I have not seen him since then.'

'I wish it had been him that I met,' Mirim told her. 'But it was another.'

As the desert woman spoke she reached across to touch Sianan gently on the arm in reassurance.

'It was an ancient hermit of the desert whom I knew,' she explained. 'There were those who said she'd lived in her cave since before Our Lord walked upon this Earth.'

'I'm not quite that old,' Sianan smiled to cover her disappointment. 'This secret of mine will not matter once we have arrived at the Killibegs. I beg you to keep quiet about it till then. I'll tell you the whole story in time, I promise.'

Mirim nodded, feeling a sudden sympathy for this strange immortal creature.

'When do you expect we will arrive at the Killibegs?' she asked.

'Tomorrow before midday,' the abbess stated confidently. 'If the rain doesn't worsen overnight.'

'Then I will tell you my story,' the desert woman offered. 'Once I have found Lord William my secret will no longer need to be kept either.'

She took a deep breath before she went on.

'My heart has only ever been home to one man. No other has dwelled there. I knew it the moment I laid eyes on him. He knew it also. That's why I agreed to marry him.'

Sianan turned to face the dark-skinned woman of the desert. The immortal one didn't shift the cloak from her head but Mirim knew the abbess was smiling broadly. And she knew she could trust this ancient kindred spirit with her heart.

***

Queen Aoife strode over to the wrecked stump of a tree knocked down by the fury of the Nathairaí in their bitter fight. She spread her gown about her and sat down as if the stump were her throne.

Although it was merely a splintered remnant of a once-great

tree, the stump took on the appearance of the richest regal seat Guy d'Alville could have imagined. The Norman felt himself drawn to Queen Aoife's side. He walked around behind the forest throne and ventured to stand there with his hand resting on the trunk near the queen's head.

It was a gesture of arrogant familiarity. But Aoife didn't protest. Guy was merely acting upon her unspoken command. She'd mastered the art of influencing others. So adept had she become that when her chosen target was compliant it was an easy matter to get what she wanted out of them. Indeed, the more arrogant her target, the easier it was to turn their will to her wishes.

Isleen and Lochie slithered around to the front of the royal seat and coiled there respectfully. As they did so Sciathan Cog hopped forward to present his report.

'All is in readiness, my lady,' the raven told her in his rough caw. 'Samhain Oidche will mark the beginning of a new age for this land. You will be our goddess and your loyal subjects will pay homage to you with love and respect for the gifts of peace and protection you bestow upon them.'

'Are the Redcaps ready?'

'They're fairly itching for a fight.'

'It may not come to that. I have a trick or two up my sleeve yet. I don't want any unnecessary killing. Do you understand?'

'Forgive me, my queen,' the bird sputtered. 'That's a difficult strategy for a raven to comprehend. What of blood and battle? What of terror and torture? Didn't we discuss this? You gave me your word . . .

Aoife smiled at the raven's protest but cut him off abruptly. 'Enough!'

They had been brother and sister long ago before enchantments had changed them. She knew well enough what was on his mind. He'd always been a bitter blood-lusting creature. A raven's clothing simply suited him better than a man's.

'Dear brother,' the queen went on, 'every living soul who worships me strengthens my power. The more adoring grateful fools there are, the greater I'll become. So there must not be too many deaths.'

'It's always an unfortunate result of war that some folk lose their lives,' Cog noted sharply. 'All the bark-splintering that has gone on since the foreigners landed has given my kindred a notion to fill their larders with fresh meat. The Raven kind who follow me would certainly see the sacrifice of a good number of the tree-cutters as just reward for their loyalty to you.'

'And what about yourself, brother?' Aoife snapped. 'What would you consider a just reward for *your* loyalty?'

'You know that well enough,' the raven cackled. 'I surely don't have to state it again.'

'Indeed not,' Aoife grimaced. 'I know what you want. But you won't get it unless I'm powerful enough to grant your desire. To gain that sort of power I need as many worshippers bowing down to me as possible. There must not be too many deaths.'

The two worms were becoming restless. They'd put their heads close together and were whispering fervently betwixt each other, vainly hoping Aoife wouldn't notice. However, the queen didn't miss a word that passed between them.

'If you serve me well you too will be rewarded,' she declared to them. 'In time I will have the knowledge and the strength to be able to release you from Danu's enchantment.'

'How much time?' Isleen enquired, suspicion colouring the question but not enough so that it could be interpreted as disrespectful.

'That depends on how many folk give me their love. It depends on the feast laid out for my Enticer. If you aid me in my quest you'll be helping yourselves.'

'What do you want us to do?' Lochie cut in.

Aoife's eye sparkled with delight. Now she had them. Her ambition was within reach. Like a war-leader preparing for a fateful battle, she issued her commands.

'Spread terror. Bring the people to their knees with fright. Try to keep your feeding frenzies under control. By all means take cattle, sheep, horses and goats, but leave the mortal kind alone. Remember, the more folk there are to worship me, the stronger my Enticer will become and the sooner you'll be set free.'

She leaned forward in her seat to make her point. 'When the time comes I'll require you to cease your rampage. Then you'll return to your well for a short while.'

'You want us to go back down that hole?' Isleen shrieked. 'Not likely.'

'Don't you see? If the mortals believe I've rescued them from the ravages of the Nathairaí they'll love me all the more. And so my strength will increase.'

'And how will it help us if we're locked within the well again?'

'You must understand that mortals will rest easier if they see you withdraw to your ancient gaol. They'll see your retreat as evidence of my influence. They'll trust me all the more if they witness your imprisonment and the end to your terrible menace.'

'How do we know we can trust you?' Lochie asked.

He instantly regretted the forthrightness of his question. But Aoife merely laughed.

'What have I to gain from breaking trust with you? In fact your loyalty can only add to the strength of my Enticer. I promise I'll treat you better than you deserve. After all, let's not forget that you two are responsible for this terrible immortality I've had to suffer. I've been trapped in this body since I drank the Brew. And the Quicken Brew was your doing.'

She was right enough. It was Lochie and Isleen that stirred

up Éremon and his brother Eber Finn to voyage to Ireland in search of new lands. And if they hadn't come along the Danaan Druids would never have resorted to using the ancient Quicken Brew to gain immortality for their people and the Fir-Bolg folk. It sounds like a terrible tangle they were all entwined in and you can be sure it certainly was. And you can be doubly sure Lochie was hoping our Aoife wasn't the kind to bear a grudge.

'You don't hold that against us, do you? We were only acting according to our nature.'

'I despised you,' Aoife admitted. 'I hated you both for longer than I can remember. But eventually I came to understand how you must have felt to be beyond the sting of death. Then I sympathised with your plight and the trick you played on the people of the Fir-Bolg. So now let's put that behind us. All is forgiven.'

'Very well then,' Isleen agreed. 'All is forgiven. But tell me something. What have you in store for him?'

The Nathair indicated Guy with a nudge of her great bulbous head.

Aoife allowed a contented smile to shape her full red lips. 'My dear friends, I would very much like to introduce you to the next High-King of Ireland and the man who will, if he proves himself worthy, become my consort.'

'I applaud your choice,' Isleen sighed. 'He's a wicked one, all right. He'll suit you well. And the highest rank in the land will likely suit him also.'

The Mouth of a Saint

t the appointed time the three travelling monks took their places in the boat to leave the island. Lewyn scowled at Finbar the boatman as he thrust his oar into the shallow waters to push the vessel along.

It was Overton who first passed a white stone to the Gael. Then he cleared his throat to ask a question.

'What happens to those souls who pass away from this life without hearing the word of God?'

Finbar raised his eyebrows in appreciation. 'That's a good question,' he nodded. 'You're obviously a man of learning, refined opinions and deep contemplations.'

The boatman stopped speaking for a few breaths in order to properly consider his answer. When at last he offered his reply he sounded as if he was reading the answer from a book.

'At the gates of Heaven heathen souls are questioned about their lives. When they've answered these enquiries, the Guardian of the Gates, Saint Peter the Apostle, reveals to them the mind and sacred purpose of Almighty God.'

He cleared his throat again, warming to his tale.

'The newly deceased must then choose. If they accept the word of God, they spend an eternity singing praise-songs among the everlasting choirs of angels.'

'And if they reject God's holy writ and purpose?' Caoimhin asked, stifling a cough.

Finbar held out his hand and winked. Once a white pebble had been dropped into his palm, he went on.

'Those poor fools who reject the word of God are granted an hour in the awesome presence of the Creator. They walk in the scented gardens of his domain, drink from fountains filled with wine and listen to joyous heavenly music resounding in their spirits. Then, just as they're getting comfortable, they're whisked away to suffer in the dungeons of the Devil deep within the dæmonic kingdoms.'

Finbar shrugged and pushed down on the oar again.

'There they live the lives of slaves, enduring the worst kind of torments until God grants them an opportunity to repent. Now and then they're given a chance to escape Hell, to taste the sweet delights of Heaven. But most fail to see the light and go straight back to Satan's sitting room to await the infinite mercy of the Almighty.'

Lewyn frowned as he held out his pebble. He might have been annoyed at the boatman but this saintly theological opinion had tempted his curiosity.

'Where is Hell exactly?' he asked.

The boat struck the black pebble beach of the mainland as Finbar answered.

'What sort of mystics are you? Don't you *know*? The realm of Satan is a place of greed, lust, envy, sloth, anger, drunkenness, deception, gluttony, pride, war and defilement. In other words, my friends, Hell is wherever you're standing.'

He laughed wildly for a few seconds. Then his features turned suddenly solemn.

'Don't forget to speak politely to Saint Peter when you arrive at the Blessed Gates of Paradise. And may this be your last stint in the Devil's own domain.'

The three monks disembarked, restraining their personal opinions on the boatman's answer. They watched in silence as he pushed off from the shore. As soon as he was a good way out Lewyn spoke in a low voice.

'What a load of rubbish! The world is also full of joy, love and the wondrous gifts of Our Lord. This can't be Hell.'

Caoimhin patted his robe where his farthing pouch should have been. Then the blood drained from his face and he cursed himself for being a dull-wit.

'What's the matter?' Overton asked.

'I've lost our last three coins,' the young scribe admitted.

'You didn't lose them,' Lewyn sighed. 'They were stolen.'

He pointed toward the boatman. Finbar was standing at the back of his boat, dangling the pouch and grinning widely.

The Welshman picked up a stone and hurled it at the boating thief. But it fell far to the left and splashed harmlessly in the water. Lewyn watched the last ripples die away before he said another word.

'On reflection, I concede perhaps we are wandering about in Hell after all,' the Welshman sighed. 'If he has the mouth of a saint then I have the teeth of a chicken.'

He was determined not to give vent to his frustration. But after a brief, half-hearted internal struggle, his temper got the better of him. The Welshman waded out into the icy lough and raised his fist in fury.

'We're writing a traveller's guide to this country. And I swear I'll tell the whole world what a bloody thief you are.'

A voice echoed back across the lough. 'Bloody mystics! You're all the same.'

'Let's find a dry place to sleep,' Caoimhin suggested. Then he coughed hard and there was pain in his chest. 'If we're lucky we'll be at Killibegs tomorrow night.'

The sun was already low in the sky, and though the rain was lifting, the air was cold. All three were damp and tired. So they trudged off into the woods again to find a sheltered spot to rest.

That evening, not far away from the lough at the verge of a wood, the next strand of my tale began to weave into the story-cloth. In a place where blackberries grew in wide hedges broader than a badger can leap, the central figure in this epic adventure entered the scene.

If you'd been there that night you would have seen an open circle of green grass bounded all around by thirteen ancient grey standing-stones. If you'd crept quietly closer you'd have noticed a fine-featured woman cloaked in a woollen garment of the brightest indigo. She was standing silently with her face toward the heavens, all alone at the very centre of the grassy patch, her hands outstretched to either side. This was the old Culdee prayer stance.

We of the ancient faith did not place our palms together when we communed with God. It was our custom to show our open hands to the Almighty as a gesture of honouring, humility, and honesty.

This woman was honest, humble and highly honoured by her kin. And if perhaps in practice she sometimes fell a little short of their praise, the folk of the community where she lived still respected her greatly.

She had eyes the same shade of green as Queen Aoife. And her hair was of exactly the same red hue as that Sovereign Lady of the Darkness. I'll wager if you'd seen them standing side by side you might have thought them sisters, they looked so much alike.

But they weren't. It was just a quirk of happenstance the two of them held such resemblance to each other. Though I suppose in one respect they shared a certain quality of character.

Binney of the Killibegs was a stubborn, formidable woman; a woman who would not shrink from a challenge. No matter how difficult a situation seemed to be, she could be relied upon to find a path through it. No matter how unfathomable the question, she would seek out the answer. No matter how dangerous the hunt, she would surely hold her quarry at the end. For she was not merely a beautiful woman capable of keeping the eyes of men transfixed when she entered the chapel. She was a wise-woman. Whomsoever heard her speak was spellbound by her words.

So it's all the more surprising that this evening found her all alone in the depths of despair. For it was not usually in her character to allow any hint of uncertainty into her heart.

Binney was singing a prayer that evening. If you'd been hiding behind one of the standing-stones you might have heard what she was saying. It was a very simple and personal offering.

'Blessings on the one. And also on the two. And in the place where the two become one may they meet with joyful hearts. May they listen to the timeless strains of the Song. May they taste the juice of the berry. And be seduced by the scent of sweet new honey.'

The woman looked into the face of the full moon. If you'd been standing beside her you might have noticed the trickle of a tear rolling down her cheek. Yes, she was softly sobbing. And in a little while the tears were flowing freely. For despite her strength of character this was often the way with her in those days when she had time to herself. And as they say, a small shower often precedes a mighty downpour.

Binney pulled the covering from her head and shook her red locks free. Then she wiped her face dry with the sleeve of her darker gown. Her sobs gradually diminished until at last the storm in her soul settled.

We all need a good sobbing now and then, man, woman, beast and bird. Even fishes cry, but sadly it is hard to tell with them so no one much notices.

Binney had every reason to be upset. For though she lived

among friends and was well loved by all, there was an emptiness in her heart. It was a void wherein nothing dwelled except a dæmon spirit of loneliness. It was probably some breed of Frightener not powerful enough to engender terror yet potent enough to draw tears.

Binney, however, had no inkling this spirit was the source of her pain. She was still a young woman in those far-off days. She'd not yet learned to recognise such creatures, though to be sure, she'd often heard stories about them.

She was loved because of the stories she knew. Indeed, there were those who called her the most gifted storyteller to have been seen in Ireland for generations.

Does she remind you of anyone yet? Isn't there someone she bears more than a passing resemblance to? Have you not guessed who this proud, lonely yet self-reliant woman might be?

I'll tell you then, if you can't guess. That woman, Binney of the Killibegs, was me.

I was adored by all the young men, I was, when I was young. I was courted by the best of them. But even the best of the best was not good enough for me. I had the notion in my head that I deserved better. And so I did.

There I stood in the centre of that archaic stone circle. Binney of the Honey Mouth they called me. Binney of the Battle Sagas. The Woman of Wise Words. The Bookbinder of Tall Stories.

But for all the fine tales I'd learned, for all the stories of love that had passed my lovely rose-red lips, I knew no fulfilment of my own heart's desire. My wonderful gift had not shown me where to find the soul-friend I sought.

Warm breath billowed steaming from my mouth. A new tear welled. And I composed another prayer with all the yearning of my very being woven into the making of it so that any who might have heard it surely would have wept with pity.

It tingles my skin just to recall it to you now. Of course I was a young thing then who didn't know that much about the world. I admit I was prone to silliness. If you can manage to see past my overdramatic delivery, you'll understand how unhappy I was.

'Danu,' I began, 'I beg you with my tears. I beseech you with my sobs. I entreat you with all the breadth of my inexpressible longing. I make this supplication with every measure of my immeasurable depths.'

I remember taking a long full breath into my lungs. I held it a few seconds, then blew it out with my words so they were formed into rolling waves of mist before my face.

'Bring to me the soul-friend of my heart. Guide the Anamchara to me so that he and I may be as one. For I am but one part of the two. And we are both two parts of the one. And without him here beside me there can be no joy in my dance steps. There can be no end to my hunger.'

I listened intently to the sounds of the night. An howl hooted in the woods. The breeze rustled the highest leaves in the branches of the trees. The wind sighed as it wove in and out of the stones.

'There can be no end to my loneliness without him. There can be only day following fruitless day and night after endless empty night. I will wither. I will shrivel. I will grow stagnant like a pond cut off from the stream.'

My nose was running from all the crying and the cold air. I wiped my face again with the sleeve of my gown.

'Hear me, Goddess of the Flowing Waters. Hear me, O Guardian of the Loughs and Rivers. Hear me, O Woman of the Everlasting Rains. It is Binney who summons you for help.'

I waited for a reply, for some sign of acknowledgment or indication of Her presence. I waited as my cheeks grew icy cold. I did not move, though my legs began to ache and my frozen feet became numb. I stood so still that after a while I lost all feeling in my fingers. And yet I waited, ever hopeful. All I knew was shivering anticipation. Until I started to doubt.

For I had heard it said that Danu of the old days had gone to sleep. I'd been told She no longer answered the call of a lonely woman standing within the stones. She was lost in goddess dreams, oblivious to any sound or summons, beyond the realm of mortals.

And though She was the only one who could help me, the only one who had the skill to grant my wish, the thought crossed my mind that perhaps She was not listening to me. That may have been unjust of me.

Maybe She did hear my words. Maybe She stirred when my prayers squeezed their way into Her dreaming. Could it be that my yearning leeched its way into Her chamber of rest?

When I allowed myself to hope again, all doubt disappeared. I took another deep breath into my body, consciously drawing in all the soul nourishment creation had to offer.

I exhaled every dark thought, every soul wound, every ache, every contamination, every weight of weariness. And then I went on waiting. But you know what I think?

I reckon Danu must have heard me. If She hadn't I'd be waiting there still and I wouldn't have this fine tale to tell.

The Woman of Blue

oife, Queen of the Night, held court there in the forest, accepting various delegations from the Raven-kind. Isleen and Lochie remained close by until every representative of the black birds had pledged their feathers in support of her cause.

Long after dark she at last dismissed the Nathairí with an order to spread their havoc in the world. She also issued strict instructions to report back to her regularly and to be ready at short notice to undertake any special tasks she might have in mind for them.

They bowed to her in worm fashion, swearing solemn oaths that they would serve her well and be forever grateful if she alleviated their suffering in return. Then they set off into the night to start their work.

Once they were gone Queen Aoife turned her attention to Guy d'Alville. The Norman moved around to the front of her throne and bowed low as she addressed him.

'You are willing to become my consort?' she asked.

He straightened up and stood proudly. For a second the Norman hesitated. He could hardly believe this was happening to him. If anyone had said to him a few days earlier that he'd be pledging allegiance to an immortal queen whose brother was a raven and whose closest supporters were two enormous worms, he would have laughed.

Guy looked around at the shattered trees and the talking raven called Sciathan Cog. He considered the high-kingship of Ireland that had been offered to him. Then he smiled as his warrior's scheming mind accepted everything he'd witnessed.

'I am willing, my lady.'

'You're ready to take command of my warriors?'

'I am ready, my lady.'

'That's well,' Aoife smiled with satisfaction. 'But first you will undergo a test of your loyalty and ability. If you prove yourself to me you will be named High-King of Ireland and you will rule under the seal of my authority.'

'As you command.'

'You'll bring me nine red berries of the holy rowan tree known as the Quicken,' Aoife commanded him.

Guy shrugged. 'I know not of this tree.'

Aoife told the history of the sacred Quicken which had been carried by the Tuatha De Danaan on their journeys across the world. When they had finally reached Inisfail, as Ireland was known in those long-ago days, they planted the tree. Within one season they'd begun to collect the sacred fruit.

You see, the red berries of the Quicken have a unique property. When the fruit is prepared in a certain manner the resulting brew can cure all ills. Those who drink the Quicken Brew live forever.

Guy listened intently to the queen's tale. He didn't have to try very hard to imagine what it would be like to be untouched by time, death or decay. For a warrior it would secure every victory and ensure unwavering valour.

'If you fetch the nine berries of that tree I will grant you the Quicken Brew,' Aoife promised him. 'You will reign by my side in the Otherworld and you will have a free hand ruling the Kingdom of Ireland as you see fit.'

'I will find these berries, my lady,' he assured her.

'You have until the feast of Samhain Oidche,' the queen

added. 'If you've not brought them to me by then, don't bother showing your face to me ever again.'

'Very well,' Guy nodded.

Just then a loud warbling cry cut through the air like a great tree-felling axe.

'My warriors are returning with news,' Aoife declared. 'And it seems they have a prisoner who has offended against the laws of my people. We may have ourselves some entertainment.'

It wasn't long before a group of Redcaps appeared at the edge of the clearing. Still panting heavily from their hard, fast journey, they unceremoniously dropped their load. Then they sank to their knees awaiting their queen's command.

These uncouth fighters were unlike any Guy had ever seen before. But he wasn't about to let Aoife think he was surprised by their appearance. They were fearsome and wild but they were still only warriors to him.

You must remember also that he'd been on campaign in the Holy Land. A man who has fought with the crusading armies isn't easily impressed.

'Bring the prisoner forward,' the queen ordered.

In no time John Toothache was on his knees before the Queen of the Night. His hands and feet were still bound tightly. His eyes flashed with fear and loathing. His skullcap and fine Saracen hat were thrown down on the ground at his feet in a gesture of contempt.

The Redcap war-leader bowed to Sciathan Cog. Then in a hoarse whisper he gave his assent for the raven to represent him. Cog coughed as he hopped across to stand in front of the captive.

'You've been charged with the murder of one of the Redcap kind,' the raven began, formally presenting the charge.

'Murder?' Aoife cut in. 'How is that possible? The Redcaps are among those who have taken the Quicken Brew. It's no easy matter to kill one of our kind. Indeed, I can't recall any mortal committing such an act.'

The Redcap war-leader stepped forward to present his version of events. Neither Guy nor Toothache understood the fellow's speech but it was evident Aoife had no difficulty following what was being said.

A few uncouth, unintelligible words passed between her and the Redcap before she turned to Guy.

'It seems this Norman has discovered a terrible secret quite by accident,' Aoife told him. 'He beheaded one of my warriors. Even an immortal may suffer death under certain circumstances. But it wouldn't do for this information to become known to the mortal kind. It's better they believe my folk are invincible.'

Now our Toothache might have seemed a simple soul with very little activity to speak of going on in his thick skull. But he had no trouble grasping the concept of Redcap immortality nor was he amazed at the sight of a talking raven. He'd been told stories of such things since childhood. So he didn't baulk when it came time to leap to his own defence.

'He didn't kill the creature!' he declared, pointing to his own chest to emphasise his innocence.

'What?' d'Alville barked.

Now Toothache fairly thumped his chest. 'He tried to kill one of them. But it wouldn't die. He couldn't have killed it. He saw that one do the murder.' He pointed at the Redcap war-leader.

Guy squinted. The fellow was obviously a half-wit to be speaking about himself like that.

'What are you doing wandering in the wild lands alone?' he asked suspiciously.

'Bishop Ollo sent him off to follow the young monk with the books. Bishop Ollo told him to kill the lad and steal the books. Then he told Toothache to bring the books back to him.'

'Bishop Ollo sent you out here?'

'That's right. Bishop told him to find Guy d'Alville too. And to report to him.'

'Well you've found Guy,' Aoife noted.

Toothache looked into the lady's eyes and began to plead for his life. 'Don't murder him. Toothache's not a bad man. He's misunderstood.'

'Silence!' d'Alville snapped.

Then Aoife cut in. 'Apparently this fellow looted the corpse of my warrior, stole a precious walrus-tooth pendant and attacked the others in the party. My captain is demanding the man be put to death in punishment.'

'But you've not made up your mind, have you?' d'Alville ventured.

The queen hummed. She was pleased Guy wasn't as slow-witted as most Normans seemed to be.

'If I allow this lackey to live there's always the risk he'll reveal this secret and thus cause me unnecessary difficulties. On the other hand, if he's telling the truth then my war-leader is lying. That's unforgivable. Such disobedience must not go unpunished.'

The Redcap stared straight ahead without flinching. He hadn't understood a word she'd said.

The queen turned her attention to Toothache. 'Tell me again. What is your version of events?'

The foot soldier swallowed hard before he replied. All the while Aoife gazed steadily into his eyes. She didn't so much as blink until he'd finished speaking.

'He did not murder the man. It's true Toothache stole the walrus-tooth pendant. But it was the war-leader who killed the other warrior. He saw him cut the fellow's head off.'

The queen knew Toothache was telling the truth. That's one of the tricks the really old Eolaí know. After you've lived a couple of hundred winters it's not difficult to tell when someone's spinning you a thread woven entirely from dried deer-droppings.

Aoife spoke a few harsh unintelligible words to the captain of the Redcaps.

The fellow opened his mouth to protest. But before he could utter a sound he was violently seized by the other warriors amidst a great commotion of guttural, cursing accusations. The other Redcaps forced the war-leader to his knees.

'I will not tolerate disloyalty or dishonesty,' Aoife declared to the Redcaps in their own language.

Guy couldn't understand the words but he easily picked up the gist of what was being said. The queen made a tiny gesture with her hand. D'Alville didn't have to question what it meant. He had the same manner about him when he was condemning a man to death.

In the next breath one of the Redcaps grabbed the war-leader's hat, stripping it from his head. Then he grasped the warrior by the hair. It was all so quick. By the time the victim understood what was happening to him his neck was bared.

A curved war-sickle was raised high in the air. The war-leader took a deep breath to cry out. But before he'd finished taking in the air the vicious weapon swung down with a whispering slice to sever his head completely. A gush of breath gurgled out of the bloody neck as the body slumped forward.

The executioner held up the gruesome disembodied artefact to show it to his queen. She nodded regally as the head dropped and rolled across the ground.

Toothache looked away. Even for a veteran warrior of fortune such as himself this was a sight too sickening to behold. And he expected no less a fate for himself.

'You'll not die for your crime,' the queen assured him, reading the dismay on his face. 'You will accompany my consort, Guy d'Alville. You will serve him faithfully and act as

345

his right-hand man. And you will keep silent about all that you have seen here.'

'He's a fool!' Guy spat. 'I'd rather have a donkey for my deputy than that oaf.'

'He'll serve you well, my lord,' Toothache promised. 'As he's served the Order of the Hospitallers these five years past. And if you will permit him to say he's already been commanded to serve by your side, my lord.'

'What are you talking about?' Guy snapped.

'Bishop Ollo is at Wexford, my lord. He told Toothache to find Killibegs then report to you.'

'Has he – Have *you* discovered where this Killibegs might be?'

'No, my lord. He was separated from the monk.'

Guy turned to Aoife. 'The man's below me. He's already made a mess of things. I don't want him working for me.'

The queen shook her head. 'It will prove your worth if you manage to complete the quest I've set you even though you are held back by a fool. It is my command. The idea amuses me.'

'Very well, my lady,' the Norman conceded through gritted teeth. He didn't need any more experience of the woman to realise it was no use arguing with her.

'I know where the Killibegs has been located this season,' Sciathan Cog declared. 'I'll take you there.'

'If you're going to pick up the trail of the nine Quicken berries Killibegs is a good place to start searching,' the queen informed him.

Guy sighed. 'Then what are we waiting for? Cut the prisoner loose and we'll set off at once.'

If Caoimhin and his travelling companions had thought they'd find the Killibegs that day, they were sorely mistaken. For you see, the community of the travelling Culdees rarely stayed put in one place for more than a dozen nights in a row, except when it came to their wintering home. They tarried there for three months beginning before the feast of Samhain and lasting until the snows had melted.

Otherwise the folk of that community were constantly on the move, cows, goats, horses, chickens, chapel and church fittings. And what was the reason for their nomadic lifestyle, you ask.

Culdees of the old faith did not take vows of chastity or obedience as do other monastics. But we did vow to poverty. A settled life with stone house, possessions and roots into the land was undesirable to the most devout followers. But to us Culdees of the clergy who had devoted our lives to the soul-journey, a settled life was utterly abhorrent. So we travelled, except during the harshest weather. For the clergy were an example to everyone. We endured hardship and deprivation to show what may be achieved when one is dedicated and self-disciplined.

We cut ourselves off from trinkets and trivial things which only bear down on your back when you have to carry them from one place to another. An uncluttered life was the ambition of all of us. Such an existence keeps Enticers in their place. Or at least it makes it more difficult for them to feed unchecked. And even Frighteners have a hard time if they're constantly kept on the road.

I have to say it wasn't a bad life either. I came to these journeying folk soon after I ran away from the convent. I had no mind to be locked away behind cold stone walls while the world was wandering by my window.

I liked the way these people lived their lives. Simple love from simple folk who revelled in the freedom God had granted them. Of course, you understand, we were all very unusual, each and every one of us. Only a somewhat strange person would consider taking to a life of everlasting travel in the first place. But it requires a *profoundly* strange person actually to commit to it.

The beautiful thing was that no two of us was ever strange in the same way. Individuality was a cherished concept among the Culdee clergy. An individual's particular strangeness was considered a deep expression of the sacred. In other words, one's eccentricities, no matter how extreme, were considered to be evidence of the hand of God at work.

Other communities practised celibacy, asceticism and reclusion. But the Killibegs was a community with a different expression of their faith. In those days before orthodoxy was forced on Ireland, our way was considered just as right and proper as anyone else's.

This is a perfect example of a major difference between the way the Normans saw the world and the manner in which the Irish experienced it. The Normans considered any eccentricity as an indication of inherent flaws or the influence of Satan. As if anything God created could be flawed. Or as if the Devil had nothing better to do than grant little quirks to people as a sign he'd had a mix-up in their lives.

Believe me, if Satan decides to mark someone, he doesn't sign his sigil in small letters. He writes it big, with illuminated letters, magnificent zoomorphic capitals and the finest array of colours available to his paintbox.

But that's enough about the Culdees for the moment. I'll tell you more about my dear friends of the Killibegs later. Suffice to say we'd just settled in our winter place in preparation for the feast of Samhain Oidche.

We had brought all our folk within the circle of the walls of an ancient rath. It was no ordinary rath, this one. It had been occupied briefly by a Norman warlord. No one knows what happened to him. He probably just decided he'd had enough and shipped himself home. Not all the foreigners were as determined to make a go of it as Lanfranc.

This rath was our secret. Finding our settlement took some effort, a little luck and a fair portion of persistence. Or if you had none of these, a raven guide would have sufficed.

As I was saying before you distracted me, Caoimhin and his companions hadn't found the Killibegs because the boatman who'd assured them they weren't far from the settlement had in fact been making it up. He didn't have any idea where the Killibegs was to be found. So it was remarkable in many ways that he'd sent the friars off in the right direction.

They trudged until it was dark. Then the three monks settled down by a hastily built fire. The rain had passed completely but the air was still chilly enough that they had to wrap their cloaks about themselves and huddle down to keep warm.

The two Welshmen fell into a deep slumber immediately. But Caoimhin couldn't sleep. His cough wasn't any worse but the tightness in his chest was making him strain hard for breath. He knew he'd be in a bad way by morning.

After lying shivering with his eyes open for an hour or so, the young scribe decided to get up. He squatted by the fireside for a while to warm his body then stacked some more timber on the flames.

As the flames crackled louder he noticed Gobann standing just outside the rim of firelight. The Druid stepped into the glow, put a finger to his lips to hush the monk then whispered, 'You must come with me. Now!'

Gobann turned on his heel and strode off into the night. Caoimhin was up and after him as quickly and quietly as he could manage. Even so he'd already lost sight of the poet before twenty paces had separated him from the fireside.

'Where are you, Druid?'

There was no reply. Caoimhin made his way alone through the woods, guessing at the path his companion had taken until he came to a stand of blackberry bushes. There was no way through them so the young scribe tried to find a way around.

The ground was very uneven under his feet but Caoimhin managed to find a gap between the thorny bushes. In the pale moonlight he could just make out a ring of standing-stones. And within the circle on the cleared ground there was a shadowy figure poised in the Culdee attitude of prayer.

'Gobann!' he called.

Well of course I heard him. He couldn't have been more than fifty paces away from me. His shout startled me. I remember that. It startled me so much I forgot about everything I'd been praying for.

'Who's there?' I called back tentatively.

I wasn't so much worried about brigands. They tended to leave us well alone. It was Normans I was afraid of. The name Gobann didn't sound too foreign to me so I was emboldened.

Caoimhin, on the other hand, froze with fear, poor boy. He was a shy one, that's for certain. You must remember he'd not had anything to do with women at that early stage in his life. Unless you counted the beautiful lady bathed in blue light who'd come to him in a vision.

So when he heard my soft feminine voice he must have shivered with apprehension. Behind him Gobann placed a light hand on his shoulder. Caoimhin wasn't surprised or shocked by the Druid's sudden reappearance. In fact he was deeply reassured. He'd grown used to the manner in which this fellow could appear without warning.

'Go to her!' the poet urged him. 'She's been waiting for you.'

'Who is she?' the scribe asked.

'Someone you need to get acquainted with,' Gobann replied. 'Don't worry. She won't hurt you. It'll do you good to get to know her.'

He pushed Caoimhin firmly in the middle of the back and the scribe took a few reluctant steps forward. Then the Druid spoke again.

'She's from the Killibegs.'

The scribe turned to look his companion in the eye. 'Why didn't you say so in the first place?'

Caoimhin moved closer to the stones as the poet whispered behind him. 'Don't tell anyone about me. Do you understand? Keep me a secret.'

'Who's there?' I called out again.

I was sure I'd heard two voices muttering in the dark. But only one fellow stepped out of the darkness. Even now all these years later I can clearly remember the first glimpse I had of him. I thought to myself what a shame it was the Church dressed up so many young men in long black robes.

I also recall wondering what a young Benedictine was doing travelling through the night in this part of the world.

'My name is Caoimhin,' he called back to me.

He waited at the edge of the stone circle. I walked over to him. Then something happened that I'll never forget. Just as I got close to him his eyes widened. He fell to his knees.

And looking like he'd seen some Enticer spirit take on human form, he uttered one faltering question.

'Who in God's name are you?'

The Killibegs

While I was out making my supplications at the standing-stones, Lanfranc's party of travellers were encountering another member of our community. And as it happened it was the old man who was our priest and our father.

Clemens was a compassionate soul but he could also be a cynical, difficult, wearisome old bugger when he wanted. And as he got older he liked to spend more and more time by himself. Not that he would have ever considered becoming a hermit. That would've been too much for him to bear. He preferred the company and security of the community over the uncertain, frightening life of one who lived alone. And it has to be said he enjoyed his privileged position. He was respected and admired by everyone. He was a wise man, after all, despite his little faults. We all have faults. In my experience it's best just to praise the good in folk and accept the annoying without a word. In Clemens's case there were many words left unsaid.

On this evening the old man had found himself a quiet place to sit by the side of a ford at the narrowing neck of a wide stream not far from the rath. He'd been there only a short while, humming a little tune to himself to settle his mind into a meditative state.

I'm sure he sensed the approach of strangers long before they noticed him. And I'm even more certain he cursed their intrusion into his private contemplations. But rather than stir himself into a lather about it, he forced himself to sit patiently and await their arrival.

Among our folk hospitality was a prized attribute. The old legends of the Gaels tell so many tales of hospitality rewarded with some boon or other. In those stories a niggardly welcome always leads to trouble. You see, the Faerie folk often travel in disguise, not so much to trick us mortals but so as not to frighten us too much. The Christian tradition tells us that Christ also uses this tactic when he journeys through the world.

So it pays to treat travellers well.

Our Clemens may have had his faults but he was a genuinely hospitable man. The truth is he loved having visitors among us. I don't know if you can imagine what it's like to be living day after day, season after season amidst the same small group of people. Their eccentricities tend to come into sharp focus. Their annoying habits start to grate on your nerves. When it's at its worst no amount of convincing yourself that these quirks are proof of God's loving influence can still your temper. Some days you pray for the strength to be able to face the other members of your community without biting someone's head off and spitting it back into their hands. After years living like this it's often difficult to find a good word to say about anybody.

I don't care what all those idealistic young mystics reckon. It's a fine idea to go off building a new life based on mutual love and respect for one another. But it's a different story when you're faced with the same old porridge every morning. Once in a while you crave a little butter and honey to go with it.

So, you understand, visitors are always a welcome relief at the Killibegs. Everyone relaxes around the feasting table to listen to a story or two. There's drinking and merriment. And there's music and dancing.

Old friends remember why they love each other. Rivals

laugh off their competitive foolishness over a few drinks. Soul wounds heal. Soul-friends sing. Yes, travellers can give a whole new life to any community.

Now it'd be true to say that Samhain is a feast of especial importance. Once a year everyone shrugs off their modesty, their humility, their personal prejudices and gets blind, falling-down-on-their-arse drunk.

One Samhain in every seven the chieftains of the clans of the west, along with their entourages, gathered with us. They brought with them food and drink and a sense of fun. They had musicians, storytellers, poets, bondsmen and serving girls in tow. Their cattle came too, so there was plentiful milk, fine fresh golden butter, honey by the barrel, white-flour bread, sweets of every kind. My mouth is watering just to recall the feasts we used to have.

This year was one of those huge get-togethers. And by the belching belly of Saint Benedict we were all looking forward to it. So as Clemens waited by the ford his fleeting annoyance fled and his excitement began to build.

We hadn't had any visitors at all since the last snowmelt. In the last few days we'd all worked hard to make the rath liveable. Everyone was tired. But not too exhausted to be eager at the prospect of fresh conversations and stimulating, if brief, liaisons of various other sorts. Strangers were just the right spice to add to our celebrations for the feast of Samhain Oidche.

It was a long while before the old priest glimpsed a sign of the travellers. Two horsemen approached the ford, scouted the banks on the other side, then rode off again without spotting him.

So Clemens crossed the ford to await the rest of the party. He didn't have to stand there long before a larger company arrived at the stream.

'Greetings,' he called out in his best hospitable, priestly voice. 'Welcome.'

A Norman warrior rode forward to inspect the old man.

'Welcome to the Killibegs,' Clemens added hesitantly, seeing the fellow was a foreigner.

The thought hadn't crossed his mind that these strangers might be Normans. Not that he minded where they came from. He just wasn't sure whether they might be a band of heretic hunters out to collect a bounty.

The Norman rider removed his helm so Clemens could see his face. This settled the old man a little because it was a sign of respect for his office as priest.

'My name is Lanfranc de Courcy,' the warrior declared. 'I'm escorting these folk to the Killibegs. Have we far to go?'

'Not far at all,' Clemens replied. 'Indeed, it is but a short ride past this ford before you'll come to the road which leads to our community.'

'Then we'll press on,' the Norman told him. 'Will you guide us?'

'My name is Father Clemens,' the priest smiled. 'I'd be happy to take you the rest of the way. And to be the first to offer you the hospitality of our humble settlement.'

Lanfranc leaned forward in his saddle to speak lowly so no one else would hear. 'Are you heretics?' he asked.

The priest caught the slightest taint of discomfort in the warrior's voice. He wasn't sure if his tone was tinged by fear.

'Some call us that,' the old man admitted. 'But you'll find we're Christian folk who'll not dishonour your beliefs by forcing you to face ours. We wouldn't press our ways on anyone.'

'I'll not be availing myself of your generous hospitality,' the knight shot back. 'Unless the lady I'm escorting requests it of me.'

From the darkness there was a cry of elation. It was a woman's voice. Then the priest saw a rider trotting forward.

'Clemens? Is that you?'

The old man frowned and squinted, trying to make out who

it was that had recognised him. As the rider drew closer she lifted her head-covering to give him a glimpse of her face.

'Sianan?' he gasped, then bowed down before the abbess. 'We weren't expecting you here for the feast. You do us great honour.'

'I haven't come for the Samhain festivities,' she told him. 'I've brought news of a war brewing in the Otherworld. Aoife has raised the hosts of the Redcaps. They're making ready to march upon us at Samhain Eve.'

Clemens's expression drained of all joy. 'Then we had should make to the Killibegs as fast as we can. Such matters are best discussed by the firelight in the safety of a large hall.'

With that he turned and marched off with surprising agility for a man of his years.

Well, I have to admit I was taken with young Caoimhin from the first moment I met him. Of course I'm willing to concede there weren't many young men his age living in our community. And the ones who did dwell in our company were really only silly boys.

So perhaps I was overly distracted. He was a handsome lad. And it suddenly struck me that I'd just offered up a prayer to Danu for a handsome lad. So I suppose I expected he'd be exactly what I asked her for.

He had the blue eyes and the corn-gold hair of a southern Gael. There was a shyness about him that melted my heart. I ended up staring at him speechless as he stood at the edge of the stone circle.

'Who are you?' he repeated.

I realised I'd got a bit lost in my dreaminess.

'Binney,' I stammered. 'My name's Binney.'

How his eyes widened. 'Are you Binney of the Killibegs?'

'I am.'

'Are you the sister of Eriginas?'

I paused, wondering how he could possibly know so much about me.

'I am.'

'Then I bear sad news to you,' he stated.

I walked straight up to the stones where he stood. 'What sad news?'

'Eriginas was my teacher. I was with him five days ago in Wexford when he passed from this life. He asked me to bring you the news. He told me I'd be welcomed among your folk.'

'You came all this way to tell me of my brother's death?'

'Actually, I came all this way to establish a Benedictine monastery,' he blurted.

I looked him up and down, hardly believing what he'd said. He didn't look as though he could have set up a butter churn let alone a whole monastic community.

But I didn't laugh. It's not right to ridicule another person's dreams, no matter how impossible they might seem.

'Come with me,' I offered. 'You look like you could do with a good meal and a warm place to sleep. We'll talk about your monastery when you've got some food in your belly.'

That's when he told me about his two companions. I thought to myself there was going to be a right good time at this year's Samhain feast with young lads coming in from all over.

Of course I hadn't any idea then that Lewyn and Overton weren't young men at all.

'Let's go fetch them,' I told him excitedly. 'The sooner we get you all back to the hearth fire, the sooner we can sit down for a good chinwag.'

Caoimhin led the way back through the blackberry bushes as I tried to make polite conversation.

'Was my brother on his way to visit me?'

'No.'

'Why had he come home to Ireland?'

'To establish a Benedictine priory.'

'My brother was a scribe. He didn't have the skill for such tasks.'

The lad changed the subject. 'Aren't you upset at the news of your brother's death?'

'We weren't close,' I explained. 'In fact he didn't approve of my decision to come to the Killibegs.'

'But he told me I'd be treated like family if I sought refuge with you.'

'What would you be seeking refuge from?' I asked.

That's when it struck me that there was more to this scribe than met the eye.

'Eriginas was a fine scholar,' says I. 'And I'm sure he was an incomparable brother. But he wasn't much of a brother, if you take my meaning. He put me in the convent when our mother died. I didn't have any choice in the matter.'

'I was put in the monastery when I was a boy,' Caoimhin added. 'And I'm glad I was. I've learned the art of scrivening and I've given my life to God.'

I stopped walking, shocked at the lad's apparent stupidity. He turned when he noticed I wasn't keeping up with him.

'Is something wrong?'

'There are more ways to serve God than wasting your days wearing the black and penning out the tales of the saints. God didn't mean us to be slaves to him. We were given this life and the five senses to enjoy, not to squander in slavery.'

The poor lad nearly choked with shock. 'We mortal kind are fallen angels who are suffering punishment here on Earth because we broke with Holy Writ.'

'What a pile of pillocks!'

He looked at me as if he couldn't understand how I could

possibly disagree.

'Who fed you that load of shite?' I asked.

'It's what the Abbot of Glastonbury taught me. It's the truth, isn't it?'

'If you believe that you'd believe anything,' I told him. 'Next you'll be telling me that visions are sent from Satan to lead us into sin.'

His eyes dropped to the ground. I couldn't be sure because the moon had moved behind a cloud, but I thought he might have been blushing. I did feel a little guilty. He'd only just met me and I was already telling him off.

'I'm sorry,' I offered.

'That's all right,' he answered. 'Hadn't we better go fetch my two friends? If they've noticed I'm missing they'll be worried about me.'

With that we went on, me biting my tongue. I thought to myself I'd well and truly ruined my chances with this one. So I was surprised when he struck up the conversation again.

'Have you ever had a vision?'

I told him I'd once seen an apparition of the Blessed Virgin Mary when I was a girl in the convent. I was very disappointed when it turned out to be old Sister Margaret sleepwalking. Other than that I hadn't had any experience of visions.

'What about you?' I asked.

He stopped in his tracks again to look me in the face. He was an intense young man then, our Caoimhin, but he had the most beautiful blue eyes I'd ever seen. The same colour as indigo they were, or the bluebells in bloom. Or the cloak I was wearing.

'I have visions all the time,' he stated.

'Really?'

But I recall thinking to myself, I've got a live one here. He's a proper mystic, this one.

I wasn't frightened of him. It's just not every day that a

stranger dressed in black who you've just met by the standing-stones in the moonlight admits to regularly seeing things that aren't really there. Do you follow me?

'I had a vision the other night,' he admitted as he turned to walk on. 'It was the most beautiful experience I've ever had in my whole life. I saw a creature of divine grace whose features shone like the stars and whose soul sparkled with a radiant love I can't even begin to describe to you.'

'Was it an angel you saw?' I gasped, for I'd heard tell of such things.

'I couldn't discern what manner of being she was.'

'She?' I noted dryly.

I knew enough about young men to draw my own conclusions.

'Were you asleep when this vision overtook you?'

'I was wide awake,' he sighed.

'What was this woman like then?'

Once again he turned to look me in the eye.

'She was exactly like you.'

By the time Clemens had brought Sianan and the others up to the Killibegs, the moon was high among the clouds, a shimmering presence behind a veil of mist. So he was quite concerned to discover I was nowhere to be found.

'We can't go out searching for her,' he complained. 'There's too much to do here and there's Redcaps abroad. What kind of a fool is she?'

But how was I to have known there'd be Redcaps roaming the countryside? How was I to know any folk other than our expected guests were going to arrive a day early? How was I to have guessed that I'd be needed to help prepare sleeping places and cook food?

Clemens was a good man, as I'm sure I've said. But sometimes he could be quite unreasonable. I'd already worked since before sun-up, thatching a temporary roof over one of the roundhouses. Then I'd spent the afternoon bringing in the cows for their second milking. When that was done I was sat at the butter churn till the sky grew pale. It wasn't as if I'd just wandered off on my own accord either. I'd been sent to gather blackberries. And as everyone knows, the best berries grow close to stone circles. It just so happened I'd stopped to offer my prayers after I'd filled a satchel with fruit.

In any case it doesn't matter now. But my absence caused quite a stir at the Killibegs. I was still in my early twenties and everyone over thirty thought of themselves as my parents. I couldn't break silent wind without the whole community knew about it. Bless him, but Clemens really was concerned for me. But of course I was in no danger whatsoever.

Anyway, soon enough the old priest had more than enough on his mind that he'd pushed me to the back of it. He always was a one who took on too much responsibility. But on this occasion he really overdid it. What with bedding folk down for the night, feeding hungry bellies, stabling horses, learning names and introducing his own people to everyone, he was fairly pressed for a spare moment.

Then he found himself taking stock of provisions, sharing polite conversation, setting a watch on the ramparts, gauging how many of the visitors could be relied on in a fight, and so on.

It was well after midnight before he had a chance to sit down with a bowl of broth by his own hearth fire to take a breath. And it wasn't till he'd laid his head down an hour later to catch some much needed rest that his thoughts returned to me.

He sat bolt upright on his straw mattress and shook his wife into wakefulness.

'Did Binney come back?' he asked her urgently.

'How should I know?' Derbáil snapped. 'I've more important matters to attend to.'

'More important matters?' he shrieked in disgust. 'What if the Redcaps have got hold of her?'

'Don't worry about that one,' his wife soothed. 'If the Redcaps have found her then I have the greatest sympathy for them.'

'The girl might be in danger! How can you be so unconcerned?'

'Shut up, will you?' Derbáil yawned. 'Binney can look after herself. And I haven't seen any Redcaps. Sianan told you the Norman called Lanfranc drove them off. Unless I'm much mistaken, it'll be a while before they risk coming out of their holes to face him again. He cut off the head of one of them!'

'I heard the story! I'm not an idiot.'

Derbáil kissed her husband indulgently on the cheek. 'Now go to sleep. There's nothing to worry about. Binney's probably just out with one of the lads.'

'What would she be doing out with one of the lads?'

His wife rolled her eyes.

'Shagging.'

The old priest's mouth dropped open in shock. He struggled to find the words to express his horror. But before he could master his tongue, his wife spoke again.

'How did you spend the evenings round Samhain tide when you were her age?'

'I wasn't out shagging. That's for certain.'

'Well that might go some way to explaining your deficiencies of character,' his wife sighed. That was the end of the conversation as far as she was concerned. She shut her eyes and let exhaustion overtake her.

But Clemens didn't sleep. He lay awake until dawn with thoughts of what the Redcaps might be up to. And worse, what

I might be up to out in the wilds with one of the lads two nights before Samhain Oidche.

When Caoimhin located his friends their fire had gone out and it was very late indeed. I helped him get the blaze going again but it was ages before we managed to stir the other two from slumber.

By then I'd heard the young scribe's story of how he'd come to Ireland with my brother Eriginas. I'd learnt how my brother had caught the fever on the journey from England. And I'd listened to his account of the journey from Wexford. I'd also realised Caoimhin was coming down with a chest cough.

I couldn't help thinking he'd left some important details out of his story. But I was content to be out under the night sky drinking up the tones of his strange accent.

Overton and Lewyn were not happy to be woken. They'd been worn down by the cold nights and lack food.

It was Overton who convinced us that it would be better to wait till first light to set off for Killibegs. He then promptly fell back into a deep sleep which was only broken when he realised we were eating all the blackberries I'd collected.

That was quite a feast too, I can tell you. The two older monks gorged themselves until their hands and tongues and lips were stained dark red. But at least their bellies were not grumbling so much.

I wasn't sleepy. Neither was young Caoimhin. It seemed to me our interest in one another was mutual. And countless times that night I silently thanked Lady Danu for sending him to me so promptly.

I suppose it must have seemed a bit heartless of me not to

have shown much grief at the news of my brother's death. But Caoimhin didn't seem to mind. Indeed, he showed as little regret as I did. And he'd known Eriginas quite well.

'What about his books?' I asked excitedly. 'Eriginas had a marvellous collection even when he was young.'

'I have them,' the young scribe nodded. 'He left them to me.' He patted the book satchel at his side rather nervously. 'I'll show you one of them,' he volunteered, pulling out a small volume no wider that his hand, though very thick, and handing it to me.

I immediately examined the binding. I had been trained as a bookbinder so that was the first part of any book I ever studied.

'The stitches are so finely done,' I noted with admiration. 'This was put together a long time ago. Perhaps a hundred years or so.' Then I read the opening page. '*Leabhar Fál.* The Book of Destiny.'

'It's a book of wise sayings,' Caoimhin commented. 'Every page offers some advice. The trick is to open it at random and it will predict the future or point you in the right direction.'

'I know what it is,' I assured him. 'These were very popular in Ireland before the Normans came.'

'Why did they become unpopular?'

'They didn't. The Normans stole them all. That's probably how my brother came to be in possession of this one. I'd say it was plundered from an Irish community in the east.'

The young scribe was suddenly ashamed. And I regretted my hasty showing-off. The book fell open then and I silently read the page that was revealed.

I was so surprised by what I saw I motioned to Caoimhin to come closer.

'Look at what it says here.'

He leaned across to read the page. '"Two lighten the load. Two brighten the Road."'

He thought about that for a moment then said, 'Someone

told me the sayings in this book are a guide to the future. He also said I should take careful note of everything the book told me.'

'That's true. This is the *Leabhar Fál*. It's a book of enchantment with a spirit of its own.'

'A spirit? Do you mean a dæmon?'

I laughed but went on to explain my limited understanding of Enticers and Frighteners. I don't think he was too impressed. But bless him, Caoimhin was a sweet lad so he didn't express his doubts.

'We'd better get some sleep,' I told him at last with a yawn.

Then, without thinking he might be shy, I threw my cloak around the two of us and settled down on the ground, snuggling against his shoulder to get some rest. I remember feeling him shake against me for a while, but I thought it was just the cold giving him the shivers.

If I'd known he was nervous I might not have been so forward. But in the end it was good for him. He later told me he'd struggled to sleep that night. While I slumbered on blissfully ignorant of his discomfort, he prayed until dawn.

So I suppose it's not surprising that when I woke up he was already packing his gear for the last part of the journey to the Killibegs.

GATHERING

The same night I was lying in the arms of Caoimhin out among the woods, Guy and his new companion Toothache were being introduced to the splendours of the Otherworld. Aoife of the Redcaps brought them to her halls deep under the forest.

In a dreamlike state they followed her through the narrow passages lit by innumerable torches. At length the three of them reached a chamber as large as the space within the great cathedral at Chartres which Guy had visited on his way to Ireland. The walls of this chamber were hung with incredible tapestries of the most vibrant colours. They reached from the roof down to the floor, entirely draping the walls in rainbows of splendour. All these magnificent artworks were woven in reds, greens and yellow richer than any d'Alville had ever seen before. Others were of darker sea blues and sky purples cunningly embroidered with gold and silver thread in such a way that the light caught every stitch. The sparkling stars were no match for these gorgeous decorations.

'This is the most beautiful room in the world,' the Norman declared, overawed at the vastness of the room and the opulence of its design. Every uncovered space was carved, moulded or painted with an intricate series of spirals. Yet there was no furniture in this chamber. Nowhere to sit. No tables. No sign that it was used as anything more than an entrance hall to an even greater room.

Indeed that is all it was. Aoife laughed at her awestruck guests, clearly delighted that they appreciated the way she'd decorated the chamber.

'We will pass now into my personal apartments,' she told them matter-of-factly. But the truth was she couldn't wait to see the looks on their faces when they saw her own rooms.

A small, modestly carved wooden door lay at the far end of the tapestry room. When they reached it the door flung open as if by unseen hands.

Aoife handed Guy a torch, telling him to lead the way. No sooner had he passed through the door than he gasped with delight. The long hall on the other side was wide enough to drive four horses walking abreast. Every surface was inlaid with countless tiny mirrors of gold and silver cut in the most wondrous shapes. D'Alville was so dazzled by the brilliance of torchlight reflected in these decorations that he had to shade his eyes from the glare.

Guy counted two hundred paces before they reached a wall also covered with small mirrors. As they approached, this wall opened up before them to reveal the wonder of wonders behind it: a vast cavern-like chamber so large that torches twinkled on its distant walls like the firelight of far-off villages at night. Once again every surface was covered with fragmented mirrors. But the colours were not merely gold and silver. There were luminescent reds, greens and yellows. There were light, bright blues. And it seemed that everything was bathed in the reflected glory of these sparkling points of light.

'It's like being in a cave made of jewels,' Toothache sighed.

'Indeed it is,' the queen replied. 'For these are jewels of the richest kind. Sapphires, emeralds, rubies, diamonds, amethysts, amber and every precious stone known to mortals are set into these wall.'

That sight fairly took Guy's breath away. He'd never seen

such riches. He'd never even dreamed such a thing was possible.

'But be warned,' Aoife added. 'Any mortal who should try to remove even a single stone from this place will suffer for his impudence. This is my palace. You may stare in wonder as long as you don't steal in envy.'

She strode off along a glittering path to where yet another small door opened in the wall. She bowed down to enter this next chamber. The two Normans followed on close behind.

This room was very tiny, barely five paces wide by ten long. But laid out on a table was every kind of food imaginable. There was roast boar, honey-baked chicken, fish grilled in herbs and butter. There were vegetables of every kind roasted, fried, boiled or sweetened. Great glass pots of honey as tall as a child stood on the floor. There were ten different colours of the sweet condiment, and breads of white, brown, yellow and red. Rounds of cheese, stacked along one wall, filled the air with their aromatic tinctures, beckoning the visitors to taste them. Smoked wild fowl were hung on hooks. Geese, swan and duck were laid out on steaming platters fresh from the ovens. Wines and mead of every variety waited in beautiful crystal decanters which reflected the light of a hundred candles set into tiny recesses around the walls. And in the middle of the table was a small fountain from which spurted the sweetest, clearest water sparkling fresh and pure like liquid diamonds.

'Eat your fill,' the queen commanded. 'I will return to take you to the Killibegs when you're done.'

Now, Guy considered himself a restrained man not given to acts of overindulgence or gluttony, but the very moment Aoife left the room he almost leaped into the feast. He ate and ate until he could eat no more. Then he waited a while to regain his composure and ate some more.

He'd never felt so hungry in his life. Nor so satisfied. The food was exquisite. Finer than the finest banquet he could have imagined. And as for Toothache, he almost forgot his pain in his haste to fill his belly.

The Normans of those days were not a people known for their marvellous culinary achievements. In that time they were only a warrior people who taught their sons and daughters to endure hardship, to go without and to suffer bland porridge for the greater good of their kinfolk. So Aoife's kitchen must have been as close as either of them could have imagined to Heaven on Earth. That is to say, Heaven under the earth, if you understand me. And wasn't she a wily one, our Queen of the Night?

Do you recall what Finbar the Boatman told Caoimhin and his companions? Do you remember how he reckoned unbelievers are given a taste of Heaven then sent back to Earth to dwell as mortals?

Well that's what Aoife had in mind for these two. She wanted to buy their unswerving loyalty. And she could see well enough that Guy and Toothache weren't philosophers or mystics. They were simple men at heart, easily swayed with minor wonders.

That's why all the tales warn folk not to eat of the food of the Faerie world or to drink the wine or to sleep in the arms of the Faerie folk. For it's all illusion created to beguile the fool and purchase the loyalty of the greedy.

Anyway, as I was saying, the two of them eventually discovered they had immeasurable thirsts to quench. Toothache quaffed a small barrel of mead without once coming up for air.

Guy sampled all the wines, finally settling on a jug that had been sweetened with the finest of golden honeys. It was unlike anything he'd ever tasted before. And what's more, neither of them felt giddy drunk, just merry and refreshed.

They must have been at it for hours. But at last, exhausted from overexerting their stomachs, the two of them fell into a deep untroubled sleep. And while they slept both men dreamed of Aoife, Queen of the Night, Sovereign of the Dark Places.

Toothache dreamed of being her servant. Guy dreamed of being her consort. She was well practised at this sort of thing, she was. I have to admire her skill even though I can't approve of her motives.

As I recall that year was the last time our people gathered in such an open spot where anyone could see the smoke of our hearth fires. Father Clemens had chosen that ancient hilltop rath thinking that the chieftains who were to be our guests would feel more at home within a fortification that had once been home to their martial ancestors.

It was a fine place to be wintering. The steep hill was surrounded on three sides by sheer rocky walls not carved out by the hand of man. At the base of the hill a path wide enough for a wagon wound its way to a small stone gatehouse slightly elevated from the surrounding countryside. The solid stone Norman walls encased this gatehouse built on the foundations of a much earlier fort. These walls led all the way up to the main walls of the enclosure. In this way archers could stand upon the walls to harass any enemy that breached the gatehouse.

The Normans had installed two squat towers on either side of the entrance path near to where the large main gatehouse afforded entry into the rath. Each of these structures had a huge iron cauldron permanently set above a fireplace. These cauldrons were used to boil large quantities of oil. Once the liquid was bubbling away, the cauldrons could be emptied down on any unwelcome intruders via a system of levers and pulleys. The Normans were old hands at siege warfare. It suited their temperament.

But it wasn't our way of giving battle. Amongst the tribespeople of the Gael the rath had been a place of refuge where the cattle could be brought to ensure their safekeeping. No war-leader ever tried to take a rath by force. It just wasn't done.

Inside the walls of this rath there was a large Norman-style hall, rectangular, spacious and built of sturdy stone. It was half hall, half keep. There were stairs down to the ancient pre-Norman dry cellars where all the produce of the community could be stored for the winter.

These cellars were spacious and by the ingenuity of their construction kept at an even cool temperature all year round. When we arrived there were supplies of butter, cheese and wine laid in, remnants of the previous occupant. In one huge room we found two great barrels full to bursting with precious cooking fat and lamp oil.

Above the dry cellars the main meeting room of the hall could hold a hundred folk or more round the central hearth. Smaller cooking hearths were set into fireplaces in the north and south walls of the building. Smoke from the central hearth was funnelled up through a chimney set into the second and third floors. On the next level up were chambers where the servants and family of the Norman knight must have lived.

The topmost floor was taken up by a chapel and the private rooms of the lord. We found abandoned wall hangings rolled and stacked on this floor, so we hung them up to cover the cold stone. This area we set aside for our guests of high rank.

Above that was the roof which doubled as a place where archers could be positioned in time of strife. The whole country for miles around could be seen from there. It was the perfect place to direct the defence of the rath.

There were other smaller buildings within the walls. Old round thatch-roofed homes of Irish design stood alongside square Norman storehouses and stables. There was a heavy pair of double doors set into the ground near the main gate. These doors led down into the dry cellars under the hall.

Some of the older thatch needed some repair, but for the most part the place was habitable and a great contrast to the life we'd been living since the previous snowmelt. Even if the sky sent us a blizzard, this was going to be a comfortable winter and we were all looking forward to the warmth of the hearth fires.

So now you know something of our rath. Well, if we thought we were going to have a restful winter we were wrong. But Father Clemens couldn't have chosen a better place for us as it turned out.

I was still sleeping wrapped in my cloak at Caoimhin's side when Clemens rose that morning. Before dawn he was already checking on the preparations for breakfast, going from house to house seeing to the fires so everyone would be warm when they awoke.

Then, as the sun rose, he set off toward the stone circle to look for me. He was a stern old man as I've already mentioned but he was very popular with the children. He hadn't made it as far as the outer gatehouse before he had a dozen of the younger ones following after him. They were all excited at the prospect of visitors. None of them suspected there could be any danger.

'Go home!' the old priest commanded. 'There are wicked folk about in this part of the world. The Redcaps will get you if you stray too far from your fireside.'

The smaller children screamed half in delight and half in real fright. Then they faltered and turned around to go home. A few of the older ones boldly beckoned them back. Then they all waited till the old priest was halfway down the hill before they followed after him again, hiding behind bushes or scurrying into the ditch whenever he turned to look back.

He was a gentle soul. He knew what they were up to. So he thought to play a trick on them to teach them all a lesson. At the very bottom of the hill he climbed into the branches of a gnarled old oak that spread out low to the ground. As I've said, he was a surprisingly agile man for his age. Once Clemens had settled himself he gathered a few fallen branches to stick in his belt. Then he tied an antler-like sprig to his head with his belt and waited.

The children didn't suspect a thing. Full of giggles they approached the tree, thinking to climb it to get a look at the progress of their beloved priest.

But as they came within a few steps of the bough, Clemens jumped up and down on the thick low branch to surprise them. He growled with all the ferocity he could muster. And bless the little ones, they were frightened all right. Two of the smallest broke out into loud wailing tears the moment he appeared. The elder children grabbed stones and sticks to throw at him. Soon the old priest was being pelted with everything the children could lay their hands on.

One stone arced high into the air and hit Clemens right on the top of his head. The old man lost his balance, fell off the branch and rolled across the grass toward the path.

In less time than it takes to yell, 'Stop, it's me!', the children fell upon him with a mixture of laughter and relief. Tears turned to delight. Tiny fists did their best to give the old man a bruising as unforgettable as the fright he'd dished out to them.

As it happened that was the very moment Caoimhin's little group, with me guiding them, appeared on the road. I ran up to the children, pulling them off the old man one at a time until there was a circle of smiling youngsters around us.

Clemens lay on his back, groaning, half in pain, half with the joyous silliness of the game.

'I scared you!' he guffawed. 'That'll teach you to go wandering out from the hill-fort with no one to keep an eye on you. What if I'd been a Redcap? What would you have done then?'

One of the older boys stepped forward. 'If you'd been a Redcap we wouldn't have stopped till you'd given in to us!'

From somewhere amongst the children another stone was thrown. It flashed by me to strike Clemens in the chest. The surprise of it knocked him over again. He groaned once more Then he stopped moving.

I looked down at the old priest, my expression full of concern.

'You've killed Father Clemens!' I exclaimed.

The children gasped. 'It was Tomás,' they shrieked as one. Except for poor Tomás, of course. He was very silent indeed.

'Step forward, lad,' I commanded. 'Look what you've done!'

The boy pushed his way to the front of the group. He was small for his nine years but he was the most difficult, mischievous, adventurous and unruly of them all.

His jet black, permanently tousled hair fell across his face but it couldn't hide his expression of horror at what he'd done. Step by step he approached while Caoimhin and the other two monks crowded round to see what could be done to help the old priest.

Clemens lay motionless, his eyes staring into space. No breath heaved his chest. No flicker of life passed across his features.

'What have you done?' I wailed. 'You've killed him!'

The lad looked down at the deceased priest with some suspicion at first. But then he plainly saw the old man wasn't moving. A look of real remorse suddenly coloured his expression.

'I didn't mean to,' Tomás whimpered.

'It's too late for that now,' I scolded. 'What are we going to do without Father Clemens? We all depended on him. He was our guide and the oldest member of the community.'

'I'm sorry,' the boy offered sincerely. 'Truly I am.'

'You must close his eyes,' I informed him. 'Since you murdered Clemens, you must put his soul to rest. You'll have to stand vigil by his body through the night. And I pray his ghost doesn't come to torment you. You'll have to pay his wife the fine for his value.'

'The eric fine!' the other children hummed in horror.

'Clemens must have been worth a dozen cows at least,' I nodded. 'Your family will be very poor. Your brothers and sisters won't have any cheese this winter. You'll have to pay Derbáil and you'll have to sell everything your family owns to be able to do it.'

The lad hung his head in shame and a few tears gathered at the corners of his eyes. He wiped them away, determined to face what he'd done like a man.

'I'll pay the fine,' he declared. 'But I'll find a way so my family won't suffer for my foolishness.'

'I hope so,' said I. 'Now close the old man's eyes and we'll go back up to the Killibegs and tell folk what you've done.'

The boy looked to the strangers for some support. But Caoimhin turned his head away so he wouldn't have to make eye contact. The other two monks simply shook their heads in disbelief.

Tomás placed a shaking finger on each of the dead man's eyelids to shut them. And just as he did so Clemens sprang to life, grabbing the boy about the waist, throwing him to the ground.

'Murder an old man, would you?' the priest screamed in a mock temper.

The lad shrieked with terror, thinking for a moment the ghost of Clemens had returned to torment him. But the other children saw the joke the moment they noticed the hint of a smile on the old man's face.

'You tricked me, Father!' the boy yelled.

'I'll teach you a lesson you won't soon forget,' the old man promised.

The two of them wrestled playfully until the rest of the children realised it was all in fun. Then Clemens had a dozen laughing playful souls gathered jumping on him again.

'Go home, the lot of you!' the old priest demanded at last. 'Your mothers will be waiting your breakfast. There's work to be done today. We have guests!'

The youngsters cheered as they ran off up the hill.

'Tomás!' the priest called out. 'You'll clean out the cattle byres all by yourself this morning. And you'll use the smallest shovel I can find for you.'

'Yes, Father,' the lad dutifully replied.

'Now go home, Tomás, before I decide on a harsher punishment. And next time I tell you to do something, make sure I'm obeyed.'

'Yes, Father.'

Tomás hunched his shoulders, turned then took his time walking back to the settlement.

'Father,' I began, 'this is Caoimhin, a scribe from the Abbey of Glastonbury.'

The young Benedictine bowed. 'This is Lewyn and Overton of Llancarfan. They are journeying through Ireland collecting travellers' tales. They're compiling a book on the people of this land.'

'You're all welcome here in our humble home,' Clemens bowed in return, but the mirth had vanished from his voice. 'I hope you'll forgive the misbehaviour of my youngest son.'

'Your son!' Lewyn exclaimed. 'I thought you were a priest?'

'I am. Among the Culdees priests are permitted to marry.'

'But Tomás wasn't born to Clemens' wife,' I explained. 'She's too old to bear children.'

There was an uncomfortable silence. I'd forgotten how staid foreigners could be. I suppose I should have been gentler about introducing them to our ways.

Clemens put a firm hand on my shoulder. 'And just where the bloody hell were you last night, young lady?'

'I went to gather blackberries and became lost,' I lied.

'Then perhaps you might tell me why this young man is blushing?'

It was true. Caoimhin's face had turned bright red with embarrassment.

'He's just flushed with the cold morning air, Father.'

'Rubbish. You'll help your youngest brother shovel out the cow shite from the byre. And when you've finished that, the two of you can offer your humble apologies to me in my chambers. I was up all night worried to death for you.'

'You shouldn't have concerned yourself about me, Father.'

'There are Redcaps abroad,' he snapped. 'There's talk they're amassing an army and Queen Aoife is behind it. It simply isn't safe to be out after dark. Do you understand me?'

'But no harm came of it,' I protested. 'I spent the night in the arms of this lovely lad. I was perfectly safe.'

Lewyn and Overton both gasped in shock at this. Caoimhin's cheeks blushed even redder than before.

'You're just like your mother,' the old man scoffed. 'Always off having a good time. Never thinking of the trouble you might cause.'

'Didn't you ever have any fun when you were my age?' I shot back, losing patience with his reprimand.

'I did not.'

'Well maybe if you had, you'd be easier to get on with now.'

Clemens's face turned a brighter crimson than Caoimhin's but it wasn't embarrassment that lit it up.

'Your old mother said that last night.'

'She's a better judge than me,' I replied. 'She's known you so much longer.'

'That's enough!' he hissed. 'Go to your work. And don't think I'll forget the humiliation you've brought upon me with your selfishness.'

'Eriginas is dead,' I told him flatly.

'What?'

'Ask young Caoimhin,' I went on. 'He was with your eldest son when he passed from this world.'

Then I stormed off to the settlement, my empty blackberry basket swinging from side to side. Just as a torment to the old man I turned to call back, 'I'll see you up at the Killibegs, Caoimhin. I forgot to thank you for a wonderful evening.'

The poor lad hid his face in his hands. I knew he was going to get a terrible time from the two Welshmen. But it was all in good fun.

I'll tell you this much. I may have seemed short tempered with old Clemens but I was glad to be with our own people. My elder brother, Eriginas, had taken me away with him when he ran off to join the Benedictines. He had that trouble common to eldest sons. He thought he knew everything and his father knew nothing. He was arrogant and self-obsessed. But he had a way with words. So when he told me he was off to join a holy order I insisted on going with him. I soon enough regretted it.

As soon as I was old enough to climb the convent walls I was off home to my own kith and kin. I left him behind without so much as fare-thee-well. Silly old bugger he was.

Anyway, after I was out of earshot Clemens asked about his eldest son, Eriginas.

'But my teacher was an old man himself,' Caoimhin protested. 'Surely he couldn't have been your son?'

'My boy, I am much older than I seem,' the priest explained. 'A wholesome life in the clean air works wonders on a man. And as we say among our folk, a light heart lives long.'

'But you'd have to be nearly ninety,' the scribe calculated quickly.

'Eighty-eight winters I've walked upon this earth, young man. Just because a man grows ancient doesn't mean he has to feel old or think like an old fool.'

' Yes, father,' the young scribe bowed with deep respect.

'Young Caoimhin,' the old man said, 'after we've eaten, you

378

can come with me to milk the cows. Then you can tell me all about my son, Eriginas.'

Then he repeated his welcome and added another touch.

'While you stay with us you may consider my people to be your family. For we are all the sons and daughters of God.'

In the great hall of the Killibegs all the folk who had so far arrived for the feast of Samhain gathered together to share news and to take their fill of breakfast. Our food was simpler fare than that offered to Guy and Toothache within the Faerie palace. There were oatcakes sweetened with honey, aged yellow cheeses and white steaming ones fresh out of the cheese cloth. To accompany this fare there were breads both brown and red, ale and generous helpings of butter and milk.

Our people were still fasting in the lead-up to Samhain Oidche, so there was no meat or fish to be had. According to tradition, until that feast we ate nothing but the simplest of foods.

There was no feast like Samhain during the whole cycle of the seasons. Even the winter-feast of Imbolc wasn't as sumptuous nor satisfying. As I've said, we never took more than we needed, though we were not as austere in our habits as some who called themselves Culdees.

Sianan, Martin, Mirim, Lanfranc and the others who'd arrived the night before were already seated around the central hearth. By the time Caoimhin and his travelling companions arrived to take up their positions, breakfast was well under way.

As I've told you before, this main hall had been built by a Norman. It took up the lower floor of a square tower, and a hundred folk could be seated in the chamber comfortably. At a pinch, another fifty could squeeze in. There was a great hearth right in the centre in the style of the Gaels. Such a hearth was known by our folk as the round table. This was where meals were shared, business discussed, stories told, songs sung, judgements passed and strategies planned.

The Norman who'd built this hall had probably had an Irish wife. Who knows, but perhaps a falling-out with her was the reason he'd abandoned this place in the end. It's more likely than any other reason I can think of.

Directly above the hearth a wickerwork chimney funnelled the smoke out to the roof so folk sleeping on the upper floor weren't choked by the hearth fire. Thirty people could be seated closest to the fire on a circular bench formed by an excavated depression in the floor. It was within this depression that the great fire was placed.

I can't say what the Norman lord must have thought of this very un-Norman feature. But I can tell you it suited us perfectly. I've never understood the foreign custom of sitting at squared-off tables with the hearth fire at your back. At a rectangular table it may be easy enough to see the eyes of the person opposite you, but if you want to speak with someone further down the bench, you've got to get up and move. No wonder the Normans spent so much time fighting amongst themselves. Either they couldn't make eye contact or they were constantly jostling for position at table.

As I was saying, by the time Caoimhin and his companions entered the hall I'd already finished my breakfast. I was due out at the byre to shovel out the manure as Clemens had commanded. But I was there long enough to notice the way Sianan looked at my scribe as he sat down opposite her at the fire. I remember thinking to myself that I'd seen him first. And how dare she cast an eye over my young unsullied Benedictine?

But there was more to her look than that, as I found out later. There was something about the lad that sparked a memory in her. Though she couldn't quite place where she could have met him or what it was about him that caught her interest.

I had to leave just then. And I was sorely upset that Caoimhin couldn't come with me.

'Enjoy your meal,' I said to him as I placed a hand on his shoulder on my way out. 'I'll talk to you later. I'd love to have another look at your *Leabhar Fál*.'

I still can't believe I fawned over him so. As if I'd never seen a young man in my life before. There you go. That's what being young is all about. I'm glad to be an old biddy, I can tell you and no lie in it at all.

After I'd gone Sianan introduced herself. Then she asked young Caoimhin where he'd come from and who were his kinfolk. He told her the tale of Eriginas and their journey to Ireland and all the sad details of his teacher's death. He told her about his fosterage at the Abbey of Glastonbury after the death of his parents. And he mentioned that the abbot had never told him their names so he knew nothing of his kin. But never once did he touch on the real purpose of his journey, nor on the quest his teacher had assigned to him.

Truth to tell, Caoimhin had begun to lose interest in his quest the moment he'd first seen Gobann in the market at Wexford. Little by little he'd started to enjoy his life on the road, despite the encroaching chest cold and the days with little food. His new-found sense of freedom was exhilarating. The excitement of meeting new people was far more precious to him than any manuscript or the machinations of far-off potentates.

So it was natural for him to react with shock when Sianan made another comment then asked a new question.

'The Abbot of Glastonbury must have thought highly of your teacher and yourself,' she began. 'To send you all the way to Ireland in order to set up a Benedictine priory he must have placed a great deal of faith in you.'

She paused, carefully gauging the young scribe's reaction. 'But tell me. Why would any abbot send two scribes to do the work of a priest?'

Caoimhin swallowed hard, certain he'd been discovered. 'I don't know what you mean.'

'You said yourself that you've never been outside the monastery. And your teacher was a renowned scholar who'd deserted his native country to study in the great libraries of the Continent.'

Once again she paused. The whole room fell silent. Her point had not been lost on anyone who'd been listening. Folk began to question whether Caoimhin was telling the truth about his purpose in their country.

'Eriginas had no experience of the day-to-day running of a monastic community. He seems a poor choice for the founder of a religious establishment. Why do you suppose your abbot chose him?'

'He was well versed in the Gaelic language,' Caoimhin offered. 'And in the ways of your people.'

Sianan smiled, certain she was on to something. 'I must compliment you on your grasp of our language. Eriginas taught you well.'

She looked him squarely in the eye to let him know she was harbouring some suspicions about him . . . 'I hope you won't think it rude of me but I've a notion that your abbot may have had some other task in mind for you both.'

'What task?' the scribe shrugged, attempting to seem surprised by her question.

But Caoimhin wasn't a very good liar. That his reaction was fake was obvious to everyone.

'It's well known that the community of Killibegs holds a library of rare and precious manuscripts. Many of the books cannot be found anywhere on the Continent or in Britain. Was Eriginas sent here to copy them? Or to plunder them?'

Clemens stood up and faced Sianan directly. 'I respect the learned Abbess of Dun Gur,' he began. 'But the breakfast hearth fire is no place to be making accusations against a guest of mine. If you have any further questions to ask of the lad you'll respectfully wait until the council meeting this evening.'

Sianan bowed her head. 'It was not my wish to cause offence.'

She turned her attention back to Caoimhin.

'Please accept my apologies. I forgot myself. So much has happened in the last few days. I've been beset with so many challenges and so much worrying news that I've unintentionally breached the etiquette of hospitality. I hope you can find it in your heart to forgive me.'

The scribe nodded.

Clemens swallowed a cup of weak ale before he spoke again. 'Caoimhin, my lad. Come with me. I want you to help me with the milking.'

Then the priest turned to his guests. 'Please accept the welcome of the warmth of this hall. Stay here by the fire for the day is cold and the weather unpredictable. As more guests arrive they'll be led in here to meet with you all. Talk, tell stories, play the Brandubh if you wish. But I ask you to refrain from speaking of great matters until we've broken bread and shared the sacrament.'

With those words he made for the door, followed closely by Caoimhin.

Cheese

When Guy awoke, Toothache was snoring heavily, buried face down in a colourful mountain of silk cushions. The room was smaller than the Norman remembered it. The tables and food were all gone. They'd been replaced with bed silks, cushions and covers.

D'Alville stretched as he yawned. He couldn't recall a sounder night of rest in his entire life. His sleep had been remarkably sweet. There'd been no blood to haunt his dreams. No plunder. No treachery. No battle. His slumber had never been so serene and satisfying.

Guy stared at the ceiling, unwilling to rise from this comfortable spot. The dazzling little mirrors reflected back every hue of the rainbow in a glittering array of sparkling wonder.

The room was light. Yet no candle burned. No torch shone. He frowned in confusion, wondering what magic had been woven about this place. Then he had his doubts. The first and only serious doubts he suffered about whether it was wise to couple his fate with that of the Witch-Queen of the Redcaps.

He'd already seen what the Nathairaí could do. They were evil enough. He'd witnessed the dæmonic powers of Aoife and he suspected what he'd seen had just been a foretaste of her capabilities. What if she were in league with the Devil? He considered the consequences for his immortal soul if she turned out to be a servant of Satan.

Then he laughed at himself for entertaining such foolish thoughts. He'd already indulged in enough evil in his life to condemn him to an eternity in Hell. Joining Aoife's cause wouldn't tip the scales against him.

His mind strayed onto more important matters. Such as what he'd do once he held the high-kingship of Ireland. He'd always known he was meant for better things than serving as a mere lackey to the Order of the Hospital.

He then considered the Redcaps. They were tough, frightening fighters. From what Toothache had told him the strange warriors were strong and fleet of foot. True enough the Redcaps could be killed if beheaded. But it was an easy enough matter to have armour constructed which would protect their necks. If they truly were immortal and impervious to all other injury, there would be no stopping the advance of an army of them.

With a force of Redcaps under his command, Guy realised he could easily conquer England. And if he could take that country, in time he might find himself seated on the sacred throne of the Holy Roman Empire.

Guy was a conceited bugger. Did I mention that earlier? Most men would have been more than content with the high-kingship of Ireland. But not him. He was already off fighting mighty battles in his mind, conjuring up the terrified faces of his adversaries when they surrendered to him.

The Norman rolled onto his side, grinning with pleasure at the possibilities laid out before his fertile, self-serving imagination. Then he noticed something very unsettling. There beside him, wrapped in the covers, was Aoife. He was sure she hadn't been there a few moments earlier.

Suddenly the Norman realised he was completely naked beneath the fine bed silks. He sat up in surprise.

'Good morning, my dear,' the queen purred. 'I was wondering when you'd cease your scheming long enough to notice I was here beside you.'

Guy was speechless. He couldn't recall how he'd ended up in the same bed as this Otherworldly woman. But his confusion didn't have the opportunity to bloom into a question.

'You don't remember our night games?' she asked him. 'That's well. I knew a bard once who told me he could always be sure when his performance had been excellent because he usually couldn't recall anything about it.'

She laughed at her own wit but her humour was wasted on Guy. He wasn't in the mood for it. He hated being caught off guard.

In the next moment the air filled with a brightness such as he'd never witnessed before. D'Alville shaded his eyes to protect them from the intensity of the light. A few moments later he sensed a change had taken place.

'You can look up now,' Aoife told him in a mocking voice. 'Who would have thought that such a vicious, fearless, unprincipled warrior such as yourself would be shy with women.'

'I'm not shy!' the Norman grunted.

As he spoke he removed his hands from his face to find the queen standing before him in her regal attire of a green gown with a darker cloak wrapped about her shoulders. Guy himself was clothed in his tunic and mail as he had been when he arrived in this place.

'What witchery is this?' he hissed. 'They're burning sorcerers at the stake in France and Spain.'

'Any practitioner of the Draoi-craft who allows themselves to be burned to death isn't much of a sorcerer,' she noted dryly. 'It'll never happen to me. My power is based on something a little more substantial than an empty ritual, a pointed hat and a book full of silly mumblings.'

She laughed with delight. 'Most of those fools who call themselves wizards have enough trouble conjuring their next meal, let alone summoning a spirit to satisfy their darker desires. Witches! You Normans wouldn't know a real enchantment if it flew down from the clouds and plucked your eyes out with its black beak.'

As she spoke the wall slid open and Sciathan Cog hopped into the room.

'Did you summon me, sister?' he cawed.

'I did,' Aoife replied. 'It's time to take these two to the Killibegs.'

The raven bowed. 'I'll fly on ahead to scout the way,' he cackled. 'Will you be wanting an escort?'

'Send a troop of Redcaps with a war engine,' she told him. 'I want them to start pounding the settlement into submission at first light tomorrow morning. Give the Gaels a taste of my wrath on the day of Samhain Oidche.'

'Yes, my lady.'

Then Cog was gone.

'What have you got planned?' Guy ventured. 'Why bother with a community of worthless heretics? What possible value could they be to you?'

The queen patiently explained her strategy, reminding d'Alville how important it was that as many folk in Ireland as possible bowed down to her in worship. To ensure this she had contrived to make herself look like the saviour of the Irish people. The Nathairaí were already spreading havoc and fear. But it was to be at the Killibegs where the full force of her fury would be unleashed. On Samhain Eve her Redcaps would descend upon the community, cutting everyone and everything to shreds.

'Of course I'll allow a few folk to escape so they can spread the news of the terrible slaughter,' she explained. 'But the rest of them will be a blood sacrifice dedicated to me.'

Her fiendish mind had planned this out well. I can truly attest that once news of the attack on the Killibegs passed around the land, folk would fairly quiver in their bedsocks at the thought of the same thing happening to them.

The cost would not be great. A hundred or so simple Culdee folk would lose their lives. They were people who would have bitterly resisted her anyway. If they were allowed to live there would always be a danger they might lead a rebellion against her. She could do without the grudging devotion of these few.

But because they were known to be so fierce in their own defence their deaths would be enough to ensure terror spread through the countryside. That's why Aoife chose them. Everyone in Ireland knew the Culdees couldn't be defeated easily. She knew they couldn't be fooled easily either.

Once they were dealt with it would be a simple matter for Aoife to step forward with a great flourish to seemingly halt the Redcaps and imprison the marauding Nathairaí. Then most folk would simply bow down to her in deep gratitude. Such worship would add to the strength of her Enticer spirit. While her Frightener would be feeding on the apprehension, fear and horror which spread with the news of the slaughter at Killibegs.

I can tell you, if I'd known she intended to murder almost all my kinfolk for her own purposes I'd have stepped up and done something about her. I would have found a way to stop her.

She was a cunning one. To make sure everyone was on edge she'd contrived another surprise. You see, in those days before the Normans held too much of our island there was a tradition attached to Samhain Oidche.

It was a ritual known as the kindling of the Need-Fire. Every year as the sun set on the Eve of Samhain all the hearth fires in Ireland were extinguished. In the days before the Christians there was a gathering at Tara, seat of the high-kings. At midnight a Druid would rekindle a new flame from flint and steel. Then the fire would be carried out from Tara to every hearth in the land. All the fires of Ireland would be lit from that one kindling. It was a beautiful symbol of an ancient concept of interconnectedness.

It made no difference where one dwelled nor what rank one held. Everyone needed fire to survive, especially in the cold winter months following Samhain. Everyone was part of a much wider community than their own hearth fire encompassed. The ritual of the Need-Fire was a reminder that help must be offered wherever it was asked. After all, at the end of the day we're all sailing along in the same fishing boat.

I don't expect someone who wasn't born into that world to understand how important this ritual was to our people. Enough to say that even when Samhain ceased to be celebrated by the Druids, Christian priests kept it alive.

Saint Patrick himself kept the tradition going, it was said. Though I can't vouch for the truth of that. Fire is life. Risk all by extinguishing your fire, then depend on someone else to light it again for you. Then you'll truly value your neighbours.

Aoife's plan was devilishly simple. Prevent the Samhain Need-Fire from being lit. Let folk do without flames for cooking and heating for a day or two. Send them a blizzard such as hadn't been seen in over a thousand winters. That'd be enough to set their nerves on edge. What with the rumours of the Redcaps and the Nathairaí to go with it, ordinary folk would be all the more thankful when heat and light were restored to them.

'I will be worshipped,' Aoife told the Norman confidently. 'I will become a goddess.'

Toothache stirred from his sleep to look up.

'He dreamed he lost his tooth,' he muttered. 'Toothache was floating in a river of bliss.'

Then he screwed up his face again into the old familiar scowl of pain. 'What have you got in mind for him today?'

Queen Aoife smiled indulgently. 'It's time you were both off to the Killibegs. You have some Quicken Berries to collect for me. And I wouldn't mind if you caused some havoc of your own while you were there. Every little rumour can only add to my triumph. When you've collected the berries and scouted the enemy encampment you will return here. My warriors will be waiting for you to lead them into battle at the rath of Killibegs.'

She pointed to Guy and added another stern command. 'During that fight you must make certain three or four folk escape that place with their lives. A couple of children, a woman and an old man perhaps. But no more. I leave it to you to decide which among those folk will live.'

As she finished speaking the room darkened. The countless tiny mirrors set into the walls and ceiling transformed into as many autumn leaves. Then the chamber started shedding its foliage like an oak tree at leaf fall.

A shower of dry red leaves suddenly choked the air. Soon enough Guy was up to his neck, drowning in them. Toothache also struggled to stay above the swelling multitude.

Then a terrible humming buzz filled the air. From Aoife knows where a massive swarm of angry bees appeared. Toothache screamed with fear. He hated bees. But he needn't have panicked. These weren't the stinging kind.

They swirled around the Queen of the Night who sang an ecstatic song to them in a language neither Norman could rightly understand. Faster and faster they flew until at last Queen Aoife was lifted up amongst the bees.

As she took to the air Guy felt his own body rise, suspended on the soaring hiss of impossibly delicate miniature wings. Leaves scattered in every direction as if a mighty wind had swept through them.

Just as he thought he was about to be carried away by this vast army of willing insect servants, a most unsettling thing happened. Guy d'Alville and his servant Toothache melted away. They became a part of the hive. Their flesh disappeared as they each transformed into a thousand little bees.

Before he knew what was happening Guy felt his body

disintegrate. Then he flew out into the morning sky, tossed about amidst a seething sea of tiny uncountable winged creatures.

Toothache would have screamed but the only sound he found himself capable of producing was a wild unbridled buzz.

Tom Curdle sat with Derbáil, wife of Father Clemens. And the two of them talked of nothing but cheese making. The old woman was a bit of an expert herself.

In her youth she'd travelled to Rome on pilgrimage. Along the way she'd stopped in the mountains north of Italy in the land called Helvetica. And that's where she'd learned the subtle art of boiling, straining, seasoning and, most importantly, aging curds.

Now you might say to yourself, what skill is there in boiling up a vat of milk, waiting till the lumps form, then draining off the whey? It's a simple task not worthy of a lifetime of study.

Well you'd be wrong.

Cheese making requires patience, experience and persistence. The only way to master the craft is to stick at it day after day, taking note of subtle variations in texture and aroma. If you're born into a curd-draining family you'll be doing it before you can walk anyway. But if you're venturing out alone into the wide world of boiled milk solids you'll need a guide. Even if you've spent a lifetime learning just the right second to add rennet to the bubbling mixture, it only takes a moment of distraction to spoil the whole thing. Then you'll end up scrubbing blackened sticky glup-leavings from the inside of your pot. And that's not even the half of it.

Real cheese craft begins with the cows. The grass they eat,

the herbs they swallow with it. Every step of the process is as important as the next. If the cows are happy they give better cream. The richer the cream, the tastier the curds. The tastier the curds, the finer the flavour of the final product.

The truly mysterious and unique thing about cheese is the mixture that causes the hot milk to curdle. It's made from two important ingredients. At least that's how I understand it.

The first part of the mixture is a powder ground down from the dried lining of a calf's stomach. It's called the rennet. The name is not so disgusting as the idea, you might say, and you'd be right. But it's rennet that makes cheese cheese. It's what gives it a fine yellow colour and keeps it from going rancid. And there doesn't seem to be anything else that'll do the job quite so well. I've known folk who tried soured wine or vinegar. Their curds were loose and runny. Trust me when I tell you that the last thing a cheese-maker wants is loose, runny curds. Especially if you're aiming to make a firm tasty cheese that'll keep for years.

A small amount of this powder is mixed with a cupful of whey from the previous day's cheese making. And that's why it takes generations of curd-rendering before a really outstanding cheese may be produced.

Rennet is easily acquired. A cupful of whey that can trace its lineage back a hundred summers is not so readily secured. Wars have begun over the theft of thousand-year-old whey. Feuds have erupted based on a jealous guardianship of a clan's curd-leavings.

So it was with a great deal of respect that Tom sat down beside Derbáil to discuss her family recipe for cheese and her precious jug of ancestral whey.

You may wonder why I've waxed so wide-eyed wistful about something as ordinary as cheese. Well I'll tell you something about the winter that you'd only know if you'd lived in a community that had to endure the snowfall without sufficient stores of grain. Toward the end of winter, when supplies of other foods may have rotted or gone bad, a goodly treasure-trove of cheese may mean the difference between life and death.

Cheese doesn't suffer from decay if its well looked after. It doesn't rot as long as its kept dry. It doesn't turn rancid as butter may. Mould can't destroy it. In fact, in a very literal sense it is mould, when you think about. You can't get any-thing more rancid than cheese.

My point is that everything in our lives had to be as carefully planned out and prepared as the cheese-maker's craft. The winter store of curd blocks had its beginnings with the cows among the sweetest grass in spring. The seasons each have their turn. The springtime grass we feast on in our youthful days may see us through to the winter of our lives. But unless one watches carefully and considers well one's craft, there may not be much of a store to see us through as we get older. Or worse still, the cheese we end up with may not be very tasty at all.

This was what Derbáil told Tom Curdle as they sat there at the hearth fire. It was her philosophy of life. She measured folk up according to the quality of their curds, if you take my meaning.

And she knew there was something unusual about our Tom.

'A man like you would do well to visit the Otherworld,' she advised. 'I've heard the cheese is incomparable there. I knew a fellow once who'd strayed into that country. He returned with an uncommon knowledge of curdling.'

'Any craftsman who dwells a while in the Land of the People of Peace is sure to learn something valuable,' Tom replied respectfully.

'Why aren't you married?' Derbáil asked him bluntly, changing tack.

'I'm a servant to my lady,' he explained. 'I'm devoted to her.'

The old woman squinted, sizing up his sincerity.

'A man in your position should be wed.'

'I'll wait till I meet a woman worthy of me,' Tom laughed.

The old woman placed a hand firmly over one of his. 'You may have fooled the others,' she whispered. 'You may have even convinced your Lady Mirim you're nothing but a cheese-maker. And I admit you have a certain rare knowledge one doesn't encounter every day. Almost Otherworldly, I'd have said.'

Then she leaned in so close he could feel her breath on his cheek.

'But you're no more a cheese-maker than I'm a Knight Templar,' she hissed softly.

Tom smiled at her and he answered in the same low tone. 'Keep my secret just a little while longer and I'll thank you for it.'

Derbáil laughed. 'I won't say anything,' she promised. 'But that doesn't mean you've much chance of remaining undiscovered very long. You have an air about you, my boy.' She paused. 'Have you told him you're here?'

Curdle stopped breathing. Then he frowned, pretending he didn't understand what she meant. But the old woman was in no mood for his denials.

'Don't play games with me. Have you told him you're here?'

'Not yet.'

'Don't leave it too long,' she advised. 'It'd do him the world of good to know you're back.'

Then she stood up to stretch. 'Would you like to come stir the curds with me?'

Tom rose to stand beside her. Then he answered with a wry smile.

'There's nothing I enjoy more than to observe the curd craft of a well-skilled stirrer.'

394

Clemens squatted on a three-legged stool, pressing his cheek against the side of the cow as he steadily coaxed the milk from her udder. And all the while he listened to Caoimhin's account of the death of Eriginas.

When the tale was done the old priest sighed heavily and spoke from the heart.

'I'm grateful for your news.' Clemens caught the young scribe's eye. 'But I'm surprised you travelled so far and through such hardship to deliver it.'

Caoimhin shrugged boyishly. 'Eriginas told me I'd be safe here.'

'Safe from what?'

The young scribe tried to think quickly but he paused a little too long for his reply to be convincing.

'Brigands,' he offered.

The priest grunted. 'You've a copy of the *Leabhar Fál*?'

'Yes.'

'Read a page from it to me.'

Caoimhin removed the book from the satchel he carried slung over his shoulder. He untied the leather straps which held the book boards closed. The manuscript fell open immediately.

'"Seeking for one thing will lead to another,"' he read.

'What are you seeking?' Clemens snapped.

The scribe smiled. It seemed every Gael he met asked him this question.

'I was told there was a copy of *The Brown Book of Aontacht* here,' he stated in reply.

'Who told you that? Was it that bloody drunken fool, Michael of the Vomit-Beard?'

'Yes,' Caoimhin admitted.

'There is no such manuscript as *The Brown Book of Aontacht*. It's just a story we tell fools to put them off the scent of the real jewels in our fine library. You've wasted your journey.'

The old man stopped milking and turned to face the scribe. 'Do you suffer from visions?'

Caoimhin nodded shyly.

'In that case you're welcome here among us. But don't get it into your head to be making off with our sacred books. You're welcome to read the Gospel of Thomas. I may even allow you to glance at the Book of Sigils once I get to know you well enough. But don't think for a moment of stealing them.'

'What makes you think I'd want to steal them?'

'I'm not cursed with the Faidh-sight as you are,' Clemens retorted sharply. 'But it doesn't take a seer to understand that my son, Eriginas, was after pilfering our treasures. What other reason could he have had for returning home after all these years? In his foolish pride he turned his back on our ways and broke faith with us forever. He must have known I would never accept him back into the fold.'

'Perhaps he simply wanted to visit you,' the scribe guessed. 'Maybe he wanted to make amends and heal the rift between you both.'

'Listen to me, young lad. You and I will get on all the better if you can manage to be honest with me. I don't take kindly to being treated like a fool.'

Clemens tapped on the open page of the Book of Destiny.

'You may have come here looking to thieve our books but you've found something else. Something far more precious than the written word.'

'What's that?'

'My youngest daughter Binney has her eye on you,' the old man winked. Then he sat back and let out a deep breath. 'The milking's done. Now let's go back to the fire. If you're going to be joining our family you'd best get to know everyone.'

Caoimhin was lost for words. He was a monk. He had vows of chastity to maintain. He laughed nervously, deciding the old man must be joking. Then he put the Book of Destiny away and followed Clemens back to the hall.

Guy d'Alville's head was spinning. He couldn't recall ever feeling this sick. His vision was blurred and his ears were ringing. The Norman felt like he'd been tossed into a raging whirlpool then left to fend for himself.

But he gritted his teeth, trying his best to hold the precious contents of his stomach from surging out in a spray of rebellion. Just when he thought he couldn't take this punishment any longer, he felt the solid Earth beneath his body.

He looked up, head still spinning. He was suffering that feeling a sailor gets when he's been at sea for months. He was so used to pitching and rolling that the firm land under his feet still felt as though it was moving.

The intense buzzing suddenly ceased and Guy caught sight of Aoife standing with her hands on her hips.

'Get up!' she demanded. 'You haven't got time to be lying about all day. There's work to be done.'

The Norman groaned as he struggled to his feet. Nearby Toothache was flat on his back, staring at the sky. He didn't seem that concerned by the flight. Indeed, after the first few seconds of mind-numbing terror, he'd come to enjoy the sensation.

'When can he do that again?' the warrior asked enthusiastically.

'Soon enough,' the queen laughed.

Then she wagged a finger at d'Alville. 'You should be ashamed of yourself. You've been bested by a mere foot soldier.'

The Norman stood up straight, stretching his back and rubbing his shoulder. 'Couldn't you have provided a more comfortable way to travel? Where are we?'

'We've come to the ford at the stream near to the settlement of Killibegs,' she told him.

Behind them on the other side of the water a dozen Redcaps were urging on a team of four horses. The struggling animals were hauling a catapult into position in readiness to drag it over the ford.

The Queen of the Night held out a long sword in a beautiful black scabbard. She gestured for Guy to take it.

'This is a gift for you. There's a spirit of fright dwelling within this sword. Its name is Maolán the Messenger. All who witness the flash of its steel will fall back before you in terror.'

The Norman received the blade from her with a respectful nod of thanks and a glint of pleasure in his eyes. He firmly grasped the hilt. As he did so the weapon leaped out of its sheath.

D'Alville had never seen such a long, fine, exquisitely fashioned sword. At first he doubted it would hold up in any fight against a typical broad-bladed Norman weapon. It seemed too flimsy. But as he swept it through the air he heard the sword sing an Otherworldly song in an ethereal voice tinged with hatred. He tested the balance, weighed it in each hand, then he sheathed the weapon once again.

'Thank you, my queen,' he said formally.

'Summon the spirit when you're ready for a fight. It will serve you well.'

She stepped closer to him, placing a hand upon his chest. Then she lowered her voice to a whisper. 'Now swear your allegiance to me.'

Guy d'Alville knelt down before her, leaning on his sword. 'You are my queen,' he began. 'My hand, heart and blade are yours. Command me and I will obey. There is no other but Aoife, Queen of the Night, Sovereign of the Dark Places, Goddess of Ireland, Lady of the Bees, Empress of the Redcaps.'

Aoife purred with delight. 'You know what I like to hear,' she told him. 'You'll be a fine high-king. Now be on your way. Let's see you put all those pretty words into practice. Bring me the Quicken Berries.'

'Who has them?'

'A woman you've already met. Her name is Sianan.'

Guy scowled with disdain. 'She won't escape me a second time,' he promised.

'You know the great secret of the Eolaí, the immortal ones,' the queen reminded him. 'Our kind may be killed. Cut off her head and she will surely perish. There are other ways to vanquish her, of course.'

'Tell me.'

'I'd rather let you find out for yourself,' she laughed. 'It's much more entertaining that way. We immortals never discuss such matters with your kind. When you're one of us, then we'll have a little chat about it. All in good time.'

She turned to Toothache, though it was obvious she was addressing them both. 'You are my eyes and ears at the Killibegs. Serve me well and you will be rewarded. Cross me and you will understand the true meaning of eternity. For you will spend an eternity suffering for your treachery.'

With those words Queen Aoife took two steps back and held her hands out to the side, palms facing forward. Then she instantly transformed into a wild swirling mass of bees.

Guy instinctively cowered as the swarm circled him closely before lifting up on the breeze to return to the haunt of the goddess-to-be. When they were nothing but a black mass far above the forest, d'Alville grunted with satisfaction.

'Come along, Toothache,' the Norman commanded. 'We have work to do.'

Three chieftains of the north-west had arrived at the Killibegs since Caoimhin had gone with Clemens to the milking. And since they each have a part to play later in my tale, bear with me while I introduce them.

Tigern Og of Connachta was an old man, though his name actually meant the young lord. He was overweight, balding and his face was covered in seeping scabs, the result of a malediction placed on him by a poet to whom he owed payment for a poem. It was said he was a tight-fisted man with a terrible temper.

The second chief was Morcán the Warhorse. He had been a fighter in his youth with a reputation for ferocity unmatched among the Gaelic war-leaders. But as he'd aged he'd fought less and taken to strong drink more. Nevertheless, in his declining years he was a stronger man than some half his age. His sword arm was legendary. His fury in battle had made his name a byword for reckless courage.

The sad fact is that even though he'd fought the Normans off and kept them from entering deep into Irish-held territory, he'd also been the first chieftain to make a treaty with the foreigners. Now his only dealings with them centred around a brisk trade in wine. Thus his people called him Marcán behind his back. This subtle adjustment of one syllable transformed the meaning of his name to packhorse. But his kinfolk were really calling him slave.

Rián Rónán Og came from the west also. His kin had lived on the Isle of Inis Muirdeach since ancient times. Since the foundation of the monastery of Saint Molaise on that island they'd lived along the coast around the Bay of Sligo. They were proud of their ancestry, and under the rule of Rónán they continued to harass any Normans who dared enter their territory.

The chieftain's name meant the Young Seal-King, for it was believed by many that he was descended from a seal-woman of the Otherworld who'd seduced his grandfather. It was true enough that he had fine folds of skin between his fingers and toes resembling those of a seal. And unlike the other two he could justly call himself young for he was a man of barely thirty summers.

It has to be said that these three did not always get on together. They had the interests of their own people at heart. And sure enough, the interests of their own hearts took precedence over the wellbeing of their kinfolk. In the manner of many rulers in those days, treachery, greed and self-interest governed their tongues. Though admittedly Rónán Og was the least offender among the three. Perhaps because he was the younger, so he was less tainted by the world.

When Clemens returned to the hall he sat the young scribe down then stood by his own place at the central hearth. He took off his milking smock and apron, folded them neatly then placed them on the bench seat behind him.

That done, he commenced naming each chieftain for all to hear. He made formal welcomes to the three of them in turn, starting with the eldest, Tigern Og. Then the old priest introduced all the other guests one by one. When that was finished he named each of his own people around the circle. This all took some time, as I'm sure you can imagine.

Clemens remained patient despite the fact he was eager to discuss the news that had come to him. To his frustration he noted Sianan was not present in the hall.

He'd just completed the formal introductions when the abbess returned, her face still veiled to conceal her Otherworldly eyes. Martin and his dog were right behind her. When she took her seat, the Breton and Oat-Beer sat down right beside her.

The dog reached across to lick at her face now and then. But she managed to keep him at bay by stroking the back of his head or rubbing him behind the ears till he collapsed in a whimpering heap of ecstasy.

'There's no time to waste,' Clemens announced in his most formal voice. 'Now the chieftains are here we should share our tidings of the world without delay. Forgive me if we speak before the breaking of the bread but some tidings cannot wait for the pretty niceties of tradition.'

The chamber hushed. This was the gathering day. The day before Samhain Oidche. It was both a celebration and a feast. The chieftains had come to waste as much time as they could manage.

'A calamity is about to descend upon us,' the priest declared. 'I fear it will test our people to the limit of their endurance. And even if we survive the first disaster, another will be upon us before we have a chance to recover.'

'What talk is this?' Tigern laughed. 'We live in peace with our neighbours and prosperity with our own folk. What calamity could strike us?'

'Hear the words of Sianan, Abbess of Dun Gur,' Clemens announced. 'She has come to us from the south-east with news.'

Sianan coughed to clear her throat as the priest took his seat again. According to custom she did not stand up. That was the right of the host, Clemens.

She began by relating the tale of the Nathairaí which pleased everyone since it was not a story that was well known in those days. A new tale is always welcome, as we used to say then.

When she'd finished describing how the Nathairaí had come into the world and how they'd been imprisoned in the well of Dun Gur, there were murmurs of appreciation.

'A Norman came to my community a few days ago,' she went on. Then she told all she knew about the arrival of Guy d'Alville and his warriors. She explained that he'd locked her in

402

the well with Martin. The Breton nodded in acknowledgement throughout the story to confirm the truth of her words.

Then she paused.

'How did you escape?' Rónán Og called out. 'It's clear the Nathairaí didn't eat you!'

Sianan didn't want to reveal her relationship with Lom Dubh or his origins. That was a whole cycle of tales in itself. It would have taken all day to relate. And believe me this audience would have demanded to hear it.

Mirim glanced up from under her own veil allowing her eyes to twinkle in acknowledgement of their shared secrets. Sianan answered her with a little nod. Then she looked out at the assembly. Lanfranc was seated beside his sergeant and the two men were silent with their eyes downcast. He had decided to wait a while here until the lady Mirim decided whether she wanted him to guard her any longer. Sianan couldn't tell what the two Normans thought of her story.

Opposite them across the fire sat Lewyn and Overton respectfully biting their tongues though both men longed to be a part of this discussion. Both brothers had an instinct they were taking part in momentous events so they each noted every word that was said and whispered to one another if a meaning in the Gaelic language escaped either of them.

Gusán Gelt the brigand sat next to them where Lanfranc could keep an eye on him. It would not have been within the allowances of hospitality for him to remain bound as a prisoner. So he had made a solemn vow not to attempt to escape the custody of his captor while they remained within the rath. Every once in a while he gave Lanfranc a little wave just to remind the Norman he was keeping his promise.

The abbess shook her head to think of all these different folk brought together under the one roof in such strange circumstances. She paused for a few more breaths before she went on.

'Martin and I made off when the two worms were distracted,' she lied.

There were muffled protests of disbelief from every corner of the hall. But it wasn't that these folk doubted how she'd escaped. They just couldn't believe the Natharaí were anything more than a story or at the very least a poetic invention. You see, in the generations since the Gaels, the ancestors of these people, had come to Ireland they'd had little to do with the Danaans, Fir-Bolg or the other ancient inhabitants of the land. The Natharaí had faded into fable. Not many Gaels had any first-hand experience of the denizens of the Otherworld. And since the coming of the Christians few folk had retained any faith that the Faeries had ever existed at all.

Tigern in particular found the whole tale a little far-fetched. And I don't blame him. Sure enough when you're a child listening to these stories at your grandmother's knee they seem real enough. But spend a lifetime fighting off foreigners, dealing with death day to day and struggling to feed your kinfolk, and you'll soon brush aside the legends as having no basis in fact. Only those who've glimpsed the Otherworld know the power slumbering therein.

Sianan for her part remained patient with these people. She'd long ago come to understand that mortals live short, brutal, painful lives full of struggle and heartache. It was natural for them to want to believe that the extent of their difficulties was limited to this world. She had no desire to bring more worries upon them. So before she went on she said a few words to soften their scepticism.

'Do not judge my tale until you've heard the full of it,' she begged. 'Then you may make up your mind.'

She launched into the story of the Redcaps who'd once been a tribe of the Sen Erainn of the Fir-Bolg folk. She explained how they had bartered their warriors' skills in exchange for the secret of the Quicken Brew and had thus become immortal.

However, they had not anticipated that immortality and eternal health could be a burden or that death might be a gift.

This may be difficult for you to grasp, but believe me there are few immortals who truly enjoy the experience of an unnaturally lengthened life. I know of only two who've made the most of their immortality right from the start. But in many ways Dalan and Sorcha were different in any case. They were just happy to be together. The fact they ended up in one another's company forever was the basting on their roast. I'll tell you more about them later for those two make a brief appearance in my story.

So as each season had passed, the Redcaps had become more and more embittered with their fate. Until at last they'd drifted into endless enmity with those of the mortal kind. Now, Sianan told her listeners, they were amassing behind Aoife, the Queen of the Night. They had their sights set on bringing war, destruction and disarray to Ireland. Such a disaster might destroy the ways of the Gael, or at the very least bring great hardship to the people of Ireland.

As she finished her speech there was silence in the hall. No one dared speak until Tigern Og made the first comment.

'Clemens,' he began, 'you are to be congratulated. As usual your hospitality is unmatched. The food is excellent. The drink is incomparable. The welcoming of your kinfolk is generous. And the talent of your storyteller is unmatched.'

'She's telling the truth!' Martin blurted, outraged that anyone could doubt Sianan's word.

In consternation he stood up, which was a severe breach of politeness. A murmur of shock passed through the Gaels. The abbess dragged him back to his seat then placed a firm hand on the back of his head to hush him.

'You should not speak,' she warned him in a low voice. 'You're a foreigner here.'

But Tigern laughed and many folk followed his lead,

relieved that such an outlandish tale had merely been for their entertainment.

'Congratulations to you!' Morcán piped up. 'You had me believing you for a while there. I was looking over my shoulder thinking there might be Redcaps about!'

'That speaks of your valour,' Tigern Og observed cuttingly. 'Or should I say your lack of it. If a far-fetched fable could test your courage, it's no wonder you'd rather drink the Norman wine than spill their blood.'

'If I made a treaty with the foreigners at least I wasn't the first to do so,' Morcán spat. 'I may have followed your lead but I'll never been known as a stingy provider in times of peace.'

Tigern fumed. 'Better to be known as a frugal father to my people than to be called slave behind my back!'

Rónán stood up. 'Silence! Both of you!' The hall hushed again in shock at the flouting of custom as the chieftain turned to Clemens. Before he spoke he realised his passion had got the better of him. He returned to his seat so as not to offend his host. 'Tell us, dear father, what purpose did this story serve? Was it meant to bring dissent to the three of us? Or have you some other lesson to impart?'

The old priest sighed as he rose to his feet. He waited till there was silence. He didn't want anyone to miss a word of what he had to say.

'Everything Sianan has told you is the truth,' he declared, but there were clearly still many in the hall who doubted it. 'We are about to experience a terrible change,' Clemens went on. 'Even if it were not for the Redcaps or Queen Aoife or the escape of the Nathairaí, there is another frightening enemy. The Normans have landed an army of black knights. They're gathering in Wexford and may already be on the march west.'

'Rubbish!' Tigern cried out. 'My scouts would have sent word.'

'It's true!' Caoimhin declared. 'I was in Wexford five days ago. I saw the warriors for myself. One knight told me they had three hundred Hospitallers in their company and more than a hundred men-at-arms.'

The word Hospitallers spread round the room from mouth to mouth.

'Be quiet now, Caoimhin, my boy,' the old priest advised gently. 'This is none of your affair.'

Sianan spoke up again. 'There may be more of them landing at Limerick where Guy d'Alville disembarked his troops.'

Tigern laughed. And his laughter was so mocking that there could be no other motive behind it than insult.

'We've stopped the Normans before and we'll stop them again,' he proudly stated. 'But don't expect any battle-hardened warrior to swallow your foolish lie about the Redcaps. The days of legend are long gone. There is no Otherworld. There is only this one.'

He stopped to make sure everyone was listening. They were. His words had struck a common sentiment with most of the audience.

'And this world is full of misery, suffering and battle. There is precious little joy to be had. There is very little rest for those who toil. No sooner is the harvest gathered than the soil must be tilled again.'

He had the ears of all the folk in the hall now. Heads were nodding. Voices were subdued out of respect.

'The stories of the old days were a gift to us. The sagas grant us some escape, however brief, from the unrelenting hardship of the day-to-day. But they are nothing more than stories. They have no more substance than the shimmering dew sprinkled across fine spiderweb. When the sun comes out the magic fades away under the light of truth.'

'You are wrong,' Sianan objected. 'There is more to creation than you can imagine. Have the Children of the Gael become stupid? Have the descendants of Eber Finn and Éremon lost their wits?'

'How dare you speak to me in that manner?' Tigern bellowed. 'I don't care if you're the Queen of the Night herself, I won't be addressed with such contempt.'

'I'm not the Queen of the Night,' Sianan replied, her voice cold. 'I am like her though. I'm one of the Fánaí. I am a Wanderer. I have seen seven hundred winters and more. I spoke with Patricius Sucatus whom you know as Saint Patrick. I walked the woods with Queen Caitlin of the Eoghanacht and feasted in the hall of the high-king at Tara. I took the Quicken Brew and vowed to protect the ways of my people.'

She waited, looking at the faces staring back at her in awed silence. Oat-Beer whined as he tried to lick her face again. She pushed him away before she went on.

'But now I'm thinking it would have been better if I'd chosen death than to see this day when the descendants of King Leoghaire and the bloodlines of the old peoples have degenerated into such pettiness and short-sighted self-importance.'

Tigern frowned, doubting she was telling the truth yet certain she believed what she was saying.

'Am I the only true Gael alive in Ireland? Is there no one who will raise themselves out of their sloth to make a stand?'

'You're no Fánaí,' Tigern Og laughed, though there was obvious discomfort in his mirth. 'The tale of the Wanderers is just a folly told to little children. The Quicken Brew is a fable. The Otherworld is a heathen place where the souls of pagans dwell forever separated from their Christian kin.'

Sianan was about to tell him he was a fat, lazy old tankard tiddler when Oat-Beer jumped up at her. The dog caught her veil and head-covering in his mouth then tore them away. In the next breath he was lavishing his attention on his beloved abbess. And though she struggled to push him away he'd got the advantage of her this time.

It was some moments before Martin was able to restrain his dog. By then everyone in the hall had got a glimpse of Sianan's wide dark eyes. Even Tigern was beginning to wonder whether he'd misjudged the Abbess of Dun Gur.

The Prodigal

s this debate was going on within the hall, Derbáil and Tom Curdle emerged from the small stone house where she'd sited the curd cauldron. The two of them were laughing at some quip the old lady had made about Norman cheese. The foreigners were renowned as a people who rarely washed, so you can imagine the nature of the joke.

Just at that moment Guy d'Alville and his servant were being led through the gates by two of the elder boys of the Killibegs. As soon as Tom caught sight of Guy he stopped dead in his tracks and grabbed Derbáil's arm.

'What in the name of Saint Benedict's boots is he doing here?' Curdle hissed.

'Who?' the old woman asked as she followed his line of sight. 'Do you know that man?'

'Let's just say I've heard a lot about him.'

She cursed under her breath. 'Another couple of bloody Normans! There's foreigners enough in this settlement. There must be something particularly rotten luring these maggots to our dunghill.'

Before Tom could make any response she strode over to the strangers, her palms held out in the traditional blessing.

'Welcome to the Killibegs. My name is Derbáil. I'm the wife of Cenn Maenach Clemens, the priest of our community.'

Guy looked her up and down with suspicion but he made no reply.

The old woman knew malice when she saw it. And it was painted all over this fellow's face. As for Toothache, he was wearing his customary scowl, though she had no way of knowing it was the result of his affliction.

'Will you come in by the fire to meet our other guests?' Derbáil offered.

'My name is Guy d'Alville. I've come in search of a prisoner who escaped my custody some days ago. I'm told she's in hiding among your people.'

'What's her name?'

'Sianan, Abbess of Dun Gur.'

'She's here,' the old woman confirmed. 'But she's under the sanctuary of hospitality. She has the protection of the laws of our people. If you wish you may present your case for us to surrender her to you. Then the council of our elders will consider your request.'

'I demand in the name of King John of England that she be given over to me.'

'King John, is it?' Derbáil retorted. 'Well he may be King of England but this is Ireland. We don't recognise his authority here. If she's committed a crime she'll certainly be released to you. But you must present your case for consideration.'

'Very well.' Guy couldn't imagine that this old woman held any authority. He decided to make his demands to someone who did.

Derbáil gestured toward the entrance to the great hall. Guy brushed past her as if he were King John himself. He glanced at Tom Curdle but didn't waste any speech on him. Toothache was close behind his master.

The Norman burst into the chamber, followed by his servant, the old woman and the cheese-maker. This brought the gathering to silence for it was considered very rude to enter the hall ahead of one's host.

Derbáil put up a hand to still the outrage. There was no one present except for Lanfranc and his people who had any affection for the Normans. And more than a few relished any opportunity to hate them even more.

'This is Guy d'Alville,' the old woman began. 'His serving man attends him.'

The knight didn't wait for her to finish. 'I've come to seize Sianan, Abbess of Dun Gur!' he declared. 'I demand she be handed over to me immediately.'

'Is she charged with a crime?' Clemens asked, forcing his own temper to be still.

'She escaped my custody.'

'Why was she your prisoner?'

'She is a sorceress who summoned two great beasts from the depths of a well. Those worms devoured my entire company of foot soldiers. The monsters are even now running amok through the countryside, causing havoc and destruction. She is a servant of the Devil. I intend to force her to dispel her dæmons.'

The gathering was abuzz now. At least part of Sianan's story had been confirmed. Suddenly the rest of her tale didn't seem too far from the truth.

'You will have your chance for a hearing,' Clemens told the Norman in his calmest, most conciliatory tone. 'But first we have other business to attend to. Please take a seat until then.'

But Guy wasn't in the mood for talk. He drew the sword Aoife had given him. I can tell you without a doubt that if he'd remembered to summon the Frightener spirit by name, he might have got what he wanted there and then. But it slipped his mind.

'Put that blade away!' the priest bellowed with surprising force. 'This is a community of Christians and this is a Gaelic hall. You will hand your weapon to my steward or you will leave this place empty-handed.'

Three chieftains rose from their seats to protect their host. This was the only occasion such behaviour was considered not only acceptable but expected of a warrior.

Tigern Og was the eldest, so he spoke for all of them. 'Your name has already been mentioned in this hall. And it was not disclosed to us with any affection. Take care what you say. The rules of hospitality protect you from harm as much as they do Sianan. Respect those rules and you may get what you want from us.'

'Aren't you a little fat to be making threats?' d'Alville shot back.

'No one draws steel in the guests' hall and gets away with it,' Tigern bellowed. 'Especially not a Norman who's outnumbered a hundred to one. I suggest you respect the wishes of good Father Clemens.'

Now Guy was an arrogant man and no mistake, but even he could see the odds were against him. So he sheathed the weapon and quietly handed the sword to a steward who took it from him with a respectful bow.

While that was being settled Toothache sought out a seat in the darkest part of the hall. He'd spotted Caoimhin, of course, seated next to Clemens. He touched the crucifix which hung round his neck as he resolved to carry out the instructions Bishop Ollo had given him. Clemens was speaking as he found a place to sit down where he could keep an eye on the young Benedictine he'd been sent to murder.

'The sword will be returned to you when you leave this hall,' the priest assured Guy, his voice quieter now the immediate danger had passed.

'Take a seat. We will come to your business soon enough. For now there are others who've been waiting to speak.'

The old man turned his attention back to the assembly. The

situation had suddenly changed. Where there had been doubt there was now evidence. Where there had been scepticism there was now corroboration for all Sianan had told them. Where there had been talk of Guy d'Alville there was now the man himself.

Clemens held up a hand to still the disquiet in the chamber.

'Clearly we are experiencing difficult and uncertain times,' he began. 'For what it is worth to you I can state that I have known Sianan since I was a little boy.'

His words quietened everyone down.

'She has not aged a single day since then. My grandmother and her mother both knew her and they also told me they had known her since they had been children. She is one of the Fánaí. I have no doubt about it.'

There was silence.

'And since she is one of the Wanderers, her word may be trusted.'

Guy laughed provocatively. 'She's a dæmon.'

No one took any notice of him. Or if they did they saw the wisdom in ignoring his words.

'What can be done about the Redcaps?' Rónán Og cut in. 'If they're truly massing for war, we must act quickly.'

The chamber erupted as everyone presented their own opinion. Guy was quiet. Toothache smiled, though the expression wasn't that different on him from a scowl so no one noticed.

'Why is the Orchard Keeper not present for these discussions?' Clemens shouted above the din.

'Who's the Orchard Keeper?' the cheese-maker asked Derbáil.

'Lord William,' she told him.

Curdle leaned closer to her. 'I'll go to fetch him,' he volunteered.

That's the moment when I returned from shovelling out the

byre. Derbáil scrutinised the cheese-maker as if she'd suddenly realised something about him. Then she told me to take Tom up to where the old hermit was staying.

'Why do your people refer to the old lord as the Orchard Keeper?' Tom asked me as we made our way to the hide-skin hut where Lord William was housed.

I told the cheese-maker that Lord Fitz was charged with taking care of our collection of manuscripts. Every book was considered to be a tree with many leaves. And if one searched diligently among the leaves, the fruits of wisdom might be tasted. So if a book was an apple tree then a library was an orchard. And the librarian was therefore named the orchard keeper.

Tom stopped me in my tracks to explain he wanted a private word with Lord Will first. I frowned, surprised a cheese-maker would have anything to say to the old man.

'I've travelled far to speak with him,' Curdle explained. 'I've come from the Holy Land hoping to hear his advice and ask his help. Mirim also hopes to speak with him.'

'As you wish,' I replied, finding the story difficult to believe.

As we set off toward the stream I made some chat about the weather, even though it's considered very rude to do so in a country where it rains almost every day of the year. I was simply avoiding the subject I knew would arise sooner or later.

At last I worked up the courage to ask Tom if he was sure he didn't want me to go in to see the old man with him.

'I have private matters to discuss with His Lordship,' Curdle repeated in a firm but gentle tone.

I coughed. I remember feeling very uncomfortable indeed.

I didn't want to offend anyone but Curdle would have to find out sooner or later. I decided it would be best to be careful telling Tom the terrible truth about old William.

'His Lordship's lost his mind,' I blurted.

'What are you talking about?'

I bowed my head a little. I was sad this duty had fallen to me. I truly loved old Lord Fitz. He was a grand old hermit who never harmed anyone. But then he rarely went near anyone either, so that may go part of the way to explaining his gentle reputation. He was a Norman, after all. And even the best of them are blaggards.

I quickly reworded my announcement and presented it in a more soothing tone. 'Lord William has the impression he's at the Battle of Hattin in the Holy Land. Whether he's caught in some dark daydream that is the result of his experiences or he's simply succumbing to withering old age no one can tell.'

I paused to see how Curdle would take this news. Tom stopped walking, turned to face me then scrutinised my expression for any hint of a lie.

'It's true,' I protested. 'He thinks everything going on around him and everyone he knows is involved in the prelude to the great battle.'

'He was at Hattin,' Curdle confirmed, worry etching into his brow with every breath. 'He was one of the few to escape with his life.'

Now I had no idea till Tom told me, but Old Fitz had actually been with the doomed forces at Hattin. That was the conflict where King Saladin of the Saracens decimated the crusader force then chased the survivors back to the sea.

'Tom Curdle, how did you know Lord Fitz was at Hattin?' says I.

The cheese-maker came over a little nervy all of a sudden. Then he sputtered a hasty reply.

'I lived on the estates of Lord FitzWilliam when I was a lad. He often told us tales of his adventures.'

Then Tom's eyes softened as the memories flew fondly home to him.

'I looked up to Lord William,' he admitted shyly. 'I wanted to be just like him. I longed to take the cross to fight for Christendom in the Holy Land where the great stories all unfolded.'

He paused, choking back the emotion of his recollections.

'Then as I grew older I learned what fighting really meant. I didn't want to go to war any more. I just wished to take the road of a pilgrim. Or to sit telling stories for the children as Lord William used to do.'

There was a tear in his eye but whether it was shed for a joyful memory or for the loss of something dear, I could not tell.

'Stories are all that is left of what I once aspired to be. Lord William told me all the tales that were ever to have any bearing on my life. It was his stories that set me off on my wild adventures.'

The cheese-maker paused, put a hand on my shoulder then said one last thing. 'And now I fear I have come too late for him to appreciate any of mine.'

I took Tom Curdle by the hand to lead him through the pastures to where Lord Fitz had erected his temporary hermitage. It wasn't hard to find. I used to take the old man his daily bread. But I'm sure I've already mentioned that.

When we got near to the simple hut Tom paused. He hesitated for another few breaths then spoke.

'How bad is he?'

'Even if he knew you better than you know him, he might not recognise you. Even if you were his own child there is no way of knowing whether he'd recall your face. Or remember it tomorrow. We watch over him. But he has chosen the life of a hermit and we must honour that.'

'Surely he lives within the community during the winter?' Curdle asked, concerned.

'He does not.'

I explained to Tom that Lord William's desire to live as a hermit on the edge of our community had to be respected. He was an old man but a very wise one. If he had no concerns about his living alone, then neither should we.

'But what if he should freeze to death?' Tom snapped. 'What if the wolves were to take him?'

I pointed out that there hadn't been any wolves in Ireland since the days of Niall of the Nine Hostages. But Curdle was determined to take issue with me.

'It's not safe for him to be out here alone in the cold with . . .' Curdle paused, searching for the right words. 'With his head not right.'

I agreed entirely of course. It certainly was more risky for Lord Fitz to be out here on his lonesome than it was for anyone else in the community. But that wasn't the point at all, you see. In the Killibegs we all knew Lord William was a man who'd faced danger, fear, death and foreign devils in his time. He'd fought the Saracens, he'd fought the Turks, he'd even scrapped once with a heavily-armed bishop from the Acquitaine. And when he'd finished with that lot he'd had to joust his fellow Normans for the right to remain in this land. If he hadn't fought for it he couldn't have held his castle. All these adventures were a risky business, each and every one.

Lord Fitz had grown used to having danger at his doorstep and chance playing her cheating games at table. He enjoyed risks. They made him more aware he was alive. A life without risks, I explained to Tom, was a worse thing than death to one like Old Will. If building his own dwelling apart from the rest of the community and living there in solitude was what he wanted to do, we would let him.

'And if he should die alone?'

'A man who desires to take such chances is never really alone. At least he never feels alone,' I replied.

I was trying to sound wise but I probably seemed a little silly talking down to this man who'd travelled with his lady all the way from the Holy Land. Truth to tell I was just repeating what my father had told me whenever I had questioned Old William's decision to remain a hermit. But I forgot to tell Tom what else old Clemens had said. William wasn't really a hermit in the strictest sense. He still relied on the folk of the Killibegs for his daily bread and if he'd fallen gravely ill we would have brought him close to the community hearth and nursed him.

'Come in with me,' Tom asked. 'I'm afraid he might not remember me.'

I let Curdle go in first. Then I waited for my summons. It wasn't proper for a woman to enter the abode of a holy hermit uninvited. But I knew I wouldn't have to tarry long at the door.

'Binney? Is that you out there?' Old Fitz called out. 'Come in here this moment!'

I bowed my head to enter under the flap of bull hide which covered the entrance to the dwelling. When I was inside I could have stood up to my full height but it was considered impolite to do so.

I immediately dropped to the floor to sit beside Tom. He was seated across the central hearth fire from Old Will. The hermit was staring at Curdle with barely restrained rage.

'This young man says he's come from Jerusalem,' the old man spat. 'He's a liar! Everyone knows the Holy City was sacked by Saladin. All its Christian inhabitants were bonded into slavery.'

'That was a long time ago,' Curdle ventured. 'Christians are permitted to enter Jerusalem once more.'

'How is that possible?' William stuttered. 'All the knights of Outremer are here today waiting to ride to battle. There's no one else who could have beaten Saladin but them. And he will never allow our folk within the walls while he lives.'

'Saladin is dead and so is King Richard.'

'I don't believe you! You're drunk.' William turned to me. 'Tell this fool to go back to the troubadour camp. There's no place for his kind on a battlefield.'

'I have come from Jerusalem, my lord,' Tom insisted. 'And I bear important news for you.'

The old man shook his head with confusion.

'No.' Then a sudden sparkle lit his eye as a tiny flicker of recognition flitted across his face. 'Who are you, boy? I'm not sure whether I know you.'

Curdle sat forward so his face was lit brighter by the flames.

'Take a good look, old man. See if you can put a name to the face.'

William squinted. He grunted with frustration. Then he snapped at his guest. 'I haven't got all day to play games, boy. What's your bloody name?'

The cheese-maker sat back, disappointment written plain upon his face.

'My name is Curdle. Tom Curdle.'

Tom told Lord Fitz that the assembly had summoned him to Killibegs. The cheese-maker then informed him there were folk who sought his counsel and others who had news for him.

Curdle was very persuasive. But Old Will was reluctant. Then Tom mentioned that on a such a cold damp day it couldn't be very pleasant to sit alone in a hut made of hides.

The lord had to agree. The old man noted it was one thing to choose to be a hermit, but everyone needs company now and then. If nothing else it is a reminder of one's humanity. A change started to come over him and he looked at Tom the same way Derbáil had back in the hall.

He was right about everyone needing company on occasion. For example, if you hadn't stumbled across my little dwelling I'd have been sitting here all alone reciting my story. I tell it better when I have an audience. So you have my thanks.

My, but it's a lovely change to have someone round to hear me speak, other than the ferrets, I mean. Or to respond now and then to some witty observation, clever remark or wise bit of advice. Not that I want you to think that means you may interrupt me whenever the whim takes you. I don't mean that at all. You just keep your place and listen well and I'll be happy. If I need an opinion I'll offer it to you.

But I was talking about Lord Fitz. The old man suddenly forgot about Hattin. He brightened up altogether as the gloom of impending battle faded away from his mind. In a moment he was telling us that an afternoon with other folk around him wouldn't hurt him none. I hadn't seen him so cheery in a long while. So I helped the old man on with his cloak to lead him back to the Killibegs.

The three of us climbed the rampart path slowly for the going was hard in the rain. And with the old boy struggling along, the journey was that much harder. We had to stop for a breather on the steepest part of the path.

'Robert went off to the Holy Land,' Old Will told us as he leaned over his knees to catch his breath. He stood up straight and went on. 'It was a long time ago.'

We both looked down at the mention of the lord's son. There was such sadness in the old boy's voice neither of us had the heart to reply.

'I used to hold some hope he would return to me one day,' the hermit went on. 'Alas I heard that my son had died of the black fever in the city of Acre.'

Then he turned to face Tom with a fierce determination.

'Have you heard what became of my boy?'

The cheese-maker blushed. Then he put a hand gently on the old man's shoulder. But he didn't look up. The words came hard for him as he struggled to answer the question.

'I was told that Robert FitzWilliam perished defending the honour of a maiden in the port city of Marseilles.'

'Don't be ridiculous!' William spat. 'There are no maidens in that town!'

Then the lord squinted, suspicion filling his gaze. 'What do you know about my son?'

Curdle lifted his teary eyes to meet those of the old man. 'I know that he wished only to come home and sit with you by the fireside. I know he would have expended his last breath in that effort and that he would have held you in his thoughts to the last. He looked up to you as a hero.'

'How do you know this?'

Curdle took a deep breath. 'Because I also looked up to you. I know that if your son were here now he would be proud of you for taking to the life which best suited your soul. He would have been honoured to stand beside you in this dark time. And he would have been confident in your leadership and counsel. But since he cannot be here, I will be proud, honoured and confident in his place.'

'What dark time are you speaking of? What's going on?'

'It is not for me to discuss that with you. Father Clemens will speak of such matters when we reach the rath.'

Once more the old man squinted.

'Do I know you, lad?'

Curdle looked away. 'It doesn't seem that you do, my lord.'

A few of the youngest folk who were playing outside the hall caught sight of us through the open gates. They ran down the hill chasing after their own joyous whooping and screams of delight. Then all of a sudden a crowd of little ones was jostling round to welcome William to our hearth. Half a dozen of the older children lifted the old lord up on their shoulders. This brought a beaming smile to the old man's face such as I'd rarely seen before.

I can recall thinking he must have been a handsome man in his youth. For though he was well into his seventies, he still had a noble bearing about him.

The younger folk carried Lord Fitz right into the hall, chanting his name as if he'd just returned from the Crusade that very minute. They set him a seat in among the soft furs by the great hearth fire in the middle of the hall.

They gave him the place of honour, ignoring the sombre mood among the gathering. Then the young ones sought out seats nearby in the hope the old lord would decide to speak. In less time than it takes to fill two bowls of broth they'd filled him one, as you would expect.

The former nobleman sat there with a great mischievous childish grin on his face, clutching his bowl of steaming broth. And I thought to myself he was such an agreeable hermit, at least compared to the descriptions of other hermits I'd heard tell of.

I knew it wasn't that William was merely being agreeable. I understood that he'd probably wandered off in his mind to walk the roads of his past. Perhaps Tom knew it too. Even so, the old boy seemed a little brighter than usual. It was only now and then he'd look across at the cheese-maker, obviously straining to conjure some memory.

'Perhaps it was a mistake to bring Lord William here,' Curdle conceded as he noticed the hermit stroking his beard in search of his recollections. Folk were already mumbling at the old man's eccentric behaviour as he carried on a conversation with an invisible companion.

I placed a hand on Curdle's shoulder. It was too late to rescue Old Will from embarrassment now.

'Let it be, Tom,' I suggested. 'Maybe having folk around will jump his memory a little and so bring him back to us.'

Suddenly the old man squealed with delighted laughter which hushed everyone abruptly. His cry was like that of a wildly excited child. He drained his bowl of broth then threw the empty vessel to someone in the crowd.

'More,' he demanded in an unexpectedly stern voice of command.

The bowl was filled. But before the old boy took it back he raised his palms in the air, threw back his head and closed his eyes. His long grey hair fell down in cascading faded curls which must have been a magnificent copper red in the days of his youth.

He took in a deep draught of air, sucking it through his nostrils until his lungs could take no more. Then a calmness descended on him as he held his breath.

When he began to let it out he opened his eyes and spoke, allowing the words to ride out with the full force of the air escaping from his lungs.

'I have seen a sight which made me lose all hope. And I have seen another thing which brought all hope back to my bosom. But who knows whether hope will flee or choose to reside in the heart? Only he who has put his spirits to rest.'

Many folk in the hall frowned. Some muttered that he'd lost his mind at last. One or two uncharitable souls laughed openly. William was born a Norman and in those few petty minds he would always be a lesser man because of it.

'It was a day so much different from this day!' he declared. 'For the days are long and hot in the country they call Outremer. There is no rain and there is no place to shelter from the scorching heat of the sun.'

The mood in the hall instantly changed. Everyone was suddenly hushed. For you see, in those days the words of an old one were valued higher than gold or jewels. Even if he were nothing but a mad old Norman his story might be worth the telling.

As far as most of those people were concerned the tales of the elder folk had to be heard, no matter what other business was pressing. For elders have lived through hard times which may come again after they're gone from us. It is our duty to listen to everything they have to say, to drink up their wisdom and hear how they overcame hardship. We must remember to listen. As you are listening to me now.

Sometimes I yearn for those days, you know. We Culdees held that the aged ones amongst us were our teachers. We believed that God spoke through them to guide us.

Besides, there wasn't a single soul in the Killibegs who could resist the lure of a good story. Especially if it was one they hadn't heard.

Among all the assembled folk both visitors and kinfolk, only Curdle did not sit down. Though he risked offending his host he lurked near the door to the hall just out of the circle of firelight. He was listening though.

And Old Will did not disappoint. He told us the tale of the Battle of Hattin, of the flight of the crusader knights and of the mercy of Saladin. But I won't repeat it here as it has no bearing on my story. I believe Caoimhin included the full account of it in his book about Lord William which he called *The Tale of the Tilecutter's Penny*. That's by the by. It wasn't the story he told that was important. It was the way Lord Fitz told it that mattered. When he spoke it was as if we listeners walked among the warriors waiting to war with one another.

'There is nothing so unnerving as the breathless trembling silence that strangles all sound in the anxious hour before battle,' he declared as a thrill of nervous tension passed through the crowd.

I saw Mirim's face light up with joy at his words. It was as if somehow William's story had conjured her lost husband to her again. I saw Shali bow his head to quietly weep as the tale unfolded into a foolish fight and bloody massacre. Toothache scowled at every word but as this was the usual expression on his face no one much noticed.

Lanfranc was silent and emotionless. Guy d'Alville was proud, staring into the flames of the hearth fire as if he could see the battle being fought out amongst the glowing embers. Caoimhin, too. His ears twitched to hear every word. This was just the kind of tale he loved to listen in on. Here was a battle and a fight between two great armies.

Sianan was the only one not watching Will. I almost thought she hadn't noticed the old man at all, her attention was so taken up by my young scribe. And I said to myself she had a cheek to be sitting there in full view of everyone with those adoring eyes bathing the lad in light.

After all, I'd seen him first. There was nothing I could do about it, though, so I had to sit there quietly fuming while I tried to hear every detail of the story. Bloody distracting it was. Nevertheless I noticed one other interesting thing.

As Lord Fitz led us into his story world, Tom Curdle was drawn ever closer to the fire. There were tears in his eyes again but I knew they were born of pride in the old man.

When at last Will finished speaking, a hushed silence descended on us all. It was as if we had been there at Hattin among the slaughter. We had heard the dying moans of a thousand men and witnessed the mindless butchery of the fight. None could find words for what they'd witnessed through the powerful words of this storyteller.

Lord William, too, was silent for a long while. He'd relived the disaster of Hattin all over again and now a calmness descended on him. He picked up the bowl of broth that had been laid at his feet, then drained it. And as the last drop gurgled down the back of his throat he put the bowl down and locked eyes with Tom Curdle.

A shadow lifted from him in that instant and it was as if he were suddenly young again. Caoimhin sat forward, stunned at what he saw. For in that instant he recognised the old knight from his dream-vision at the abbot's door in Wexford. He would have stood up but Clemens held him back with a firm hand.

As I watched a smile gradually spread across the old man's face, brightening his expression as much as if the fire had been suddenly built up into a blaze.

'I have visited that battlefield for the last time,' he declared. Then Will stood up. No one dared to reprimand him for the breach of custom. They were all still in awe of his tale-telling and everyone could plainly see the change that had come over him. It is said among our people that a trouble shared is a burden halved and a joy shared is a happiness doubled.

'Is that you, my boy?' Lord William asked Tom.

The cheese-maker nodded.

In a few moments the old man had walked round the fire to where Curdle waited for him. All the way his steps were faltering. But this wasn't the result of his advanced years. It was disbelief that unsteadied him.

'How do you know so much about my son?' he repeated.

'I know him better than I could know a brother,' Tom replied. 'If you asked him he'd say the same thing about me. Though oftentimes of late I've wondered whether Robert FitzWilliam was nothing more than a dream.'

The gathering was hushed save for those few who understood what they saw and heard. *They* were dumbstruck. William opened his mouth to laugh but tears flowed freely from him and it seemed he could just as easily have cried like a little baby.

'Is that really you? Or am I dreaming again?' Lord Fitz managed to ask. 'Curse this old man's eyes and his foolish mind for I see you as if you were a boy again long before you took the vows of the Temple or ever grew your hair and beard. Is it truly you?'

'It is I,' Tom managed to reply, tears of his own to contend with.

The old warrior placed his hands on the cheese-maker's shoulders.

'I never thought I'd see you again,' he declared hoarsely, scarcely holding back the emotion though he struggled with all his might. 'I have dreamed you would return. My dreams have often been of you. My prayers have been for you also.'

Guy d'Alville felt a shudder of recognition too. But he didn't understand what was taking place before his eyes. It was as if some spirit had whispered the truth to him but he hadn't been listening.

Lord William hugged the serving man close to him. And as he drew Tom closer the old man's heart nearly burst with joy. His cheeks shone with silver tears of gratitude and his smile broadened even further into an expression of overwhelming thanksgiving.

'My son. Robert, my son. You've come home at last.'

'At last,' echoed Guy d'Alville under his breath. 'At last.'

The Bookbinder's Blessing

ll eyes in the gathering of the hall at the Killibegs were fixed on the cheese-maker. And well enough he knew why. It was a great offence to everyone to give a false name.

Guy didn't move a muscle. His expression was inscrutable, his attitude outwardly calm. But he must have been seething with excitement at this revelation.

Of course he hadn't recognised the son of the FitzWilliam until he'd heard the name. Robert had shaved his beard and cut his hair short so he'd not be recognised by his enemies.

'Are you Tom Curdle?' I asked before anyone else had a chance to voice what was on their minds.

'My name is Robert FitzWilliam,' he stated. 'I'm a knight of the Order of the Temple.'

I went on to ask him why he'd lied to us, pointing out that this deception was a grievous insult to the hospitality of our people.

It goes without saying we were suspicious of Normans in general and their warriors in particular. But to have one masquerading as a cheese-maker so he could walk among us undetected was of concern to everyone. I had no idea then that Guy was a greater threat to our future than Robert would ever be.

As I spoke Robert scanned the chamber, observing every face in turn.

'I have been sent by my Templar brothers to ensure the collection of books which were given into my father's care some years ago and the sacred books of this community are kept safe. I have also brought another manuscript to add to your collection. It was necessary I cloak myself in this guise to allow me free passage through the Norman port of Wexford. There is a great Hospitaller force assembling there ready to sweep through the land in a campaign to rid the country of heretics. They are seeking to destroy any manuscript which has not been ratified by Rome.'

I told him I didn't care what his reasons were for this ruse. He should have informed us straight away who he was. It was then Guy d'Alville rose from his seat. For the second time this arrogant man insulted the hospitality of our hearth. He ignored the derisive shouts that demanded he sit down again.

'Do you know me?' the Norman noble bellowed over the throng.

'I know you well enough,' Robert replied.

Folk were throwing their broth cups at the fire in outrage, shaking their fists as they screamed at the Norman to leave the hall.

Guy knew he was outnumbered. He could see folk were barely holding back from tearing him to pieces. This was obviously the wrong moment to confront his rival.

'I will await you outside on neutral ground. We have a score to settle.'

'Indeed we do,' the Templar agreed. 'I was told I could expect to find you in Ireland. I had no idea I'd cross paths with you at the Killibegs.'

Father Clemens rose to hush the crowd. 'What is the nature of your quarrel? Why would you seek to spill one another's blood?'

D'Alville merely stated that his adversary had treated him with disrespect, sullied his name and falsely imprisoned him. His words were sombre and full of hatred. But when Robert spoke his tone was coloured by regret.

'I am commanded by the Grand Master of the Order of the Temple of Solomon and the Poor Knights of Christ to end the life of Guy d'Alville. His crimes are too many to mention here. Suffice to say he has been convicted by an ecclesiastical court in his absence.'

'An ecclesiastical court?' d'Alville raged. 'Seven so-called warrior-priests who indulge in heresy with their daily bread and pay homage to the Devil. The inspiration for both the charges and the sentence was Satan himself. I do not recognise the authority of the court.'

'Nevertheless fate has brought us together,' Robert noted. 'We have a grudge to bury. And I won't shirk from my duty.'

'Fate has certainly brought us together,' Guy nodded. 'Only here beyond the civilised lands could we have resolved our old quarrel in an honourable fashion, as equals on the field of valour.'

'I will draw swords with you when I have given account of myself to these good people.'

With that d'Alville left the chamber, taking his sword as he passed through the door. I followed him, anxious to prevent bloodshed on the holy ground where we'd settled our community for the feast of Samhain Oidche.

Once outside the Norman turned to me. He must have known what I intended to say.

'Fear not. I have no intention of challenging him here in this place. We'll go out into the wilds far enough that no one in Killibegs will hear the ringing of our blades. I'll meet him at the shrine to Saint Bridget on the road to the ford.'

Then he marched off to prepare himself for the fight. I watched him go and I knew in my heart that if Robert did not dispatch this warrior to the afterlife, Guy would certainly return to persecute my people at the tip of his blade.

By the time I returned to the hall everyone was talking at once. A heated discussion had erupted with suspicions boiling over into outright antagonism.

It took me a good while to call everyone to silence again for no one was taking any notice of Clemens. By then it was evident that all our visitors had fallen under suspicion.

'Who else is pretending to be someone they are not?' the old priest demanded to know.

The desert woman stood up and an awed silence descended upon the chamber.

'My name is Mirim. I have no need to hide behind another name. I have come with Robert to give the book he spoke of into the care of William FitzWilliam. It is a holy book. And it must be preserved from the enemies of truth.'

Clemens frowned at her. 'Give him the manuscript then. And we'll thank you to leave our community in peace when you've done that. We have no wish to have strangers among us acting out their own petty quarrels.'

Derbáil, his wife, laughed. 'We've enough petty quarrels of our own to deal with, if you don't mind.'

A ripple of amusement passed through the crowd. These two could be very entertaining when they held opposing views.

'Normans are not to be trusted,' Clemens stated flatly.

'Yet William is a Norman,' his wife pointed out. 'Would you banish him from our company also?'

'William is no longer one of them. He is one of us.'

'We cannot refuse hospitality to anyone,' Derbáil declared. 'For Christ often goes in the guise of a stranger. If anyone seeks refuge among us we must offer it willingly. For who can say that we may not stand in need of the same help ourselves one day?'

'They are foreigners!' Clemens spat. 'They seek to change

our ways. They aim to hammer us into accepting their rules.'

'There are six or seven of them,' Derbáil countered, 'and a hundred or more of us. If we allow our faith to be strained or our lives to be disrupted by so few, then it is because we are weak in our hearts.'

'We must know the truth about them! How can we judge them if we don't know who they are?'

'You're always quick to judge,' Derbáil laughed mockingly. 'You should be thankful no one cares that you're a lazy old drunkard who thinks of nothing but bedding his poor old wife.'

The old man was outraged. 'If she spends so much time amongst the bedclothes with him, there must be something which lures her there.'

'It's a little thing,' Derbáil stated, and the room hushed for now the banter was getting very personal.

'What is?' he stuttered, shocked that she would make such a comment.

'Our quibbling is a little thing,' she answered quickly. 'The important matter is that we must not refuse hospitality to anyone. Charity, compassion and trust are the basis of the life we have chosen. Even when we are certain distrust is justified, it is still our duty to offer the hand of friendship as Christ would have us do.'

Mirim coughed before she interrupted. 'I have come here with Robert for another reason also.'

Shali sat forward, beads of sweat forming on his brow and running down his cheeks.

Mirim went on to tell the tale of her husband Alan de Harcourt, a noble knight of the Temple who had strayed into the territories of her people with a book in his possession. The elders of her oasis knew this manuscript was too dangerous an item for them to keep safely at their settlement. So they sent her in search of the traveller Robert FitzWilliam who was well known to her people. The Order of the Temple commanded him to escort her to Ireland with the manuscript since she was determined to bring it herself.

Clemens asked her why she had come all this way with the book. Why hadn't she simply stayed at home? What purpose had been served in her long arduous journey from the Holy Land?

'My husband was struck by an affliction when he stumbled upon our oasis. There is a tradition that any who drink from the Well of Shali without first asking leave of the Woman of the Well will be struck down with a terrible curse.'

'What is the nature of this curse?' I enquired.

'The spring which serves my people is known as the Well of Forgetfulness,' she explained. 'My husband was a sworn knight of the Temple before he tasted those waters. But his vows of chastity, poverty and obedience meant nothing to him when the forgetfulness laid hold of his mind.'

'This does not explain your presence among us, lady,' Clemens cut in.

'I heard tell that in this country there are those who have knowledge in such matters. So I brought my husband here with me to find Lord William. I was told he might know of someone who could restore my true love's memory.'

Shali stood up now and to the surprise of all, especially Lanfranc, who'd been told the man was mute, he spoke.

'My name is Alan de Harcourt. Or at least that's what they tell me. I have no recollection of anyone by that name. And if the truth be told I do not wish to recall him. For if I remember my vows to the Temple I will be bound by them. And then I will have to leave my wife, the only woman I have ever loved.'

Everyone fell silent. Except me of course. There's not much can silence me.

'Why have you gone to so much trouble then? Wouldn't it

have been better to stay at the oasis and live out your life in ignorant bliss?'

Mirim spoke up. 'The man I love has already chosen me for his wife. We were married before I realised that he might one day regret his marriage vows. I would never have peace in my mind if I thought he might wake one morning with a full memory of his old life and thus be filled with remorse.'

She sighed and cast a loving glance at the man who had been posing as her servant.

'It is better we resolve this matter early. If I'm going to lose him, let it be now. I'm grateful for the time we've had together and he will always be my husband in my heart but I will not hold him to a promise that is at odds with his conscience. For in later years I do not wish to be living in fear that he will leave me.'

'Anyone else got a story to tell?' Clemens asked, shaking his head. 'We've had a tall tale or two already this morning. We might as well bring everything out into the open before we share the bread and the wine of the holy feast.'

Lanfranc stood up, his eyes staring blankly at Mirim's husband.

'Sit down, my son,' Clemens advised him gently. 'You're causing offence. You may speak from the place where you're seated.'

'Why didn't you tell me?' the Norman stammered, ignoring the advice. 'You pretended to be a mute. You gained my sympathy for your false tale of woe. I fell in love with this lady. And all the while you saw the way I looked on her. You must have known how deeply she was drawn into my affection. You were laughing at me all along.'

Alan lowered his gaze so he didn't have to meet Lanfranc's eyes. 'I'm sorry,' he stated sincerely. 'It was necessary to concoct a story so we would not rouse suspicion as we travelled.'

De Courcy strode across the chamber to the door where all the weapons were stacked.

'That's enough!' Father Clemens bellowed. 'When will you foreigners learn some manners? Sit down!'

But before he'd finished speaking Lanfranc had picked up his blade and drawn it from its scabbard. There was a hushed murmur of horror as it became apparent he meant to do some harm.

Then there was a general gasp of awed wonder. The whole company were transfixed by the abrupt transformation which came over Lanfranc. Instead of a clumsy, awkward knight they were confronted by a handsome, valiant warrior in shining armour.

His eyes were piercing now and everyone who glanced at them had to look away. No one dared protest at this insult to their hearth welcoming. The very firelight seemed to diminish before the illumination which emanated from his face. All were stunned, all were silent.

Except old William.

'Where did you get that sword?' the old lord asked.

Lanfranc was surprised at the question. No one ever spoke back to him when he had his blade drawn. Unless you counted those disrespectful Irish brigands who'd been with Gusán.

'My grandfather left it to me along with this suit of mail, my helm and shield.'

'And does your weapon have a name?'

'Grandpa called this blade Tóla. I believe it means the flood or abundance.'

A muffled hum of understanding spread through the chamber.

'Will you put the weapon away?' Lord Fitz asked. 'It's considered very impolite amongst the Irish to draw a sword in the hall of your host. If you have a quarrel with someone it's best settled outside.'

Because it was William who addressed him Lanfranc shrugged in agreement and immediately sheathed the blade. He'd never met the old knight before but he'd heard enough tales about him to respect his wishes without question. And truth to tell, Lanfranc wasn't such a fool that he couldn't admit he'd gone too far. He didn't really want to do any harm to Alan de Harcourt. His temper had just got the better of him.

As soon as the blade was safely returned to its scabbard the light of enchantment around him dimmed. Lanfranc hardly noticed the change. He'd probably grown accustomed to the effect this weapon had on him. But everyone else recognised an Enticer spirit when they saw one. And they also knew that such a strong spirit as that would not be content with someone like Lanfranc for long.

You see, powerful spirits need more nourishment than their lesser counterparts. A truly formidable Enticer is usually quite impatient. They can make or break a man's life depending on whether he chooses to take up the challenge of the spirit's particular gift.

Lanfranc didn't come across as the sort of fellow who'd give this Enticer much opportunity to feed. So it was only a matter of time before it found a new master. One more willing to exercise its power and reap the rewards.

William motioned to Lanfranc to come sit beside him. Then the old man caught my eye.

'Fetch me my blade will you, Binney? I have a feeling Robert may stand in need of it.'

Without hesitation I went out to the house where weapons were kept, retrieved the sword the lord had deposited with the weapon-keeper when he joined our community, then made my way back to the hall.

Sianan was waiting for me at the door.

'Lom Dubh tells me that the big Norman who calls himself Toothache has been sent here to murder Caoimhin.'

I couldn't believe my ears. Why would anyone want to kill the lad?

'When this discussion is ended it is Clemens's intention to share the wine and bread,' Sianan went on. 'I want you to stand by Caoimhin to make sure all is well. I have a terrible intuition something is about to happen and it's not going to be pleasant.'

The sharing of the wine and the bread was an ancient ceremony among our people which had originated long before Patricius Sucatus brought Roman Christianity to these islands. It was a symbolic feast shared in trust between folk who may not have the opportunity to again share meals together for some time. The idea that someone could take advantage of such a sacred ritual to further their own ambitions or cause havoc made my blood run cold.

I nodded to the abbess then entered the hall with her close behind me. And if you're having trouble keeping up with all these sudden developments, imagine how I must have felt. Robert was waiting to receive his father's blade. I handed it to him with a bow as William began his declaration.

'This weapon is known as Órán. It was forged for me by a blacksmith skilled in the arts of fighting steel. It has dwelling within it a minor Frightener spirit. But as I have an Enticer attached to me, the two have always balanced one another out. So I've had no trouble. That is to say I've had none to speak of.'

Robert tried to interrupt to say he really didn't hold with such heretical and heathen notions. But his father stopped him, reading his son well.

'I was the same once,' the old man admonished. 'I had no faith in what was told to me about the spirits of this world. But I have a different view now.'

He paused as the crowd quietly acknowledged his wisdom.

'It matters not whether you believe what I tell you about this sword. It is yours. May it serve you well. And remember, if you should stand in need of a little more strength, a measure of courage or a touch more endurance, call on the spirit of the sword. For that Frightener saved my life more than once. And I would not be here today had it not been by my side at Hattin.'

Robert bowed. 'If you will excuse me, I would like to withdraw to prepare myself for the fight with Guy d'Alville.'

'Why waste your time with him?' his father asked. 'You're among friends now in this place. Enjoy this short rest from the duties of your profession.'

'I am under strict orders, Father,' the Templar explained. 'I may not rest until I have fulfilled them.'

With that all attention turned back to Clemens who stood up to wish Robert well.

'May the blessings of your God go with you,' he said simply.

Then the priest turned to the assembled guests.

'Let us share the bread and the wine.'

The assembly rose together to take up their positions for the Feast of Friendship. Lewyn and Overton were summoned to assist Father Clemens. This they gladly did when it was explained to them what a great honour was being paid in the invitation. Gusán went to stand beside Lanfranc in readiness for the rite.

For among our people it was the custom to take the opportunity to reconcile with one's enemies through the sharing of the bread and wine. Even if the truce lasted only as long as the ritual, it was considered to be a blessing. Perhaps it had been that way once in the Roman Church. I don't know. But it seems to me it has been turned into an empty mumbling sideshow in the hands of the priests of Rome.

Our lives were harsh, make no mistake. Winter was a time

of hardship and hunger. A cold season that outlasted the supply of food meant a high toll of sickness. Many older folk succumbed to such deprivations. So Samhain Oidche, which marked the start of the coldest weather, was a time for making some show of reconciliation with neighbours, friends and rivals who might not be met again on this Earth.

Lanfranc had no idea of all this so he was taken aback when Gusán slapped him on the shoulder with a blessing.

'Let's break bread together and pray we both live into ripe old age so our rivalry never weakens for an instant,' he offered. 'I'm proud to call you my enemy. I've seen you in a fight. I've witnessed the strength of your sword arm and the influence of your weapon spirit. I thank the Lord for sending me such a worthy adversary as you.'

'What are you talking about?' the Norman asked, mildly confused.

'I'm grateful for your company,' Gusán explained. 'We're going to have a lot of satisfying adventures in the future if we concentrate on fighting one another. I have to tell you I'm happy to call myself your enemy.'

'I'm your captor,' Lanfranc pointed out. 'You're my prisoner.'

'For the moment,' the brigand winked. 'For the moment.'

As folk were taking up their positions Toothache saw his opportunity. He edged his way around to where the sacred chalice had been placed behind Clemens in readiness for the sacrament. He'd already removed the crucifix from around his neck, ready to deposit the poison powder in the sacred vessel. However, he couldn't be certain Caoimhin would take a drink from the chalice so he had to wait his moment.

What could he have been thinking? It's one thing to plan to murder a man. But to be willing to risk the chance of killing others in the process is reprehensible in the extreme. I can't for the life of me imagine what made him think he'd get away with it. Perhaps he didn't care. It's hard to say for certain whether he'd even considered the terrible repercussions of his actions.

I took my place beside Caoimhin to share the wine and bread of the holy feast. Lewyn and Overton flanked Clemens as the three of them chanted the Latin Pater Noster.

I was so surprised at this concession to the foreign clergy I didn't even notice Guy's servant standing so close behind me. Indeed my attention was sorely distracted by the proximity of the young scribe. My heart was beating in my throat at the thought that our hands might brush against one another or that our eyes might meet.

It was a tradition among our people that a man and a woman assist the priest to serve at this ceremony. Bless him, but old Clemens had seen the way I'd been looking at Caoimhin. He must have thought we'd make a good match. He wasn't the only one. I hadn't been able to get that thought out of my mind since I'd met the lad.

'I invite our guest, Caoimhin of Glastonbury, to help my daughter Binney to serve the Feast of Friendship,' old Clemens declared.

Toothache made his move then. In the next breath he poured out a draught of wine and handed me the great silver cup from which it was to be distributed to the people. I thought nothing of it at the time, despite Sianan's warning. It didn't strike me as remarkable that a stranger was standing so close or that one of our own people had not done the job. I was so bloody smitten.

Caoimhin held the platter for the bread. Clemens blessed both. Then, as was the tradition, he indicated to us to begin passing around the holy feast.

I offered the cup to Caoimhin. He offered the bread to me. I took a mouthful of the dry, hard morsel. He took a deep draught of the wine. Then he handed the cup back to me and I gave him the platter.

But something unexpected happened as he swallowed the wine. The young scribe suddenly turned pale in the face. Then he coughed as if he was about to bring up whatever was in his stomach. The cough was hacking and painful.

'What's the matter?' I whispered. 'Is it the pain in your chest from the cold?'

'It's the wine,' he hissed.

'You Normans certainly don't know how to hold your drink,' I scoffed.

But before I'd finished speaking Caoimhin had dropped the platter of bread. In the next second he'd fallen to the floor, blood at his nostrils.

'He's been poisoned!' Clemens gasped.

Lewyn was at the lad's side in a second; he cradled Caoimhin's head in his hands and turned his face to one side. Overton stood over them both protectively, warding off any who tried to approach, including Father Clemens.

'Is it poison?' the large monk asked his companion.

He was answered with a sharp nod.

'Who would do such a thing?' Overton cried in distress.

Behind me I heard a low laugh.

'May your God bless you, heretic,' Toothache declared. 'That poison will bring you before him in a short while. So may God bless Toothache too who brought you to him.'

I must have lost my temper at that second. Red rage clouded my vision. Unchecked anger raised a storm of humming confusion in my ears. I don't really remember what happened next. Though I'm reliably informed that I turned to Toothache with the wine cup still in my hand. I'm told I spoke a few words to the warrior, my voice perfectly controlled and serene.

I said something like, 'You've asked for God's blessing. Now take mine.'

Then I swung the cup round hard onto the side of John Toothache's head.

What happened next is a little clearer in my memory. I recall standing there with the great silver cup still in my hand. It was dented out of shape from the force of the blow. But the Norman foot soldier was as tall as ever looking down on me. And do you know something? He seemed even bigger and broader than he had done before.

He clutched at the side of his face and ran his tongue around the inside of his mouth. Then to my horror he spat out three teeth, followed by a large amount of blood.

Toothache began laughing like a wild man, screaming the roof off our hall with his ecstatic guffaws. Outrage overwhelmed Overton. The large monk screwed up his fat hand into a tight ball of flesh and bone. Then, with a deep grunt, he brought his fist down on the Norman's head so hard I swear I heard the murdering bastard's skull crack.

'Who sent you to do this?' the monk cried out. 'What dæmon could have put you up to this task?'

Toothache ceased his laughter for a few breaths. He considered the question. 'It was Bishop Ollo,' he replied. 'He wants the books that lad was carrying.'

The poor man slumped forward a little with a dull expression on his face. He laughed a little again before he added another thought.

'But I reckon even old Ollo is nothing more than a servant to Aoife the Queen of the Night who saved my life and sent me here as her eyes and ears on your people.'

He started to laugh again but before he knew what was happening he was seized and restrained by the brothers and sisters of Killibegs. It took twenty of them to drag him outside to where they could tie him down. And all the while the fellow laughed like a madman which just outraged everyone even more and cost him many more bruises than if he'd stayed quiet.

Everyone in the gathering had suffered enough of foreigners breaking with our traditions. A few folk went outside to where

Toothache was being restrained to vent their frustration by sticking their boots into this stranger.

Once he was out of the way I was able to turn my attention back to Caoimhin. I looked into that dear sweet face and I cursed myself for not noticing Toothache slip the poison into the wine.

I had no doubt but there was little we could do to save him. There was already blood in his mouth and nostrils. His breathing had slowed to the point where he was hardly drawing air at all.

It was Sianan who gave us hope. She knelt beside the scribe to check for signs of the poison.

'He may live,' she announced. 'But we must act with all speed. Take him to a house where there's a fire, plenty of hot water and a cooking pot. I want water that has been boiled then allowed to cool. Then I want a fresh calf's liver.'

She touched his forehead then examined the whites of his eyes before she spoke again.

'Hurry! If we are to have any hope of saving the lad we must work quickly.'

We did as she instructed. Though it cost us dearly to slaughter one of our younger beasts, it was done. For Caoimhin had been a guest beneath our roof. According to the law we were responsible for any harm which came to him.

He was taken to the building that was set aside for treating the sick during the coming winter. The best warmest house was always chosen for that purpose. I followed to help lay the scribe out by the fire. The liver was brought to the abbess while it was still steaming with the warmth of life.

Sianan cut it up into small pieces. Then, without a word of explanation, she filled his mouth with as much of the offal as she could. She lay his head to the side so he couldn't swallow any of the liver. After a short pause she cleaned each piece of it out of his mouth and threw the remnants on the fire. Then she filled his mouth again. Five times she repeated this procedure until there was no offal left.

'Let us hope we reached him in time,' she stated to me. 'If I've managed to leach out the poison from his tongue, he may live.'

'And if not?' I asked her with tears welling up in my eyes.

She shrugged. I remember thinking there was very little compassion in her voice. But I didn't know her well in those days. I had no idea what thoughts might have been going through her mind.

'I'm sorry, Binney,' she soothed. 'All mortals must die. It's your lot.'

'But you can save him,' I pointed out. 'You're a Fánaí. You know the secret of the Quicken Brew.' I'd heard enough stories of the Wanderers to know that much about her. Sianan pursed her lips tightly together, obviously striving to control the tone of her voice so she would not be misunderstood.

'That is not something I can just dish out to anyone,' she explained. 'Caoimhin has not undertaken the proper training nor has he expressed any desire to attain to immortality.'

'Would you have granted it to him if he had?'

'Of course not. It's no blessing!' she snapped. 'It's the worst of all curses. If you had any inkling of what it means to live without illness or injury, to have to go on with living after you've watched everyone who ever mattered to you pass away in pain, you wouldn't even consider asking this of me.'

She caught her breath, struggling to hold back her emotion. But the flood had begun. She could not hold it back.

'If he were to die now it would be a better thing than to have to live endless days on this Earth witnessing the petty strife and petulance of the mortal kind who never learn the lessons of their forebears. I've seen enough of wars and death. I've heard enough cries of dying anguish brought about by selfish acts.'

She took another deep breath through her mouth, struggling hard so she wouldn't succumb to her sadness completely.

'I've said enough farewells. I've closed too many eyelids rendered lifeless by the terrible consequences of greed. If I were young again and knew what I know now, nothing in this whole world could convince me to take the Quicken Brew. So I will not grant it to anyone for any reason so long as I live.'

She placed a hand on Caoimhin's forehead.

'Even if this lad were able to beg for the Brew, I would not grant it to him. Even if the fate of hundreds of other folk depended on his survival I would not have him sip from that cup. What can you mortals know of the Fánaí? Your lives are built on your own selfish fancies. You see the Brew as bestowing a gift but you cannot imagine the reckoning that must be paid for it.'

'Will you truly let him die?' I sobbed. 'He's an innocent caught up in the troubles of this land. Do you have the heart to allow him to pass away? What wrong has he done?'

There was immeasurable sorrow in Sianan's voice when she replied. It was anguish drawn up from the depths of the Well of Grief. And it was bitter to my ears.

'Each mortal has their time. It is not for me to grant him life any more than it is my place to decide the hour of his death.'

Guy strode off down the path that led out from the rath. He was headed for the roadside shrine where he was to meet Robert in man-to-man conflict. His thoughts raced to the preparations he must make for the coming contest.

At last, at last the score would be settled. The festering hatred that had driven him on for years would be expunged from his soul. He would be free of its dark vengeful stain. And Robert FitzWilliam would die by his hand as he should have done in the Holy Land when they had first met.

In the back of his mind there was a nagging little voice which asked over and over what he'd do with his time once he'd concluded this business. His whole life had been consumed by the desire for revenge. It had become a travelling companion of sorts.

Aoife came to mind. There was a new life waiting for him as high-king of Ireland and consort to the Queen of the Night. But taking second place to a woman, even an immortal one, rankled his Norman sensibilities. It just didn't seem right to gamble his future on the intrigues of a mere female.

His steps became more confident as he decided to find some way to wrestle control from Aoife. A smile of satisfaction spread across his lips as he imagined himself seated on the throne of Ireland while Aoife begged for his mercy. At that moment Sciathan Cog appeared on the path before him amidst a tremendous fluttering of wings. The bird cocked a head to get a better look at him through one eye.

'I hope you've got those rowan berries the queen was after,' the raven reminded him. 'You don't want to see her when she gets her fine red hair in a tangle.'

'What are you talking about, bird?' d'Alville spat. 'Does everyone in this heathen country talk in riddles?'

'Have you the rowan berries?' the raven countered.

'No!' Guy shrieked.

'I wouldn't want to have to be the one to face my sister with that admission. I've seen what havoc she can raise when she's just being mischievous. I'd hate to have to watch what she does to you if you stoke the coals of her rage.'

'That's my affair! And surely none of your concern. I've more important matters to deal with than your sister's scorn.'

I should mention two points here. First of all, Guy would

447

never have said such a foolish thing if he'd known Aoife any better. Second, he was certainly distracted by the scent of revenge. Sciathan Cog cackled with amusement as he always did when confronted by the short-sighted foolishness of mortals. One thing that eternal life grants you, his twin brother Lom used to say, is a sensitivity to long-term consequences.

'On reflection it might be entertaining to see how she punishes you,' Cog commented. 'She's a good girl at heart, our Aoife, but she's also one of the most inventively cruel creatures it's ever been my misfortune to encounter.'

'You can save your breath,' Guy cut back sharply. 'I must prepare to meet Robert FitzWilliam in single combat. When that debt of honour has been repaid then I'll think about the rowan berries.'

'Good luck to you, then,' the raven cawed. 'I understand vengeance well enough. One such as myself burns with its heat by day and by night. But I have to say you Normans give a whole new weight to the word.'

D'Alville did not reply. He simply drew his blade to face Sciathan Cog with the tip.

'I may just warm up for the fight by separating that evil black beak from your long pointy skull.'

The raven stepped back. 'It'll do you no good. I'm immortal. You can't kill me that easily.'

'But you'll suffer a hellish pain for a while at least. And who knows, if a Redcap can be put away by the severing of his head, who's to say you can't be dealt with just as easily?'

'Don't be like that!' the bird spat at him. 'It's me you have to thank for introducing you to Aoife in the first place. I put it into her head to make you high-king of Ireland. You should be grateful.'

'Leave me alone,' the knight hissed, taking a step forward.

'I have some information for you,' Cog cackled. 'I know where the holy books are kept. They're unguarded at this moment. Just waiting for some questing knight to pick them up. Imagine what an army you could barter for those manuscripts. I'm sure every bishop from Ballyhooley to Bethlehem would pay handsomely to have a peep at what secrets they hold.'

He paused, seeing he'd got Guy's attention.

'And I'll wager there's a few dark-hearted Draoi-masters who'd pay you even more,' the bird added. 'The Book of Sigils is crammed full of magical spells.'

'Where are the manuscripts?'

'I'll take you to them.'

The two of them covered the short distance to Lord William's little hermitage. A bubbling stream gurgled away beside the humble hide hut singing its merry tune, ignorant of the vile act of thievery about to take place or the trouble that would surely result.

As soon as Guy was sure no one had spied him approaching the hut he drew his blade. Then he was inside the hermitage turning everything upside down in his furious determination to find the precious books.

He tipped the bed over. With stabbing thrusts of his sword he tore the straw mattress apart. In his blind frustration and unbridled haste he wasted quite a bit of time. But I suppose he had to vent some of his pent-up emotion. Warriors can be like that. Even knights like Guy who really should know better can often act like petty-minded little children when pressured.

Give anyone a sword and they'll likely misuse it. Give anyone a sword that's been forged in the furnaces of the Faerie world and there's sure to be trouble.

The truth is the fool needn't have bothered with all that destructive raging. The books he was searching for were wrapped in a large leather satchel made of two huge pockets designed to be slung over the rump of a horse.

The saddlebag had been sitting by the door all along. When

Guy noticed it he growled with satisfaction. Then he pulled out a book to get a closer look. He flipped the catch that held the book boards together, then opened the manuscript.

Unlike many Norman warriors d'Alville was a well-read man. He could understand letters in Latin, Norman-French, Greek and some Arabic as well. He even had a basic understanding of the Saxon language. But he couldn't make head nor tail of the words written on those pages. For you see, the book was written in the old Gaelic language. But even if he had been able to understand the words, the whole work had been transcribed into a cipher. Only those who knew the key could ever tell the truth of what had been put down in ink on that vellum.

He skimmed through the pages, his frustration building.

'What heathen scrawl is this?' he asked himself aloud.

'Queen Aoife will thank you for that book,' Cog told him. 'That manuscript holds the invocation which summons the Goddess Danu out of her sleep. And Danu is the only serious threat to Aoife's strategy.'

Guy threw the book down, scoffing at the notion it could be valuable. He pulled out another from the saddlebag and read a line from one page to himself.

'"Jesus said, 'Whosoever drinks from my mouth will become like me. I myself shall be that person and those things which are concealed will be revealed to him'."'

He turned back to the opening of the book, discovering the title to be the Secret Book of Thomas. Under the title there was an explanation which stated this to be a collection of the true sayings of Our Lord.

D'Alville slammed the book boards shut in disgust, though not so hard as to do any damage to it.

He may not have agreed with the sentiment but he certainly recognised the value of such an heretical work. This manuscript alone would fetch him a fortune with the right buyer. Satisfied, he stashed it back inside the saddlebag.

Then the Norman grabbed up the other manuscript to pack it away. But as he did so the whole book opened wider; its spine broke and the pages fell from the rotten stitches of the binding.

Guy swore under his breath then quickly shoved the individual leaves of vellum back into their boards. He was tiring of this search. He had enough already to make him a wealthy man.

So he didn't notice one page that had escaped. It fell down among the pieces of the straw mattress he'd hacked to pieces with his sword. And there it remained as he left the hut with the leather satchel slung over his shoulder.

SIR ROBERT

Believe me, I've met some awful characters in my time. I've known folk without the spine to own up to their own hideous misdeeds yet ready enough to condemn others for trifling misdemeanours. Those who are loudest in accusation are usually the ones with the most to hide. Or as Sianan used to say, the crow that caws the loudest has the freshest, largest, tastiest carcass to guard.

But Robert FitzWilliam, son of William FitzWilliam, was not amongst those people. I never heard him level any accusation against man or woman. Except one. And no one at the time would have said he wasn't well justified.

While all the other inhabitants of my tale had been getting themselves into one kind of trouble or another this knight had been indulging in a quest. He'd done it without letting anyone but Mirim and Alan know his true identity. And he hadn't even let them know the nature of his mission.

He'd cut his hair and beard so he wouldn't be recognisable as a Templar knight. This was done at the insistence of the Grand Master of his order. He'd taken up the art of cheese making and excelled at it so that none would question his identity. He'd even adopted the air of an overfamiliar servant to encourage the contempt of his betters so they would never guess he'd been born into a noble house.

All these many months since they'd left the Holy Land he'd

kept his secret. He was a man of amazing self-discipline. Yet who could have imagined he'd run into Guy d'Alville in this place? Who could have predicted that his quest would end here? He contemplated the coincidence as he walked down to the shrine dedicated to Saint Bridget, may she forever sit at the table closest to God's kitchen.

I suppose I'd better tell you something more about Robert's side of the story. You see while Guy and his rival were set on murdering one another, in many respects they weren't really that different. Both men had been devoted members of their respective orders. They both took their duties seriously and respected the commands they were issued with.

Five years earlier Guy had been sent to the Outremer to track down the fabled Holy Grail and the Ark of the Covenant. The Pope had heard a rumour these sacred treasures were in the keeping of the Temple and the Grand Master of the Hospital was determined to have these mystical items for himself.

Our Robert got caught up in Guy's plan to wrest these relics from the guardianship of the white knights. He ended up a prisoner of d'Alville in a strange castle in the mountains at the edge of the desert. And no one would have ever heard of Robert FitzWilliam again had it not been for a strange twist of fate that delivered him from his captor.

It was this quirk of happenstance that left Guy d'Alville in a Templar prison for twelve months waiting the payment of a ransom. And it was those twelve months that ruined d'Alville's reputation and his hopes of one day attaining to the rank of Grand Master of his order.

The thought crossed Robert's mind that Guy was a much more experienced warrior than he. If he was defeated, the Temple would surely feel and mourn his loss. But it was thoughts of his old father that plagued the good knight's mind the most.

To Robert's way of thinking his father needed someone

around to look after him. The strange lapse of memory William had suffered was, as far as his son was concerned, obviously a symptom of old age. But you must remember that the Normans didn't generally respect their elders in the same way our folk did. So our Rob felt it was his duty to take care of his apparently ailing father in his dotage. Of course, as you'll see, William wasn't on the dote at all. He hadn't slipped his verve or limped off to light the loony lamp. He'd merely started looking at the world a little differently.

His father wasn't the only reason Robert had for wanting to live on. He had another compelling motivation for staying alive. He hadn't worked out the answer to the great mystery. And being a man *inspired* by the mystery, he couldn't let go of it without at least having come up with a workable theory about why everything in creation was arranged the way it was.

So he determined he had to defeat d'Alville as much for his father's sake as for his own. Though he didn't necessarily have much confidence in his ability to achieve that goal.

When he reached the shrine he stood for a long while contemplating his predicament. Then the young FitzWilliam placed his father's sword on the ground beside him. It was still in its scabbard. When he'd stared down at it for a while he placed his own sword alongside it.

After a short pause to bring his thoughts to stillness Robert knelt before the sacred statue of Saint Bridget draped in fine blue robes of silk which had been a gift from some grateful supplicant. He crossed his breast and bowed his head in deep contemplation.

Even before he'd arrived at Killibegs we'd all heard something of this nobleman. Who hadn't? He was as famous as his father. He was usually spoken of as Sir Robert of Jerusalem. He had little time for titles himself; besides, he was sworn to the order of the Temple and so was not permitted to use them.

He never spoke of his heroic deeds in the Holy Land. He was

too humble for such idle talk. Nevertheless the tale of his life passed around Ireland like duck-down caught up on a feather-catching breeze.

He'd fought alongside King Richard at the Battle of Jaffa. He'd been captured not by Saracens but by the wicked emissaries of the Knights of the Hospital. Just because the Templars wore white and the Hospitallers preferred black doesn't give any clue whether either order was bent on good or evil. There were good and bad in both, as there are amongst any folk in the rest of the world. But Robert FitzWilliam was one of the best of all of those warrior monks and his captors just so happened to be among the worst.

So the story goes, he and his squire escaped to liberate the fabled Holy Grail from the hands of the Hospital. It was said of him that when he'd passed that sacred treasure into the keeping of his Grand Master, he took up a travelling life as a special emissary of the Temple. If you wish to know more of him his tale is well known.

Ask any storyteller to speak of the Tilecutter's Penny and you'll hear it. I may tell you some of it another time if you've a mind to listen. But as I've already said, Caoimhin wrote it all down so seek out that manuscript if you must.

Though Sir Robert always laughed when anyone spoke of the Grail and his part in its rescue, the fact remains he was knighted by the King of England. And Richard Lion-Heart didn't dish out dubbings to everyone he met, so there must have been good reason for it.

As a famous gallant knight Robert was highly respected among his peers. As a kind, generous and just man he was admired by the womenfolk. As an honest, pious warrior monk he impressed everyone who met him. As a cheese-maker he hadn't really made his mark in the world. But that was just a disguise after all. Still, as far as cheese-makers go, he wasn't a bad curd-collector either.

As I was saying, it came to pass that Robert had been charged as a special emissary by the Grand Master of his order. His mission was simple: to discover the whereabouts of an old enemy of the Templars, track down this adversary and put the man to death.

Now it would be remiss of me if I didn't mention that this command didn't sit well with Sir Robert. He was a man who believed in the Holy Writ of the Ten Commandments. In his view the word of God forbade killing of any sort.

You'd be right if you thought that was a strange thing for a Templar knight to be thinking. But Robert had witnessed plenty of war in his time. He'd seen enough fighting and bloodshed to last him the rest of his life. He yearned for a peaceful existence entirely taken up with quiet devotion in search of the mystery.

He oft times repeated his favourite phrase in Latin. *Omnia quaecunque vultistit faciant homines ita et vos faciatis illis.* Every good deed you desire to be done to you by men let it be that you do unto them.

Or in plain language, don't go sticking a sharp farming implement up anyone's bum if it's not something you'd particularly like them to introduce into your own seating arrangements.

So you probably understand it was to Robert's dismay that he found himself in the service of God acting as an assassin. He'd sought the counsel of his superiors of course. And his Grand Master had explained the situation to him this way: in practice there is no difference between living a life of devotion in the monastery or offering one's skill in the service of the Lord Almighty. A scribe uses his craftsmanship with the pen to praise God. A warrior brings his sword to the same task.

If a silly old fool like me can perceive the faulty reasoning in that argument, I'm sure Robert could too. Indeed, his mind was not put at rest whatsoever by his Grand Master's words.

Our good Templar was much troubled by the duty allotted to him.

So at every opportunity along his road he'd stopped to pray, seeking guidance in this matter. He'd knelt before numerous stony-faced sainted sentinels of the road. He'd asked them each a question. Was it right to murder a man simply because the superiors of the Templars ordered him to do so?

To his bitter disappointment no statue ever spoke to him, no saint appeared to light his way, no answer was offered from on high. Robert was beginning to fear God had abandoned him altogether.

There was no reply this time either, so he stood up from his prayers. He crossed himself as he muttered a few words. 'Thou shalt not kill.'

There was silence for a long while. No intervention. No admonition. Not so much as a sneeze.

He brushed the mud from his long grey cheese-maker's tunic, then picked up his father's sword enclosed within its black leather scabbard. As he began to fall into a deeper meditative state he grasped the sheath in his left hand.

Robert placed two fingers over the hilt so the weapon didn't slip from its hard leather coat. Then he stood for a long while in the pose Gaelic warriors adopted when travelling armed.

The Irish of those days didn't carry their weapons slung across the shoulder on a baldric or strapped to their belt at the side as is the fashion now. They always had their sword in hand with point high and hilt low to announce their profession. This stance clearly showed they meant no aggression toward anyone. A warrior Gael of those days would rather remain at the ready than risk the humiliation of being caught without a blade. There were some who wouldn't go swimming in the summer without their war axe or pigsticker. Others annoyed their womenfolk by insisting on sleeping with weapon on one side and wife on the other.

Robert felt the weight of the blade and smiled in appreciation of the well-crafted sword. The hilt, pommel and blade of this weapon were of finely polished steel unadorned by any decoration. The scabbard, like the handgrip, was wrapped in tight black leather.

Sir Robert slowed his breathing, preparing his mind for the coming fight, but his thoughts were racing. It was good to be home in Ireland, he realised. Though his blood was Norman it was the land of his birth. He realised he'd been away too long. I don't know exactly how long he'd been off adventuring but it must have been more than three years. His father had come to the Killibegs then and young Robert had never visited us before.

Since he'd landed at Wexford with Mirim and Alan he'd been too preoccupied with their safety to appreciate the place. This was the first chance he'd had to be by himself. It was time to retrieve the customs of the native Gael from his earliest memories. And most importantly it was time to recall what was expected of him as a warrior in this land. For though the troubadours do sing of the gallant knights of France, they know nothing of the traditions of the Irish.

And our gentle Robert understood that Guy d'Alville had also studied the ways of the Sword Dance. So the community of Killibegs was in for a rare show: two foreigners who'd fight in the style of the ancient Gaels.

Sir Robert cradled the upturned sword in his left arm. This was a sign to all who saw him that he had no intention of harming anyone. He practised his bow, concentrating on every nuance of movement. All warriors bowed to one another upon meeting, whether they were friend or foe. But this same move was also used to prepare for the drawing of the sword.

With a broad sweep of his arm over his head Sir Robert released his blade from its confinement. Then he levelled the weapon at his imaginary opponent and raised his left leg, bending it at the knee. This stance represented the warrior's vulnerability. No contest could begin until both warriors had their feet firmly planted on the ground.

Órán was a light weapon. Robert judged it would be very effective if wielded from high upon horseback, for it was broad and deadly sharp. The handgrip was long enough for the weapon to be grasped with both hands if necessary. If used on foot to bring down heavy blows, this sword would likely split a man's helm in half.

It was a fine example of the swordsmith's workmanship. It had served his father well. It had earned Lord William a fearsome reputation in battle.

Órán. Robert knew the word inferred greatness or majesty but he couldn't be sure of the exact meaning. His father had once told him it was a name from the ancient Norse speech of his ancestors. But to Robert's ear the word sounded Gaelic.

As the Templar ritually lay the scabbard down upon the ground at his side he continued to point his weapon at the invisible enemy. It was at this moment, whilst down on one knee, that the two opponents would make eye contact.

Since he was merely practising the moves he rose from his knee again to take up the first pose of the battle dance.

And why was it known as the Sword Dance?

My people have a saying. Don't give a sword to a man who hasn't learned to dance. A warrior who cannot master this war dance is not considered fit to bear weapons. But the saying also has another deeper meaning. A fighter who has no respect for the joy of life cannot be expected to honourably wield the tools of death.

I can't tell you where Robert learned the dance. Many Normans favoured the Irish customs but few went to the extent of incorporating our ways into their day-to-day lives. I don't know what inspired him to do so but it may have been his dissatisfaction with the Norman approach to life as much as a willingness to try anything that might help him solve the mystery of life.

In any case the younger FitzWilliam continued to practise the movements, correcting his small errors here and there to focus his concentration. Now and then when he needed a short rest he leaned on his weapon.

Don't imagine a sword is an easy thing to throw about. You try swinging a heavy stretch of steel around all day fending off blows or striking with a broad sweep. You'll soon find out how hard the labour can be.

Even a strong veteran needs to stop to catch his breath every once in a while. To the Irish warriors of those days there was no shame in ceasing the conflict for a few moments. Any fighter who leaned on his sword was respected in his right to do so. His opponent would mirror the gesture, politely waiting for the enemy to regain his strength or breath.

No one, no matter how bitter the feud, wanted the death of another man on his conscience. It's one thing to kill an enemy over a petty quarrel in a fit of temper. It's quite another to have to face his wife and family and to pay the fine for his death with a herd of cattle.

You see, in that long-gone time before the Norman laws were taken up, it was the duty of the murderer to compensate the family of his victim on pain of banishment and remission of honour. Whether the tragedy occurred in stealth, revenge or fair fight made no difference.

Death used to be taken seriously. Before the foreigners came, that is. And murder was not only a crime but also a sure way to bring hardship on your own family. Fines were paid in cattle according to the worth of the man or woman. This was the eric fine.

The consequences of an eric are far reaching. For if you've no cattle left, you've no milk. If you've no milk, you've no cheese. Believe me, when the winter comes and there's no cheese to be had, you'll wish you hadn't taken a life.

That's why war was frowned upon. Every hand was needed to bring in the harvest or go out into the snow to hunt at midwinter. War could so easily lead to famine. The lack of one man could prove disastrous to a small community. The lack of five could seal the fate of many more folk under the tyranny of hunger and cold.

Sir Robert must have been considering all these matters. His conscience nagged at him constantly. On the one hand his oaths to his superior were clear. On the other hand his duty to his fellow human beings and to his God weighed heavier each day.

He ended the dance with a short salute to his imaginary enemy. Then he knelt down to pick up the scabbard and with a flourish returned his new blade to its home.

'Thank you, Órán,' he whispered.

He placed the weapon down by the shrine then picked up his other sword. This blade was short, heavy and not very well balanced. It was designed for close-quarter fighting on foot. The contrast between the two was remarkable. But Guy hadn't dared carry a better sword on his travels lest he betray his knightly origins. Even this one was worth more than most cheese-makers could have afforded to own.

This weapon was called Bláni, which means Daughter of Renown in the Gaelic language. The scabbard was plain brown, functional, a primitive covering to protect the steel from the rain. Even so, rust and other subtler signs of wear marked the blade. It was a weapon unworthy of expensive repairs. The hilt was poorly made so Robert wore leather half-gloves when he wielded it. This sword may have lacked the balance and precision of Órán but it had a devastating effect on an opponent. The weight of it could tear a wooden shield in two.

It took a strong arm to swing Bláni for more than a short while, so it was a last line of defence. Besides, it was little more than a flat iron rod sharpened on both sides with a wooden grip added to make it safer to pick up. You wouldn't want to try shaving with it.

With meticulous attention to detail Robert performed the Sword Dance again. He was slower about it this time. He'd neglected the use of this blade for many months and he needed to familiarise himself with its ungainliness again.

When the dance was done a second time he sighed with satisfaction. Then he packed Bláni away in its rough brown scabbard.

After taking some bread and a draught of water from a leather skin, Robert knelt down in front of the shrine again. He prayed for strength. He begged all the saints in Heaven for guidance.

Another doubt crossed his mind. He'd made a rash decision to leave his mail coat in England to save the effort of carrying it. Now he wished he'd thought that decision through more carefully. He wrapped his belt round his tunic to make it look bulky; as if he were wearing mail underneath in the custom of the travelling brigands. Satisfied that at least Guy would not notice his weakness immediately, he sighed with acceptance of his fate.

Of course Robert hoped that however this fight turned out it would be for the best. Why was he so concerned about this scrap in particular? Why was he forced to question himself again and again? Why was he so nervous about the outcome?

I'll tell you. The warrior Sir Robert FitzWilliam had been sent to Ireland to eliminate and who had earned the hatred of the Grand Master of the Order of the Temple was none other than Guy d'Alville.

While Robert was off getting ready to fight Guy and Toothache was being secured by strong ropes to the gatehouse, I sat in a corner of the small Norman stone house where they'd laid Caoimhin.

Sianan had already refused my pleas to use the Quicken Brew to save his life and she remained determined not to do so. There was nothing I could say to persuade her.

I reckon she just wanted some peace in which to work at saving the lad from pain if at all possible. She must have felt my eyes burning into the back of her neck. I wasn't surprised when she eventually commanded me to leave her with the lad so she could concentrate on doing what she could for him.

'I'll do my best,' Sianan assured me as I departed. 'I've been practising the healing arts longer than anyone I know. If it can be done I will bring him back to you. Now the best thing you can do is calm yourself. If the Redcaps are going to fall upon us we'll need your cool head and strong hands.'

She was right. I knew it. If the Redcaps attacked there really wasn't much hope any of us would survive. Except her of course. She was a Fánaí. She wouldn't suffer the fate that awaited we mortals.

The chieftains were already marshalling their warriors and seeing to the defence of the rath. Fortunately for all of us it had been abandoned only a few years before, so the ditch and palisade were in good order, as were the walls and gatehouse.

If Toothache's rash act had achieved anything it had galvanised the Gaels in their determination to resist the foreigners. If they could treat Caoimhin, who was one of their own, with such contempt, there was little hope for people they considered less than savages.

The chieftains had now thrown off all their doubts about Sianan's story and had banded together against the common enemy. Their fury at Toothache's admission he was a servant of both Bishop Ollo and Aoife masked a deeper sense of dread.

For who could hope to stand against the might of the Otherworld when allied with the devious wiles of a ruthless churchman?

All these matters were beyond my understanding at that moment. Even if I could have grasped the full meaning of everything that had been said in the hall that day I couldn't begin to consider how it might affect my kinfolk.

I was beside myself with the shock of Caoimhin's poisoning and thus no use to Sianan. So I went off to watch the fight between Robert and Guy. The outcome of that fight would decide a few matters. And there'd be work enough for us all once the duel was ended.

I left Sianan praying for the young scribe's recovery. She did that for a long time before she looked once again at his features, wondering where she could have met him. Why was he so familiar to her?

The lad stirred in his fever as the sweat began to pour off him. Whatever poison had been used it was a slow-acting, painful death-bringer. The abbess shook her head. She had never been able to understand how mortals could bring themselves to murder one another.

Sianan had seen so much death in her long life. So many friends had departed to the Halls of Waiting. For the first hundred winters after she'd taken the Quicken Brew she'd found it difficult to become attached to people. It was simply too painful to part with her friends when they inevitably passed over.

The death of Queen Caitlin of Munster had been particularly saddening for her. This great lady had looked after Sianan in her youth. If it hadn't been for Caitlin she might not have had anyone to guide her after her teacher, Gobann, was killed in battle.

A Druid woman known as Síla had also been one of her closest friends. Síla had lived into her nineties but had lapsed into a personal dream of visions and memories in the last three winters of her life. Sianan had cared for the old woman to the last, though it had broken her heart to do so.

The abbess had been tempted to share the Quicken Brew with both those women, yet she had refrained from doing so. She'd made a promise to the Danaans who had granted her the Brew that no other mortal would taste the Water of Life at her hand. That promise had been the most difficult oath she'd ever taken.

Sianan sighed deeply as she stroked Caoimhin's hair. He was so young, she thought. He'd experienced so little of life. A thought struck her.

She searched through the pouch tied to her belt. Inside was a square of leather in which she'd wrapped the nine berries of the Quicken Tree. She poured them out into her palm to examine them. Each one was a dark blood-red shrivelled lump slightly smaller than a pea. Their outer skins were quite hard with age. Strange, she thought, that a fruit which grants eternal life should be subject to the passing years in such a way.

She counted them, though she knew exactly how many were there. She sniffed them but couldn't detect the sweet fragrance that had once surrounded the berries.

At last she laid them back on the square of leather and wrapped them up again. Just as she did that Derbáil entered the healing house carrying a black pot of boiled water that had been allowed to cool a little.

Sianan thanked the old woman then dipped a wooden cup into the pot. She tasted the water, nodded her head to signal that it was sufficiently cooled, then put the cup to Caoimhin's lips.

The lad was already drenched in sweat but he managed to take in a small amount of liquid. This was all that could be done for him. It was important to keep the flow of water into his body to make up for the loss from his fever.

Derbáil asked if there was anything else the abbess needed. Sianan shook her head. Then the old woman said she'd stay a while to help keep watch over the young scribe.

The abbess smiled in thanks but nothing was said between them for a long while. They both sat and stared at Caoimhin as the strength drained from his body.

It must have been a sad sight to see. For Derbáil told me afterwards that her eyes had been so filled with tears she could hardly see her own hand in front of her face and that from a woman who'd witnessed more than her fair share of death and suffering so was somewhat hardened to grief.

Sianan was bathing the lad's head in cool water when he stirred briefly from his distress. She recognised this stage of a poisoning. She'd seen it enough times before.

'Where am I?' the young scribe asked in confusion as he stirred from his delirium.

'You have been brought to the house of healing.'

'Why?'

'You're ill.'

Then the lad opened his eyes wide and stared at the door as if someone he recognised had just walked in. Sianan looked up, but there was no sign of any visitor.

'What have you seen?' she asked the scribe. 'What are you looking at?'

'I knew he'd come to sit with me,' Caoimhin muttered. 'He's been watching my every move since Wexford.'

'Who?'

'Gobann,' he replied. 'Gobann the Druid has come to sit beside me and keep me from death.'

Thou Shalt Not Kill

uy d'Alville concealed the saddlebags of precious books in the hollow stump of a venerable yew. Then he made his way down to the shrine where Robert had been praying.

He stood on a hillock above the spot for a long while, watching the Templar practise the Sword Dance. The Norman couldn't help wondering why the fellow was putting so much effort into this fight. In d'Alville's mind there was no question the Templar would not be defeated. Put simply, he knew Robert's skills couldn't possibly measure up to his own. As I've said, he was arrogant. But on this occasion his confidence was well justified.

Guy had waited a long time for this opportunity. He'd honed his warrior craft. He'd mastered the art of the blade. He hadn't met a man who could best him in weapon play.

All the humiliation he'd suffered since he'd first encountered Robert FitzWilliam was about to be assuaged. The Norman could already feel the dead weight of dishonour being lifted from his shoulders.

The death of this Templar could not possibly make up for the damage that had been done to d'Alville's reputation, but Guy could sense a breeze rising and it heralded a wind of change in his life.

The Norman waited till Robert knelt down again to pray.

467

He noticed folk from the community starting to gather near the shrine. So he chose his moment to proudly march down to the open stretch of ground where the fight was to take place.

Cradled in his left arm, in the manner of the Gaelic warriors, d'Alville carried the sword Aoife had presented to him. She'd told him there was an enchantment laid on this blade but it was of little consequence to him.

His vengeance was such that he felt he could have beaten Robert with his bare hands.

'Calm yourself, Guy,' he admonished under his breath. 'You've waited for this. You've been patient. Savour every sword stroke. Enjoy every thrust of the point. Don't rush. The longer this takes the more you'll have to think back on with fondness.'

Robert rose from prayer. He'd not seen the Hospitaller arrive, instead he'd sensed the presence of his hatred. As he turned to face his rival the young FitzWilliam recalled with intense clarity the last occasion he'd met with this proud, cruel man. Since that time Robert had heard so many stories of d'Alville's evil. He'd witnessed the destruction Guy had left in his path. He'd seen the anguish on the faces of those who'd suffered at his hands.

He knew that every act of violence and cruelty had been calculated to draw him closer to this vengeful creature. D'Alville had always mentioned Robert's name, asked his whereabouts or told some untruth about him so the witnesses became a bait on Guy's hook.

It was only a matter of time before the Grand Master of the Temple sent Robert out to clear his name of d'Alville's slander. Yet our lad could not bring himself to hate Guy. Nor could he summon up the desire to kill the man.

Not even the stern command of his master inspired Robert to want to eliminate this enemy from the face of the Earth. Without the will to fight and lacking sufficient practice in his warrior craft the young FitzWilliam faltered. For the first time since he'd marched alongside King Richard in the Crusade, the Robert wondered whether he would live to see another day.

'If it be your will, O Lord, to take my life today, let my passing be honourable,' he whispered.

The two adversaries faced each other now, mirroring each other's stance. No words passed between them as each prepared himself to meet with destiny. Both men sank into a fathomless trance-like awareness of the other man's eyes. These men were not Gaels who would have waited till their scabbards were lain on the ground. They were two souls whose destiny was rushing at them with the force of a tidal wave.

As they stood regarding each other in this manner the gathered spectators seemed to vanish, becoming no more significant to them than as many trees in the woods. Neither man heard the excited chatter or perceived anything else in this world but his opponent.

Guy was surprised. He hadn't expected Robert would be able to allow the weapon trance to descend upon him so completely. He wasn't worried though. In truth, he was overjoyed there would be some element of challenge in gaining this victory.

With studied grace the two men silently began to move, preparing to engage in battle. They bowed to one another, never once breaking eye contact. Murmurs of appreciation rippled through the gathering of women and children who'd come to watch. Three older men who were not helping prepare the defences came down from the rath to adjudicate. All three gasped at the total focus of these two opponents.

Then each drew his blade with a broad sweep like a farmer cleaning cobwebs from the high ceiling of a barn. Each man knelt to lay his scabbard down on the ground, arose, then bent the left knee to lift that foot off the ground.

By the rules of the Sword Dance the fight could not begin

until the combatants had both feet firmly on the Earth. Neither moved for a long while.

Two sword points wavered slightly. Even a strong man cannot keep a blade perfectly still in this position. The crowd hushed, transfixed by the intensity of the confrontation even before a blow had been struck.

I arrived at the shrine just as Guy spoke the name of his sword.

'Maolán the Messenger,' he said with a firm challenge.

'Órán the Dark One,' Robert replied, though he couldn't be certain of the meaning of his sword's name.

Now that the spirits of their weapons had been summoned it would be impossible for either warrior to hold back from a bitter fight.

I remember very clearly the next thing that happened for it came like a lightning bolt. Each man stamped his left foot on the ground then charged at his opponent with a war cry.

A ruddy flush painted Guy's face as he slashed his weapon round toward the Templar. Robert parried the blow then managed to stab the point of his sword into d'Alville's right thigh.

A hint of concern passed across the Norman's face, but he'd not been wounded. His long mail coat had saved him from injury. But he must have been shocked that his enemy had struck a successful blow so early in the contest.

What happened next was a blur of flashing steel and grunted retreats, punctuated by the ringing of metal and heavy exhaled breaths. And I knew then why this mode of fighting was called the Sword Dance.

If it had not been for the fact they were trying to kill one another, or if they had not wielded weapons, they might have been engaging in some elaborate courtly set-dance. Both men were so finely attuned to one another's movements they seemed to be as one.

I'd never seen such a sight and I'm certain I never will again. There was something Otherworldly about the whole conflict that defies explanation. Witnesses gasped in awe and exaltation. I lost sight of Guy or Robert. I merely saw one creature bathed in the light of a mystical hatred.

I suppose I should have taken into account that each man carried a sword reputedly inhabited by a Frightener spirit. But I didn't know very much about such matters in those days. As I think back on it now, though, there were two unusual ghastly shadows cast by the combatants. I guess these must have been some reflection of the Frighteners at their work.

As the fight progressed, both warriors received cuts and grazes to face, hands and neck. But it was only when Robert stabbed the point of his blade hard into Guy's mail coat at the chest that my heart jumped with hope.

The Norman wasn't injured, of course. He knew how to fall back before such an attack so he wouldn't be bruised or winded. But something significant happened in that instant. The connection between the two opponents was broken for a moment.

D'Alville broke eye contact for no more than a moment. But it was enough to notice something remarkable about his opponent. Robert's tunic was torn open to waist under the right arm revealing his weakness for the first time.

'You came to this fight without donning any armour,' Guy observed, in surprise. 'You have a high opinion of yourself!'

We'd all assumed Robert was wearing a mail coat under his simple cheese-maker's clothes. It would have been suicide to face an opponent without it. But there was nothing between Guy's blade and Robert's chest save a flimsy strip of torn linen.

D'Alville placed the point of his blade down on the earth to lean on his sword more than merely confident of victory now. According to custom Robert mirrored him. Both men took the opportunity to catch their breath. But the build-up of nervous energy wasn't going to allow them to rest for long.

Nor were the Frightener spirits which dwelled within their weapons.

'I've had enough of this game,' Guy stated flatly. 'Let's finish it.'

'I will kill you,' Robert gasped. 'I'm the better swordsman.'

D'Alville stared at his opponent in utter disbelief, uncertain whether the Templar was mad or simply overcome with battle lust. The Norman laughed.

'You'll not kill me,' he assured Robert.

'I will cut you into a thousand pieces if you let me.'

'I won't let you.'

You must understand that although Robert had entered this fight unsure of his chances of victory and unwilling to spill his enemy's blood, the Frightener spirit within Órán had descended upon him. It was lending him an arrogant courage which was uncharacteristic to say the least. As for Guy, he just seemed more arrogant than usual with his Frightener about.

Maolán wasn't as experienced a spirit as the one which inhabited Robert's sword. But it had a few tricks hidden up its invisible tunic cuffs. Guy suddenly seemed to grow taller and darker as if he'd been engulfed in a mighty storm cloud of rage which was on the very point of bursting its fury in a wild torrential downpour.

Robert wavered. He could clearly see the Frightener taking shape, fed by the fear of all those spectators and spurred on by a desire to feast on some fully fledged terror. No one else saw it. That's for certain. I was there and I spoke to many of those folk afterwards. No one mentioned it but Robert.

The spirit rose up around Guy in a twirling whirlpool of leathery wings, long teeth and lizard skin. It was like a dragon out of the troubadour romances. And it was seething with the ecstasy of battle, hatred, anger and fear.

The sword point of Órán faltered as Robert began to seriously doubt whether he could face such a spirit working its will through the sword arm of one such as d'Alville.

If only he'd known that Guy was experiencing exactly the same doubts. For the Norman could see the spirit of Órán, a Frightener that had never known defeat in the hands of a FitzWilliam. And Órán was no less awe-inspiring or ugly than Maolán. Indeed it was much larger and immeasurably more ghastly to look upon.

The two spirits must have decided to take a short break from the conflict, hoping to settle this with a retreat or withdrawal rather than death or damage. When Robert and Guy spoke they were simply voicing those thoughts their Frighteners had inspired them to express.

'I'm stronger than you are,' Órán said through Robert.

'Perhaps you are. But I am swift,' Maolán countered through Guy.

'Lay down your fury and I will spare you,' Robert warned.

'I will feed from you first,' d'Alville replied, and a shudder of disgust touched my stomach.

'You'll be shattered,' the young FitzWilliam warned.

'You will.'

'Return to the one who made you or I will send you home with your tail between your legs.'

'She that brought me into the world would not have let me live if she suspected I would turn out to be a coward,' Guy answered coldly. 'Enough talk. Let's do battle. I hunger.'

In the next instant both men swung their blades high again in unison. They doubled their rage and trebled the pace. Each attack was parried by an expert tactic. Every slash was disabled with a furious sweep.

Robert sweated so profusely that his tunic was drenched. And though the air was crisp the perspiration rolled off his forehead in great rivers. The exertion of the fight was beginning to tell upon him.

The Templar's responses were slowing. Once or twice he barely managed to save himself from a death blow. But he would not put his sword point down to rest. He was determined to go on with this foolishness to the end driven by the awful spirit which dwelt within his blade.

Once again it was Guy who brought the conflict to an unexpected halt. He was wearing a mail coat. So the strain was great on him also. Both men panted heavily as they leaned hard on the hilts of their weapons.

'Now I will finish you off,' Robert declared confidently through his heaving breaths. 'Unless you submit to me. This is your last chance.'

Guy threw his head back with laughter. He'd never heard any words so defiant, foolish or unrealistic. Suddenly he recognised a little of himself in this old enemy. And that was the moment when the finely woven cloak of arrogance started to unravel for Guy d'Alville.

Never doubt the power of a Frightener spirit. Even a man with a good heart and a clear conscience can be drawn into acts of dishonour by these fiendish feasters of the soul. As Guy's laughter rang out it stung his opponent's ears. Robert felt a fury rise in him such as he'd never known. All questions of right and wrong vanished from his mind. Órán shrieked with delight but it was our Robert's voice that did the crying out.

All consideration for his honour shed away from him like petals falling from a flower once it has bloomed. And the bud which remained was made of murderous malice.

Robert lifted his sword, not waiting for his opponent to ready himself. Then he charged forward with such a vicious war call that Guy fell back in shock.

The Norman tripped and fell heavily on his back with his blade raised across his body to repel a deathly slice. The

Templar screamed an unintelligible curse that echoed round the shrine. Then he brought his weapon down with such a force that Guy's sword shattered into shards.

The Norman cried with outrage. The rules had been broken. Conventions had been breached.

But Robert paid him no heed. Before d'Alville could roll out of the way the Templar had the point of his sword pressed so heavily down on the Norman's throat it cut slightly into his flesh.

A light went out in that moment as surely as if someone had blown out a candle on a moonless night. And the darkness was as deep and all consuming for Guy as if he'd suddenly been dropped into a cave far within fathomless parts of the Earth.

D'Alville could not speak. His eyes widened as he faced death. The shock of his Frightener's demise was utterly shattering. Yet even at this moment Guy experienced no fear. Indeed, a part of him welcomed this release.

Though there was a risk it might be said of him in the future that he'd buckled under the trickery of a dishonourable man, Guy let go of all such concerns. There was nothing to do now but face his end with courage.

But the fit that had taken hold of Robert dissolved the very moment his opponent's sword shattered. The Frightener spirit within Maolán rose up out of the shards of the blade within which it had been trapped. Robert watched the spirit shake off the bonds of enchantment which had imprisoned it within that weapon.

Maolán was suddenly free. It looked down on Robert as it rose up and spoke once more through Guy addressing Órán.

'You are the better of we two. You have proved yourself in this fight. I bow down before you and relinquish the field to you.'

'Go now,' Robert replied. 'This fight is done.'

The young FitzWilliam felt a pain in his chest. He released

the pressure of his blade tip upon Guy, though he didn't remove the point.

'What are you waiting for?' the Norman gasped. 'You've beaten me. It's time to finish the job.'

Robert stared wide-eyed at his enemy.

'Go now. This fight is done.'

'What?'

'You will leave this country immediately,' Robert declared. 'Return to the land of your fathers and never set foot on the soil of Ireland again.'

'What are you saying?' Guy gasped. 'You've beaten me. Now end it like a warrior. Finish what you started.'

'I will not kill you,' Robert stated calmly as he regained control of his senses. 'But I will certainly humiliate you further if you don't submit.'

'What further dishonour could you do me?'

'I'll hand you over to the people of Killibegs and let them decide your fate.'

Guy frowned with indignity. He could see he had little choice. Better to live to fight another day. Better to have another chance to bring revenge to this fool. Better to back down than to end up a slave to these savage heretics.

'I submit.'

'Swear it!' Robert screamed, the wildness in his eyes the last flicker of battle frenzy.

'I swear!'

Robert removed his blade, saluted his opponent and sheathed the weapon.

'Go now,' he demanded. 'Leave this place and never return.'

Guy d'Alville rolled onto his side clutching at his throat. Then he stood up and stared around him disdainfully.

No one made a sound. Except for Robert. He whispered one phrase under his breath which I barely heard.

'Thou shalt not kill.'

Guy d'Alville summoned what dignity remained to him. He brushed the mud from his sleeve. His expression was full of contempt but he was not about to risk his life only to be overwhelmed by the large number of heretics who'd watched the fight.

He rightly gauged the Culdees would have torn him to pieces if he'd reneged on his promise to withdraw honourably from Killibegs. Yes, we were a peaceful bunch, but by Saint Patrick's pockets we were all in a dark mood that day. He might have cut a few of us down with his knife before he fell, but he wouldn't have been able to visit his revenge upon Robert FitzWilliam. That would have to wait for another day. This encounter had merely ensured his vengeance would be keener than ever before.

And of course he felt he'd got one up on Robert anyway. He possessed the books which had been in the old lord's keeping.

Guy decided to make a show of his departure by way of gloating a little. Being the kind of fellow he was, you could hardly expect less of him.

'You have offered an immeasurable insult to me,' the Norman noble stated as he faced his rival for the last time before leaving the Killibegs. 'No man may do me such injustice and yet expect to live.'

Robert didn't want to provoke Guy any further. He was simply grateful the matter had been settled without too much blood being shed. He had more pressing matters to attend to now.

Guy waited a few moments to see whether his words would be acknowledged. Robert bit his tongue. He didn't want to waste any more time with this black-hearted Norman.

Fortunately d'Alville wasn't going to wait forever. He looked toward the afternoon sun then turned to take the road which led east toward Wexford.

He marched a hundred paces before he was out of sight of the Culdees. Along the way he picked up the saddlebags of precious manuscripts he'd hidden. With his plunder retrieved, another thousand steps brought him to the ford where the Redcaps were waiting with their catapult. He tried to order them to advance across the stream but they didn't understand a word he said. They obviously had their orders from Aoife. Guy gave up on them soon enough.

Then he walked on, following the path to the edge of the great oak forest. He paused at the place where the road entered the woods between two standing stones. The pillars were adorned with carved strokes down their sides which the Norman knew were a form of writing but could not interpret.

The sun was already low in the sky by that time. He realised how far he'd walked from the settlement. He caught his breath as he turned to look back down the path toward the Killibegs. Then the quest Queen Aoife had set him came to his mind.

'I suppose I'll have to go back to get those wretched rowan berries,' he hissed in a low tone of frustration.

'It's too late for that,' a familiar feminine voice informed him.

Guy turned round with a start to see Aoife standing between the pillars. Behind her the forest rustled as if it were a massive creature stirring from sleep. And though she was smiling, d'Alville had the distinct feeling she was not happy with him.

'Too late, my lady?' he ventured. 'I merely have to wait for darkness to fall, then I'll return to Killibegs to retrieve the berries as you requested.'

'I didn't request it,' she corrected him. 'I *commanded* you to bring the rowan berries to me. Don't forget your place, dear warrior.'

'It seems a strange command,' the Norman shrugged. 'Surely there are rowan trees in this forest. Could you not collect some fruit from those boughs?'

'They're not ordinary berries I asked you to bring me. They're the fruit of the Quicken Tree. They are perhaps the only Quicken Berries to have survived the long passage of the seasons since the great tree was cut down.'

'I've never heard of the Quicken Tree.'

'It is the tree of life. It's the tree of eternal health and the bough which banishes injury. None who drink the Brew made from its berries will ever taste death.'

'The berries grant immortality?'

'Indeed,' Aoife nodded. 'How many times do you Normans have to be told a story before you remember the details?'

D'Alville recalled to mind the strange Abbess of Dun Gur whose appearance had so frightened his warriors. He wondered whether this queen was telling him the truth. Could it be that the weight of the years left its mark on these immortals in some other way? Why didn't Aoife have that strangeness about her eyes such as Sianan had.

'I'm not touched by time because I'm older and stronger than she is. I first saw the sunlight at least a thousand winters before she was born,' the queen told him as if she had been listening in on his thoughts.

Which she had. She was able to do that because she was older and stronger than him. She'd applied herself every day of her life to learning the secret things of the world. She hadn't wasted a moment of the endless moments at her disposal. Overhearing the inner musings of a mortal wasn't much of a mind task for her.

'If the berries are so important to you I will retrieve them,' Guy cut in, thrown off balance by her thought-listening trick. 'I promised I would and I intend to keep that promise.'

'I've already told you,' Aoife laughed wagging a finger at him as if he were a naughty child, 'it's too late for that now. You'll have to face a punishment for failing to fulfil my wishes.'

'What punishment?'

'You can't be worried about that now,' she scolded. 'You should have done as you were told in the first place. I'd dearly love to give you another chance but that just wouldn't do. I couldn't have my Redcaps thinking I was being soft with you. They might start to expect the same treatment. Then the whole fabric of my reign would be rent into tiny pieces.'

As she spoke Guy noticed a numbness in his toes that spread slowly to his feet and lower legs. He looked down, but disbelieving what he saw, he rubbed his eyes and looked again.

Where his boots should have been, the roots of a tree were splayed about digging themselves far into the earth. And though his toes were numb he could sense they were burrowing into the soil, seeking out a deep source of life-giving water.

'What's happening to me?' he gasped, dropping the saddlebags of books.

'Don't ask stupid questions,' Aoife scolded. 'You're far too evil-hearted to waste your breath with such things. My but you Normans do love to talk, don't you? Well it's too late for words now, my poor warrior nobleman.'

Then the queen relented a little as she understood she could have some really satisfying fun with him.

'Oak trees may live over a thousand summers. Some grow tall, others grow short and squat. Many rot from the inside so that by the time they're ancient they have a great hollow space inside which may prove an ideal den for foxes or a home to badgers. I like the poetic tragedy of that, especially in your case.'

She smiled a wicked smile, enjoying his discomfort. But Guy was not a man to show fear, even if he had been suffering from it. In fact he was not at all afraid of the transformation overtaking him. He was fascinated and quite uncomfortable, possibly in pain, but he certainly wasn't frightened.

In my opinion d'Alville had faced his own Frightener spirit when he was still a young man. I'm talking about the spirit which fed off his soul energy. I reckon he was one of those rare folk who'd recognised the creature living within him and had come to some sort of an agreement with it. Not to the extent that Aoife had, of course. I'm not suggesting that at all.

Probably in return for all the fear he inspired in others, his Frightener had likely conceded not to feed off his soul, just off the souls of Guy's victims. Well that's how I've explained to myself why nothing ever terrified that bastard. You can judge for yourself as the story goes on.

One thing is for certain Guy was changing into an oak tree. He told me about it not long after. And though I know him to be a liar and a blaggard, I could see in his eyes he was telling the truth.

'You don't mind the ravens roosting in your branches, do you?' Queen Aoife teased, moving closer to grasp his fingers tightly.

She raised his right hand and arm above his head.

'Stand like that for me,' she ordered, as if she were asking him to arrange a piece of furniture in her underground palace.

Then she took his left hand and drew his arm out parallel to the ground.

'Hold this arm here,' she commanded gently.

Guy stared her straight in the eye, determinedly unflinching. The numbness had already spread to his belly and was moving up to his chest. He gasped for breath as his body became the trunk of a sturdy oak.

His skin was now a rough dry bark. His hair was an unruly clump of mistletoe. His heart was an empty space reminiscent of those rotting hollow hearts the oldest trees hide within them. Where his ribs had been there were branches sprouting new leaf cover and buds. His hands were already wooden, his arms the main limbs running out from the trunk of the tree, each thick enough to bear the weight of a man.

Aoife watched greatly amused. But she couldn't help respecting the Norman's steadfast refusal to beg for mercy.

'If you apologise to me now I'll let you go free,' she cooed, touching a finger under his chin.

Guy was in obvious distress from the pain of the transformation. Yet he did not call out. He mustered all his stubbornness, refusing to give in to her torturous game.

Three hard deep breaths drew into his body then his features contorted with his frantic struggle for air. And as his mouth gaped open the place where his eyes had been became two small blemishes in a knothole that had been his face.

The wind picked up to rustle through his newly acquired foliage. But if you or I had stumbled upon him then, we'd have had no inkling this was Guy d'Alville. Nor that this oak had ever been a man at all.

Aoife stepped close to the newly created oak-noble. Then she wrapped her arms about him and pressed her cheek to the rough bark near to his knothole face.

'Your skin is so wrinkled,' she mocked. 'That's what comes of a warrior's life out in all weathers. I must admit I have to admire your stubbornness.'

The queen closed her eyes.

'I used to do this when I was a girl,' she confided. 'I would go into the forest to find an ancient tree. Then when I'd chosen one I thought must be particularly venerable, I'd press my body close and listen to its soul.'

'I will not submit,' she heard Guy's innermost being whisper to her. 'You may do with me as you wish but I won't give in to you.'

She pushed away from the tree to stand a few paces distant.

'I love that sensation you get when you're so close to a mighty bough that you could swear you can hear it thinking.

'Goodnight, Guy d'Alville. If I were you I'd be praying that your tree-splitting brothers don't come out here looking for timber to build new ships or stoke their fires. Wouldn't it be unfortunate if you fell to the axe as so many oaks have done since the coming of the Normans?'

If Guy had any reply to offer it was not about to be expressed. He forced his mind to stubborn silence, though he was still in shock at the transformation. The new experiences of water being sucked up through his roots and the delicate sensations of wind and cold on his leaves were captivating and intense.

'Maybe that's how I'll stop you foreigners cutting down all the trees,' Aoife opined. 'Perhaps I'll turn all you Normans into a vast forest to replace the timber you've felled so viciously and indiscriminately for the last thirty summers.'

Then she added one more thing.

'Sweet dreams, man of oak.'

In the next instant a great buzzing cacophony rang through the twilight air. Aoife's body transformed into a seething black mass which swirled and dispersed to form a dark, swarming cloud of bees.

The insects lifted up on the wind led by a magnificent queen bee. They encircled the new oak briefly, then they were off into the forest, headed for who knows where. But she left the satchel of books he'd dropped by his feet and by midnight on Samhain Oidche she'd regret that oversight.

COBANN

I'm sure you can imagine the scene back at the guests' hall when everyone gathered after the fight. Robert FitzWilliam was given pride of place among the people. For he was already a legend among these folk.

And there's nothing like a living legend to give people hope. His father sat beside him, tall and straight as he'd ever been in his youth. The change that had come over the old man was incredible. Alhough he'd stayed at the rath to help the chieftains organise the defences, he acted as if he'd stood beside Robert throughout.

The threat of impending bloodshed and the need to think like a strategist again had given him new life. It was as if the years had dropped away from Lord William. I suppose he'd realised his battle skills were going to be needed, so he'd rallied his scattered thoughts to the fray.

'The Redcaps can be dealt with!' Lord Will declared once Clemens had called the gathering to order. 'We know they can be defeated, though the taking of heads won't be an easy thing.

'There's no guarantee we'll be able to stand against a massed forced of their warriors,' he went on. 'If we are to strike off every head it will be a hard-won fight.'

'They will beat us!' Tigern shouted. 'Perhaps it would be better to scatter before the hordes descend upon us.'

There was a hiss of derision from every corner of the hall.

'Tigern Og speaks the truth,' William declared and everyone was shocked to silence. 'If we stand we may well be slaughtered. But we need only strike at one head to end this fight. Without Aoife to lead them the Redcaps will disperse to their underground homes. It will take them centuries to recover from the loss of their queen.'

'How do we deal with her?' Tigern scoffed. 'If she's as powerful and invincible as we've been led to believe, it won't be an easy task.'

There were reluctant murmurs of agreement. William put up a hand to ease the disquiet spreading round the hall.

'It is a very simple task,' he told them. 'I am the Orchard Keeper,' he reminded them. 'One of the trees I watch over is a book of enchantments. This manuscript is full of songs, poems and incantations for dealing with spirits of enticement and fright.'

'How can that help us?' the old chieftain cut back quickly. 'Poems don't win battles. Words don't win wars.'

'Enticers and Frighteners may be brought to heel,' Lord Fitz went on. 'If we can but summon Danu she will put things aright again. Only she can entirely dispel the spirits which are the source of Aoife's influence. A direct appeal to the Goddess of the Flowing Waters is our only real hope of salvation.'

'If there ever was any such being as Danu she is asleep. None can wake her,' Morcán stated confidently. 'Don't waste our time with such trifling hopes. They will amount to nothing and we will not think well of you when we are being hacked to pieces by Aoife's Redcaps.'

'Listen to you!' William laughed. 'You have no trouble believing in the bloody-hatted minions of the Queen of the Night yet the Goddess Danu is difficult to reconcile? I'm a Norman and I have more faith in the stories of the Gael than all you Irishmen put together. We'll summon her here, then we'll see what you have to say about her.'

His son shifted uncomfortably in his seat. Clearly all this talk of goddesses and enchantments didn't sit well with him. But if William noticed the distaste in his Robert's expression, he didn't draw anyone else's attention to it.

'Your book truly contains an enchantment that will summon Danu?' Rónán cut in.

'There are many fruits upon this particular tree,' the lord confirmed. 'And any one of a dozen of them might aid us in our task. But it is the song to summon the Goddess Danu I recommend we make use of. And Samhain Oidche is the best time to raise such an enchantment.'

'That is tomorrow night,' Morcán reminded the assembly. 'Even if it were to work, have we enough time to weave such magic?'

'Are you certain that once Danu is called upon this threat will be done with?' Tigern Og interrupted.

'It will take someone of a stout heart to summon the goddess with the incantation,' William conceded. 'A soul made of stern stuff, without fear and unswayed by any enticements. Sianan is an immortal for whom the shadow of death is not a consideration. She would be my choice.'

Clemens searched the room but the abbess was still with young Caoimhin. He summoned me with a wave of his hand.

'Binney, go to the Orchard Keeper's home,' he instructed me. 'Fetch the book of which he speaks. Do you know the one?'

'I'll bring back the whole saddlebag.'

'On your way back bring Sianan to the hall. We have need of her.'

'Yes, Father.'

Then I was off. I hadn't got out the door when I decided once I'd found the book I'd give it to the abbess to bring to Clemens. Then I'd be able to sit beside the young scribe for a while.

Sianan knelt beside the Benedictine brother, wondering if she'd heard him correctly. Derbáil had muttered something about the fever setting in, then had left to go off and watch the fight. The old woman hadn't returned.

The abbess pulled the cowl up around Caoimhin's head so that it framed his face. She wanted to see how he looked with the black outlining his features.

It was remarkable. Now the idea had been triggered, she realised that the lad reminded her of Gobann. The black cowl was so like the jet-black raven-feather cloak her teacher had always worn.

She stared at him for a long while, hoping, wishing, praying that this fellow might have some connection with her beloved Gobann the Poet. Then, when she saw no flicker of consciousness in his face, she began to berate herself.

'I'm a fool!' she whispered.

She was disappointed with herself for allowing her longing to cloud her judgement. There couldn't possibly be any connection between this dying lad and her teacher who had departed so many winters ago. And even if there were, this young scribe wasn't likely to live. The poison he'd swallowed was unlike any she'd ever seen before. It had been quick to sap his body of strength but slow to kill him. To her way of thinking this was a very bad sign.

His death was likely to be long and lingering. At least he wouldn't suffer too much pain, she thought.

Sianan wiped away the perspiration from Caoimhin's brow then dipped another cloth in the water and placed it in his mouth. A little of the moisture seeped into his body but it was nowhere near enough to replenish what had been lost.

He muttered again in his fever. And then he eyes shot open again.

'Gobann? Is that you?'

Sianan mopped his brow.

'Gobann isn't here, my boy,' she soothed.

'He's always here.'

Then Caoimhin's eyes rolled back as he lapsed again into unconsciousness.

The abbess let him be and moved closer to the fire to warm herself. The lad was burning up with the effects of the poison but the chamber was icy cold.

She stared into the flames, exhausted from the long journey to the Killibegs, worried about the Redcaps and despondent that Aoife's star was on the rise. As she drifted for a few short moments, caught up in her anxieties, she sensed another person's presence in the room.

She looked up at the door as the fire died down, plunging the chamber into gloom. A cold chill swept over, her tainting the air with a taste of winter's breath.

'Who's there?' she asked. 'Who's standing there in the shadows?'

A figure dressed in a long tunic and cloak shimmered in the dark. A soft blue light danced about it. The glow was steadily growing with every breath.

'Aoife?' Sianan whispered. 'Is that you?'

The figure glided forward, the blue luminescence intensifying. A muffled voice spoke a few words the abbess couldn't understand.

Another garbled phrase followed hard upon the first but Sianan couldn't make any sense of what was being said. She stood up but as she did so the shadowy blue creature retreated in alarm.

'Don't be afraid. I mean you no harm,' she softly assured the visitor. 'I can't understand you. You must speak more clearly.'

Once again the room was filled with a muffled voice but this time there was greater urgency in the tone. She sensed the shadow was fearful and desperate. Then in a flash the bluish shadow leaped toward the dying lad.

Sianan didn't have a chance to cry out or to protect the scribe. The spirit had entered Caoimhin's body and he stirred slightly.

'Gobann,' he muttered. 'My name is Gobann.'

She was at the lad's side instantly, grabbing a strip of linen to mop his brow.

'Are you speaking to me through Caoimhin?' she asked.

'Yes, Sianan.' Caoimhin's voice was deep and resonant now, exactly as the Gobann's had been in life.

'Is that really you, Gobann?'

'Yes, Sianan. It is your teacher, Gobann of the Silver Branch, Ollamh Poet, bearer of the raven-feather cloak. Greetings, my student.'

The perspiration broke out anew across the young scribe's face and neck. Clearly the strain of this encounter was sapping the last of his strength.

'Caoimhin will die if you continue this,' she stated.

'He is already dead,' the visitor declared through the dying lad's own mouth. 'He drank the poison.'

'Why have you returned?'

'Returned?' He laughed a little. 'I never went away. I've been asleep. Now I'm awake for a while.'

A shadowy blue mist floated around the scribe, encasing him in its mystery. Sianan looked into the blueness of the ethereal mist, searching for Gobann's face. But there was nothing she could recognise there. The thought crossed her mind that this might be a trick of Aoife's to gain her confidence.

'Prove yourself to me,' she demanded.

'Would you like to know where Mawn has got to?'

She nodded, speechless.

'He's away in the Otherworld sleeping. Flidais the Goddess of the Hunt has him. She's a jealous lover. She won't let anyone near him and she won't let him wake. She intends to keep him there forever.'

'How can I find him?'

'I'll take you if you wish. It's no easy journey. And it will be a trial to release him from her enchantment.'

'I'll go with you.'

'Then give the scribe a portion of the Quicken Brew.'

'What?' the abbess gasped.

'Grind up the berries,' Gobann told her. 'Make up a measure of the Brew. Let him drink of it.'

'I can't do that,' she protested. 'I promised not to use the Brew, only to keep the knowledge of it.'

'What good is it to keep the knowledge if you never use it?' Gobann pressed. 'You're wise. You've kept your promise. But this is something I ask of you. As your teacher. As your friend. As a soul seeking fulfilment I beg you to grant Caoimhin the Quicken Brew.'

Sianan shook her head. 'I can't do that.'

'You must! It's my only hope of ever seeing my true love again.' There was a sudden melancholy in his tone. 'Would you take away our only chance of happiness? Would you keep us separated for the rest of eternity? We sacrificed our love for the good of our people. We surrendered our own dreams so that you and Mawn might live. How can you refuse us an opportunity to live also?'

'I don't know what you're talking about,' the abbess replied, confused.

'Do you have no memory of Síla? The woman I loved? My soul-friend? The Druid woman of the Cruitne folk who took you to her people in the lands of Alba and taught you her wisdom?'

'I remember her well,' Sianan affirmed.

'She has returned at last. Her name is Binney.'

'Binney?'

'The soul of Síla dwells now within a new cloak of flesh. And that cloak calls itself Binney.

'I have had a terrible time tracking her down. But now I've found her. And I don't wish to be taken from her again. The poison will kill me!'

'Kill *you*?'

'Can't you see? I dwell within the cloak which calls itself Caoimhin. I am Caoimhin. If I die I may have to wait a thousand years before we are both born together. If I go to the Halls of Waiting now, our paths may never cross again.'

'But would you truly consider taking on the weight of immortality? The burden is terrible.'

'I would do anything for the opportunity to live out a life within the circle of her arms.'

The blueness brightened around the scribe's face so that Sianan could make out the indistinct form of a face. One of Caoimhin's hands lifted up and the clenched fist opened. He was holding Gobann's Druid cross, an equal-armed cross with a perfect circle spanning the arms.

'This is our time. This is where our circle is crossed and our cross may be encircled. Would you deny it to us? Have we not earned our happiness?'

Sianan mopped Caoimhin's face with the linen. She was confused. All her heart spoke to her saying she must help her teacher. But she of all people knew the consequences of the drinking of the Quicken Brew.

Immortality was a terrible fate. The soul needs rest. The Brew would snatch the opportunity for soul-renewal from Gobann's grasp forever.

'You will never sit again in the Halls of Waiting,' she reminded him.

'I would barter the very essence of my soul for this chance,' he replied without hesitation.

'I can't be held responsible for the consequences,' she added.

'No one is asking you to. I have requested this gift from you. I will answer for it to the ancient ones. I will bear what punishment must be paid. And I will thank you with all my heart and praise your name forever.'

'Let the lad rest now,' Sianan advised. 'I will do as you ask. But there are two things I ask in return.'

'Name them.'

'If I grant you life you will lead me to the place where Mawn sleeps. For he is my soul-friend as much as Síla is yours.'

'Agreed.'

'You will play for me upon the harp,' she sighed. 'For I have missed that about you more than anything else in this world.'

'I would gladly do so,' the teacher assented.

'Then you shall have your wish.'

'Thank you, my dear. You have proved yourself worthy of the Brew and of the duty you bear. Do not forget me, though I may not remember you whilst dressed in the flesh of Caoimhin the Monk.'

The scribe offered the Druid pendant to her. The abbess hesitantly held out her hand to receive the circle and cross Gobann had worn as a sign of his office and his vocation.

'Do not question the wisdom of your actions,' he told her finally. 'Your compassion will bring immeasurable joy to both Síla and myself. And for that you will be blessed.'

The apparition faded and the flames of the hearth fire rose high in the room, banishing all darkness.

When the fire settled again the ghost of Gobann the Poet had melted within the body of Caoimhin the Scribe and the blue light was gone.

AN ORCHARD PLUNDERED

 could feel in my bones that was something wrong. Before I'd pulled aside the hide cover to the entrance of Lord William's hut I knew something terrible had happened.

Even so I wasn't prepared for the sight that met my eyes when I got inside. The fire was just a smoky memory of warmth. The bed had been slashed into shreds. The saddlebag of books was gone.

I couldn't believe it. I searched through the wreckage of the lord's personal possessions hoping without hope to find the one book I'd been sent to retrieve. The only thing I found was one tattered page with letters on each side.

I could read the words but they made no sense to me. The tears ran down my face. This awful discovery must have released all the pain I'd held back when I saw Caoimhin swoon under the effects of the poison.

I folded the page, tucked it into my tunic and ran back to fetch Sianan just as the heavens rained down their own tears upon me. By the time I'd made it to the house of healing I was soaked to the skin.

I burst in, sobbing.

'Sianan!' I cried. 'Someone has made off with the orchard! Every tree.'

She looked up from her patient with a puzzled expression. 'What are you talking about?'

'The books. All the books Lord William was caring for. They've been stolen.'

'Everything?'

'All except this page,' I told her, pulling out the dampened sheet of vellum. 'Clemens has summoned you to the hall. I was supposed to fetch a book of incantations. But every book is gone.'

She stood up and took me by the hand.

'Sit here by the fire. Warm yourself. You've been drenched. I'll go to see Clemens now. There's nothing more I can do here.'

'Nothing?' I replied as the tears began to flow again. 'Is there nothing you can do?'

'Young Caoimhin has been through a terrible ordeal,' she gently explained. 'He has travelled to the brink of death. I don't know anyone who could have survived the poison he was given.'

She sat me down with an arm around my shoulders. I could see the young scribe lying there motionless. His skin was as pale as death.

'He is at peace,' Sianan stated.

Then she took the vellum sheet from my clasping fingers and kissed me on the forehead.

'Is he dead?' I whispered, fearing to hear the worst.

'No, my dear,' she assured me as she held me close. 'He will live.'

I held her closer, hardly believing the joy those words brought to me.

'Thank you, Sianan.'

Then she pushed me away and looked deeply into my eyes.

'You must promise me you'll look after him,' she said sternly. 'He will need all the care and love you are capable of in the next few days. His recovery may be unexpectedly swift but he's not to be allowed to leave this bed for a week. Do you understand?'

'Yes, Sianan.'

'Then I'll leave him in your care,' she told me.

I was already peering past her at the sleeping form of the young scribe.

'He's very important to me, Binney,' she went on. 'So look after him. Do you hear?'

'That's easy enough, Sianan,' I replied. 'He's very important to me too.'

Lord Will was his old self again and no mistake. With his son seated beside him the old man had a sparkle in his eye such as he hadn't had for years.

And his mind was sharpened, for as I'm sure I told you he lived for the challenges of life. The existence of a hermit may have suited him in many respects, but it was the music of adventure that sang to his heart.

So by the time Sianan entered the hall the old lord was already advising Mirim and Alan how to solve their dilemma.

'I have read of a place named the Well of Many Blessings,' he told them. 'That's where you may find the cure for the loss of your memories. A draught from those waters is said to restore a mortal by driving out all maladies.'

'Where can we find this well?' Mirim asked excitedly.

'I believe it may be found in the realm of the Otherworld,' the old knight told her. 'The journey there is perilous. No one who dwells there may be trusted to tell the truth. No one who travels there can expect to return. Finding the well is only half the challenge.'

He took a deep breath, not eager to be the bringer of hard news.

'First find the place. Then you must deal with the Keeper of the Well. I can't say whether she will be agreeable or not. She may set you a test or require of you some token in exchange for her healing water.'

Mirim's expression hardened. Lord William could see the determination written on her face. She'd come this far. She would go on. It was Alan's expression which surprised him. There was doubt painted there and reluctance also.

'Once you have a bottle of the waters you must find the way home. That is not as easy as it is to stumble on the road which leads to the Otherworld. Many mortals have set out for that country. Few have ever returned. None return home unchanged. Most are not changed for the better.'

'What do you mean?' Alan cut in.

'The mind of a mortal is often not so sturdy as the body. Though you may have the gifts of intelligence, education, knowledge of every sort; though you may be talented or quick-witted, these things will amount to nothing.'

'Nothing?'

'But if you possess resolve, determination and persistence, you will not fail.'

'Then we will not fail,' Mirim declared. 'We will find this Well of Many Blessings and we will cure the malady that has taken my husband's memory from him.'

'I have one warning for you,' William added sternly. 'If you should find the well against all odds, bring the waters home with you. Do not drink from the cup at the well.'

'Why not?' Alan asked.

'Two reasons. First, it is most unwise to eat of the food of that country or to drink of anything which is offered to you. Such an act may mean you can never leave the Otherworld at all. Second, if the waters restore all memory of your old self there may be a price.'

'What price?'

'Everything that happened since you arrived at the oasis of Shali may be driven from your mind forever. You may not recognise anyone you've met since then, including perhaps your dear wife Mirim. For though love is powerful, it too may be forgotten. Are you willing to pay such a price?'

'We are,' Mirim stated before her husband had a chance to speak. 'We have journeyed halfway across the world to find the answer to our riddle. We will not turn back now. I will not lose him.'

She turned to Alan, squeezing his hand tightly. 'I will not lose you,' she repeated.

'We'll talk later,' Old William told them. 'When Binney returns with my books I'll show you the one in which the road to the Otherworld is described. You'll have no trouble finding it if you follow the instructions contained in that manuscript.'

'The books are gone,' Sianan declared, cutting through the conversation.

William stood up in shock.

'They been stolen,' she added.

'Guy d'Alville,' Robert said with certainty. 'I should have guessed something was up with him. He gave up the fight far too easily. He's not known for his willingness to walk away from a humiliating defeat.'

'We must catch him!' Tigern bellowed. 'Fetch my horse!'

The hall erupted with cries of outrage. While the gathering shouted to one another, venting their anger at this act of thievery, Sianan handed William the one page that had fallen from the manuscript.

The old man perused it quickly then held up his hand to quieten the people.

'All is not lost!' he exclaimed.

Once again the gathering fell silent to hear what he had to say.

'Two incantations remain in our possession. They are not

497

the two spells which will provide the solution we had planned on. But as chance would have it they may yet serve our purposes.'

'We haven't time to chase after the Norman,' Clemens agreed. 'Even if we found him in time he may have already disposed of the books. Tomorrow night is Samhain Eve. If Aoife is going to put her plans into effect it will be while all the fires are extinguished. We must use what weapons have been left to us if we are to have any chance of defeating her.'

'These two song-poems may yet be enough to turn the tide against her,' William went on. 'Though they do not summon the Goddess Danu herself, they may tip the balance in our favour.'

'What are these poems?' Tigern demanded to know.

'The first opens the doorway to the Otherworld. This will save us much effort and precious time. The second is a song which lulls Enticer spirits and Frighteners alike into sleep. It may be enough to disarm Aoife so that she can be imprisoned. Without her at their head, the Redcaps will surely capitulate.'

'Once she is dealt with we need only concern ourselves with the Normans,' Rónán Og observed. 'My fellow chieftains will prepare to fight the foreigners for that is the skill we've spent our lifetimes perfecting. And we will leave it to others to travel to the Otherworld to face the Queen of the Night.'

'But if they fail we will be ready to face the Redcaps also,' Tigern promised. 'Aoife will not have her way.'

'So be it!' Clemens decreed. 'Who will offer their sword arm to this quest into the Otherworld?'

'I will,' Robert replied without a moment of hesitation.

Sianan stepped forward. 'I will go also.'

Alan raised his voice next. 'I will go since my road leads in that direction anyway.'

His wife said nothing, though none questioned whether she would be accompanying him when she put her arm about him, her green eyes flashing with fire.

'I will go,' Lanfranc declared and he felt everyone's gaze turn upon him.

'You may not go,' Clemens informed him flatly. 'I'm sure you're a man of honour. But you're a Norman. Your place is with your own people.'

'Robert FitzWilliam is a Norman. Alan de Harcourt is a Norman. Yet they have not been refused.'

Mirim noted the change in Lanfranc. He wasn't as jittery as he had been when she'd first met him.

'Robert is my son,' William told the knight. 'He was born in this country and I raised him with a thorough knowledge of the laws and lore of Ireland. Alan has his own quest to fulfil. But you are a newcomer to this land. You are still too much a Norman.'

'I have a good sword arm and a fine blade,' Lanfranc protested.

'No one is doubting your gallantry or your skill. You've proved them already. But you must go to your own folk now,' Clemens told him. 'If you do not raise your arm against us you will have done enough.'

The Norman let his gaze drop to the floor. And then he left the hall to make his preparations for departure.

The Cow and The Catapult

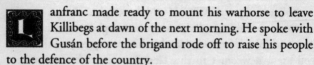anfranc made ready to mount his warhorse to leave Killibegs at dawn of the next morning. He spoke with Gusán before the brigand rode off to raise his people to the defence of the country.

'I am willing to forgive you your thieving ways on the condition you promise you'll abandon them and lend your sword arm to the folk of the Killibegs.'

Gusán smiled, winked and took Lanfranc's hand in a firm grasp.

'I promise I'll do as you ask, my enemy. For you're truly a worthy one as I said before.'

'I'm not your enemy any longer,' the Norman corrected him.

'Yes you are.'

'No I'm not!'

'You know you'd like to be,' the brigand insisted. 'We'd make such a good team. Imagine the songs they'll sing about us. Brave Gusán the outlaw who outwitted the valiant Redcap-killer Lanfranc time and time again.'

'I don't like the sound of that,' Lanfranc objected.

'Well I'm no troubadour. In the hands of a professional storyteller or song-maker it'll sound so much better. The point is we'll both be remembered. If we set about it the right way our legends will live on long after we've turned to dust.'

The Norman shrugged, unconvinced. 'So you're proposing that we pretend to be enemies?' he asked.

'Not exactly,' Gusán replied. 'We certainly won't be able to be seen drinking in the same tavern. But we wouldn't want to hurt one another either. The longer we keep up the adventurous sparring the more ingrained our saga will become in the minds of the general populace.'

'Why would I want to take part in such a hollow, meaningless deception?'

Gusán leaned in closer to whisper. 'It works wonders with the ladies.'

He winked. Then he slapped his former captor on the shoulder.

'I must be off now. I've got lots to do. Don't worry if you don't get the hang of it straight away. You'll pick it up in time. Take care!'

Lanfranc had to laugh a little at the brigand's slant on their relationship but it didn't raise his spirits at all. He had a heavy heart, that was plain to see. For the rest of his farewells were very formal.

By the time he was ready to leave he'd spoken with almost everyone he'd come to know. Everyone except Alan and Mirim, that is. In the short time he'd travelled with the desert woman he'd developed a deep affection for her. That's what he probably would have called it. But the fact is he was entirely infatuated by her.

He wasn't so much in love with the lady as in love with the idea of her. He was a fragile soul, our Lanfranc. Years of dealing with the Enticer which dwelled in his sword and the Frightener that lived in his heart had confused him terribly. He was easily hurt. Especially when he allowed himself to fall in love. The disappointment he'd suffered when he'd found out that Shali was Mirim's husband had cut him to the very core.

If a soul could have bled he would've spilled its life-blood everywhere and expired in a state of messy bewilderment. So it's just as well souls don't bleed the same way the body does.

Mirim noticed she'd been left out of his round of fare-wells. And being the kind heart she was she decided to make her apologies before he departed. As he was putting his foot to the stirrup she approached him, her soft voice preceding her.

'Gentle knight,' she began.

He turned, surprised she'd been able to sneak up on him like that.

'Good morning, my lady,' he replied.

'I'm sorry for my deception.'

'That's perfectly all right, lady. I understand your reasons for deceiving me. I'm not upset by that.'

'You saved our lives,' she went on. 'If you hadn't dealt with that Redcap we might have all been slain.'

'I'm a knight. I'm sworn to guard the weak and any who cannot protect themselves.'

'But there are few who follow the code of chivalry in these dark days. You are a rare one.'

'Thank you,' he bowed.

'Will you not stay for Samhain?'

'I must return to my own lands. If there is to be a war it is my duty to patrol the roads and watch over other travellers.'

'I have a gift for you, in gratitude for your courage and determination.'

'There's no need. I sought no reward when I promised to escort you.'

'Nevertheless you placed your life in peril to protect me. And I would like you to accept this as an apology for the harsh words which passed between us.'

She opened a black velvet pouch and poured out a handful of dark red stones each larger than any of his knuckles. Mirim chose four then passed them to the Norman.

He held out his hand, fascinated by the sparkling jewels.

'They are rubies,' she explained. 'They were given to me by my father before I departed from my home.'

'They are exquisite,' the knight gasped. 'But they are too precious a gift for me to accept.'

Mirim closed his hand around the gems.

'It is you who is too precious for one such as me. Take them. Give one as a token to the fortunate woman who becomes your wife. But the other three will help pay for your castle.'

The Norman swallowed hard, weighing the rubies in the palm of his hand.

'Thank you,' he stammered, overwhelmed at her generosity. 'If ever you or your husband should stand in need of help, you have only to ask me. I will be at your side if you give the word.'

'Dear sweet Lanfranc,' she sighed. 'You are a jewel among men.'

Then Mirim kissed him lightly on the cheek, turned and walked back to the great hall where her husband was waiting.

Before she disappeared from view she called back to add one more thing.

'Safe home and God speed.'

Then she was gone.

'My lord?' Stephen cut in. 'It's time we were leaving. We've a long road ahead of us, and who knows what dangers lie ahead.'

The Norman nodded. Then he chose one of the red jewels and tossed it to his sergeant-at-arms.

'At last I can afford to pay you for your loyalty and hard work,' he smiled.

Stephen caught the ruby. He held it up to the light in disbelief.

'Thank you, my lord,' he exclaimed. 'Thank you very much.'

Look at my long grey hair. It was a lovely shade of chestnut red once. All the lads thought I was the pinch of spices when I was a girl. But my imagination let me down. I never thought for a moment that I could stay young forever if I simply put my mind to it.

So how could I have dreamed I could take whatever form my whim decreed? How could I have comprehended that every desire that ever raised my eyebrows could be mine? If only I'd known then as I do now the one unquestionable truth of existence. If you can conjure an idea in your head you can make it real. As real as everything else in the world at least. If not more so.

You're looking at me with scepticism dripping from the corners of your mouth. Don't let it dribble off your chin onto your cloak. I mean what I say. You may not understand the concept but it is an incontrovertible fact.

Have you heard the story of the cow and the catapult?

I'll tell you then.

A farmer was on his way home after going to watch a battle. It was when the Normans first came here so it was a pretty one-sided affair. He thought he'd better not get caught by the invaders after they'd finished their slaughter.

So he was hoofing it along over the fields. And didn't he look just like a man who has something to run from? If he'd walked, no one would have noticed him and he'd have got home without any bother.

Cursing his ill luck and his short legs, this runaway was spotted by a band of Norman knights who rode him down on horseback. When they found he had nothing of value about his person they were mighty upset. So they tied him to a tree while they went off to chase other runaways, hoping to poach a few full farthing pouches.

Our farmer was propped there bemoaning his fate and the cruelty of misfortune's messengers when a raven appeared beside him.

Now it is said that ravens may sometimes be convinced to help a man whose life is endangered. For they are clever carrion creatures and brilliant bargainers to boot.

So the farmer begged the bird to chew away at his bonds. He pleaded. He bawled like a baby. But to no avail.

The raven sat there observing him coldly through his bleak black eyes. And when the bird spoke his voice was emotionless and entirely devoid of compassion.

'If I wait a few days you'll be dead. Thereafter I may feast on you at my will and your flesh will have dried out to a nice firm stinking biscuit.'

'But the warriors will come to fetch me and they'll chase you off,' the farmer countered.

'So I'll take out your eyes and peck on the tasty organs at the back of your throat until you're dead enough the warriors won't want you any more.'

'If you do that you will have to pay my kin a penalty under the law for my murder,' the farmer shot back.

'And what is the penalty?' the raven cawed.

'You must pay a fine.'

'What sort of fine?'

'The amount of my worth within the law.'

'And what is a farmer worth these days?' the raven enquired.

The bird's beak watered to think of squashing this poor man's eyeballs in his mouth then holding the two sweet delicacies at the back of his tongue before swallowing them.

'What are you worth?' the raven asked.

'A cow.'

'One cow?'

'No more, no less,' the farmer admitted, seeing no sense in lying.

Now the thought of a cow for supper really got the raven worked up. Cows are much tastier than men. Ask anyone you know, I'm certain they'll tell you the same thing.

But where would a bird get hold of a cow to pay the fine? The raven realised that if he was strong enough to catch a cow he wouldn't be sat here wasting his breath on a mere man.

And ravens being the cunning creatures they are, an alternative presented itself to the bird.

'I'll let you go if you give me a cow,' the black bird offered. 'That's my price for helping you escape certain hanging at the hands of those bark-splitting Norman bastards.'

The farmer thought about it for a moment then quickly agreed. Before you could say, 'It doesn't do to promise a raven anything if you don't intend to keep your word,' he was off over the fields a free man.

And the raven smiled or as close as a raven can approximate to a smile. But on the way home, as so often happens in these sort of stories, a strange thing came to pass.

As our farmer neared his cottage he stumbled across a two-man, stone-throwing catapult that had been abandoned by the Norman knights in the heat of the battle. The cow-keep slapped his thigh and thought to himself that even a bitter battle may bring some blessings.

He dragged the siege engine home. And when he got there he set about piling stones into the leather flinging pouch.

'What are you doing?' says his wife.

'I'm keeping a raven away. He'll be coming for his cow and I have a notion not to give it to him. Get our three beasts indoors and brace yourself for the attack.'

The woman did as she was told. But no matter what she tried, only two cows would fit inside their little round cottage. The third beast wandered into the oat field and rummaged about while the farmer blessed his wits and his wife questioned them.

Before long the raven appeared on a nearby branch and the catapult was put to the test. But the stones flew only a short distance and landed harmlessly beneath the tree.

Perhaps if he'd known something about catapults the farmer might have had a hope of hitting the bird. But he didn't know more than how to load it and set it to flinging.

Of course creatures of the air have the nous to know when to leave a stone-throwing cow protector well enough alone. So the raven settled down to wait until the farmer ran out of rocks or got tired and went to sleep. But the farmer didn't sleep.

He started to worry. He knew he was going to lose his cow and he marvelled at his own stupidity that he'd made such a bargain with a carrion bird. When you're likely to end up a dead man, a cow seems a small price to pay for your life. But when you're a living man with a wife to feed and placate, a set of udders is worth the world. The farmer thought himself a fool.

His wife thought even less of him. The both of them struggled to imagine some way of making room for their third milk-giver in the tiny cottage, but there was no obvious solution at hand.

So the farmer set the pulley that hauled back the rope to ready the catapult for another shot. And just as he finished, the most curious thing happened. The third cow, which had been wandering in the oat field, ambled over toward the war machine. She bumped the trigger handle and set off the catapult just as the leather strap wrapped round her back feet. In a second she was flying. Up, up, up into the evening air she went, doing her best impression of gossamer lifted in a light breeze.

I didn't say it was a good impression. It was just the best she could do considering she was a cow. In any case it was as astonishing to see how high she flew as it was to observe where she came down again.

With a last frightened bellow she landed slap on the thatch of the farmer's cottage which promptly collapsed. By the time the farmer had got his screaming, distracted wife out of the wreckage and rescued his two surviving cows, the raven was already feasting on the deceased third.

The next morning the farmer bowed his head when he surveyed the destruction of his cottage. And because he'd had his wife bellowing in his ear all night he ruefully rubbed his forehead. But the pounding across his brow would not abate.

Among the torn thatch the raven perched, well fed and preening. The farmer didn't bother to throw a stone. In fact he realised he'd probably deserved to lose his home for breaking such a solemn bargain.

Now, there's two things about my story I'd like to point out. First, as I said earlier, as soon as you imagine anything, it becomes real.

The raven imagined a cow for breakfast. And because he went about getting it, never doubting his ability to do so, it was easily his without too much effort or any cost to his dignity.

The farmer, on the other hand, imagined his freedom but wasn't willing to pay the price agreed upon. Then he and his wife pictured some way they'd fit their third cow into the house. And one way or another that problem was solved when the beast brought down the thatch and broke her neck.

The farmer ended up relinquishing the cow as agreed. Though he had a roof to mend once the mess was cleared up.

So heed my advice. Be careful of your thoughts, won't you. Don't imagine you can trundle round the countryside confounding ravens.

The other thing I have to say is in the form of a warning. Catapults are bloody dangerous devices. Take me at my word. If you see one lying about after a battle don't work up a sweat to drag it back to your humble cottage.

It'll only bring you trouble.

Lanfranc de Courcy and his men marched off down the hill, homeward bound. The Norman had more than a few regrets about leaving the Killibegs. But he couldn't remain there while the Gaelic chieftains were planning a war against the other Norman lords of Ireland.

Truth to tell he'd become quite confused since he'd got to know the Gaels. He liked them. He admired the way they stuck together when challenged. Despite their outward differences they were capable of working with one another for the common good. Normans rarely thought about the common good, unless you count plunder to be a virtuous pursuit.

Lanfranc found he was ashamed to be associated with Guy d'Alville. Though Guy was a wealthy cultured nobleman he was a deeply unsavoury character at heart, a man with no qualms. And Lanfranc had always thought that every man should have a healthy store of qualms to carry about with him.

As his little group of warriors came to within sight of the ford Stephen dropped back to ride beside his lord.

'There's something going on down by the stream,' he reported.

Lanfranc stood up in his stirrups and squinted.

'It looks like a siege catapult,' he commented. 'And a full team of four draught horses dragging it along.'

'It seems they can't get the animals to cross the ford,' Stephen added. 'The beasts are too skittish.'

'Who are those warriors?' the Norman asked. 'Can you make out whether they're our people?'

'They look like Redcaps to me, my lord.'

'Redcaps!'

Now it was a fortunate thing for our lad Lanfranc that Aoife had only sent a small party of her warriors to harass the

Killibegs in preparation for a full-scale attack the following evening. If there'd been any more Redcaps it might have all ended in disaster.

As it was they were few enough so that any opponent with a knowledge of how to deal with them wouldn't have baulked. Lanfranc's face lit up with excitement and he drew his sword quickly. The Enticer spirit engulfed him completely, so that even those of his warriors who harboured some trepidation about encountering these foes sat high in the saddle.

It was as if the Norman were lit by a great flame of courage, valour and beauty. His warriors gasped with amazement at their lord's charismatic presence. The spirit within the weapon seemed more powerful than ever before. And the lord felt a surge of invincibility and recklessness such as he'd never known. He'd dispatched one of these immortals easily enough. He didn't even question whether he'd be able to do it again.

'Do the men know what to do?' Lanfranc asked his sergeant.

'They're to take off heads,' Stephen replied, drawing his own blade from the scabbard.

'Then let's start a hat collection,' the Norman declared. 'Tóla!'

With that he spurred his warhorse down upon the dozen Redcaps. And he was followed, though not too closely you understand, by his warriors.

Lanfranc's party were only six so they were outnumbered two to one. But they had a reputation galloping before them.

Redcaps never shy from a fight and these fellows were no different. The very moment they noticed the Normans riding down toward them they raised their awful sickles, abandoned their draught horses and leaped into the fray.

Lanfranc had the heads off two of them before they knew what had happened. The others faltered and in no time six more were lying about headless.

The other four weren't hanging about to find out the name

of this knight with the Enticer dwelling in his sword. They were off abandoning the catapult, the horses and the fine red hats of their surprised, demised companions.

Eight caps were washed out clean in the stream. And each man who'd felled an enemy warrior pinned a doeskin hat to his saddle. Lanfranc himself had three from this fight and he wished he'd thought to keep the first cap he'd knocked off the head of an Otherworld warrior.

'What shall we do with the catapult?' Stephen jubilantly asked his lord. 'Shall we take it back to Killibegs?'

'It's no use to them,' Lanfranc noted. 'This is made for breaking down walls. The best thing we could do is take it as far away from here as possible.'

Stephen laughed. He whooped to let out his joy and exaltation. Then he gave the orders to bring the horse team round to take the siege engine home.

'It might fetch us a few marks in the market at Wexford,' Lanfranc shrugged. 'You never know.'

The Norman sheathed his sword. As you'd expect, the awesome air of enticement which had engulfed him drained back into the scabbard with the blade. But a residue of soul-light lingered about him. And he could feel it bolstering his resolve. Fear had no chance to creep back into his being. His Frightener did not re-emerge but cowered somewhere deep within him, shivering because he had stood up to it.

Lanfranc took a deep breath and shook his head to clear his thoughts. An idea formed in his mind. He put a hand on the two rubies inside the pouch within his tunic. Then he smiled to himself.

'My lord,' his sergeant cut in, interrupting his master's thoughts. 'What do you say we go sort out that bloody lion?'

'I was just thinking the same thing,' the Norman replied. 'I was just thinking the same thing.'

But that wasn't what he'd been thinking at all.

The Well of Yearning

So that was how I met Caoimhin of the Killibegs, who was later briefly known as King Caoimhin. But that's another story and I don't have the inclination nor the inspiration to tell it to you now.

At the time I was overjoyed he'd survived the poisoning. I was so happy I didn't once question the manner of his cure. And because she'd so adamantly refused, I didn't for a moment think that Sianan might have used the Quicken Brew on him.

In later life I often thought I must have been bloody desperate to have fallen for him like that. What a narrow-minded one-sided story he told in his silly books. I've read his tales, the ones about the Fánaí, the Nathairaí and his rendering of Sir Robert's story. His inaccuracies and his turgid prose were hard enough to swallow. But his foolish romantic notions of our Irish customs and traditions were unbearable. I suppose he had no love for the Church of Rome and he likely looked up to our heroes with too much enthusiasm.

He'd had precious little experience of the world when he came to us. And though he'd been taught by the Benedictines what to think when he was young, he never quite mastered *how* to think.

His heart was in the right place. I'll give him that.

So I can forgive his rather silly assertions and all his other faults. Even the fact that in his stories he painted some folk as black-hearted and others as faultless. In truth the world is not such a simple place. For there are spirits of enticement and of fear everywhere. And as I've said before, they're neither good nor evil; they simply are.

He never quite grasped that. So we had more than a few fallings-out about the finer points of storytelling. In those early days, of course, when love was still fresh, I didn't concern myself with such matters. I was infatuated with the lad, I freely admit it. And I arrogantly believed he could learn the art of storytelling from me.

Sadly he'd spent too much of his youth among the Normans and the Saxons. You only have to read the silly book Overton and Lewyn wrote about their adventures in Ireland and the Otherworld to know such an education must have put Caoimhin at a distinct disadvantage. Those Benedictines didn't know what the folk of the Killibegs instinctively understood.

Stories are glimmering treasures heaped upon us by the inhabitants of the Otherworld. The People of Peace whisper their tales to us unceasingly. They fill our hearts with cupfuls of the mystical waters drawn from the Well of Yearning.

My kinfolk of the Killibegs were already a rare breed even in those days. We lived to travel as our ancestors had done in the times before the Normans or the Christians came to this land. We journeyed on eternally, moving from one place to the next as a queen might wander between the rooms in her palace.

The land of Ireland was our palace. Every camp we made, each chamber of that home, revealed something new about the nature of the architect.

That year we settled for the winter within the walls of an ancient rath that had been inhabited for countless generations. A Norman hall stood where the simple round stone clachan-homes of the ancestors had once been.

Not far from that place a trickling stream narrowed before it poured into a pool. At that spot a rocky ford reached the sand on the other side of the water.

And there, almost smothered by blackthorn bushes, lay the beginnings of a road. This was no ordinary road. To my people it was *the* Road.

It was our link to the world beyond. It was our lifeline and our purpose.

Would that you ever find yourself walking this Road, trudging tirelessly, seeking some journey's end, I give you this warning. The Road is a living being. She's an enchantress. And she has a long reach.

The best of all stories are like unto the Road. They will lead you on to the edge of the world into the lands of light. Aye, and beyond to the darkest corners of creation.

Story tales hold a secret unseen current within them which draws you to their holy shrines. There, when you're caught up in the travel trance, you may well become lost to all your fellow beings even though you are surrounded by them.

Know then, in that moment, you have crossed into the Otherworld. The gate is easily found. It's not locked. But beware.

Once you are wandering in that enchanted country, the days pass differently from the world of mortals. If you're not careful a hundred winters may pass before your heart finds the way home to your own hearth.

The paths of a story lead in many directions. Explore them as you wish. For like the Otherworld, a story has no bounds. It is limitless, immeasurable and enticing.

Yet there are also fears to be found in the kingdom of tales. For the Otherworld is the natural domain of Enticers and Frighteners.

Go there if you dare. Do not be lulled by beauty nor dismayed at any terror you encounter. And when you return make sure you tell your tale to everyone you meet.

I'm tired now. I must have been up all night with telling you this part of my story. But like all the best tales, it isn't finished yet. Not by any measure. I haven't told you how Overton and Lewyn came to be lost in the Otherworld after Caoimhin was healed. And I haven't told you how Aoife set about putting her plans into action.

Let me sleep a while. When I awake I'll tell you more about such things.

There never was a tale without a quest. There never was a story without a transformation. There never was a hero without a longing in the heart that burned like liquid fire.

For all of us are questing. Each one will be transformed in time. And if you draw breath it's certain you've tasted of the precious waters of the Well of Yearning.

Goodnight. Sweet dreams. Tomorrow starts another chapter.

And by the way, have you seen what became of my ferrets?